ANDRE GONZALEZ

Never Look Back

For Natasha.

It hasn't been easy, but here we are.

"If you only do what you can do, you will never be more than who you are."

—Master Shifu

GET EXCLUSIVE BONUS STORIES!

Connecting with readers is the best part of this job. Releasing a book into the world is a truly frightening moment every time it happens! Hearing your feedback, whether good or bad, goes a long way in shaping future projects and helping me grow as a writer. I also like to take readers behind the scenes on occasion and share what is happening in my wild world of writing. If you're interested, please consider joining my mailing list. If you do, I'll send you a free time travel thriller as a thank you!

You can get your content **for free,** by signing up at bookhip.com/KAWWBK

Chapter 1

The man across the bar would be dead in fifteen minutes. He had been staring at me since I walked into the Ocean Wave Tavern. It happened often, though. A side effect of being a six-foot-four Mexican man with all my intimidating tattoos and scars. What if I was just a cat guy with a dozen furry friends at home who liked to scratch my arms?

I'd wandered around Central and North America for the last few years, and I got the same reaction whenever I strolled into a new town. People stared like I was some anomaly. One time I stepped into an upscale restaurant in Los Angeles, and it was like one of those scenes in the movies where everyone stopped mid-conversation to gawk at me.

That's when a harsh truth finally settled in. If I couldn't blend into a major city like Los Angeles, there was nowhere in the world for me to fit. The smaller towns suited me better. Sure, rumors spread much faster about my arrival, but I didn't stir up any shit and people let me be.

I preferred coming to hole-in-the-wall bars like this one. Small town bars typically had a higher concentration of freaks and weirdos, so it was the closest thing to my natural habitat.

I left Los Angeles a couple of days ago, hitchhiked north-bound with a couple of truckers, and they dropped me here in

Hillcrest, promising it was a quiet little town.

A ten-minute walk from the beach, so I had little to complain about. Hillcrest had the perfect blend of small-town America that I had grown to love, mixed with the laid-back vibes one would expect so close to the ocean in California.

Best of both worlds. If I had any interest in permanently living somewhere, this place would fight for a spot at the top of my metaphorical list. But I couldn't settle. Not with my past always following me around like a starving stray dog.

Nope. I usually found some manual labor job to help cover the costs of a motel for three to four weeks, then I'd be off. Part of me wanted to get comfortable and settle down. Smoke cigars on the beach and drink glasses of whiskey without a care in the world. But I'd done too much. The screams of my past always seemed to creep back into my mind like a gentle breeze.

The man across the bar sat surrounded by four other men in a corner booth. They were all of Latin descent, and I could hear them speaking Spanish. But the speakers in the bar were blasting a Jimmy Buffett playlist, and I couldn't quite make out what they were saying. They *seemed* suspicious, but I admit to jumping the gun on my initial judgments at times.

But why the hell was this guy staring at *me*? If he wanted to dance, I wasn't sure he'd like my tango. None of his friends—associates?—paid me any attention. They were all dressed in cheap black suits, scavenging two flatbreads and a single bowl of peanuts in the middle of the table like it was the last meal of their lives. Well, it *was* the last meal for Mr. Stares-a-lot.

I examined the bar like I do any time I step into a new place. That's a benefit of having grown up around violence in the border town of Laredo, Texas.

"Know where your exits are," I could hear my late mother telling me. "Identify any objects that can be used as a weapon. Look for obstacles down low that can block you from crawling toward the exit."

I missed her. My mother was the most incredible person I'd ever known. I supposed her lessons were the reason I was still alive today. After all the dangerous shit I'd lived through with the Navy SEALs and the CIA, I was still here and in one piece.

I sat at the bar and studied my routes to the two different exits. The main doors were fifteen feet to my right. There was also a green, glowing exit sign above the hallway next to the men in the corner. The restrooms and kitchen were back there, along with the back door where the cooks stepped out for a smoke break.

No obstacles between myself and either exit aside from plenty of people. I found it odd the bar was so crowded on a Tuesday night but have since learned beers were buy one, get one until nine o'clock. The demographics were all over the place inside Ocean Wave Tavern. Older couples. Younger groups of friends. Whites, Asians, and Latins. My kind of place. When there was a good mix, people were less judgmental when they saw me.

When I sat down ten minutes earlier, I'd ordered a margarita to appear less threatening—along with a plate of nachos. Both arrived, and I almost forgot about the man glaring at me, even though I felt his gaze burning into the back of my head. A plate of tortilla chips smothered in shredded beef, queso, pinto beans, sour cream, and guacamole was just what I needed to feel at peace.

The bartender slid over. She was middle-aged with lots of

makeup caked on her pale face, but she spoke in a caring tone as she planted her elbows on the bar top and leaned in to me. "How's your food, dear?"

I swallowed my bite and offered a polite smile. "Fantastic," I said. "Hitting the spot. I know the drink specials are popular, but is it always this lively during the week?"

The bartender leaned back and topped off a glass of water for the gentleman two seats down from me. She wore a black apron tied snugly around her pudgy midsection, pens and papers stuffed in the front pockets. "Tuesdays are the busiest weeknights, but the others aren't too slow, either. Not too many spots for people to just hang out in town, so most come here. I take it you're from out of town. Visiting someone?"

I took great pride in being off the grid. No cell phone—I'd buy a burner for the rare instances I *needed* one. No driver's license. Not even a home address. And definitely no social media presence. None of that shit. I carried around a backpack with two extra outfits, a toothbrush and toothpaste, a pair of wired headphones, and an old iPod containing a variety of music in its eight hundred songs stored from a decade ago. But I knew this bartender was just making small talk, wanting to improve her tip. I couldn't tell people I was homeless. That was an automatic guarantee to get treated like shit for the rest of my stay. I wasn't poor—I just didn't have a home address.

"I'm in town from Texas," I said. "Left L.A. a couple days ago and wanted to travel up the coast. See what else California has to offer besides the big cities."

"Well, you've come to the right spot. I was born and raised here in Hillcrest. Took a stab at acting in my twenties. Bussed tables in Hollywood and all that typical jazz. Nothing panned out, so I came home and opened this tavern. Go figure, the food industry is what I learned the most about in Hollywood, and Hillcrest needed something fresh. Been in operation for twenty years this upcoming summer."

"Congratulations," I said, finally taking my first sip of the margarita. Wow. I'd had margaritas from all across the continent, and this one had the perfect flavor. I couldn't even taste any tequila, but knew it was there because of the slight tingle it left on my tongue.

She grinned at me. "Thank you. Let me know if you need anything else."

She strode down the bar, tending to the other patrons. The man to my right gazed at his half-eaten burger, debating whether or not to finish his meal.

The chatter behind me rose, and I looked over my shoulder to see the group of men from the corner booth standing up. The suits looked even worse at full length. One man tossed a fifty-dollar bill on the table, and I noticed none of them had ordered any alcohol. Not a crime, but suspicious considering it was the hottest happy hour in town. Five glasses of water. Two partially eaten flatbreads, and the bowl of peanuts. What were these men really here for?

The one who had been looking at me the whole time gave one last glance as they filed out of the front doors. And that was that.

No drama or bar fight that typically followed the long stretches of obsession over my behemoth body. Thank God for small favors. I could really enjoy my nachos and marg in bliss.

I grabbed a chip and scooped the appropriate blend of meat and cheese, raising the perfection to my lips—

Pop! Pop! Pop!

The small windows high on the walls exploded into fragments. Shrieks erupted around the bar as a handful of people sprinted down the hallway toward the rear exit. Others fell to the ground and climbed under tables. A few scurried behind the bar to take cover.

The gunfire continued outside. I counted at least eighteen shots fired. Thank God for the building's brick exterior, or people inside would have definitely been injured.

I stuffed the nacho into my mouth and stood up. No one else was visible as I grabbed the backpack I had slung over the back of the chair and raced toward the main doors. Inside, the bar was quiet enough to hear a mouse fart, but outside I heard angry voices shouting and rubber burning as a car peeled away.

I stepped outside in time to see a black truck already fading into the distance down the street. Due to the darkness of the night, I had no way of figuring out the make or model. A guttural moaning sound came from my right, and I looked over to see two men lying on the ground, blood pooling on the concrete beneath them. The bar's exterior light splashed across the men like a Klieg searchlight.

The one nearest was the man who had been gawking at me. He wore two silver chains that now clumped over his throat. Blood spilled out of his quivering lips as his eyes stared lifelessly into the night sky. He was gripping a gun, fingers loosening.

I took a step closer and squatted down. The metallic scent of blood filled my nostrils, mixed with a poignant stench of the man's cologne.

"Who are you?" I asked.

But the man could only stare. He was dying, had only a few

seconds left. His grip on the gun completely loosened, and I saw it was a Glock 17. Why would this man in this supposedly safe, charming town be carrying such a high-quality firearm?

"Who are you?" I asked, knowing no response was coming. The man locked eyes with me one last time before the remaining life slipped out of his body. He had three entry wounds across his chest, his shirt and jacket drenched in blood.

I stood up and stepped over the man to examine his friend. This guy was already dead, lying on his side with both arms splayed out in front of him. Sirens wailed in the distance, a reminder to not get my fingerprints on any evidence. I squatted again and patted down the dead man. Pistol tucked into the back of his waistband, but I left it.

An engine around the corner of the building roared before a black car screeched out of the parking lot. I knew it was the other three men who were sitting at the table. The car had no license plate, and I could tell it was a Mercedes sedan before it also disappeared down the road.

The sirens grew louder, and I saw the flashing red and blue lights appear a half mile up the road. I could run, but that would only make me look suspicious. I already knew I'd get questioned when the police arrived. Big brown man from out of town strolled into the tavern moments before two men were shot. Not the best look for me.

I drew in a deep breath as I shuffled back into the bar. The salty odor of the ocean filled my nose. Fresh. Comforting. Why did trouble follow me everywhere I went? I was already planning on spending extended time in Hillcrest, but it looked like I wouldn't be smoking cigars on the beach.

Chapter 2

Back inside the bar, most of the patrons were still hiding beneath tables. The ones who had hidden behind the bar gradually stood up and watched me with suspicion in their eyes.

"There is no more danger," I said in a confident tone. "It appears to be a drive-by shooting. The police will be here any second now."

The shattered windows allowed the screaming sirens to be heard by everyone. Jimmy Buffett continued to play through the speakers throughout this whole ordeal. A chilling detail that would haunt me as I tried to fall asleep later. Hearing him sing about a beach in heaven while two men lay dead outside was a sick irony.

The sirens approached the building, police cars screeching to a halt outside. The red and blue lights flashed within the tavern like a nightclub. Commotion ensued outside. Dozens of stomping boots. A cry of "Oh fuck!" as they discovered the dead bodies. Two officers blasted in through the main entrance, pistols held at the ready.

"Hillcrest PD!" one shouted. "Is anyone injured?"

"Is there an active threat?!" the other hollered.

More sirens in the distance. The ambulances and probably

a fire truck.

The officers lowered their weapons as they stepped deeper into the bar. Their presence allowed everyone to come out from hiding. A man and woman broke into hysterical sobs, embracing each other. Most everyone else looked pale as ghosts as they gazed around the bar, dumbfounded.

The first officer moved toward the windows and examined the shards of glass on the floor.

The second approached the bar, sizing me up as he kept two hands on his gun.

"Kelly?" he called out, looking behind the bar.

"I'm over here," the bartender replied from the hallway.

"Kelly, what happened?!" the officer asked in a panic.

The beauty of a small town was most people knew each other. I now knew the bartender's name without having to ask.

Tears welled in Kelly's eyes as she took trembling steps toward the officer, hands clutched over her mouth, shaking her head. "I don't know," she said. I could tell she had a lump in her throat. "We were just having a usual happy hour, then the shots were fired, and the windows were blown out."

She tried her best to not cry, but tears streamed down her face.

"And everyone is okay?" the officer asked. He took another step toward Kelly and was directly next to me. I glanced at his nametag. Collins.

"Is anyone hurt?" Kelly shouted, and now Buffet sang something about wrinkles and smiles. "Cut the damn music!"

A rattled woman who had taken refuge behind the soda gun turned around and smacked the power button on the stereo system, draping the bar in silence. The sirens had stopped, but anxious chatter continued outside.

A paramedic barged in. "Is everyone okay?" asked the young man with curly hair.

"Everyone is fine, Bobby" Kelly assured him, letting out a deep sigh that she must have been holding in for the past five minutes.

"Alright, folks," said the first officer, turning his attention away from the windows. "We're going to have a long night of taking statements from everyone here. We need to know everything and everyone you saw in here tonight. Who wants to start? Preferably anyone who might have important information."

All heads in the tavern turned to look at me. Dammit. My curiosity always got the best of me. It didn't help that gunfire no longer bothered me. Why couldn't I have just pretended to be scared and hidden like everyone else?

The officer cleared his throat and took steady, cautious steps toward me. "And who might you be, sir?" he asked, thumbs hooked into his belt loops.

"He showed up a few minutes before the gunshots," someone shouted from the back hallway. The light back there was too dim for me to see who it was.

I wore a shirt with no sleeves because I was in a California beach town and that's how it's done. The officer studied the Aztec tribal tattoos and scars on my arms, and I could practically feel him jumping to conclusions.

"My name is Jonny, sir," I replied calmly. "Jonny Mendez."

I saw this officer's name was Matthews. He scrunched his brow. His eyes were level with my throat, and he had to look up to meet my gaze. "Is this true about you arriving moments before the gunfire?"

"It is," I replied. I'd been in these situations in the past and have since learned telling the truth will get me out of jail the quickest. "That's just a coincidence. I was passing through town and stopped here for dinner."

"Dinner?" Matthews asked, taking a step back to feel less emasculated.

"Yes, sir," I said. "Incredible nachos, by the way. Thank you, Kelly."

Kelly wiped her tears away as the slightest hint of pink flushed her cheeks.

Officer Matthews wasn't impressed. He glared at me like a child who just talked back to him. I knew we'd get along well.

"Why don't you come with me?" he said, turning around and taking two steps toward the exit.

"I'm sorry," I replied. "Did I do something wrong? Am I under arrest?"

He stopped and spun back around. His hand twitched slightly toward his service pistol but never landed on it. "If you were under arrest, you'd be face down with your hands behind your back."

"I don't know what kind of stuff you're into," I said, and out of the corner of my eye I saw Officer Collins bite his bottom lip to keep from laughing.

"We got a smart ass," Matthews said to Collins. "If you're smart, you'll keep your mouth shut until we ask a question. Are we clear?"

I nodded. We both knew I could pick Matthews up and toss him through the busted windows. But this was his town, so I played by his rules. For now.

"Good," he continued. "Now follow me. I just want a word with you outside."

He didn't wait for me and shuffled out, Officer Collins looking up at me with a red face. I winked at Collins before following his colleague out the doors, where a clusterfuck of law enforcement officers gathered around the dead bodies.

I saw ten patrol cars, two ambulances, and two black town cars with government license plates. A man and woman were leaning against the hood of one of the town cars, both wearing navy blue jackets zipped up snugly to their throats. Feds. But which department?

Why the hell were federal agents in this small town?

Officer Matthews stopped just shy of the perimeter around the deceased and turned to face me. He fished a stick of gum out of his pocket and popped it into his mouth.

"Do you have any identification?" he asked, crossing his arms.

Dammit. I was going to jail tonight.

"I don't," I replied. "Not on me, at least."

Matthews frowned and started chomping his gum like a pissed-off horse. "You're passing through town with no ID. Homeless?"

"I prefer to be called a drifter."

Matthews chuckled and rolled his head around like he'd had enough bullshit to deal with today. "Drifter. So you don't have a home."

"I don't have a permanent residence, if that's what you mean." Matthews was maybe a few years older than me. Early forties, I'd guess. I had noticed his fingernails were regularly chewed upon when he put the gum in his mouth. And now he chewed even faster. I smelled the faint bubble gum scent every time he spoke. This guy had no control over his stress.

"No ID," he repeated. "Nowhere to stay. You show up here

tonight. Shots get fired and two men are dead. There hasn't been a murder in this town for almost five years. What do you want me to believe about you?"

"I have no involvement with what happened here tonight," I said. "The dead guy—the one on his back—was staring at me. Never seen him before, and I have no idea why he was looking at me, but I'd like to find out."

Matthews uncrossed his arms and planted his hands on his hips. "*You'd* like to find out? I'll be damned. Just an outstanding citizen, are you?"

"I'm a former Navy SEAL, sir," I said. "Also worked in the CIA. I know my way around a crime scene."

Matthews pulled out his chewed gum, rolled it into a ball, and threw it over my head into a dirt field next to the tavern. "SEAL and CIA...and no ID to prove either of those things is true. You can't bullshit a bullshitter. Didn't your mother ever teach you that?"

My flesh instantly flushed with a raging heat. I hated when people mentioned my mother. But throwing this cop through his own windshield would surely get me off on the wrong foot with the rest of his colleagues, so I bit my lip. Besides, I knew he was speaking in generalities and didn't actually know anything about my mother.

"I prefer to live off the grid, sir," I said. Calling people *sir* had gotten me out of situations like this plenty of times, but I didn't get the sense Matthews was buying any of it.

Matthews let out a heavy sigh, and I heard a slight wheeze. He pulled out another stick of gum and continued chomping. Not only was he stressed, but he was a former smoker. The gum had replaced his bad habit but didn't quite fill the void.

"I have to take you in for questioning," he said, almost

ashamed. "You're not under arrest, but given the scenario and your untimely arrival, I have no choice. Can't let you walk."

"I understand," I said. "And I'm happy to cooperate."

Matthews snorted and shook his head. "I need to check in with Collins inside, then you and I will head down to the station. Don't move from this spot, you understand?"

I nodded and watched him return inside the tavern, mumbling something under his breath.

More officers worked their way into the tavern over the next couple of minutes, and I slid over to lean against the brick wall. I counted eleven holes in the facade where stray bullets had struck.

The feds approached the dead bodies, and I heard them speaking.

"You don't think this is related to them?" the woman said in a low whisper.

The male agent shrugged. "They're saying no one inside recognizes them. They were either passing through, or recently arrived."

"Shit," the woman replied. "They're Hispanic. Dressed the same. And according to the witnesses, were with other men dressed the same. That's not a group of friends cruising down the coast for vacation. They're not even friends if they left the scene."

"My thoughts exactly," the man said, lowering his tone. "This is officially out of control."

A man cleared his throat from my other side, and I whipped my head around to see Officer Matthews, eyebrows cocked as he looked up at me. "Ready?"

"Yes, sir."

He grunted as he pushed past me and trudged to one of the patrol cars. I followed him to the vehicle, where he held open the back door like a valet.

"Won't I seem like a criminal in the back?" I asked.

"You must be out of your damn mind if you think I'm letting you ride in the front with me," he said. "I can put you in handcuffs if you'd like to feel like a criminal." His eyes fell to my wrists that were as big as his biceps. "Or zip ties, I suppose."

I let out a laugh, but he didn't care. "Fine. Back seat it is."

He slammed the door shut a split second after I pulled my feet in. So rushy.

I watched him circle back to the front of the car to say something to the federal agents. He nodded toward me, and both of their eyes immediately darted to find me in the backseat. Like a criminal.

They nodded, and I knew I'd see them soon.

Officer Matthews opened his door and fell into the driver's seat, the chomping of his gum continuing with no end in sight.

He fired up the engine and backed out of his parking spot, keeping a close eye on the rearview camera before pulling onto the road and heading northbound.

"Do you always greet new guests in your town with such hospitality?" I asked.

He looked at me in the rearview mirror. "Only the ones that cause trouble when they show up."

Touché.

"I didn't get a good look at the truck that sped off after the shooting," I said. "Not sure I can be of too much help."

"Save it for the station," he replied. "I can't take notes right now."

Matthews flicked on the emergency lights and sped up. He clearly wanted to get out of this car as much as I did.

I looked out my window for the next five minutes, oblivious to what road we were on. There was little on either side of the street. We passed a gas station and a general store, both of which looked closed for the night. A tire shop next to a mechanic's garage.

It was too dark to see if there was anything between these buildings, considering this road had no streetlights.

We pulled up to the station, gravel crunching beneath the tires as Matthews pulled into the spot closest to the entrance.

The size of this police station surprised me. In most small towns I've visited, the station was typically no bigger than the tavern we had just left. But this one was roughly twice the size.

Matthews killed the engine and unbuckled his seatbelt. "Let's make this quick. I have a long night ahead."

Chapter 3

I followed Matthews inside. We passed only two other officers as he took me down a long hallway. Everyone else was at the tavern.

He opened the door at the end and gestured for me to enter first. When I saw the metal table in the center, I said, "Really? An interrogation room. I thought I wasn't a suspect."

I went in and took the seat facing the two-way mirror. I'd been in these rooms plenty of times before and was familiar with the process.

"You're not a suspect," Matthew said, following me in. "But you're suspicious. Plus, the conference room I wanted to use is undergoing some renovations. Burst drainpipe. Unless you prefer the smell of shit, we'll be staying in here."

I let out a genuine laugh. I wasn't nervous. Obviously, I knew I hadn't killed anyone. Not tonight, at least. They'd ask me questions. I'd give some answers, and I should be on my way in two hours, tops.

"You like to laugh, don't you?" Matthews asked me. He didn't sit in either of the two chairs across from me, instead leaning on one with his elbows.

"I've seen the absolute worst the world has to offer," I said. "Laughing is the only thing that keeps me from losing whatever remaining marbles I have."

"I see. Well, in the name of moving things along, can you provide me with your full legal name and social security number?" Matthews pulled out a notepad from his breast pocket, along with a pen.

"My full name is Jonathan—with two A's—Christian Mendez," I said, and watched as Matthews jotted this down, along with my social.

"Thank you," Matthews said, snapping his notebook shut and struggling to stuff it back into his pocket. He had to move around his handy pack of gum to get it to fit. "I'll be back in a few minutes for actual questioning. Just want to make sure you are who you say."

I said nothing as he left me alone in the interrogation room. He didn't believe me one bit, but that didn't matter. I'd been on the other side of the glass of these interrogations plenty of times. The common tactic was to let the suspect sit alone for several minutes, sometimes up to an hour, to allow the nerves and guilt to settle in. I had none of that, so instead, I leaned back in my seat, pondering why the hell I found myself in yet another situation.

It made me wonder if God had a sick sense of humor. Always dropping me in these scenarios where I seemed like a bad guy. My mother wouldn't have liked that remark. But aside from my tattoos, I couldn't claim ownership over any of the details that painted me as a stereotypical bad guy. Sure, I could kill a man with my bare hands, but was that not a *gift* from God?

Sitting alone in a room was awful.

Forty minutes passed of dreading my decision not to run when I had the chance. When the door swung open, Matthews entered with the two feds I had seen at the tavern. Called it.

"Mr. Mendez," Matthews said. Oh, how the tone had changed now that he found out I was being honest. "These are special agents Sutton and Duncan from the DEA. They'll be taking over the interrogation. You're in good hands."

Officer Matthews didn't wait for a response and left the room.

The two agents strode to the two chairs across from me.

"Good evening, Mr. Mendez," said the woman first. She seemed too petite for someone who spent their life chasing drug dealers, but I'd encountered plenty of these women in my work. She was likely equipped with a skill set to pin her partner to the ground with nothing but her pinky finger. Plus, she looked to be in her thirties, so she had plenty of energy to kick ass. She held a stern expression, like her jaw had been clenched for at least two weeks. Her blonde hair was up in a ponytail sticking out the back of a navy blue ballcap. I loved a beautiful blonde woman.

"Hello," I said. "I can't lie. I'm surprised to see the DEA. What's really going on?"

"Why don't you leave the questions to us, Mr. Mendez," said the man. He was slightly older than me. Mid-forties, I presumed. Streaks of gray were taking over the sides of his head and nearly all of his goatee. He looked at me from tired, brown eyes that still held an edge. I got the sense he didn't want to be in this room any more than I did. I noted the wedding band on his finger and could see the tip of what I assumed was a tattoo on his wrist, but his jacket sleeve cut it off.

"I understand the locals wanting to pin these murders on me," I said. "But with the DEA involved, I'm more confused. Definitely not caught up in any drug action. What were your names again?"

The man spoke first. "I'm Agent Duncan, and this is my partner, Agent Sutton."

Agent Sutton had sat down, and I could feel her scrutinizing me. I suppose she hadn't understood how much space I took up at the table until I was two feet away.

Agent Duncan remained standing, swiping on a tablet. "Quite the background you have, Mr. Mendez. Four years studying criminal justice at Texas State University. Ten years with the SEALs. Then five years with the CIA. And now here you are in Hillcrest, California."

He paused and glared at me.

"Is there a question?" I asked.

"We're trying to understand your background and what led you to being in this city tonight," Agent Duncan said. "You may say it's a coincidence, but there are more questions than answers from what we can tell. Let's start with your childhood, shall we?"

"My childhood?" I said. "What the hell does that have to do with anything?"

Agent Sutton must have heard the anger in my voice because she quickly interjected. "We don't need to discuss your childhood." She shot a look toward Duncan, who finally sat down, sure to keep the tablet propped up where I couldn't see it. "Let's start with your education. Why criminal justice?"

Sutton's stern face dissolved into a softer one that matched her tone. I'm not sure if she was trying to charm me to get me to answer their questions, but I instantly trusted her over her partner.

"Well," I said, growing more frustrated but knowing I needed to cooperate if I wanted to get out of there. "The reason for criminal justice actually stems back to my childhood. My mother was killed when I was ten years old. We were walking down the sidewalk downtown when a car parked along the curb exploded. It killed my mom instantly and left me with several of the scars I have, including the one on my face."

Both of their eyes moved up and down my arms, studying the scars intertwined with the tattoos. Sutton's eyes fell upon my cheek, where the lone, hook-shaped scar below my left eye was less subtle.

"It was the Mexican cartel," I continued. "They had planted that bomb, and it went off early. No one was even in the damned car. They never found anyone to pin the crime on. From that moment, I knew I wanted to dedicate the rest of my life to hunting down murderers and bringing them to justice. No ten-year-old should ever have to go through what I did."

"So, how did you end up in the Navy SEALs?" Agent Sutton asked. Duncan was taking notes, and they seemed to have their good-cop-bad-cop routine down to a science. I didn't care. I still had nothing to hide.

"I didn't really know what I wanted while I was in college," I said. "I was looking into joining the police force or FBI. Those seemed like logical ways to get a foot in the door. There was a Navy recruiter on campus one day, and I visited his table. I was more interested in the travel the military could provide, and the potential of having them pay for a master's degree. Instead, the recruiter sold me that day. Before I had left his table, I filled out an initial application to join the SEALs. He promised an excruciating challenge where the grand prize was hunting down terrorists all over the world. How could I say no to *that*?"

Sutton's eyelids fluttered. "That's...a wild story."

I sighed.

It always feels like a weird relief whenever I tell that story. Perhaps I'm supposed to let these things out, but that's impossible when I'm constantly by myself. I could try to see a shrink, but that would put me back on the grid. So I'm stuck dealing with my problems the old-school way: killing thugs who deserve it.

"Fun story," Duncan said mockingly. "Inspiring even. But it doesn't explain why you're here in Hillcrest."

I had a quick flash in my mind of strangling this twerp and bashing his head into the steel table. Poor Sutton wouldn't know what to do, and I'd be stuck here longer for assault. So I let my desires slide.

"My mother always told me to stay on the move," I said. "My father left us right after I was born. Joined one of the cartels, claiming he needed the money to support the family. My mother refused to join him, but he went anyway. That's why I don't have a permanent home. I bounce around North America so that I'm never settled into one place for too long. Six months max, but I'll usually leave after three."

"I don't understand," Agent Sutton said, concern slipping into her voice. "Why move around? Was she expecting your father to come find you?"

I nodded. "Yes. She didn't believe he was out to harm me, but that he'd want to find me one day, likely as an adult. And she swore no good could come from meeting this man."

"So you've never met your father?" Agent Duncan asked, leaning forward.

I shook my head. I hated talking about this asshole, but the sooner I answered their questions, the sooner I could leave.

"Everything I just told you is the full extent of what I know about him. I don't even know what he looks like. Never seen a picture. My mom completely erased him from our lives."

The two DEA agents exchanged a curious glance.

"Do you still have the home your mother left you in Laredo?" Duncan asked, and this question made my face prickle with heat.

"You're not supposed to know about that," I said. "I scrubbed that information from my file when I was with the CIA."

Duncan put his tablet down, screen powered off, and folded his hands on top of it. "We know that, but we still have access to the scrubbed files. We're working out of the same database you would have been using in the CIA."

I stood up, and my chair tipped over, creating a loud clatter. "If you can find that out, then anyone can. Why does anyone need to know about that house?!"

Duncan and Sutton looked at each other, uneasy.

"Mr. Mendez, please," Sutton said.

I started pacing. My childhood home was technically under my name—my mother had left it to me in her will. The keys were in a safe deposit box in Laredo, but I'd never gone back. I stood outside the house once, but the memories were too strong, and I left. I didn't think I'd ever be ready to actually step foot inside.

"You don't understand," I said. "If you found out about that house, so can my father."

"Mr. Mendez," Sutton cried out. "Your father doesn't have access to the U.S. government's database."

"That's what you think!" I shouted. "These cartels plant people all over the world, especially within governments. I can't have my father knowing about our old house. That was the last big secret my mother left behind, and it was my job to protect it."

"We can help," Duncan said.

"The fuck you can!" I shouted. I felt the veins bulging in my arms and forehead, and at this point didn't mind if one of them burst.

"SIT DOWN!" Duncan screamed at the top of his lungs, his words piercing through the tension filling the room. He had risen to his feet, fingers clutching the edge of the table as if he intended to flip it over.

I was panting for breath and pulled my chair off the ground to sit on it.

"Thank you for sharing all that information, Mr. Mendez," Duncan said, coming down from his own outburst. "We knew about your ties to the Mexican cartels and wanted to see what you could shed light on. Forgive us for jumping to conclusions, but I'm sure you can imagine why we thought you might be involved with a cartel."

"Involved?" I asked. This guy was fucking kidding me, right?

"Yes, involved," Duncan replied. "We're here because we've detected a Mexican drug cartel in Hillcrest."

Chapter 4

They let me go after another twenty minutes.

Naturally, there was nothing they could pin on me. I was in the wrong place at the wrong time. A Mexican cartel in Hillcrest, California.

Jesus Christ.

I started walking down the same road that had brought me to the police station, no idea where I was going. My initial plan when I had arrived was to ask someone at the tavern for a good motel to stay at for the night. But that had all gone down the shitter when these cartel bastards opened fire, which somehow made me look like the culprit despite being ten chips deep into my nachos. I wondered if anyone finished those, or if they got tossed out.

That would be the true crime on this fucked up evening.

The clock hanging on the wall in the police station showed it was a few minutes past ten o'clock when I strolled out the front doors. I'd only been walking for five minutes when headlights appeared behind me. I stepped more to the side, nearly falling into the ditch next to the road. The last thing I wanted was to become roadkill.

The headlights grew brighter, the accompanying engine humming as it approached, and eventually slowed to a crawl next to me.

"Want a ride?" a woman's voice called out.

I looked over to see Agent Sutton behind the wheel of a black town car with blacked-out windows. She had rolled down the passenger-side window, and the glow from the dashboard illuminated her face enough for me to see.

"Are you allowed to?" I asked, approaching the car. "I'm a dangerous man hitchhiking down the road."

Sutton cracked a smile that showed the beauty beneath her rigid exterior. "Just get in, tough guy."

I opened the door and lowered my head to clear the ceiling as I sat down. "I appreciate it."

"It's the least I can do after we berated you back there," she said. She had changed into faded jeans and a purple T-shirt. The cap was gone, and she let her hair flow naturally to her shoulders. "So, where can I take you?"

"I'm not actually sure," I said. "I just arrived here today and haven't found anywhere to stay."

Sutton laughed to herself. "I'll never understand how someone can live like that. No idea where you're staying. Where your next meal is coming from. Just completely winging it."

"It's a pleasant life. Food and shelter are really my only worries...and avoiding the police, apparently."

She laughed again. It was the sound of a woman who hadn't enjoyed a genuine laugh in quite a while. Almost forced, like she was making up for lost time. "Well, there are two hotels and two motels in town. None of them are anything to write home about, but I don't get the idea you're looking for a five-star presidential suite, either."

I chuckled. "Just a bed and bathroom. TV is nice to have,

but not a requirement."

I held my backpack on my lap as she drove off, and she stared at it for a moment. I could tell she wanted to ask what was inside, but she never did. Not that it was anything exciting.

"Do you care if we grab a drink?" she asked.

"Are you allowed to drink with a potential suspect?" I asked.

"You're not a suspect," she replied.

"Then sure," I said. "But your partner seems to think I am. He also seems like a dickhead."

Sutton burst into hearty laughter at this. "You're not far off the mark. Okay, I'll take you to the hotel on Main Street—the Hillcrest Hotel. That way tomorrow morning you'll have some options for breakfast and can poke around more of the town. Plus, they have a bar that should still be open."

We drove for five minutes, Sutton filling me in on what she knew about Hillcrest. She had been on assignment here for the past two months, trying to hunt down the cartel with no luck.

When we arrived at the hotel, the parking lot was nearly empty, so she found a spot near the front entrance. We entered the lobby and took a left down a hallway that connected to the Ridgeway Lounge and Grill.

It was a room with TVs hanging along the walls and fifteen dining tables spread across the floor between the entrance and the bar on the opposite side. Only two tables were occupied, one by a lone businessman enjoying a bottle of beer and watching sports highlights, the other by a tired-looking couple poking at the remnants of French fries on their plates.

"Do you care if we sit at the bar?" Sutton asked.

"Let's do it," I said, leading the way and pulling out a

barstool to allow her to sit down first. My mother raised a gentleman.

We took our spots, prompting the bartender to glide over. He was a younger man, probably bartending his way through college, with jet black hair pulled into a messy bun.

"Good evening, folks," he greeted. "Want to let you know our kitchen closes in about ten minutes if you're wanting to place a food order. Can I start you off with any drinks?"

"Dirty martini," Sutton said without hesitation, like she had been waiting all day to say those two words.

The bartender nodded and looked at me.

"I'll have a whiskey and Coke," I said, and the bartender shuffled away to start on the drinks.

"Did you want to eat something?" Sutton asked.

"I think I'm okay," I replied. "Had started on some nachos at the tavern, but don't feel much like eating right now."

"Me neither. Seeing dead bodies usually kills my appetite."

I agreed. There was a misconception about people in our particular field. That we were numb to all the death and destruction we regularly encountered. Bullshit. Seeing a dead body never became easier. We only knew how to better cope with it after increased exposure. For Sutton, she probably found herself at a bar after seeing a corpse. I usually looked for a gym to lift weights and sweat out the nasty feeling that accompanied such macabre visuals as bullet holes through flesh and bones.

"So," I said, turning in my seat to face her straight on. "Agent Sutton. Did you bring me here to ask me more questions? Off the record, of course."

She pursed her lips into a tight smile. "First off, just call me Lily. And yes, I want to hear more. Now that we know you're not involved with the cartel, and considering your background, I'd love your insight."

"My insight?" I asked, cocking an eyebrow. "I only got here a few hours ago. Can I at least get settled in before investigating what the hell's going on around here?"

Lily laughed. That sweet, pure sound again. "Fair enough. Are you going to leave town tomorrow?"

"Why would I do that? I just got here."

"Well, I figured with everything that happened tonight…I'm surprised you're not already running for the hills. I would be."

I chuckled. "I'm not one to run from danger. Not that it matters. It seems to follow me, regardless."

The bartender dropped off our drinks, and we thanked him. Lily pulled her martini glass to her lips like she had just gone a month in the desert. I took a sip of my drink to discover the bartender used Jack Daniels. Good man.

"On the contrary," I said. "I actually like it here. At least, everything I saw before the shots started pouring down on the tavern."

"Where did you come from last?" Lily brushed her hair behind her ear and took a long drink.

"Los Angeles," I said. "I've found I can stay in the bigger cities longer. Easier to move around different parts of the city and experience entirely different cultures. Took a job washing dishes in Chinatown for a couple of months. I definitely stuck out there. Bounced around the L.A. area for about ten months before I tired of the bustle. Headed up the coast and wound up here."

"This is a pleasant town," Lily said. "They got me in a short-term rental while we work on this case. Don't even have to live with Hunter—er, Duncan—although he's just one block over. Have had some time to explore and get acquainted with the locals."

"You've questioned me all night," I said. "Tell me about you. How does one end up in the DEA?"

Lily pushed her glass back and turned more to face me. The tip of her shoe brushed against my shin, something we both felt. She blushed before talking. "Well, I started as your everyday police officer back in Cleveland—that's where I'm originally from. This was after graduating with a degree in criminal justice. Worked my way up to detective after three years and got assigned to the narcotics unit. Found I really had a knack for it, and after four years in that role, a recruiter from the DEA reached out and asked if I'd apply. Been in this role ever since."

"And you're how old?"

"Thirty-four."

"Wow," I said, taking a sip. The whiskey made my throat tingle. "You've really been at it since college."

Lily nodded with a wide grin. "Sure have. And it's all thanks to *Criminal Minds*. I watched that show when I was young and became obsessed. Made me dream of hunting down criminals for a living. And here I am."

"Criminal Minds," I repeated, nodding along. "Good show."

"I know it's silly and not nearly as powerful a story as yours. But it's mine." She shrugged and finished her martini, waving at the bartender for a second one. "So you don't even know if your dad is still alive?"

The change in subject caught me off guard, but I figured this was what she had given me a ride for. Information. And she was just tipsy enough to have the courage to go for it. I respected it.

"No clue," I said. "I've presumed he's dead. I'm only two years from turning forty and he's yet to get in touch. Maybe I've been running from the ghosts of my past this whole time. But I don't want to stop and find out."

"You don't even know his name?"

I shook my head. "My last name is my mother's. She never so much as told me his name. As far as I'm concerned, the man never existed."

"No siblings?" she asked as the bartender brought her refill.

This question shot a pain into my chest. I'd become so accustomed to stuffing my past into a bottle that I sometimes forgot about the life I once had.

"I had an older brother," I said. "Manuel. He was four years older than me. We lived with my mom's sister after she passed. Manuel felt greater devotion toward our father, even though he had only known him for the first four years of his life. When he turned sixteen, he got into a big fight with our aunt about his future. He wanted to drop out of high school and join the cartel, and that's exactly what he did. Packed up a suitcase and left us a note that he was going back to Mexico to 'look for work.' But we knew what that really meant. He wanted to find our father and work for him. Or with him. Who knows?"

"Where was your brother when that car exploded?" Lily asked. She moved to the edge of her seat. Her foot kept brushing against my shin, but neither of us seemed to mind now.

"He was fourteen at the time," I said. "Was already doing a lot of things on his own. Might have been working or playing soccer." I shook my head. "He's such an idiot. He had college scouts talking to him during his sophomore year of high school. Probably would've had a full ride to the school of his choice. Threw it all away for nothing."

We nursed our drinks in silence for a moment. Lily gazed at the TV above the bar. I couldn't help but steal a glance at her slender curves. Two men entered the bar holding hands and took a seat at the table next to the tired couple, giggling and whispering.

"Why are you here?" I asked Lily, snapping her out of her daydream. "If it wasn't for the shooting today, I'd have a hard time believing the cartel is in Hillcrest."

Lily let out a deep sigh. "You and me both. We track drug usage all across the country. When the rate of overdoses climbs too high for a certain area, we head out and investigate. When we arrived, we had no suspicions of a cartel. But the more we poked around, it became clear something was going on. The overdoses continued to rise, and there were reports of suspicious men spotted around. That's the thing about the cartel, though. They know how to keep a low profile, especially in these small towns. They're loaded with money, but you won't catch them driving fancy cars or wearing lavish outfits and jewelry. That's something reserved for the big cities where they can get away with it."

"The men in the tavern were all wearing cheap suits," I said. "Tacky. That had to be them, right?"

Lily took a sip, put her glass down, and twirled her finger around the rim. "We have a short list of suspects. And it's only from taking pictures from a distance. Further, it's only the drug dealers. We still have no idea who's calling the shots."

"What kind of drugs?"

"Opioids brought us out here. But we found a baggie of meth on one of the dead men tonight. That and a burner phone on the other man."

"Any numbers to trace on the phone's history?"

Lily shook her head, and I saw the focus return to her eyes. Even while slamming down two martinis, she couldn't help but give deep thought to her case. "Nope. All inbound calls from a restricted number. We're holding on to it with hopes of someone calling. Unlikely, considering the dead men's acquaintances got away. I'm sure word has gotten around about the two deaths."

I leaned back in my seat and looked up at the TV. Spring training was underway in the baseball world, and all eyes were on the Dodgers and their new Japanese pitching phenom. I didn't want to get tied up with the cartel and their crimes. I'd seen plenty of times how ruthless they were. But apparently, I'm a sucker for this stuff. Why waste my God-given talents sitting on the beach while innocent people were in danger?

The DEA had been here for two months and made virtually zero progress. That was the problem with the bureaucracy and rules set in place by these government agencies. Sure, they kept their agents safe, but it always slogged the moving of the needle. I had no rules to follow and could force the matter.

"Let me help," I said, leaning forward again and taking another drink.

Lily laughed, then blinked her eyes in confusion as she realized I was being serious. "We can't just hire you on to help because you happen to be in town. You know that's not how this works."

I nodded. "Sure. You have protocol to follow. But imagine

if you didn't...like me."

Her eyes fluttered again. "What are you getting at?"

"I don't need an official title. Or money. Let me do some digging and see what I can find. I can even pose as someone wanting to buy drugs so I can get a better look at one of these dealers. If I can, I'll follow them back to wherever they stay."

"That's ludicrous!" Lily cried. "People don't just sign up for some dangerous case out of the goodness of their heart."

"I'm not some random person. This is what I do. No matter where I end up, I'm always finding myself face to face with danger."

Lily frowned as she pulled out her stick of olives from the martini and chewed on the first one. It didn't matter what she said, I was going to do this either way.

After a few seconds of consideration, she looked at me and said, "Okay. I'm not responsible for your safety. Let's be clear about that."

"Crystal clear," I said, smiling.

"Okay, is there anything you need from me?" She reached across the bar where they kept a bowl of breath mints. The red and white peppermint ones you find at most restaurants.

As she popped one into her mouth, we locked eyes. There was a burning tension between us, but it could have just been the alcohol.

"All I need is a gun."

Chapter 5

I spent the night at the Hillcrest Hotel and enjoyed a deep sleep. No dreams of dead cartel members or shattered windows. That was always a bonus.

When I woke, I showered and dressed before heading down for the continental breakfast. I ate three croissants, one chocolate muffin, and a banana. All washed down with a bottle of orange juice. Continental breakfasts were one of the finer things in life. At least for someone like me who lived on the road.

Before parting ways, Lily and I had made plans to meet at nine o'clock before she headed into the police station, where she and her partner had been conducting their official business since arriving in Hillcrest.

I wandered out of the hotel's doors with my backpack slung over one shoulder and slipped on a pair of sunglasses. Spring-time on the coast had cool mornings and suitable daytime temperatures in the mid-sixties. I wore the windbreaker I typically kept in my backpack, which made me perfectly comfortable.

Lily had been right in having me stay on Main Street. Just walking one block, I passed a pizza parlor, surf shop, two bars, and my home away from home: the local gym. Most of the businesses would open their doors at ten o'clock, so it was still a ghost town while I explored.

The gym was open, however, and I looked through the window to see a small but reasonable space. Plenty of weights, treadmills, and machines to maintain my strength.

A car honked from the street, and I turned around to see Lily, back in her DEA uniform. Now that I had seen the beauty behind the stern exterior, she seemed much less intimidating.

"Hop in," she said through the rolled-down window.

I settled into the passenger seat, and she greeted me with a cup of coffee.

"Apologies," she said, handing it over.

"What on earth are you apologizing for?" I asked, graciously accepting the gift.

"Last night," she said, the corners of her mouth turning into a frown. "We shouldn't have done that. Unprofessional on my part. If I wanted to ask you more questions, I should have just got you to come back to the station."

"Apology not accepted," I said, grinning. "I wouldn't have agreed to go back to the station. I much prefer the atmosphere of the bar. Laid back. No pressure. You seemed like you had a good time."

"I did," she replied, cracking a smile. "I'll admit I've had little fun since coming to Hillcrest. It's not exactly easy to make friends while on assignment. And Hunter never wants to do anything."

"*No bueno*," I said, earning a playful giggle. "Besides, I meant what I said last night. Let me help."

Lily had driven us three blocks, turned off Main Street and parked in front of a used car lot that wasn't open yet. "I thought you might say that. Open the glove box."

I furrowed my brow at her before turning my attention to the glove box and pulling open the small door. Staring back at me was a black pistol. I reached out and grabbed it, holding it up to find it was a Glock 48.

"It's my backup," she said. "So don't go losing it. There's a box of ammo in there, too."

I fished out the ammo and dropped the box into my backpack, along with the gun.

"That's pretty trusting of you to hand over a gun to someone you just met," I said, admiring the Glock in my grip.

"I read through your government files." Lily replied with a tight-lipped smile. "Well, what exists of them. You're as straight of an arrow as they come."

"Thank you," I said. "I never plan on using a gun. It's always my last resort."

"Right after beating someone to a pulp?"

I laughed. "No, I actually try to use my words first. You'd be surprised how well I can sweet talk a criminal."

That wasn't true. What usually happened was I made them more agitated to the point of having guns drawn.

"I'm sure," she said. "What's your plan for today?"

"You tell me. Where should I start? Any way you can point me is much appreciated."

"Well, lots of the overdoses are high schoolers, yet we've never seen a transaction occur on school grounds."

"Kids aren't *that* dumb," I said. "Usually."

"The meth is a surprise we came across last night, so your guess is as good as mine. Hunter and I plan on canvassing the neighborhoods for any homes that might look like meth labs."

I took a sip of my coffee. It had a hint of hazelnut that I

didn't normally enjoy. But it seemed okay this morning. I thought driving around looking for a meth lab was a waste of time, but I had no grounds to tell them what to do.

"Sounds like a good plan," I said. "I'll keep exploring town today and see what I can find. I need to at least get familiar with this city and its people. Maybe develop some trust with a few locals. Plus, I need to find somewhere to stay."

"Sounds like you have a busy day ahead, then," Lily said, drinking from her own coffee cup. "I need to head into the station, though. How can I get in touch?"

"Leave me your card," I said. "I'll grab a burner phone today while I'm out."

"Sure thing."

Lily opened the center console and pulled out her wallet. Dark purple with overlapping L and V letters. She had style.

I took her business card, which listed her full name as Lillian Sutton, along with her phone number and government email address.

"I'll be in touch," I said. "Thank you for the gun. I promise to take good care of it."

She smiled at me as I opened the door and stepped out. "Don't go getting in too much trouble out there."

"Wouldn't dream of it," I said as I closed the door and she drove off.

There I stood with a laundry list of things to do, and nowhere to actually go yet. Lily had dropped me on a side street, and I looked ahead to see another three blocks of businesses. Main Street was behind me, but I now saw a brewery, an indoor play center for children, and, most importantly, a grocery store.

I continued down the sidewalk as an empty school bus

passed by. The brewery was still closed, but I caught the slightest whiff of the yeast oozing from within its confines. I knew the scent all too well, having worked at a brewery while in college. It made me rather popular, having discounts at a place where practically every cash-strapped student spent their free time.

The play center was open already, as I saw a mother with three kids pile out of a van, sack lunches and water bottles in hand.

I arrived at Fresh Valley Grocers, a local chain I had seen across California. I knew they were open thanks to the massive sign in the front window advertising fresh coffee and doughnuts.

When I stepped in, I welcomed the mixed scents of bread, baked goods, and the aforementioned coffee. The combination was intoxicating. If I didn't have so much to do, I'd have spent a good portion of my morning sitting in the corner cafe next to the entrance.

Instead, I took a right and headed down the aisle behind the checkout lanes. The prepaid cell phones were usually in a locked case near a customer service desk and that proved true once more. They had lots of flip phones to choose from, and only one brand of smart phone. I didn't *need* a smart phone, but I never complained when I could connect to a free Wi-Fi.

"Can I help you, sir?" an older man asked me from behind the customer service counter. The lights gleamed off his bald head as he cracked a toothy grin at me.

"Yes," I said. "I'd like to get this phone."

He waddled over like a penguin, suggesting knee or hip pain. I pointed to the phone I wanted, and he raised his head to see through the glasses perched on the bridge of his nose. "Very good."

He wore a red apron with his nametag clipped front and center. Richard. When he reached into the front pocket of the apron to fish out the keys, I noticed a tattoo on the inside of his forearm. An eagle with the words Semper Fi scrawled above its outstretched wings.

"Thank you for your service, sir," I said.

Richard pulled out the keys with a shaky hand. "Why thank you, young man. Are you military?"

"Ex-military, sir. Ten years with the SEALs."

Richard raised his eyebrows. "The SEALs? I'll be damned. Thank *you* for your service."

I nodded in appreciation as Richard turned his focus to the case, opened it, and pulled out the package with my newest cell phone.

"I'll check you out over here," he said, locking the case back up and continuing his pained strides toward the register. I followed him and waited as he pushed buttons on his screen. "Sixteen dollars after the military discount."

"You didn't need to do that, sir. But I appreciate it."

He waved me off. "We've got to take care of each other, right? Always a soldier until our last breaths."

"Yes, sir. Do you mind me asking if you've lived here long?"

I pulled my backpack in front of me and took out my wallet, where I kept three hundred dollars cash and an assortment of Visa gift cards. Richard removed the security magnet from the phone's packaging and bagged it up for me as I slid a twenty across the counter.

"Spent my last four years in the Marines down in Pendleton," Richard said. "Moved here after I retired, which was twenty-seven years ago. Christ, where did all the years go?

Why do you ask, son?"

"I'm new to town," I said, and lowered my head and voice. "Working on a special assignment. Do you know the town's population?"

Richard nodded and lowered his voice without skipping a beat. "Last census said fifteen thousand, but I'd guess it's closer to twenty-five. Lots of undocumented folks living and working here."

"I see. Is this the only grocery store in Hillcrest?"

"We're the *main* grocery store, I'd say. The only all-purpose one, if you will. There are some other specialty stores like delis and bakeries. And two of those vegan stores all the hippie dippies like to go to." He shivered at the mention of such an atrocity in his city.

I chuckled at this. "Thank you, sir. I was just curious what all the town has to offer."

"Is there any danger I should know about, son?" he asked me. I didn't know how to answer that, considering I was a walking danger magnet. My mere presence in front of Richard was enough to warrant a yes to that question, not that an ex-Marine would shake in his boots at the mention. Unless a vegan grocery store was involved, of course.

"No danger, sir," I said. "That's why I'm here. To make sure it never gets to that point."

"Well, God bless you then, young man. You come see me if you need anything."

We shook hands, and I left the store. I sat on the bench outside the storefront and ripped open the box containing my new phone, powering it on to find a fifty percent charge. Not bad, but I'd need to plug it in before dinner time.

Richard might come in handy further down the line. People

needed to eat, and they didn't like to go out of their way for food. If there was only one grocery store in town, then the cartel was getting their food from Fresh Valley Grocers, like everyone else. The store offered delivery service, but I doubted these guys wanted anyone knowing where they lived. Not even the pimple-faced teenager smoking pot between deliveries.

I opened my phone, connected to the store's Wi-Fi, and searched for my extended stay options in Hillcrest. I found two. The StayComfort Suites and the Ocean Breeze Inn.

The Ocean Breeze Inn was more on the outskirts of town, and without a vehicle, that wouldn't work for me. The StayComfort Suites, however, was three-quarters of a mile north of my current location. And it was roughly a half mile west of the police station.

While it was technically a hotel, the suites had separate rooms, like a kitchen and living room, aside from the bed and bathroom. I usually stayed at these spots because they had the best pricing. Their cheapest room was advertised at seventy dollars per night. With four thousand dollars on those Visa gift cards, I could stay two months. I'd need to find work if I wanted to stay longer.

I plugged the address into the map, then took out Lily's business card to enter her phone number into my empty contacts list. I'd have no one else to add if I played my cards right for the rest of my time in Hillcrest.

With another search, I looked up the local high school and all the bars and restaurants within Hillcrest. If those men at the tavern last night were part of the cartel, then they clearly had no issue sitting in a public place where anyone could see them. I'd visit different spots throughout the week until I saw them again, though I suspected they might lie low for a while after the double murder.

I stood up and pulled the backpack over my shoulders, starting my brief walk to the StayComfort Suites. Several of the bars and restaurants I had pinpointed on my map were closed, but I could at least put a face to the name for when I'd return later.

As I passed by several more businesses, and eventually through a neighborhood, I couldn't help but feel like I was being watched.

Chapter 6

Two hours later, I was back on Main Street. I had checked in to my new home at the StayComfort Suites and talked the girl at the front desk into tossing me a free two weeks if I booked two entire months in advance.

"The worst they can say is no," my mother used to say. She swindled her way through more farmer's markets than you might believe. But she always got a deal, and I supposed I was keeping her spirit alive by doing the same.

I had lain down for thirty minutes after settling in my room to figure out how the hell I wanted to approach this ordeal. Stopping at the high school seemed like a bad idea. A big hunk like me lurking around all those teenage girls only spelled trouble, and probably another visit from Officer Matthews, who may or may not have been briefed on my secret involvement with this case. Probably not.

None of that mattered at the moment, and I needed to dig into whatever crime lurked beneath the surface of this peaceful town. Richard from the grocery store had mentioned several undocumented people living in Hillcrest. If the cartel was here, they could recruit from this pool of talent in desperate need of earning money under the table.

My mother spent the first six years of our life in Texas

undocumented. She had no choice but to take on the jobs no one else wanted. Washing dishes at restaurants, cleaning houses, offering childcare. Anywhere she could make a dollar, she'd take the opportunity.

I knew where to find these people, but I couldn't just barge into the back kitchen of a restaurant and start asking if anyone knew about the cartel presence in Hillcrest. That was the perfect way to scare off potential information. Or catch a slug to the face.

No. I needed to be patient and calculating.

Everything was open on Main Street, so I wandered into the first bar I came across. The sign outside was tattered, and the name of Ted's Place was barely visible thanks to the fading of the colors from constant sun exposure.

I pulled the door open, and a bell jingled from above. The space was cramped and narrow. The bar stretched all the way toward the back wall, and to the left, there was one row of five tables, one billiards table, and two restrooms in the back.

The man tending bar looked to be in his late fifties. Messy gray hair, lots of stubble on his double chin, and a classy T-shirt one size too small that read, "What the fuck do you want?"

I'd found my place. And on the first try. If I had to put any odds on it, I'd guess there was an eighty-five percent chance drugs were sold in this bar. Not necessarily by the bartender, although he might know which way to point me.

There was only one other person in the building. A man I would guess to be close to my age but looked much older thanks to the dark bags under his bloodshot eyes. He wore baggy clothes, but I couldn't tell if he lived on the streets.

"Well, ain't you a big motherfucker!" the bartender called

out, passing across a bottle of beer to his lone customer. He let out a hoarse chortle, which the other man copied while slapping the bar top.

"Do you greet all your new customers so kindly?" I asked, taking two more steps in. A normal person would have gladly turned around and gotten the hell out of this place. Good thing I wasn't normal.

"Relax, Sally," the bartender replied. "I'm just fuckin' with you. Come on in and have a drink. What's a man like you take, one of those floozy drinks with a pineapple on the rim?"

The customer let out a laugh that sounded more like a cry as he continued slapping the bar. I got the sense these two men were friends of some sort, or the man was at least a regular. Passing around their cheap jokes all day for a quick laugh.

"I'd like a glass of the best scotch you have," I said, pulling out a seat four spaces down from the drunken man. He had two empties in front of him as he grabbed the fresh bottle. "Neat, please."

The bartender stopped laughing and crossed his arms, gazing at me. Sizing me up. "Whatever you say."

He turned around to fix my drink, and I admired the bar's decorations. The walls were covered with a mixture of scantily clad women, some entirely nude. Posters for Budweiser and Coors Light. A Harley Davidson neon sign that wasn't yet turned on suggested bikers most likely frequented this bar.

Behind the bar hung a flat-screen TV showing Fox News on mute. An American flag next to one of those "Don't Tread on Me" flags. Precisely the people I preferred to tread on.

The bartender approached with my glass of scotch. "Here you go, big guy. Grants scotch. Neat."

As if I needed any more confirmation, this verified I was in a dive bar. I wouldn't call myself a scotch snob, but I knew Grants was the type of bottle broke college kids bought to make themselves feel classy drinking out of their red Solo cups. It would probably cost me five dollars and leave me with a pleasant headache.

"Thank you," I said, pulling in the glass and taking a sip. It stung my gums and throat on its way down.

The two men watched me drink, staring at each other every few seconds as I looked mindlessly at the TV showing a commercial for Taco Bell.

"What's a big wetback like you doing here in town?" the bartender asked.

I took another drink, trying to make sure I heard the man correctly. I really hoped he didn't want to go down this path with me. Taking offense to people's words was not in my blood, but I believed in teaching people a lesson whenever they felt they could get mouthy with a stranger. And this time, *I* was the stranger.

The drunk man whistled at me. "Hey, bean boy, we're talking to you!"

Bean boy. That one made me giggle. I did love a good bowl of refried beans with cheese and rice. They got that part right.

I cleared my throat and stood up, the feet of the barstool screeching against the wooden floor.

"Gentlemen," I said, finishing my scotch before slamming the empty glass back down. "Why so much name-calling? It's not polite."

The two men grabbed their bellies and howled with delight. I could have taken the high road and left the bar without a fuss. But I wanted information that I was fairly sure these men had. And now they owed me.

"Polite?" the bartender asked. "What would be polite is for you people to get the fuck out of my city and country."

"You people?" I asked, rolling my head from side to side. These men wanted a fight, and I was happy to oblige, even in the middle of a weekday afternoon. "And what people is that, exactly?"

"All you dirty Mexicans," the bartender said, hocking up spit and sending it my way. Lucky for him, it landed short, but the sentiment wasn't lost on me. "You spics have been sneaking in and taking over. You're everywhere! Fifteen of you crammed into one tiny little house, up to no good."

"Spics?" I asked. "Wow. Do you even know how to spell that word?"

"Don't get smart with me, boy," the bartender grumbled through clenched teeth.

I glanced at my backpack that I had left on the stool next to where I was sitting. My new gun was in there, and I didn't think I'd need it so soon. But considering this unfolding situation, I'd bet this gentleman kept a shotgun or two beneath the bar.

"Well, *sir*," I said. "I'll have you know I served this country for ten years of my life. I may have been born in Mexico, but I was raised in this country since before I could even walk."

"Bullshit," the bartender snarled. "Get the hell out of my bar before this day goes a hell of a lot worse for you."

The bartender's fists balled up, and the drunk hopped out of his stool, swaying a moment before gathering himself.

"Is this really what you want?" I asked.

"Let's go, bean boy!" the drunk hollered, taking two steps toward me.

Bean boy again. Too funny.

The drunk lunged, surprisingly quick on his feet. He reared back a fist and swung it forward when he was within two feet of me. I sidestepped like a matador toying with a pissed-off bull. The drunk tumbled off balance and crashed forward, taking down a barstool with him. He moaned something I couldn't make out as he scrambled to get to his feet. I dashed down the bar and grabbed the two empty bottles he had left behind.

The bartender ducked low, and I knew he was going for his gun. In his mind, I was now the one threatening him, and he had every right to shoot me. The moment his head came back up, I flung the bottle and watched it connect squarely to his right temple.

He shouted in agony. "Dammit! You motherfucker!"

His little goon had finally regained his footing and charged at me once more. This time, I held my ground and grabbed the man by the throat. His measly fist connected with the side of my neck in what felt more like being hit by one of those foam balls kids played with in the giant ball pits.

I seized his wrist and twisted it outward until I heard the popping sound of his elbow dislocating. The drunk wailed in pain, clutching his arm as he collapsed to the floor. To my left, I grabbed a second empty beer bottle and cocked it back, waiting for the bartender to get back to his feet. But he never did, and after waiting twenty seconds, I leaned over the bar to see him also on the floor, head bobbing from side to side as he uttered incoherently.

"Let me help you up," I said, tossing the beer bottle on his chest for good measure. People playing hurt had tricked me in the past, but I doubted this gentleman was playing that game. Still, I could never be too sure.

He didn't react when the second bottle struck him on the sternum, so I knew he really was injured. I circled the bar and found a shotgun just out of his reach, lying on the floor by the man's sprawled out feet. A Remington 870. One of the finest pump-action shotguns that was sure to tear apart a human body at close range.

I kicked the shotgun aside and crouched low to pull up the bartender from his shoulders. He moaned, his head rolling around like he had no control over it. I spotted the stool he must have used further down the bar, and dragged him to it, propping him up like a useless dummy.

I slapped his face gently to help coax him back into consciousness. That first bottle had hit him perfectly in the temple, and I knew he wasn't feeling anywhere near his best. I didn't always have such impeccable accuracy, but of course I did on the day when I needed to extract information from this racist excuse of a man.

"Let's go, buddy," I said, tapping on his cheek.

He snorted and let out hot, sour breath. Pistachios and beer. Did no one ever tell this man to not get high off his own supply?

"Wake up, asshole," I said again, peeking over the bar to check on his friend. Poor bastard had fainted from the pain. He was lucky I didn't dislocate both elbows.

The bartender blinked his eyes slowly, so I grabbed a couple of rags from the bar and tied each of his wrists to the barstool, sure to triple knot them.

Eventually, he became alert enough as his eyes focused on me, surely trying to piece together what had just gone wrong in his attempt to exterminate me.

"You're going to be fine," I said, lowering my face to his.

The man drew a deep breath.

"What's your name?" I asked.

He cleared his throat three times before responding, "Ted."

I scoffed. "Ted? As in Ted's Place? You're the owner of this bar and insult a brand-new customer like this." I shook my head. "Oh, Teddy. You must have never taken a business class. You're not supposed to insult your customers, dumbass. Bad for business. I could have had friends I wanted to bring back here, and you just lost out. How the hell are you still in business?"

"Who are *you*?" Ted asked, his voice sounding almost confident.

"I'm bean boy, remember?" I replied with a wide grin. "Enough about me. I came here today looking for drugs, and if you want any chance of getting out of this chair, you'll tell me how."

Ted scrunched his face like he had just bitten a rotten apple. "Drugs? Do I look like a drug dealer to you? I run a legit operation here."

"Yeah, for whites only, apparently. Seriously, though. I'm new in town and am looking to score. Where do I go?"

"I told you, man, I don't have any drugs."

I stepped back and sighed, crossing my arms. "Look, we can do this the hard way, where I'll break your fingers one by one. Or you can just tell me."

Ted let out a laugh that he immediately tried to pull back. He wasn't sure if I was bluffing or not, so I had to reassure him.

"I took out you and your friend without even pulling my gun out of my backpack," I said, lowering myself to get eye to eye with him again. He glared at me, and I could tell he wanted so badly to spit in my face. But he knew better now. "If you think bending your fingers backwards is out of my comfort zone, you're sorely mistaken. So what's it going to be?"

I stepped back again. It was only polite to give a man space to think and consider his options, especially when it involved retaining his body parts.

Ted looked me up and down twice, probably trying to figure a way out of this mess. But he'd reached a dead end.

Me.

Bean boy was the dead end.

He gulped before speaking. "Hamburger Stand."

"Excuse me?"

"Hamburger Stand," Ted repeated. "On the corner of Seventh and Orchard. Go inside and order a triple deluxe. They'll serve you a regular burger with fries, then you go around the back to meet a guy named Ben. He'll take care of you."

Burgers. Triple deluxe. Ben. Got it.

"Is he the only one in town?" I asked. "Or can I find someone else if he doesn't have what I need?"

"Fuck if I know, man," Ted replied. "He's the only one I know, and that's his process."

"I'll tell him you said hi," I said, turning away to exit the area behind the bar. "Thank you for the info. That's all I wanted."

"Hey!" Ted cried desperately. "What about letting me free?"

I stepped over the knocked-out drunk and swooped up my backpack as I headed for the door. Without looking back, I called out, "Maybe when you upgrade your scotch collection!"

Chapter 7

I hated starting off a perfectly beautiful afternoon that way, but old Teddy left me no choice. In any case, I had my answers, and after dashing two blocks away from Ted's Place, I sat down on the curb along Main Street to pull out my phone to search for this Hamburger Stand.

I had fled to the north from the bar, and it must have been a subconscious fate at play, because that was exactly the direction I needed to go. Three more blocks north, and two west would take me to the intersection of Seventh and Orchard.

My motivation increased after seeing I was well on my way, and the GPS suggested it was a fifteen-minute walk to complete the journey.

I made it in ten and stood in front of the most peculiar looking fast-food joint I'd ever seen. Next to me stood a towering pole with a sign thirty feet in the air that simply said, "Hamburger Stand" in bright orange lettering that looked too similar to Whataburger.

Ahead of me, however, was a light tan building with a tall, triangular roof that stretched nearly as high as the sign. The roof was too narrow to house office space or anything of importance. It was apparently a design decision that probably should have been reconsidered. It looked like an awkward birthday party hat on top of the actual restaurant portion below, which had several large windows that allowed me to see inside.

Only two tables inside were taken, and one man stood in line at the counter to place his order. When I searched this place, all I had seen were rave reviews.

Best burgers in SoCal!

I would die for one of these juicy patties of perfection!

Shit like that.

People are funny in how passionate they can get about food. I've traveled the continent and can count on six hands how many times I've eaten at a local diner advertising the world's best pie, or soup, or burrito. Marketing at its finest, I suppose.

Regardless, the word of mouth of total strangers on the internet had my mouth watering at the thought of trying one of these burgers.

I strolled up to the doors and pulled them open, welcomed by a rush of warm air. Why did they have the heater blasting so intensely?

I couldn't deny the smells filling my nose. French fries, grilled beef, and onions. Is there a better combination? Washing it all down with a fountain Coca Cola was the cherry on top.

No, I didn't indulge like this often, but when I did, I made it count.

I approached the counter, keeping a safe distance to study the menu before they called me up and expected me to know what was going on. There was no triple deluxe on the menu, a good sign. Ted could have made up the entire story to get me out of his bar, but a secret menu option only proved his honesty. He couldn't have made that up on the fly. Not with his phalanges at risk.

A young Latino man stood behind the counter, dressed in his uniform of all black clothes with an orange apron draped over, complete with a matching visor that reiterated the name of the restaurant. He finished with the customer in front of me and offered a pleasant smile in my direction. "Good afternoon, sir. Are you ready to order?"

I grinned back and stepped forward. No way this kid was involved with any of the shady drug dealings. He seemed too straight, judging by the first impressions.

"Hello," I said confidently. "I'd like to order the triple deluxe, please."

His eyes flickered so subtly that I wouldn't have noticed if I wasn't looking him straight on. He looked me up and down, then nodded his head as he started pressing buttons on his register. "One triple deluxe coming right up. Will that be all today?"

Apparently, I had jumped to a conclusion too soon with this kid. He was definitely in on the whole thing and didn't skip a beat.

"That's all," I replied, pulling out my wallet.

"Great. That will be nine-fifty total."

I slid over a ten, and he was already handing me a receipt. On the back was messy handwriting that said *Head out back in five minutes.*

I turned it over and found the receipt wasn't actually from my order, not even the same day. And apparently I wasn't getting my fifty cents back in change, as the kid had vanished into the back. Fuckers.

I stepped aside to the area in front of the soda fountain

machine and waited. Ranchera music blared from the kitchen in the back, and I enjoyed listening to the cooks whistling and singing along. It reminded me of home, where pretty much any public place in Laredo had ranchera music playing in the background.

The kid returned from the back and took his position behind the register, smiling ahead and acting like I didn't exist. I assumed he went back to inform the supposed Ben that I had ordered the triple deluxe.

A moment later, another employee came from the back with a white paper bag and placed it on the counter. "Your triple deluxe," he said in a heavy accent that was undoubtedly from Mexico.

He pivoted and disappeared without waiting for me to react. I felt rather uneasy about how open and simple this process seemed, but I couldn't deny this drug dealer had his system efficiently in place.

I grabbed the paper bag and peeked inside to see the burger and fries. When I glanced at the kid, he kept staring ahead. At least it was awkward for him, too.

The burger was calling, but I had business to attend to. With the bag clutched in my grip, I exited the restaurant and promptly circled the building to the back. I passed a dumpster, the lid pressed upward by overloaded bags of garbage. Against the building stood a storage crate of propane tanks with a heavy padlock keeping it secure. Next to the crate was a lone door that led into the back of the restaurant.

As I approached, the door swung open and out stepped a Latino man with jet-black hair slicked all the way back, a perfectly trimmed goatee, and sunglasses so shiny I could see my reflection perfectly. He wore jeans and a leather jacket over a white T-shirt, several rings decorating his fingers.

"Who sent you?" he asked, stepping up to me, completely unbothered by my ten-inch height advantage over him.

"Hello," I said, sensing this guy's distrust. "Ted. From Ted's Place. You must be Ben."

He took a step back and looked up at me. "What were you doing with Ted? That guy's a racist piece of shit."

I heard the disdain in his voice and could safely assume he had also been called bean boy by Ted at some point.

"Yeah, I figured that out real quick," I said. "I'm new to town and wandered into his bar looking for some pills. He sent me your way."

The man said nothing and continued gazing in my direction, although I had no idea what he was actually looking at thanks to the sunglasses.

"You a cop?" he asked after a few seconds.

"They wish," I replied. "I'm ex-military. Got hooked on Vicodin after suffering an injury. Still use it to keep myself calm."

"When did you get here?" he asked, crossing his hands in front of his belt buckle.

"To Hillcrest? Just a couple days ago. I move around a lot, don't really settle in one place for too long."

"You looking for work?"

"Not at the moment, but that may change in a couple of months."

I knew what he was doing. He had to ask me random questions to see if I would stumble on any answers or contradict myself. All I could do was answer with confidence.

I apparently passed the test, as he nodded.

"My name's Ben," he said, which I knew was a lie. No drug

dealer, especially one this organized, ever gave out their real name to their customers. "Vicodin all you're looking for?"

I nodded. "That or anything similar."

Ben hadn't moved in the last minute and continued watching me from behind his shades. "Lift your shirt for me."

"Excuse me?" I asked, sounding more defensive than I had intended.

"Relax, guy," he said calmly. "Just making sure you're not strapped or wired."

"I see."

I felt ridiculous pulling up my shirt behind this odd building in front of this random drug dealer I'd just met, but I did just that.

He nodded and turned around. "Be right back."

I watched him go through the back door and waited by stuffing my hands in my pockets and kicking some rocks on the ground. I'd never done anything like this before. The last time I bought drugs from a dealer was at a college party. Just some weed, so it wasn't a big deal and fairly straight forward. Hiding out behind a fast food joint definitely added to the criminal sensation of my current endeavor. Some might call it a rush.

Two minutes passed before the door swung open again, and Ben returned.

"Hundred for ten," he said once the door glided shut behind him. He returned to stand three feet in front of me.

"That's a bit steep," I said. "My guy in L.A. was getting me ten for fifty."

I had no idea what the going rate for opioids was from a black-market dealer, but I figured he would at least try to hustle me, since it was our first encounter. Drug dealers had to set the bar from the first meeting, and I at least knew that much.

Ben licked his lips, frustrated I didn't fall for his offer.

"Ninety," he said, and now I had *him* on the hook.

"Fifty," I repeated.

"Fifty is absurd. Your guy was probably selling some off-brand shit. I have the real thing. I'll go down to eighty."

By now, Ben knew he couldn't lie to me, and I trusted he had authentic Vicodin. I also heard the slightest murmur of frustration in his voice, so I pounced.

"It's fine," I said, turning and walking away. "I'll keep looking elsewhere."

I took fifteen steps and reached the corner of the building, thinking he was actually going to let me walk.

"Sixty!" he shouted. "Final offer."

I grinned to myself before turning around and showing him a flat expression. "Deal."

I shuffled back to him, kicking up a storm of dirt I hoped would powder his leather jacket. My wallet was still in my pocket after ordering inside, the scent of the burger still tempting me with each step I took. The sooner we got this over with, the sooner I could sink my teeth into this world-renowned beef.

I pulled out three twenties and handed them over. Ben grabbed the bills and stuffed them into his pants pocket, then reached into the inside pocket of his jacket, where he pulled out a small baggie with ten white pills inside. "Pleasure doing business," he said, extending his hand like he wanted me to shake it.

We did the classic move, posing as old friends clapping hands, and I felt the baggie slip into my palm as he pulled his hand away. This guy had swag and confidence. In some other life, I'm sure I'd want to grow up to be like him.

I moved the baggie into my pocket and said, "Is this where I can find you all the time?"

Ben nodded. "I'm usually here. If not, someone here will know where I am and can get in touch."

Noted.

"Thank you, Ben," I said, grinning to his face now. "I look forward to seeing you again.

Ben nodded at me and we both turned away from each other at the same time to head our separate ways.

I returned to the front of the building and crossed the street without looking back. Ben couldn't possibly live at the Hamburger Stand, so I found a bus-stop bench to sit on catty-corner from the restaurant. Now that I knew what the drug dealer looked like, I just needed to keep track of him. There had been no car parked around the back of the building, but I counted four vehicles in the restaurant's main lot. With two customers inside, that left two other cars belonging to the staff. I had seen the young man, a cook, and Ben. It was possible two of them had carpooled to work, but I still couldn't know if there were other employees I hadn't seen.

With a clear view of the Hamburger Stand, I opened my bag of food and unfolded the paper wrapper holding my burger. It was still a decent warmth, considering almost fifteen minutes had passed since I received it.

The burger made my day, and I couldn't help but be frustrated by the fact. Lettuce, tomato, onions, pickles, and a mystery sauce swirled around with a perfectly juicy patty of beef in my mouth. The bun was crunchy on the outside and soft in the middle. My head spun while this first bite went down.

Dammit.

I'd really hoped the burger from a joint being run by a drug dealer was going to taste lackluster, but that couldn't have been further from reality.

An hour passed, and I didn't leave a single crumb of burger or fries behind. I even sucked the salt right off my fingertips because I liked to live on the edge. I was pissed at myself for forgetting to order a Coke and had nothing to quench my thirst. Fuck.

With the trash balled up and lying by my side, I jumped off the bench when Ben exited through the restaurant's front doors. He walked alone and got behind the wheel of a black Chevy Silverado.

If only I had known that was his truck, I could have hidden in the bed to find out where he was going. Maybe some other time.

I pulled out my cell phone and dialed the only number saved in it.

After six rings, Lily answered, "Agent Sutton."

"Hey," I said. "It's Jonny."

"Well, you got a phone pretty quick."

"I've had an interesting day," I replied. "I have some info worth sharing. Can we meet tonight?"

"Okay," she said. "I've already had to skip lunch today. Do you mind if we have dinner when I get off? Let's say six o'clock at Carlo's?"

I had seen several restaurants while browsing the map and Main Street and remembered seeing Carlo's Italian Ristorante.

"I'll be there."

Chapter 8

My new home at the StayComfort Suites was only a seven-minute walk from the Hamburger Stand, so I stopped there to lie down and freshen up before meeting Lily for dinner.

Carlo's was on the central part of Main Street, sandwiched between a barber shop and an accounting firm. I had to pass by Ted's Place on my way and stayed on the opposite side of the street. The lighting inside was dim, but I saw a handful of people sitting at the bar enjoying a cold beverage at the end of the workday. I supposed Ted didn't share what had happened to him earlier that afternoon. Or maybe he had. I didn't particularly give a shit at this point.

I arrived at Carlo's five minutes before six and leaned against the brick exterior. The backpack wasn't necessary for dinner, so I left it in my room, bringing only my wallet and cell phone. I'd considered bringing my gun, but I was going to dinner with a DEA agent.

I must have looked like a bouncer, as several people paused to look at me before entering the restaurant. Most smiled and nodded when they realized I was just a regular guy loitering around and went about their jolly evening.

I checked my phone at 6:12. No message. No Lily.

But I expected as much. Law enforcement seemed to be

late to any personal matter, especially if the plans were after work. There was always one last thing they needed to review or some paperwork to submit. I was glad to be out of the CIA. The paperwork was damn near suffocating.

Lily finally arrived at 6:19, hurrying down the sidewalk from a block further down.

"Sorry, I'm late," she said. "I got caught up with some things at the station."

Of course.

"Still had time to change, I see," I said.

Lily was again in jeans and a button-up blouse with no sleeves. Her silky hair flowed, and I couldn't help but notice a faint scent of lavender.

"Of course I needed to change," she said. "This is a fancy restaurant. Well, fancy for a small town. Beats eating more fast food at my kitchen table alone. I never get to go out like this."

Lily was in desperate need of fun, and surely saw me as that outlet, now for the second night in a row. I was happy to oblige.

"I'm just teasing you," I said. "You look nice."

She blushed at the compliment and broke eye contact. "So do you."

I laughed. "I don't exactly carry around a suit in that backpack of mine. Jeans and T-shirts for me, but I at least did some laundry earlier."

"Let's head in," she said, starting for the door. "Then you can tell me all about your day."

I leaped ahead to open the door for her, and she offered a cute smile while passing me by. It was at this moment I noticed her light red lipstick. Was I on a date? Because it was starting to feel like one.

Lily spoke with the hostess, a high school girl with a welcoming smile, and we followed her to a table for two along the wall.

We sat down, welcomed to the table by a flickering candle as the centerpiece. Soft Italian jazz played through the speakers, mostly inaudible because of the hum of conversation in the restaurant. Laughter, clinking of glasses, and the clatter of silverware on plates filled the room. The heavenly smell of freshly baked garlic bread lingered in the air.

"So, tell me all about today," Lily said, grabbing one of two glasses of water that had already been set out on the table.

She sipped while I told her about Richard at Fresh Valley Grocers, checking in to my new place at the StayComfort Suites, and, of course, the fight with Ted.

"Jonny!" she cried. "You can't just walk around town beating up the racists!"

Her tone suggested she was quite satisfied with what I had done.

"To be fair, I didn't beat him up because he was racist. I beat him up because he was going to shoot me."

She cackled with delight and called over our server to order a bottle of wine.

"There's more to it," I continued. "I asked Ted where I can find drugs, and he directed me to the Hamburger Stand."

"The Hamburger Stand?" Lily repeated.

"Do you know it?" I asked.

"Of course," she said. "When I'm having a good week of self-control, I'll only eat there once. Don't go back for dessert, though, or you'll be addicted."

"Well, I think some people *are* going there because of their addictions," I said. "Sure enough, I bought ten Vicodin pills from a guy named Ben. Had me meet him around the back of the building after ordering a triple deluxe. That's code, of course."

Lily nodded and reached into her purse to pull out a notepad. She jotted down what I was saying, and that made this feel like less of a date. Fine by me, either way.

"Hamburger Stand," she said again. "Really? We're going to have to take another look at their financials."

"Why is that?" I asked.

"Well, one of the first things we do when arriving in a town is look at the businesses. Where there are illegal drugs, there's usually money laundering. Bars, restaurants, casinos, and strip clubs are the favorites for laundering. Basically, anywhere that has a lot of foot traffic or transactions. We found nothing out of the ordinary for any business in town, and we've sort of pushed that priority to the back burner."

"Forgive me for not being too familiar with this stuff—I used to hunt terrorists," I said. "But would someone dealing drugs conduct that business from the same location they're using to launder the money?"

"Absolutely," Lily said without hesitation. "That's why I'm so intrigued."

"That explains why the burgers are so good," I said, more to myself. "They need customers coming back for more and more."

"Exactly. You said this guy's name was Ben. Did you get a last name?"

"Afraid he wasn't exactly up for getting personal," I said. "And I doubt Ben is his real name. Not to stereotype, but he didn't exactly *look* like a Ben."

"Latino?" she asked, and I nodded.

Lily sighed just as the server returned with a bottle of wine and a basket of garlic bread.

"So, was any of this information useful?" I asked, taking a slice of bread and spreading butter over the surface while our server poured our first glasses of wine.

"It's very helpful," she said, then waited a moment for our server to step away. "None of our intel has pointed back to Hamburger Stand. We've been wasting our time at the high schools and looking for meth labs. I'll be honest, Duncan has been pretty checked out during this assignment. I think he has some issues back home. Heard him on the phone with his wife, and the call did not sound pleasant."

"Life on the road can put strain on a relationship," I said.

"Oh? Do you speak from experience?" Lily asked as I pulled my glass closer.

"Always. Tried it when I first joined the SEALs, and the relationship fizzled out after six months. It's nearly impossible to keep the romance alive when you can't physically see each other every day. Paranoia creeps in, accusations get thrown out. Messy stuff."

Lily nodded. "I don't doubt it. I can't fault Duncan if that's what he has going on, but I feel like I'm shouldering the load of this entire assignment. He's doing the bare minimum to save his ass, but he's not as enthused as he's been in the past."

"Have you mentioned me assisting to him?" I asked, taking a sip of the wine. It was fruity, and I didn't exactly like it. But I had to be polite and keep sipping.

"Yeah..." she said, taking an extended gulp.

"Oh boy. He didn't take it well?"

Lily chuckled. "He lost his shit. Said I must be out of my

mind letting a citizen put themselves in danger on our behalf. I stressed you had volunteered, and I can't actually stop you from doing anything."

"He can throw me in jail if he feels I'm getting in the way," I said. Again speaking from experience.

Lily shook her head. "That's not going to happen. Like I said, he's too checked out. I think his reaction was because he felt undermined. Maybe if he was actually helping me, I'd consider what he had to say. But I *need* the help, and you seem plenty capable. No matter how unorthodox this is."

"It's only unorthodox because there's no paper trail approving what I can and can't do. You work by the book, and there's nothing wrong with that. But I know that doesn't always get things done. Had you ever considered barging into Ted's and asking him where to find drugs?"

"Well, no," she said. "We never had a reason to even question Ted about anything. He's not involved. We've poked around some other suspects, but have come up empty."

"Exactly. When you've lived my lifestyle, you develop an instinct for finding things. Look at today. In a matter of two hours, I found a cell phone, a place to stay, and where to find drugs in this city."

Lily grinned. "Imagine what you can do with a week."

I nodded. She wasn't wrong.

"What's your plan for tomorrow?" she asked.

"Is there any chance I can get a car?" I replied, stuffing a fresh slice of bread into my mouth.

"For what, exactly?"

I swallowed and took a sip of water. "Well, I found Ben today. Saw what he drives. Would have been nice to follow him. If I can track him to where he lives, who knows what doors will open? I assume he's not working alone, so tracking him will be key to finding who else is involved."

"I'll see what I can do."

The server returned to take our orders. Our conversation about the drug ring in Hillcrest subsided after that, and we chatted more about our lives while waiting for dinner to arrive. Twenty minutes later, my plate of lasagna appeared along with Lily's baked ziti. We feasted, and the wine gradually disappeared. It actually tasted much better paired with the entrée.

After we finished, the server dropped off the check, and Lily snatched it up immediately.

I reached across the table for it, sensing my mother turning in her grave at this disturbing possibility of me not paying for dinner with a beautiful woman.

Lily smacked my hand away. "I'm covering this. It's a job expense."

"Fine Italian dining and wine is a job expense?" I asked, crossing my arms.

"Did we not discuss the case? Did we not make progress on it?"

"Well, yes," I said.

"Okay, then. It's a job expense. I get a daily stipend for meals and have never come close to spending it all. We could do this a couple more times this week, and I'd still have a surplus."

I tossed up my hands. "If you insist. I'd like to contribute somehow, though. It's how I was raised."

"Fine. Go get me a couple of those mints from the host stand up front. They were in a bowl."

"The red and white mints? Are you addicted to those or

something?"

Lily grinned. "Would it be wild if I said they were my favorite candy?"

"Wild? No. A bit unusual, perhaps."

She let out a hearty laugh as I stood from the table and crossed the dining room to grab a handful of the mints.

When I returned, the check had been settled, the plates removed, and the wine officially polished off.

I dropped the pile of mints onto the table and watched her face light up with sheer joy. "Thank you," she said. "For everything tonight. I feel like I have an actual partner again. Want to grab some ice cream? There's a parlor across the street that's just to die for."

Ice cream. Maybe this was a date again.

We went and talked the night away until they kicked us out at closing time.

Chapter 9

My buzzing phone woke me the next morning. I'd kept it on vibrate overnight, and the steady hum alerted me to an incoming call.

It was Lily, and it was already nine o'clock.

"Hello?" I said, clearing my throat.

"Wow, still asleep?" she said, a slight cheer in her voice.

"Like I said, I'm not tied to any work schedules." I sat up, shaking my head free of the fog following such a deep night of sleep. "I was out late last night. You know, big dinner and ice cream. The usual."

"Oh, is that right?" I could hear the smile in her voice. "I haven't had a full night's sleep in six weeks. Last night may have been the final nail in the coffin. I'm *exhausted.*"

"Why's that?"

Lily sighed. "I got home and was so energized by our conversation. You gave me new hope for this case, so I spent hours on my computer looking into all sorts of matters..."

She trailed off, and I wouldn't put it past her to have fallen asleep on her keyboard if she really had pulled an all nighter.

"Are you there?" I asked.

"Yes, sorry." Lily sounded more awake than me somehow. "I was debating if I should tell you this over the phone or not.

It'll be better in person. Can you meet me at the police station this afternoon?"

"Afternoon? You're going to tease me with mysterious information and make me wait all day?"

"I'm afraid so," Lily said. "I'm going out this morning with Duncan to canvass more neighborhoods. Then the police chief wants to have lunch with us to discuss the case. He's done this every couple of weeks. I'll keep my afternoon clear, if you can meet me at three?"

"And what am I supposed to do for the next six hours?"

"Look, Jonny," Lily said, lowering her voice. I could hear chatter and phones ringing in the background. She was already at the police station. "Cases like this can be a little slower paced than what you're used to. Not every second of the day is going to make progress. Enjoy the morning and afternoon, then come meet me. I think I'll have a car for you this evening, too. Then you can really hit the town and work your magic."

"I'm not a magician, but thank you."

She laughed, a lazy sound that showed her true fatigue. "Just be here at three, okay? It's important."

"You got it. I'll see you then."

We hung up, and I lay back down. She was right. I could use some rest. I'd practically been at it since the minute I arrived in Hillcrest. Bullets in the tavern. Two dead bodies. Questioning at the police station, followed by the whirlwind of activities yesterday. As much as I wanted to go back to the Hamburger Stand to check on Ben—okay, and *maybe* grab another burger—there was little I could do aside from hiding in the bed of his truck and waiting.

That option simply wasn't efficient or smart.

Something in Lily's voice—not the sleepiness—suggested I needed to brace myself for bad news. It was the same tone my mother had used when I was a child. The *I need to talk to you after school* tone that caused a day of dread and the inability to focus on any single task while at school. Why did parents do shit like that?

I'd always been a straight shooter and couldn't tolerate such madness. I pushed the thoughts aside. It was not like Lily had any personal bad news to deliver to me. She likely found something sensitive in her research she wanted to discuss in private. And that was fine.

Killing time posed no challenges. I threw on some clothes from my dirty laundry pile, headed downstairs for the continental breakfast, then returned to my room, where I fell asleep for another three hours. Apparently, having no immediate worries allowed my mind to relax and catch up on the overdue rest I needed.

I woke again at 12:30, took a shower, put on fresh clothes, and watched TV for the next ninety minutes. The local news mentioned warming temperatures over the next week, and thoughts of the beach came calling me back. That's why I had come here, after all.

When the weather segment ended, the anchor discussed another teenager in the hospital after taking pills at a party. The kid's name was Dominic Evans, and he was only three months away from graduating high school with a full-ride scholarship to play basketball at the University of Wisconsin. Instead of enjoying the last months of his senior year, he now lay comatose in the hospital with an uncertain future.

They kept his picture from the yearbook on the screen. Letterman jacket, short spiky hair, and a charming smile.

I saw the innocence behind his eyes. So young. So much potential. The easy access to drugs in Hillcrest had derailed another bright future. Hopefully a case like this would scare the other kids from taking drugs, but I knew that was a stretch. Human nature left us with the belief of *It will never happen to me.* And that was only amplified when you were a young and careless teenager.

I remembered getting into fights in college. They were easy for me. I never sought a fight, but if I saw someone getting picked on, I stood up for the innocent and left their bullies wishing they had never stepped out of the house.

I'd always wanted to use my size and strength for good, and protecting the innocent is the only way I'd ever known how. Having no parents by the age of ten left me to protect myself in this unfriendly world, and as an adult, I've found my joy in offering that protection to others.

I turned off the TV at 2:30 and started my journey to the police station. I made it in fifteen minutes, taking my time to enjoy the beautiful day. The neighborhood I passed through made it impossible to believe drugs were running rampant in Hillcrest. Perfectly manicured lawns, kids playing in the front yards, couples out for walks with their dogs. No way crime lurked a few blocks away at the Hamburger Stand. No way an innocent boy fought for his life because of the infiltration of poison from a highly organized crime ring.

When I reached the police station, I sat on the bench out front and sent a text message to Lily. I had no interest in going inside on my own. What would Officer Matthews say if he saw me?

I only waited five minutes before Lily came outside and sat down next to me. Her eyes were bloodshot, dark bags hanging below.

"So, how's it going?" I asked as she stared blankly into the distance. All her energy from her phone call this morning had vanished, replaced by exhaustion. "I take it we're not going out to dinner tonight again?"

She snorted, then let out a long yawn like a cat. "Nope. I'll be going straight to bed when I leave here."

"We're not young enough to stay up all night," I said, playfully nudging her in the arm with my elbow. "What were you thinking?"

She shook her head like she had been asked this same question a dozen times today. "I guess I wasn't thinking. Just got caught up in the heat of the moment. Now I'm paying for it. I'm about as useless as Duncan today."

"It can't all have been a waste, though," I said. "It's not like you were partying until four in the morning—you were working."

She bobbed her head slowly up and down, like it weighed a ton. "Oh, I found some juicy stuff. Just wish I had the energy to explore it more today. But it's been a wash. I got you that car."

Lily nodded to the parking lot, where a handful of police cruisers were parked, along with Lily's car, and another that looked identical.

"You got me the same as yours?" I asked.

"That's what I have access to," she replied. "Apparently can rent them as I please. All I had to tell my boss was one of the officers wants to help our case and needs to drive around more discreetly than his patrol car. I was expecting a long list of questions, but I think with the news this morning about the kid in the hospital, our case took on more importance."

"I saw that," I said. "Terrible situation. Poor kid."

Lily nodded. "It's fucked up. Kids can't even party today like we used to. I remember high school parties. Senior year, there was one pretty much every weekend. Lots of beer, maybe some weed. Kids got drunk and sloppy, but no one ever ended up in the hospital. Now it's all about these damn pills. They're easier to hide and consume, which is what kids want. But they don't realize the risk they're taking."

Lily was right, times had changed, and there was nothing we could do about it.

"Well, I'm going to follow Ben next time he leaves the Hamburger Stand."

Lily patted her pants pockets and let out a frustrated moan. "I left the keys on my desk. That's fine. I want to talk to you inside, if that's okay. The sun is too much for me to handle right now."

Lily stood up, and I followed her into the police station. I didn't recognize any faces from the other night, but that was an entirely different shift. During the day, the station had a less threatening feel. I saw a trio of police officers sitting at their desks in the bullpen. The scent of freshly brewed coffee filled the lobby area, and I couldn't help but assume Lily had kept it going all day.

The officer at the reception desk gazed at me for a few moments before returning to his book of crossword puzzles. Lily led me down the same hallway I was familiar with and turned into an office two doors before the interrogation room.

It was the DEA's makeshift workplace. Two desks crammed into opposite corners of the room. One mini fridge and a coffee pot that was indeed completing its newest batch. Agent Duncan sat at his desk, hammering away at an email on his laptop.

He stopped the moment he looked over his shoulder and saw me.

"What the hell is *he* doing here?" he asked, slamming his laptop shut. His desk was covered in loose papers and torn-open envelopes. A coffee ring formed on an application for couples' counseling.

I raised my hands to show I came in peace.

"We talked about this," Lily said through gritted teeth. "Jonny is no threat and has offered to help where he can. He has plenty of expertise—it's not like we plucked him off the street."

"That's exactly where he came from," Duncan replied, standing and putting his hands on his hips. "You have no right to snoop around this case. We can get into so much shit if our boss finds out. We could lose our *careers*. Have you not considered that, *Lily*?"

This must have been a fun room to sit in every day. Shit, no wonder Lily raced to meet me for dinner last night. She'd been putting up with this guy for two months in these closed quarters. I'd only been around him for thirty seconds and was ready to get the hell out.

Fortunately, Duncan felt the same and stuffed his laptop into a briefcase.

"Where are you going?" Lily asked.

"Not here," he responded without looking at her. "I will not be an accomplice to whatever the hell is going on. When this *thug* turns out to be trouble, don't come crawling back to me."

Duncan snapped the briefcase latches closed with authority and exited the office.

Lily sat at her desk and took a sip from her DEA coffee mug. "Don't mind him," she said. "Just how he's been lately. Hates pretty much everything and everyone, so don't take it personal."

"Wouldn't dream of it," I said. Duncan was going to cause me problems the more I got involved in this case. Technically, he had rank over me, but if he was as checked out as Lily had mentioned, maybe he wouldn't get in the way.

"I have your keys," Lily said, pulling them out of the desk's top drawer and dangling them toward me.

I shuffled to her desk, which was against the window overlooking a small courtyard where two officers were enjoying a smoke break.

"Look," I said, staring outside. "If you need me to back off, just say the word."

Lily jerked her head from side to side. "No. To hell with Duncan. He hasn't done a damn thing since we've been here. Two months, mind you. He's produced zero leads. Hasn't even questioned a person of interest aside from you. It feels like he's just taking the free trip. No work getting done."

I cleared my throat. "Okay then. I'll stay out of his way as much as I can. You take tonight off, and I'll get to work following Ben."

Lily sighed and rubbed her temples. "About that..."

She let the silence hang for far too long. I thought it was the exhaustion. Surely her mind was moving at a snail's pace. But as the silence stretched to forty seconds, I suspected she was holding something back.

"What is it?" I asked. "What did you find?"

"Lots," she replied quickly. "You were right. His name isn't Ben. Thanks to your tip about the Hamburger Stand,

I dug up information on that property and that's what led me through the rabbit hole all night. His real name is Javier Ocampo, and he's part of the Mexican cartel based out of the city of Eldorado."

I nodded as I listened. "So it's confirmed. The cartel has operations here."

"Yes, but there's more. The leader of the Eldorado cartel is a man by the name of Rafael Cortez. Are you familiar with the name?"

I shook my head. "Doesn't ring a bell."

Lily looked at me through her sleepy eyes, but I could tell there was plenty of gravity inside. "Rafael Cortez is your father."

Chapter 10

I couldn't concentrate for the rest of the afternoon.

Lily had to run to a final meeting before wrapping up her day but had made copies of the documents outlining the Eldorado cartel, its members, and its leader, Rafael Cortez.

I returned to the StayComfort suites in my new car. It had the faint remains of a new car smell. Overcome with so much energy and emotions, I could have sprinted back in five minutes. Probably could have won a marathon in that moment, or at least run through ten brick walls.

My father was still alive. It had always been easy to assume he was dead—that was the eventual fate for most cartel members. All these years later, and the opposite had happened. He had worked his way up through the ranks and was the leader of a cartel responsible for about two thousand murders across the Mexican state of Sinaloa.

His nickname was El Fantasma, which translated to "The Ghost." He had never so much as been spotted by the authorities in Mexico, earning him the nickname. His cartel had survived many sting operations—Cortez always a step ahead. He had a reputation for planting insiders in all the Mexican government agencies.

The DEA had just one picture of Rafael Cortez, a candid shot of him at age forty-three, sitting behind the wheel of a black Cadillac DeVille. The resemblance of his facial features to my own made my stomach sink to my knees.

I stood up and paced circles around the dining table in my suite. I had all the files splayed out, but his eyes in the picture seemed to follow me no matter where I stood. Wasn't that only supposed to happen in paintings?

Photo aside, the DEA had tons of information on El Fantasma. They created files on every cartel member they heard about, and Cortez had first been discovered working for a cartel in Guadalajara thirty-five years ago. Whoever had compiled the information back then had found Cortez was married to Elena Mendez, who gave birth to two sons, Manuel and Jonathan.

Just reading this tidbit made me want to hurl. My name had been in a government database since childhood. Years before I joined the SEALs or CIA. Yet no one ever bothered telling me the truth. I knew these databases were checked each step of the way through my employment under Uncle Sam.

"Fuck!" I screamed, grabbing a stack of papers and hurling them across the room. My breathing grew rapid, and I was losing my grip on reality. My entire life had been a quest for answers, and they were in plain sight the whole time.

Only they weren't.

When I was part of the CIA, I had looked through all my files. Nothing about Rafael Cortez was ever mentioned. It was like no one wanted me to know the truth about my father. But why? Did they think I might one day find him and join his cartel? Anyone who knew me would have known that was utter nonsense. I despised criminals and murderers and wanted nothing more than to give them a taste of their own blood. Literally.

I couldn't dwell on these details for too long. There was nothing I could do about any of that shit in the past right now. All that mattered was that I still had a father. And if I saw him, what then?

I'd have questions, but I'd also want to kill the man. Not for what he did to me—although, that would be a tasty bonus—but for all the innocent lives he had taken and destroyed.

I gathered up the loose documents and sorted them back into a neat pile. I stuffed the picture of my father into the back so it could stop staring at me. Thousands of thoughts rushed through my mind. I wanted to talk to Lily, but she needed rest. If we started, I'd have her up all night telling me what else she had found. Finding this connection probably made her second-guess my involvement, prompting her to stay awake until she had a conclusive answer.

We could talk tomorrow.

Tonight just became a lot more interesting.

Ben was no longer Ben, but Javier Ocampo. And he worked for my father.

Could he have seen the resemblance when we were talking behind the restaurant? Is that why he didn't take off his sunglasses? Maybe his eyes were bulging in fear. He caved during our price negotiations much easier than I'd expect from a professional drug dealer.

Granted, the picture of my father was from twenty years prior. He had surely aged by now, so maybe the resemblance was no longer as prominent.

Still, I couldn't help but wonder, and let my thoughts carry me through the process of confirming my gun was in the backpack before slinging it over my shoulder and heading out the door.

I returned to the car and took a deep breath while starting it up. It rumbled to life, adrenaline coursing through my veins. Damn, it felt good to be back behind the wheel. It was a freedom many people took for granted. As much as I'd love to have a vehicle of my own, that required registering said vehicle with the state and needing a driver's license. That was simply too much information that could be traced back to me, especially now, knowing my father could be on the lookout for me.

I drove through town and pulled into the Hamburger Stand lot five minutes later. There was a dinner rush, so a lot more cars filled the lot than last time. I found Ben's Silverado—I would still call him Ben until I confronted him directly about his name—and parked in the row behind it, four spaces further down. Perfect for pulling out to tail him when he left.

My stomach grumbled the moment I parked. Not a coincidence. I'd be lying if I said I hadn't thought about one of these burgers since my last visit. It was in my best interest to eat before this evening progressed any more. There was no saying when my next chance to eat would come once I followed Ben out of here.

It felt wrong to go back inside and essentially give my money to my father. I jumped to the conclusion that the Hamburger Stand was a front to launder the money for his operation. Lily wanted to wait to hear from her forensic accountant—boringest sounding job if there ever was one—for a concrete answer.

Let's not kid ourselves.

My option was Hamburger Stand or a vegan hamburger joint one more block down. Was that a fucking joke? I'd rather eat drywall.

Two minutes later, with much angst, I was back inside Hamburger Stand.

It was the same kid running the register as yesterday, but they were swamped. He either didn't recognize me or was still playing the game he had started when I ordered the triple deluxe a day ago.

No triple deluxe for me today, however. Just a double with extra of whatever that crack sauce was.

I was in and out in ten minutes, stuffing my face in the car and consequently destroying the new car smell with the stench of French fries that would take a week to air out. I only took two sips of my soda, not wanting my bladder to protest at the wrong time later on.

The next three hours were excruciatingly boring. Diners came and went. Cars pulled in and out. The Hamburger Stand could have done themselves a favor by opening a drive-thru window, as the peak of the dinner crowd saw a line out the door. Business was booming. I couldn't deny it. They had quite the operation slinging burgers.

I watched the blue skies give way to orange, then purple, and finally complete darkness. The parking lot was down to six vehicles by 7:45, Ben's Silverado included. I wished I had brought a book or something to do. Instead, I had been trapped in a car with my thoughts after the bombshell Lily had dropped on me a few hours ago.

I hadn't heard from her and trusted she got back home to sleep off a rough night. I'd kept my windows cracked the whole time and now listened to the early chirping of crickets singing into the night air. The moon was fierce and felt like it might fall out of the sky and smash my car. Hillcrest had little ambient light, but a thick coverage of clouds blocked my view of the stars.

I leaned back in my seat, rearview mirror adjusted at the perfect angle to alert me whenever someone came out of the restaurant's front doors. At exactly 7:48, Ben appeared, whistling and twirling his keys around his index finger while he moseyed through the parking lot.

He went straight for his truck and fired up the engine before pulling out of the lot and onto the road. Just seeing him zapped a fresh wave of energy into me, and I promptly turned on my car to follow Ben.

He took an immediate right out of the lot and had to stop at a red light one block down. I waited at the lot's exit until the light turned green before pulling onto the road, catching up close enough to stay roughly two hundred feet behind my target.

Traffic had died down. Aside from the few restaurants in Hillcrest, the rest of the town had shut down by this time. We drove down Seventh for two miles when the road curved into a quiet neighborhood. I thought we might stop at one of these ranch-style homes, but Ben kept driving at a steady thirty miles per hour until we cleared the neighborhood and ended up on a southbound road called Greenview Way. We traveled for the next half mile through open fields on both sides of the road. I thought I saw a barn in the distance, but it was too dark to be sure.

I pulled back even more, considering we were the only two vehicles on the road. A football field of distance separated me from Ben, but I could still see the red glow of his taillights in perfect contrast against the blackness. We were now three miles east of downtown Hillcrest, in the middle of nowhere.

Ben kept driving, and after another mile, we entered an area with more houses, but not exactly a neighborhood. These houses were also ranch-style homes but had massive yards surrounding the properties. Each house was spaced apart by a quarter mile.

My stomach churned as I realized we were surely approaching our stop. Where else would a drug dealer from a foreign country live besides out in the open?

I turned off my car's lights and sped up to narrow the gap between me and Ben, the darkness engulfing us. Staying extra cautious of any wildlife that might venture onto the road, I drove sixty to close the distance and remained a steady hundred feet behind the Silverado.

We passed six different houses, each of which had an outside porch light, providing weak illumination. At the seventh house, Ben's brake lights splashed across the road, prompting me to follow suit. I could only hope he didn't notice mine trailing behind him.

The Silverado stopped and turned into a driveway, and Ben parked it right along the side of the house. I slowed to a crawl and coasted toward his property, coming to a complete stop fifty feet before the driveway, where I still had a clear view of the house and truck.

I killed my engine immediately and flicked the inside light switches into the off position. The last thing I needed was any light turning on when I opened my door.

The news of my father wasn't allowing me to think straight. Typically, I knew exactly how I'd approach Ben, especially since there were no witnesses around. I could knock on his door, barge into the house, and tie him up until he answered my questions. But that seemed too aggressive. Besides, a lot of these guys were brainwashed to accept death over ratting out their leaders. If I started asking about Cortez, that could end any chance of getting an answer from Ben.

Maybe I needed a different approach. More friendly. But how would I explain my showing up on his doorstep? I lost the pills and needed more? Saw you leaving, and followed you?

That was psychotic shit and would get me nowhere just as fast.

Fuck.

I unzipped my backpack, pulled out the gun, and made sure the safety was off and this baby was ready to fire.

Just in case.

I opened the car door and stepped out. The side of the roads were all dirt, but spacious. I took soft steps and gently guided the door closed, not even forcing it all the way shut. Not like anyone was going to steal it out here. I slid the gun into the back of my waistband. Walking up with a weapon in hand wasn't going to make me any friends.

Ben finally opened the Silverado door and hopped out. The light from the porch cast a wide glow across the front lawn and driveway, and I could see he was talking on his cell phone. That would be a phone worth bugging. I'd have to see if Lily had the equipment to do such a thing. I had experience with that thanks to the CIA.

Perhaps intercepting Ben before he could reach the front door was my best bet. Catch him off guard. Not like whoever he was talking to could get here anytime soon if they heard a commotion. Sneak attacks were effective. They made people nervous and left them with no time to think. Imagine being approached by a monster like me in the shadows of this deserted area. The Hillcrest police might get calls for a Bigfoot sighting.

Ben strolled toward the back of the truck and turned along the front of the house, still talking into his cell phone. I broke into a sprint, knowing he wouldn't hear me if he was engaged with the phone conversation. Right before I reached the edge of the driveway, a pair of headlights flicked on from the opposite side of the road.

I screeched to a halt, sliding in the dirt like a baseball player stealing second base, then rolled to my right into the small ditch. The tires belonging to the new headlights squealed as the car's engine roared, howling into the still night like a pack of wolves.

I scrambled to my feet and dove to my right, further away from the road. The car lunged forward and jerked into the driveway, its headlights landing on a startled Ben, who had just reached the front door of the house.

He squinted into the headlights, then his face loosened into a smile when a man jumped out of the driver's door and tossed his hands in the air.

"What the fuck, bro?!" Ben cried out, hanging up the cell phone and stuffing it into his pocket.

I crawled backwards toward my car, keeping my eyes ahead at the unfolding scene.

The man reached Ben and threw his arms around him in a bear hug. The two slapped each other's backs before pulling apart. I was too far to hear or see anything. The silhouette of the mystery man showed he was the same height as Ben, but much more built. Might give me a few seconds of trouble in a fight.

The two carried on a conversation, refusing to take it inside.

That meant Ben didn't fully trust this person. If he were comfortable, he would have invited him inside instead of talking under the porch light for five minutes.

I doubted cartel members had friends outside of their gang, so this new person was of interest. If only I had a clear shot, I could snap a picture to send to Lily tomorrow morning.

There wasn't a sign of immediate danger, so crouching low, I inched forward again, desperate to hear what they were talking about. The best I could make out was that they were speaking Spanish, yet their tones were too hushed to hear the specifics.

Sweat had formed around my forehead, and I wiped it away with my arm.

Apparently, this was just a quick meeting between two friends, because the two gave another quick hug before parting ways.

Ben fidgeted with his keys in the doorknob. When the mystery man reached the driveway, he stopped, turned around, pulled out a gun from inside his jacket, and fired three shots into the side of Ben's head.

Chapter 11

I remained frozen in front of my car. Sweat seeped between my lips and the taste of salt brought me back to the horrifying reality unfolding on Ben's front porch.

The man who shot him tucked his gun back inside his jacket and hurried over to Ben, hoisting him up from his dead shoulders to drag him across the lawn. Blood splattered across the front door and parts of the house's siding like a painter had gotten pissed off and thrown his tools in a fit. A chunk of brain clung to the porch light like a piece of bird shit.

I'd seen worse during my time in the SEALs. But gruesome scenes like this were different when you were *expecting* to see them. This was supposed to be a friendly chat between myself and the Mexican drug dealer known as Ben.

Instead, Ben was dead and getting stuffed into his murderer's trunk like a sack of groceries. I was right in assuming this mystery man was strong. I'd moved plenty of dead bodies in my day and knew how deceptively heavy they could be. Even the little guys like Ben.

But this dude moved the corpse with ease, twisting the body at the limbs so he could properly close the trunk. Five seconds after that, he was speeding out of the driveway, filling the abandoned road with smoke from burning rubber and leaving me a statue.

Naturally, I wanted to follow this man, but I'd learned from mistakes in the past. Doing so would be an impulse decision. The man who killed Ben was certainly involved with the cartel, meaning he wasn't leaving town anytime soon. Who would run the Hamburger Stand?

I presumed whoever filled Ben's role would provide a fresh batch of information for this case. In addition, it wasn't wise to follow an unknown person. Especially with so many questions still unanswered. The last thing I needed was to get tangled up with the potential leader of the cartel, or even a crooked cop. I played the long game and felt more comfortable making snap decisions with more information in front of me.

Besides, my purpose for being at Ben's house was to learn more about his role in all this. Now that I couldn't directly ask him questions, I could still do the next best thing and scope out his house.

I waited another two minutes, mainly to allow my heartbeat to return to a normal pace. It had been pounding in my ears ever since Ben got shot.

Feeling more in control of myself, I stood up, shook my legs to regain the feeling in them, and strolled up to Ben's house.

"First things first," I said, pulling out my cell phone to use its flashlight. The three shots fired were too close in succession. He had most likely used a semi-automatic, meaning three shell casings should be in the area—typically to the right of the shooter.

Sure enough, my flashlight caught the glint of two casings that had rolled into the driveway. I knelt down to examine them. Ruger nine millimeters. Best for close-range shooting, as just witnessed.

I didn't touch the casings. The last thing I needed was my fingerprint on a piece of evidence less than fifteen feet from a blood-splattered door. I didn't see the third casing, either. It likely rolled into the grass or got kicked aside during all the commotion after the murder. It could have even been dragged along the way with Ben's body and was rolling around in the trunk with him.

I stood up and proceeded to the front door, sure to step around any pools of blood on the ground. My footprint in a bloody mess had put me in jail more times than I could count. I learned as I aged. Some people called that wisdom. Don't step in pools of blood you didn't cause.

Much to my delight, Ben had actually just opened his door before catching those slugs to the head. It stood ajar an inch, the keys still dangling from the knob. I pushed the door open with the toe of my shoe and stepped into darkness.

I reached around the wall to my right using my elbow—no fingerprints from me. I found the light switch and moved it up, bringing a living room to life. The place smelled of stale cigar smoke and French fries. The coffee table confirmed this. A half dozen of crumpled bags from Hamburger Stand were scattered around two ash trays full of half-smoked cigars.

A TV was mounted to the wall, so this was clearly where Ben liked to eat dinner and unwind after a long day of selling triple deluxes. I couldn't stay long. There was no saying if someone else might stop by.

The house was small. A short hallway branched to the right of the living room, leading to an office, a bedroom, and a bathroom. Behind the living room was the kitchen with a small dining table that had even more Hamburger Stand wrappers splayed in every direction. If the bullets hadn't worked on poor Ben, then surely clogged arteries would have taken him soon enough.

I kid myself. Those burgers were fucking gold.

Having minutes to spare, I checked Ben's office. If there was anything to learn, it would most likely come from that room over any of the others.

I shuffled into the office and turned on the light with my elbow again. Apparently, dealing with money made Ben a more organized person. The office was meant for business. Filing cabinets stood in the corner. The main desk overlooking the front yard was clear of papers. An opened laptop was front and center, its screensaver of bouncing bubbles trying to hypnotize me. The walls were made of wood paneling like it was an old mountain home. Perhaps the cartel had been running their operations out of Hillcrest for decades.

A mini fridge hummed in the corner to my left. There was a space heater with its cord wrapped up in another corner. A diffuser with essential oils sat on the window ledge. Ben liked his comfort when working from the home office. Who didn't?

I spotted a tissue box on top of the filing cabinets and whipped out two before sitting down behind the laptop. I used the tissues to grab the mouse and jiggled it to bring the computer to life.

Password protected. Fuck me.

I used my fingernails to type the standard guesses.

12345. qwerty. password. Iloveburgers.

None of them worked, and I had to fight my urge to throw the laptop across the room because it wouldn't cooperate. What did I honestly expect? Cartel members had shit to hide and wouldn't leave anything to chance like a simple password. And that was fine. I'd tell Lily about the laptop and shell casings, and she'd be able to get us answers.

I stuffed the tissues into my pockets and stood up from the desk. The chair's wheels squeaked as I pushed it back. I spun around and heard a series of rapid chimes coming from the laptop. Like it was teasing me. I recognized the tone as an instant messaging system. There were so many these days, it was impossible to know which one it belonged to. But the constant *ding, ding, ding,* told me someone was trying to get in touch with Ben. His cell phone had been in his pocket when he got stuffed into the trunk. I wondered if the killer was aware of that, because if not, Lily just might have an easier time tracking down a location.

The notifications continued even faster. Someone had to be sending Ben an absolute onslaught of messages. The fucking thing was chiming every two seconds, playing in my head like a song you can't erase.

"Enough!" I shouted, as if the sender on the other end could hear me.

The chimes stopped, as if they had heard me, and this sent an uneasy chill down my spine.

"Hello?" I said, not even sure who I was talking to.

Five seconds later, the laptop responded with a *ding!*

"Okay, this is getting weird," I said. "Time to get the hell out of here."

And it was. I had found nothing of significance, though I was sure there was plenty of juicy information on that laptop. When I turned back around to exit the office, I froze in place. And I mean, every blood cell in my veins stopped cold in its tracks. The open laptop distracted me from checking my surroundings as I should have done. Staring at me, from high in the corner above the office door, was a security camera.

Chapter 12

I left like a bat out of hell.

My head spun as I sped back to the main part of Hillcrest. Once I was at least a mile away, I slowed down and focused on my breathing. Seeing that camera was not the rush I needed. Who was watching on the other side? If the cartel now had my face plastered across their screens, how much longer would it be until they found me and hunted me down? The cartel could always find a person—I had no doubt.

It wasn't even ten o'clock, though I would've guessed it was well past midnight. I couldn't call Lily yet. She needed to sleep. I didn't want to risk calling the police station, either. They'd likely wake up Lily, regardless. Plus, I wasn't entirely sure who I could trust there yet. Officer Matthews seemed exactly like the type of shithead to get caught up in a small-town scandal. But that was just me judging the book by its cover. I had no proof.

The cartel was going to find me. I had to come to terms with that reality. My safest bet was to leave town right now. Vanish by the morning, and they'd never track me down. But my mother didn't raise a coward. And I certainly wasn't going to back down after learning of these ties to my father. I believed little in fate, but I had no other explanations for how

I ended up in this random small town with connections to my estranged dad.

My current purpose was in Hillcrest, and running away would only eat away at me until I drove myself crazy. I raced back to the StayComfort Suites and bought a package of melatonin gummies from the small convenience store in the lobby area.

I was asleep within the hour.

One little gummy knocked me out solid until nine o'clock, when my cell phone buzzed to life on the nightstand. I reached over and grabbed it, brain still foggy from the deep slumber, and saw Lily's name flashing on the screen.

"Hello?" I answered, clearing my groggy throat.

"Jonny!" she cried, sounding back to her normal self. "Thank God you're okay."

Witnessing Ben's murder last night felt like a distant dream, but all the details rushed back into my thoughts. I hadn't even taken my shoes off before jumping into bed, small blades of grass still clinging around their edges.

"Yes, I'm okay," I said, sitting up. I had apparently taken my shirt off at some point and slept in my jeans and shoes. Hadn't done something that absurd since college. "I need to talk to you."

"I'll say," Lily replied, concern slipping into her voice. "Where were you last night?"

"What do you know already?" I asked, keeping my voice level. I could deceive my way past a lie-detector machine. In fact, I did once.

"What do *I* know? What's that supposed to mean? I woke up to the news that four dead bodies were found early this morning. Do *you* know anything about that?"

"Four?!" I asked, spinning my legs to dangle over the bed's edge. "I know of one."

Lily sighed. "What did you do, Jonny? I know you like to take justice into your own hands, but I can't cover up for you."

"I promise I didn't kill anyone. I was at Ben's house last night to confront him. Before I did, someone sped into the driveway and shot him dead on his front step. Stuffed his body into the trunk and left."

"Jesus Christ," Lily whispered. "You didn't get a look at the killer?"

"Afraid not. It was too dark, and I was too far. The guy was short but stocky—that's the best I could make out."

"Did you see anything else?"

"There are shell casings in the driveway. I left them for you. Ruger nine mills. Also, the front door was open, so I looked around. There's a laptop in the office that was password protected. It was going off like crazy while I was there. You'll need to check it out."

"You better not have left fingerprints on everything."

"Do I look like an amateur?" I asked, sure to let the snark shine through.

Lily sighed. "I'm heading to the morgue to look at these four bodies. I sure hope one of them is Ben, because if not, then that means there were five murders last night. If you can, I'd love for you to join me. These murders were...gruesome."

"What are we talking, exactly?"

Lily gulped. "It's the cartel, Jonny. No more doubt. One body was hanging from a telephone pole. One had both hands chopped off. We got lucky, though. A patrolman spotted the body on the telephone pole. It was outside of town, so no one saw it. They were able to block the roads and get it taken down.

The panic that would have spread across Hillcrest would have made our jobs a living hell. But we're in the clear. For now."

"And you found out about this from who?" I asked, wanting to understand all the moving parts.

"Duncan called me an hour ago. Officer Matthews found the body while he was patrolling the area and kicked everything into motion."

Matthews.

Coincidence his name came up? Why would he have been patrolling a remote area in the middle of the night?

More questions than answers. A recurring theme.

"Okay," I said. "I'll go with you to the morgue."

"I'll be there in ten minutes to pick you up."

Lily disconnected the call, leaving me ten minutes to scramble and get ready. I changed clothes, brushed my teeth, and splashed water on my face. I smelled like a swamp and wished I had time for a shower, but I decided grabbing a bite from the continental breakfast downstairs would be more beneficial to my morning. The lemon cake was calling, so I swiped a slice along with a banana nut muffin and a bottle of orange juice.

I sat outside the hotel and ate my breakfast on the bench while waiting for Lily to arrive. She didn't ask me to drive to meet her at the morgue. She'd insisted on picking me up. Was she sensing the elevated danger we all were in now? I hadn't even mentioned the camera that captured my face in Ben's office.

She pulled up two minutes later, like clockwork. I brushed the muffin crumbs off my shirt before climbing into the passenger seat.

The bags were gone from Lily's eyes, and her smile looked completely refreshed.

"Hey," she said. "Sorry if I woke you, but this is important."

"No need for that," I said. "I was just about to get up."

"How late were you out last night?"

"Not too late. All this happened before ten. There is something I left out when we were talking just now—wasn't expecting you to hang up so abruptly, by the way. Kind of hurt my feelings."

Lily laughed, the sound sending a flutter into my chest. "I think you'll be okay."

"I don't know," I said, looking down at my lap. "There was a camera in Ben's office. It saw me the whole time."

Lily had just started driving away, then slammed on her brakes at the news. I flung forward and stuck out my arms to keep from crashing into the dashboard.

"You're on *camera* in that house?" Lily asked under her breath. She shook her head. "Jonny, I can't get you out of that. The team is going to tear that house apart and look for every little thing. They *will* find out where that camera is feeding to and trace it. Shit."

"I can leave town if it helps you keep your job," I said. And I would. Lily didn't deserve to have her job at risk because of my boneheaded mistake. I'd have to take my life elsewhere. Seeing Lily this morning reminded me the world didn't revolve around me. It was okay to put others first.

"No, you're not leaving," she said through gritted teeth. I could feel her rage radiating from the driver's seat, and she drove ahead onto the main road. "Let's go to the morgue, identify what bodies we can, then we'll head straight to Ben's house and establish your presence there last night. It's best to come clean now and not wait for the video footage of you to appear. Besides, no one has mentioned anything about Ben's house, so we should be the first ones there."

"Okay," I said. "Only if you think that's a good idea, and you won't lose your job."

Lily laughed again. "I'm not losing my job. Remember, I'm the only one doing anything here. If they take me off this case, the whole thing is going to unravel. Duncan is in no position to handle this on his own."

Lily drove us to a part of town I was not yet familiar with. Half a mile west of the police station was the rest of Hillcrest's government offices. Courtroom, library, town hall, and even the fire station all lined the city block called Hillcrest Avenue.

We drove to the end of this small strip where a one-level brick building waited. Hillcrest Mortuary were the only words on the white sign protruding from the edge of the parking lot.

There were two other vehicles in the lot, one of which was a police car.

"Who's all here?" I asked.

"Duncan and Officer Matthews," Lily replied, parking and turning off her car. "C'mon, let's go. And don't mention anything about where you were last night."

I followed Lily inside, her scent wafting into my nose and causing a moment of delirium.

We stepped into a lobby with an unattended desk. Lily marched around the desk and knocked on the door to the side. She stepped back and crossed her arms.

The door swung open, Agent Duncan's head popping out. He offered a forced grin to Lily. Then he locked eyes with me.

"Really?" he said to Lily.

"Please don't start, Duncan. Jonny has already proven helpful on this case." I could hear the disdain in her voice. She wanted to throw it in his face that I'd been more help than him. And I just got here. But Lily was a good person. Duncan was going through some shit and she wouldn't dare pile anything on top of that. The man looked in worse shape than Lily had yesterday.

"I'm only here to help," I said, crossing my arms in front of my stomach.

"How do we know it wasn't you who put these four men in here?" Duncan asked. His eyes were bloodshot, and his face had a scattering of gray stubble along his jaw and cheeks. Perhaps he had been jerked out of bed this morning, too.

"If I was going to kill four men, you'd never find the bodies," I said, smirking at the tired bastard.

Duncan snorted, rolled his eyes, and stepped aside to allow both me and Lily to enter.

"I love you, too," I said as the door closed behind me.

We entered a long hallway that stretched to the back of the building, four doors on each side. Duncan led us through the first door on the right.

The temperature dropped in this room the moment we stepped in. I saw Officer Matthews with a man I presumed was the mortician examining a body lying on a pulled-out refrigeration table.

This was a first for me. I'd never been inside this part of a mortuary. The giant freezer on the wall looked like a cabinet with all its doors.

Officer Matthews looked up and saw me. "What the hell is he doing here?"

"You must be a popular man around town," Duncan said sarcastically, turning away to join Matthews beside the corpse.

"He's with me," Lily said sternly. "Mr. Mendez has a

long history of hunting criminals and terrorists. He brings a lifetime of knowledge and expertise to this case—which we clearly need. He has no links to the murders that happened at the tavern, and I suggest you all put your egos aside so we can understand what's happening in Hillcrest. Can you boys handle that?"

She directed her question to Matthews and Duncan, but I spoke first. "Sure can."

Duncan nodded quietly to himself. Matthews glared at me, chomping on his fucking gum.

He never answered Lily's question and returned his attention to the dead body.

Lily shuffled forward. "What have you found so far?"

The mortician spoke up. He was tall and balding, the bright lights in this room gleaming off the top of his head. He wore a white lab coat and a matching surgical mask and rubber gloves.

"Let me show you," he said, taking out a pair of glasses from his coat pocket and sliding them up the bridge of his nose. He left the body they were all standing around and worked his way down the freezer, pulling open three more doors and sliding out the tables. "We have four Hispanic men, aged between thirty-five and forty-five."

I looked at the dead men. They all had black hair, and their once brown skin had a slight tint of grayness. Maybe it was the lighting.

The men were nude, except for a cloth draped over the lower half of their bodies. I recognized Ben immediately on the table directly in front of me. The three bullet holes in the side of his head were a helpful clue.

The men each had a variety of body ink across their arms

and torsos.

"These were all violent murders," the mortician said. "I've determined the man hung from the telephone pole was still alive when he was hung. I'll speak of them in numbers since we haven't identified any of them yet. Number one is at the end in front of the two officers." He nodded to Matthews and Duncan, Matthews still glaring at me from across the room like he wanted to put me on one of the tables. "Victim one was hung. Victim two is missing both hands. Precisely sawed off at the wrist joint, which means these people understood basic anatomy."

Or have done it multiple times before. How many hours did it take to master a craft?

"Victim three suffered three gunshots to the head, though he would likely have been dead after the first one. And victim four..." the mortician gulped. "You can't see it from here, but let's just say they removed his privates."

"Jesus Christ!" Lily cried out.

The thought was disturbing, sure, but this was nothing new for the cartel. They liked to send messages. Intimidation was just as important as the actual killings they carried out.

"Tell them about the link," Duncan said, looking at the floor. The scene inside this room was a lot to take in. Even my stomach twisted at the thought of getting my fun parts cut off. All I could think about was the cartel having my face plastered across their screens somewhere.

"Certainly," the mortician said. He pointed to a small tattoo on victim four's chest. "Each victim has a tattoo of a ghost on their left breast, about two inches above the nipple. Same design and location on all four men."

I felt Lily's stare burning into me. But I didn't look back. I had no idea how much Duncan and Matthews knew about my father's nickname. El Fantasma. The Ghost.

I assumed none. If Duncan or Matthews knew I was related to the leader of this cartel—nevermind that I'd never met the guy—there was no chance I'd be standing in this room right now.

I kept my mouth shut but took a step closer to examine Ben's tattoo. It was half an inch, black outline with a white filling and two black dots for eyes. It was the makeshift ghost people made from a white bedsheet. Not scary. The same tattoo might even be cute on a woman's hip.

But Lily and I knew what it meant. All four men had worked for El Fantasma.

Lily coughed. "I need to get out of here. Think I'm going to be sick."

The cough was fake. I could tell, but the others in the room could not.

"Duncan," Lily said, sounding like she was on the verge of vomiting. "Can you write up the report for our findings here and add it to the file?"

Concern swept over Duncan's face. Lily had mentioned they'd been partners for a while, so obviously he still cared for her.

"Of course," he said tenderly, the most human he'd sounded since we had the pleasure of meeting.

"Jonny," Lily said, turning around and heading for the exit. She nodded toward the door for me to follow.

I bowed my head to the other three before pivoting to tail after Lily.

When I closed the door, I caught one last glimpse of Officer Matthews watching me, a wide, malevolent smile on his face.

Chapter 13

"What was that about?" I asked once we stepped outside into the fresh air. I welcomed the crispness of the ocean breeze blowing over Hillcrest right now. That light scent of salt in the air.

Lily hustled to her car and got behind the wheel. I had to jog to keep up. She turned on the car and pulled out of the lot in a hurry.

"I didn't like the vibes in there," she finally said.

"Well, no shit. There were four dead bodies."

"Not that," Lily replied. "Matthews. The whole time the mortician was explaining things, he was just staring at you."

I laughed and rolled down my window. We both needed more of the fresh air. "Matthews believes to his core that I'm involved with all this. We didn't exactly start off on the right foot. Is that why you didn't mention anything about Ben? The mortician said none of those men had been identified."

Lily nodded. "Exactly. I'm testing Duncan. He has access to the same report I shared with you. I alerted him when I had uploaded it into our shared folder. If he couldn't identify Ben—or Javier—then I know he hasn't read the report. Plus, all this about Rafael Cortez being your father just proves it further. I'll try to finish this case on my own, but at some point, I have to tell my boss what's going on with Duncan."

I nudged Lily's arm with my elbow across the center console. "You're not alone in this case, so stop saying that. I don't care how dangerous this gets; I won't leave your side."

The ends of her lips curled up, and her cheeks flushed a soft pink. "Thank you. That means a lot."

She turned onto the long stretch of road that would take us to Ben's house. The scenery was much more enjoyable during the day. The open fields were turning green thanks to the early hints of spring. There was a barn with a farm stretching as far as I could see. Cows and horses grazed beneath the pure morning sun.

"Do you have concerns about Matthews?" I asked, watching Lily out of the side of my eye. She drew a deep breath.

"I'm not sure," she said. "I don't think he's involved, if that's what you mean. But it definitely feels like he has his own agenda. And he might. This is common when the feds arrive in a small town. The local police always resist our presence."

"That's natural," I said. "Pecking order and all that. They don't technically *have* to listen to you, but they also can't overrule you. A classic impasse."

"Well," Lily said with a sly grin, "we *could* force them to do things. Just need some papers signed. The federal government can trump a local government whenever it needs. I'd just prefer Matthews not be involved. At least with four murders to solve, six counting the first two, he may be out of our way for a bit. We're not here to solve murders but to find the drugs and bring down that operation. The murders are just extra clues at this point."

"Did you drive by Hamburger Stand this morning?" I asked.

"Curious what's going on there after Ben's death."

Lily shook her head. "Why don't you call them? Just see if it's business as usual."

"I suppose."

I pulled out my phone and did a Google search for their phone number, calling it immediately. The phone rang six times before someone answered, and it sounded an awful lot like the young man who had helped me.

"Thank you for calling Hamburger Stand. How can I help you?" he said over blaring background noise.

"Hello," I said. "I just wanted to make sure you were open before I head down there. Will I be able to get a triple deluxe?"

Why not ask what I really wanted to know? This question would have been better face to face, so I could see the kid squirm.

Instead, he answered with no hesitation. "I'm sorry, sir, but we don't have a triple deluxe on our menu."

"Really? I was just there the other day and ordered one."

"My apologies, sir. That must have been processed in error. That's not a menu option we have."

"So I ordered a triple deluxe and whoever took my order just went along with it and took my money?"

Lily side-eyed me with a puzzled look on her face.

"That appears so, sir. I apologize for the inconvenience. I can offer you a free meal as compensation the next time you come in."

Oh, shit. I'd absolutely take a free burger.

"I appreciate that, young man. What's your name, so I can ask for you when I go in?"

"Andres."

"Thank you, Andres. I appreciate the help."

I hung up.

"What was that about?" Lily asked, half smiling.

"Ben's death has disrupted the drug operations at Hamburger Stand, but not their burger business. And I got a free burger."

"You jackass!" Lily said, slapping me on the arm. I liked the way it felt.

"Maybe I'll split it with you. We'll see. The kid's name is Andres. Not sure if that's his real name or just the one he uses while working. But he's been there both times I've gone in. He must be part of the cartel, even if it's just operating their front."

"How old?" Lily asked.

"I'd guess he's twenty at the oldest."

"Think he's worth following?"

I shrugged. "I suppose he's as good as anyone to follow right now, but I have my doubts he's tied up in the actual crime portion of the cartel. If he was, he'd have filled in for Ben when I ordered the triple deluxe."

Lily nodded in agreement, then rolled down her window. The whipping sound of wind filled the car as we cruised down the back road and approached the row of spread-out houses. Lily's hair swirled around until we pulled to a stop in front of Ben's house.

She parked along the curb, and I immediately noticed the front door had been wiped clean.

"Shit," I said, jumping out of the car.

"What is it?" Lily asked, jogging to keep up along my side, two pairs of rubber gloves in hand. She gave me a pair, and we put them on, sure not to leave a trace of our presence behind.

"The door," I said. "There was blood all over it last night."

I hurried to the door for a closer look, now questioning what I had seen the previous night. It had been dark, sure, but there was no mistaking the blood. Or the chunk of brain.

I planted my hands on my hips and shook my head. "The door isn't just clean—it's been completely replaced. That's not the same doorknob from last night."

The one from last night had been the basic round knob with a keyhole. Now it was the type with a lever and long handle. The door in front of me now was white as snow. Immaculate.

"What the fuck?" I whispered to myself, looking up at the porch light fixture, which had also been replaced.

I rushed down the walkway and stopped where it connected with the driveway. I knew exactly where the shell casings were and squatted down to find them.

Nothing.

"These guys are good," I said, standing back up and scanning the nearby area. It was possible a strong wind could have blown the casings to a new location, but it wouldn't have taken them far. They weren't feathers.

Lily shuffled over to me, arms crossed. "You're sure Ben was murdered here last night?"

"I'm not crazy," I said, pointing down the driveway to the left. "I was crouched down right there and saw it all happen. Ben drove a black Silverado. It was parked here when I left. Where is it? Where's the blood? And the casings? I know what I saw."

Lily raised a hand. "Calm down, big guy. I believe you. They're called cleaners. Most organized crime rings have them. They clean up murder scenes and make it look like nothing happened. They're some of the highest paid people on the payroll."

"I see why," I said, rage building up within. If I had known I was coming back to this, I would have picked up those casings and taken pictures of the scene. "Where's all the blood? There were pools of it all along this walkway and in front of the door."

Lily turned and looked back at the pristine concrete. "Looks clean. I'm sure if we swabbed it, we'd find traces of hydrogen peroxide or bleach. Wouldn't be able to track anything once either of those chemicals mixes with blood."

"We need to go inside," I said. "I'm going to rip that camera off the wall and send these guys a message. They picked the wrong guy to fuck with."

"We can't just go inside," Lily said. "That's something I need a warrant for, and I'm not sure I'll get one because we haven't officially identified Ben as one of those dead bodies yet."

I laughed. "I'm not asking for permission. You can either help me get in the house, or I'll break the door down myself."

"Okay, slow down." Lily looked down at the ground, contemplating. "Fine. I have a lockpick we can use. No need to damage the house, especially if there will be others here to investigate later."

She jogged back down to her car, fished around the glove compartment, and returned with the lockpick. She held it out to me. "If you know how to use these—"

I snatched it out of her grip and returned to the door. "Thank you. I've picked dozens of locks before."

All locks used similar mechanisms, just different patterns. I could visualize exactly what the pick was doing inside the lock as I got to work, pressing the pins one by one until I heard that final *click!* of success.

"Jonny, wait!" Lily said as I reached for the handle. She pulled her gun from its holster on her hip, buried beneath her flowing DEA jacket. "Let me go first, just in case."

Normally, I wouldn't have allowed such a thing. But Lily had such an infectious confidence in her abilities and lacked any fear. Just like me.

I stepped aside and said, "Ladies first."

She reached out for the handle and pulled down the lever, pushing the door open. Lily raised her gun and took the first step in. "What in the world?" she said, steadily lowering her gun.

She passed through the doorway, and I trailed behind.

We stepped in to find the house completely cleaned and deserted. No furniture. No burger wrappers. Just white walls and immaculate hardwood floors. I ran into the office.

Empty. The camera was gone from the wall; even the holes where it had been were filled in. I looked to the window ledge and saw a small piece of paper, like a sticky note. I shuffled over and picked it up.

Looking back at me was a hand-drawn image of a white ghost.

Chapter 14

We drove in silence back to downtown and parked at Jo's Diner, a local spot that took pride in being open twenty-four hours, serving breakfast, lunch, and dinner.

We arrived between the breakfast and lunch rushes and had the place mostly to ourselves. An older Black couple sat along a window booth, the woman reading a raggedy Dean Koontz paperback, the man working on a crossword puzzle in the newspaper spread across the table.

What's a six-letter word for what I am?

Fucked.

The cartel knew I was in Ben's house—*their* house—last night. From this point on, I had to assume they'd have eyes on me. Six total dead bodies and my cover blown. Not the best start in this new town, but I've had worse. I once crashed into a police car in bumfuck Nebraska. During a murder investigation. Yeah, that was my worst entrance.

We took the corner booth away from the windows, furthest from the door. Whatever we were about to discuss was sensitive, and we didn't need any locals overhearing it. I'd prefer the diner was busier, to bury our discussions with other people's chatter, but I couldn't control that. And something told me Lily didn't want to go back to the police station.

A woman, I'd guess in her early sixties, shuffled over to our table with a coffeepot in hand. "Good morning, Lily," she greeted, eyes scanning me while she spoke. "Who's your friend?"

"Good morning, Jo," Lily replied with a warm smile. "This is Jonny. He's helping me with work."

Jo studied me, picking me apart and making her judgments in about five seconds. "Well, any friend of Lily is a friend of mine." She put the coffeepot on the table and extended a hand to me. "Jo Ellen Walker at your service. Everyone calls me Jo."

I forced a grin, not in a particular mood for meeting a new person and the pleasantries that followed. For the first time since I'd arrived in Hillcrest, I feared for my life. "Nice to meet you, Jo," I said. "Love the diner. Has a real homey feel."

"Oh, thank you, dear," she said, flipping over the two coffee mugs that were upside down on our table and pouring us a fresh brew. "I'll be back in a couple to take your order."

"Thanks, Jo," Lily said, wasting no time pulling her mug in for a drink.

"Come here a lot?" I asked.

Lily laughed. "You could say that. Every day for the first month after I arrived. There's something about Jo's hash browns. Irresistible."

"I'll try them."

Lily pushed her mug away and looked me dead in the eyes. "Jonny, what's going through your mind? I could tell you were upset back there."

I drew in a deep breath and took my sweet time exhaling it. "Lots of emotions this morning. First, I hadn't been to a mortuary since my mother's death. Just being in there brought back a lot of memories I've tried to push out of my mind."

Lily reached out and caressed my forearm, rubbing it up and down. Her touch was magic, sending sparks throughout my body. "You don't have to bottle it all up. I know you macho men like to think you have to, but it's okay to mourn your mother's death. Even all these years later."

My throat was tensing, and I had to gulp down the saliva pooling in my mouth. Lily's simple touch had opened the gates to my soul, and everything wanted to come bursting out. But I had to slam those gates closed. Lily needed my help on this case, and I couldn't be of quality assistance if my mind was elsewhere. "I accepted my mother's death many years ago. I still dream of avenging her but am aware her killer is most likely dead. Do you ever reflect on your life and look back at that one moment that made you who you are?"

Lily's eyes welled with tears, and I felt her fingers trembling on my arm. She wiped her tears away with her free hand, refusing to break her physical contact with me.

She nodded. "I lost my dad at a young age, so I know exactly what you mean."

I wasn't expecting that, so I leaned forward and extended my free hand to grab hers. Now we sat with both of ours arms intertwined across the table like a couple out on a romantic date. "So we have this shared trauma in common. No wonder we get along."

Lily managed a smile through her crying. "My dad was a police officer in Cleveland. Was killed by a local gang during a shootout. I was twelve years old. Having to live through that while giving my first real thoughts to what I wanted to do with my life led me to this career. All I ever wanted was to make sure no other families had to suffer like mine did. It broke us all. I have an older brother. He was a junior in high school at the time. Pretty much crawled to the finish line and moved away after graduating. He took to booze and fell into a heavy depression. He's fine now. Happily married with two kids and working as a real estate lender in Cincinnati."

"And your mom?" I asked, rubbing the inside of Lily's wrist. Her skin was soft and silky.

Lily sniffled and wiped her eyes again, sure to place her hand back so I could caress it. "My mom also fell into depression. They were soulmates. Together since their freshmen year of high school. She completely broke. Lost her identity and purpose. Her will to live. I had to grow up fast. Since my brother moved away, I was taking care of my mom. Cooking, cleaning, all while trying to navigate my new life in high school."

"And mourning."

Lily shook her head. "I wish. I was too busy to mourn. Didn't really get the chance until I got to college. When I sat there in my college dorm for the first night, it was like those past six years came crashing down on me. Hard. I'd cried plenty before that, but mourning is more than just crying. A lot of people don't realize that until they go through it themselves. Mourning is all the feelings. The sorrow. Rage. Regret. It's a physical sickness that needs to be addressed. And if you don't...well, let's just say it's a miracle I was invited back for a second semester. Those were some dark days. I can't even imagine you having to deal with these things as a ten-year-old. What a horrible way to be introduced to how fucked up this world is."

I saw Jo approaching from behind Lily, but she turned

around before reaching the table. We were obviously in the middle of an emotional moment.

"I'm sorry," Lily said. "This was a lot to unpack for a lunch outing."

"There's nothing to apologize for," I said. "We're two broken people who've found someone who understands. We don't even need to talk about the case if you don't want to. There will be time for that later."

Lily looked down and shook her head. She stopped crying, wiped her eyes clear one final time, and pulled her mug in for a long swig of coffee before placing her hands back in mine. "I'm not sure we have as much time as you think."

"How do you figure?"

"Well, I received an interesting email last night," Lily said. "From my boss."

Lily shifted in her seat but kept her hands with mine. "Is something wrong?" I asked.

"Yes. His email said the home office is growing frustrated with the slow movement on this case. Especially now that they know Rafael Cortez is involved. He's been on our wanted list for about seven years, but the Mexican nationals can never locate him—or so they say. They're threatening to pull us off this case and bring in a new unit."

"After you've been here for two months?" I asked. "Can they do that? Don't some of these cases take years to solve?"

"Yes. And they can do whatever they want. It's the DEA's case, not mine personally. It seems too early to pull me off, though. That's why I've been preparing information to share with my boss about Duncan. I've been putting in the work. *He has not.*"

I let go of Lily and leaned back in my seat. I rubbed my

forehead. "Remember what you said about Cortez? He has a reputation for planting his people inside different government agencies."

"Sure, but we've only found proof of that in the Mexican government. That's why he's so well protected. No one there is going to extradite him to the U.S. because they're all on his payroll."

"And you don't think it's possible he's done the same here? Think about it. Cortez is operating out of the U.S. Why wouldn't he cover his bases here as well? Maybe he has someone in the DEA who is trying to make this case go away."

Lily licked her lips and sighed heavily. "I can't rule it out as impossible. But the background checks here are so intensive. They look into *everything,* even your family's past and ties. Interviews with lie detectors. The whole works."

"I can beat a lie detector," I said.

"Bullshit. Those things are almost one hundred percent accurate."

"Ninety percent, give or take," I said with a grin. "I guess that makes me a unicorn."

Lily let out a hearty laugh, a delightful sound after sharing about her troubled adolescence.

Hearing the laugh, Jo returned to take our orders. Lily asked for the breakfast special of eggs, hash browns, bacon, and toast. I ordered the same to get a wide sample of Jo's offerings.

"So, what's your plan?" I asked. "Did they give you a timeline for when they expect you to make progress?"

Lily ran her finger along the rim of her coffee mug. "No plan. I'm going to keep doing my job and taking notes on Duncan's lack of effort. Between last night and this morning, I'd say this case has taken a turn. It may not be progress, but it's opened more options to look into. I'll do what I do best and hit the files. I don't mind getting lost in lengthy documents. It's soothing."

"Weirdo," I said, earning another laugh. "I much prefer to follow people and beat them to a pulp. Once I know they're guilty, of course."

"Of course. So you're going to follow this Andres kid? Then what?"

I shrugged. "Not expecting much out of Andres. I'm more intrigued by the police department. I'm sure I don't need to tell you, but organized crime rings like small towns like this. They almost feel off the grid. And I should know, that's why I prefer to stay in small towns during my travels. But it's also easier to corrupt the locals. Whether it's a mayor, city councilor...the police department. Folks can be bought cheaper in small towns. What's a million dollars to a cartel if it means having cooperation from local law enforcement? It allows them to operate without worry. And a million dollars is absurd money to a police department of this size. How many officers are there in Hillcrest?"

"Twenty-five," Lily said. "And that's including the chief."

"Who's the chief? I'm surprised I haven't seen him yet."

"Oh, you have. It's Matthews."

"Matthews? Nothing about that guy screams police chief."

"Exactly," Lily said. "It's a recent development, and one he tries to play down. Asks to not be called *chief* by his peers, because he still sees them as his peers."

I frowned, my mind spinning with possibilities. "And no one has thought to look into this? Where is the old police chief?"

"He retired." Panic slipped into Lily's voice. I think she

was piecing this together at the same time as me.

"Retired, huh? And was he near retirement age?"

"He was, yes. Already qualified for a pension, too. But everyone I've talked to said he wasn't planning on retiring for another three years."

"Did you ever meet him?"

"No, Matthews was already the chief by the time I arrived. I believe he was sworn in the month before I showed up."

I chewed the inside of my lip, and Jo brought our breakfast. The bacon was still sizzling, and naturally, I drooled at the sight. The famous hash browns were the stringy kind, crispy on the surface, soft on the inside.

Shit.

I could see why Lily came here every day.

While chewing on a bite of eggs and hash browns, I considered why a police chief would suddenly retire earlier than originally planned. I'd met plenty of police chiefs in my day. These were men and women of conviction. When they said something, they meant it. If this man was going to retire in three years, then, dammit, he would retire in three years.

"Do you have access to any information about the prior chief?" I asked. "Did he have health issues? Family matters?"

"I can access his files," Lily said, not having touched her food yet. "From what I remember, he moved to Arizona for retirement."

"Married?"

Lily nodded.

"So," I said between bites, "why would a respected police chief suddenly retire way before he intended? And a month before the DEA arrived in his town?"

Lily drew a deep breath. She didn't even see her food on the table. Her mind was elsewhere, probably flipping through the mental notes she loved to get lost in.

"Shit," she said, finally picking up her fork, but only twisting it around in her fingers.

I waited. No need to force anything.

"Shit," she said again. "We monitored Hillcrest for six months before deciding to come out here. That's standard. And it's usually a month between that decision and us actually moving to our location. The chief would have retired right around the same time that decision was made."

I nodded. We were just about on the same page.

Lily slapped her forehead. "I can't believe I overlooked all of this. How could I be so stupid?"

I was glad Lily was taking so much time to herself. It let me scarf down the incredible meal. I soaked up the remains of egg yolk with my toast to finish, pushing the plate back in total satisfaction.

"Have you worked on cases involving a cartel before?" I asked, finishing my coffee.

"No, this is my first time," Lily said, scooping her first bite of hash browns and still not taking it. "I've done plenty of work on small drug operations, but never a cartel. But we also assumed this was just a local operation as well. It wasn't until we got out here that we started suspecting something bigger at play."

I brushed my chin while I thought. "I don't throw this around lightly, but I think Cortez may have someone in the DEA."

Lily's eyes bulged. "Excuse me?"

"It's a theory that's probably impossible to prove. At first, I thought it was only the locals that were corrupted. Pay off the chief to retire early, make sure he leaves town, then implement someone else who will cooperate with the cartel. But the timing of it all makes me question the DEA. The early retirement was likely always the plan, but it didn't get set into motion until they knew you were coming to Hillcrest. That can only mean the DEA tipped the cartel off, right?"

Lily shook her head. "I refuse to believe it. Our office would have been in contact with the Hillcrest PD as soon as the decision was made. That's how we got accommodations like space in their offices."

"Right where they can keep an eye on you," I said.

"I've dedicated my whole life to get to this point with the DEA," Lily said, her voice trembling with rage. "I'm not naïve—I know corruption is real. But to this extent? Am I just here as a pawn?"

"That's why I say this theory is impossible to prove. How many people work for the DEA?"

"Over ten thousand," Lily said, shaking her head. "Offices across half the world."

"It could be as simple as having an informant in the DEA," I said. "Anyone who has access to the system and can see who's getting which cases assigned and what the plans are. Or it could be someone with influence over who gets assigned which cases. So, it can be anyone from the IT guy up to the chief of the DEA."

Lily snorted. "Well, I know it's not Chief Goodman. I've had several talks with her personally and trust her thirst for justice."

"I'm not making accusations, just offering food for thought. Speaking of, you were right about these hash browns."

I made the chef's kiss motion, and this seemed to relax Lily enough to eat her meal that had probably gone cold by now.

"Look, Lily," I said. "There's more at play than we think. I'm sure of it. But I don't want you to spin out of control. Let me handle following these local police, starting with Matthews. If they get the sense you're sniffing around them, well, you'll probably be sent home the next day. Keep doing your job, and I'll let you know what I find. Deal?"

Lily nodded. "Okay. But we need to make some moves. Well, *I* do. Or they're going to send me back, anyway."

"You'll be fine. Don't worry about it."

I watched Lily finish her meal, veering the conversation back to personal matters. The weekend was coming up, and Lily invited me to her house for a Sunday afternoon barbecue, just the two of us.

"I'll absolutely be there," I said with a wide grin. I couldn't deny an opportunity to hang out with Lily. I had thoroughly enjoyed every moment we'd spent together so far. Maybe she shared the same attraction I was feeling. Plus, it had been months since I'd socialized at someone's house. It was a different dynamic compared to grabbing dinner or drinks in town. Relaxing.

Jo dropped off the check, along with a pile of at least two dozen of Lily's favorite breath mints.

"So that's why you come here so often," I said, snatching up the check before Lily could.

She popped one into her mouth and smiled back at me. My insides melted a little.

Ten minutes later, we left the diner, arm-in-arm, unaware of the van parked across the street and the two men watching us.

Chapter 15

Lily returned to the police station, and I used the free day to explore more of the town now that I had a car. I drove up and down every city block, making myself familiar. I found the vegan grocery store Richard had mentioned to me and couldn't help but chuckle as I drove by.

I was intrigued after learning more from Lily at breakfast. If the cartel had known the DEA was arriving, then I assumed they'd been working out of Hillcrest for much longer than the six months the feds had been tracking the flow of drugs in this small town. What other places could they be operating as fronts to launder their money through? The burger business was booming, but I passed bowling alleys, arcades, a fun center, and a handful of pizza parlors along the outer edge of town. Many businesses that could easily be used as a front.

I drove west and spent an hour at the beach. That's what I had come to this town for, yet this was my first chance to spend uninterrupted time with my toes in the sand. The sun battled against clouds for most of the afternoon, but the temperatures remained comfortable. The ocean water was icy, so I only got in up to my knees.

I took off my shirt and went for a run up and down the beach. People were watching me, mostly the ladies. I was well aware of the effect I had on women, especially being topless on the beach. Typically, I might have pursued one of these wandering pairs of eyes, but my thoughts were tangled up with Lily. We'd only met a couple of days ago, but I already felt like we had somehow known each other for a lifetime. Bonding over childhood trauma had that effect, I supposed.

My run lasted an hour, thighs and calves working up a good burn. It'd been a week since I last lifted some weights, and I'd need to get back in the gym to maintain my strength.

I left the beach and explored the boardwalk. It had the typical surf shops, beach attire stores, and a smoothie stand with a long line.

And that's when I spotted him. A man who looked completely out of place. Black jeans, black button-up shirt, dark wavy hair, sunglasses, and three chains hanging around his neck. The man stood in the smoothie line but was facing me. His hands were crossed in front of him, and he might have blended in had he worn flip-flops and swimming trunks.

My paranoia had been getting the best of me since being spotted on that fucking camera at Ben's house. But I felt this man's gaze burning a hole into my skin, even from behind his sunglasses.

I needed to test him and wandered out of his line of vision by stepping into a store called Breezy Beachwear.

The place was empty, except for a young Asian woman working behind the counter. Her work consisted of flipping through a thick textbook on quantum physics. Brainiac shit. Good for her.

I browsed a rack of shirts, finding some I actually liked. I could use some extra clothes. Having to wash my wardrobe every two days was exhausting. But at forty dollars per shirt, this store could fuck itself. California.

"Excuse me," I called out to the young woman. "Do you have any shirts in triple XL?"

I was sure they did, and those uncommon sizes were usually kept somewhere in the back.

She closed her book and took out a pair of earbuds I hadn't noticed she was wearing. "Three X? We have the big and tall rack over there." She pointed to the back corner.

"Thank you," I said.

If the man was following me, he'd be entering the store any second now. I wanted to be more in the back in case he strolled in. There was an open doorway behind the checkout counter that I was sure led to an emergency exit in the back.

Sure enough, the man dressed in all black strolled into the store and stopped to look at the first rack of clothing. He kept his head pointed toward the clothes, but I knew his eyes were scanning the room from behind those shades. Looking for me. Finding me. And seeing me looking right back at him with a wide, shit-eating grin.

He stopped pretending to look at the shirts that were much too colorful for his palette and turned his body to face me straight on. He was here for me, and he was clearly of Latin descent. The cartel moved quickly in this town. And how long had they been following me? Fuckers.

Did they know where I was staying? That complicated matters. It was hard to be on the run in such a small town with limited options for hotels.

The young woman paid neither of us any attention as she returned to her quantum physics.

It was a classic stare down. Wild West shit, only without the saloons and an audience. No, our crowd was racks of shirts with Hawaiian designs, bikinis, and sun hats covering every damn inch of the walls. The man moved to the next rack and positioned his face behind a *CLEARANCE* sign. His hands dropped to his sides, and I already knew what he was doing.

I shifted around my rack for a better view, but he also moved to keep the bright red sign between our stare down. He whipped out a pistol and fired a shot. I had already ducked when I saw the first twitch of his arm. The bullet whizzed by and shattered a mirror along the wall behind me.

The girl behind the counter shrieked and dove to the floor. I stayed low and lunged around to the checkout counter. I popped my head up and saw the man starting for the rack where I had been. He must have seen me from the corner of his eye, because he spun around and fired a second shot. This round met the cash register, causing shards of plastic and metal to fly in every direction.

While I was on the floor behind the counter, I saw a dismembered mannequin. The limbs were piled up neatly to the side of where the woman had been sitting. I grabbed a plastic arm with each hand and stood up to throw the first one at the man like a spear.

He dodged the fake flying limb, knocked over a rack of sunglasses, and fired a third shot in my direction. Dude wasn't a very good shot. I'm not sure exactly how tall he thought I was, because the bullet exploded a panel with a light bulb above my head in the ceiling. This ass hat was going for a head shot.

In a swift motion, I moved the second plastic arm to my right hand and reared back again. This time, I had a clear view of my target and had the two seconds needed to put all my body's weight behind my throw. The fake arm soared through the air like a javelin, its solid fingers like the tip of an arrow.

It connected square in the man's chest, knocking him backward, and sending his arms flailing as he fired a completely errant shot to his right.

"*Cabron!*" the man shouted, regaining his balance and looking at the plastic arm in surprise.

Yeah, buddy, anything could be a weapon if used properly. Death by mannequin! Sounds like a cheesy horror B movie.

I turned and ran through the back door. Sure, the man had spent four shots, but with each miss, he got closer to a successful one landing somewhere on my body. And since I didn't have my gun on me, I'd rather take my chances running with his shitty aim.

Note to self. Bring the gun every day now.

It was a short hallway in the back of the store, and through a tunnel of boxes bulging with clothes and accessories, I saw the exit door.

Before I reached it, however, the young lady jumped out from the side—where the fuck did she come from?—with a baseball bat in her two-handed grip. We were both moving too fast, and I saw the recognition in her eyes as she realized the mistake she was making.

But it was too late.

She had already loaded her swing—great form, by the way—prepared to swing away at whoever came running into the back. The aluminum bat connected with my stomach, knocking the wind out of me and sending me into a spiral to my left. I crashed into a stack of boxes, and they collapsed like an avalanche over my body.

The man ran into the back and made the mistake of focusing his attention on the girl with the bat. That, combined with me being buried under the boxes, bought me just enough time.

He raised his gun to the girl's face. "Drop the bat."

I knew he wasn't going to kill her. She had nothing to do with this. All he wanted was me, but this young woman was proving quite the roadblock. I couldn't waste another second. If she took a swing, then maybe he would pull the trigger.

I grabbed the box nearest my hands, pain still shooting up and down my gut, and tossed it in the man's direction. I just needed the distraction, and it worked.

He moved his gun from the girl as he spun around to see the box sailing his way. He fired a fifth shot into the box— perhaps he was even more paranoid than me—but I stayed low, starting in a crawl and eventually getting to my feet just in time to throw myself forward and tackle him.

Shoulder into his thighs, arms around the knees. He had no chance and came crashing to the floor. He swung the gun downward, and I grabbed his wrist, twisting it backward until hearing it crack into several pieces. His fingers immediately loosened their grip on the gun, which I now saw was an FN Five-seven. It had an extended magazine holding at least twenty rounds. A fine weapon. Used by the Secret Service. If it was good enough to protect the president, then it was definitely good enough for the cartel.

The man shrieked, immediately clutching his broken wrist with his free hand, rolling back and forth on his back while tears streamed down his face. The pistol remained in his hand, but he had zero control over his fingers, deeming it useless. I stood up and kicked it out of his grip anyway, sending a fresh jolt of pain up the bastard's arm.

It was times like these I remembered how much I loved my life. The horrified woman had just witnessed a gruesome scene, but I kept her alive. And myself. I crouched down, pressing my knee into this guy's forearm, which caused another piercing shriek.

"Who sent you?" I asked calmly.

I'm not sure he even heard me. He only kept screaming and crying like a constipated newborn baby. Sometimes I felt bad for guys like this. He was just a man on someone's payroll, ordered to carry out dirty work on behalf of some pompous drug lord. He probably had a family, a whole life outside of the underworld of crime.

But this was not one of those times. This guy tried to shoot me in the face. What if he had ruined my hair? Or added another scar to my chiseled countenance? Not cool.

"*Please*, tell me who sent you," I said. "I used the magic word."

His crying had stopped, but he was still panting. Hell, so was I.

That young woman had done a number on me. A man half my size would have been knocked out cold if he had taken that same blow. She could hold her own in this fucked up world. Good for her.

The man smiled, then spit in my face. If there hadn't been innocent ladies present, I would have ended him right there. It was probably best to send a message, anyway. A dead man couldn't relay what I had done. At least not entirely.

I wiped the spit off my cheek, feeling the groove of that scar below my eye, and patted my hand dry on the man's shirt.

"Well, amigo," I said, "you can tell whoever sent you that I said hello."

I stood up, raised my foot over his face, and stomped down as hard as I could. I'm not entirely sure what all the crunching sounds were, but I assumed one was his jaw breaking, considering his next scream came out as more of a mumbled wail. Maybe his neck was broken. He wasn't moving. Just lay there, head cocked to the side, blood shooting out of his nose and mouth.

I didn't really care. Message sent.

The Asian woman hadn't dropped her bat but lowered it after I turned my attention back to her.

"Sorry about the mess," I said.

Her jaw hung open, and she kept looking from me to the man choking on his own blood.

"Do you have cameras in the store?" I asked.

She nodded. Speechless. The shock would take a few minutes to wear off.

"Go save that camera footage and call the cops," I said. "They'll need to see it if I want to be cleared of any wrongdoing."

I turned for the exit door, and she finally spoke again.

"But what about him?" she asked, pointing her bat at the writhing man on the floor.

"Oh, he's fine," I said. "He can't even wipe his ass right now, so you have nothing to worry about. The cops will take him off your hands." I rubbed my stomach. "I'd hang around, but I need to go lie down. You got me good."

She blushed. "Sorry about that."

I raised a hand. "Don't worry about it. All is fair when a coward barges into your store with a gun. Keep being awesome."

I left the store through the back exit and went straight to my car in the nearby lot. The only way to fight off the urge to vomit was to recline my seat and fall asleep.

Chapter 16

Knuckles rapped on my window, startling me back awake. I had no idea what time I had returned to my car and didn't have a clue how much time had passed since. The sun was still out, though it was lower. Maybe four or five o'clock.

Officer Matthews stared through my window, his gaze burning like a beam of sunlight through a magnifying glass. And I was the poor ant getting fried.

"C'mon, big fella," he said, knocking again.

I sat up, my abs feeling like I had just done a million crunches with no rest. In front of my car stood Lily and Duncan in their DEA uniforms, and several yards behind them I saw a huddle of police officers and paramedics taking a man on a stretcher into an ambulance. His arms and face were wrapped. *Poor guy. I wonder what happened to him.*

I opened my car door and stepped out.

"Good afternoon, chief," I said.

"Chief?" he replied, taken aback. "How did you—" He turned and looked at Lily. "God dammit! Can't you feds keep your mouth shut about anything?"

He turned back to me, face red, and I saw Lily suppressing a grin behind him. Matthews pointed a shaking finger in my face. "You haven't even been here a week, and every time something happens, you're right there. What do you have to say about that?"

I cleared my throat. I wasn't a fan of having a finger in my face. The urge to pick up Matthews and break his back on my knee was overwhelming. But I couldn't do that. Not until I had proof.

"I know you're not referring to what happened inside that clothing store," I said, crossing my arms. I flexed, knowing my bulging muscles made men like Matthews feel emasculated beyond repair. "Because that was self-defense. Guy had a gun. I did not."

"We saw the tapes," Matthews said. "At least, everything that happened before you went into that back room. That's not the issue. If you weren't here, that store would still be operating as usual. Undisturbed. But your presence doesn't allow that. Why the hell was that guy after you? What are you hiding?"

"I'm not hiding anything, chief," I said. "I asked that man who sent him. He didn't answer, so I broke his jaw."

Duncan looked at Lily with a disturbed look.

Matthews turned and spit on the ground, then pulled out a stick of gum to chew on. If only I had a cigarette, I'd light it up in front of this asshole and sell it as the best thing to ever fill my lungs.

He held his gaze on me, fury burning behind his little brown eyes. "I'm watching you," he said. "Nobody fucks with my town and gets away with it. You hear?"

Matthews pivoted and stomped away, brushing by Lily as he went to join his fellow officers near the ambulance.

Lily and Duncan stepped toward me in unison.

"Impressive to see you in action," she said. "Even Duncan

couldn't help but admit you'll be a fine addition to the team."

Duncan nodded. "I'm sorry if we got off on the wrong foot. Got a lot going on, and I don't know who to trust."

He extended his hand to me, and we shook. "Save the apology, Agent Duncan. I completely understand. Between the SEALs, the CIA, and trying to find any sort of personal life, a person can snap easily. Besides, I don't trust *anyone*, so I can't blame you there."

Duncan laughed. A sound of relief. Maybe seeing me take down a gunman with a mannequin, a cardboard box, and my bare fists took some of the pressure off him. If I was available to help their case, that just meant he could zone out even more than he had been.

"We've been doing some research the last couple of hours," Lily said, jumping right back into business with her professional tone. "Identified four of the six dead bodies. One is Javier Ocampo, also known as Ben, the owner of Hamburger Stand."

I looked at her, confused, then realized she was painting a formal picture in front of her partner. So she hadn't told him about our trip out to Ben's house earlier this morning. Maybe she was still hesitant about Duncan knowing how involved I'd been so far.

"You mentioned you attempted to buy drugs from him, correct?" she asked me.

My brain fog was clearing up from my nap, which I now estimated had lasted a whole thirty minutes. "That's right," I said, rubbing my stomach. Fuck, it hurt. "I found out from the kind gentleman down at Ted's Place how to score drugs in Hillcrest, and he pointed me to Hamburger Stand, where I had to order a triple deluxe. I was asked to go around the back of the building to meet Ben, and we bartered until he sold me some drugs."

"Do you still have them?" Duncan asked, looking intrigued by the story. Maybe the opposite would prove true. Perhaps my aid in this case reinvigorated his passion for justice.

"I do in my hotel room," I said. "Vicodin. Which, ironically, I could use right now. Took quite the blow to my gut."

Duncan's eyes fell to my stomach. "You sure you're okay?"

I nodded. "Good girl back there. How is she?"

"She's fine," Lily said, placing her hands on her hips. "She's closing up early to call it a day."

"What's the deal with Hamburger Stand?" I asked. "Have you questioned any of the staff?"

"Not yet," Lily said. "We're exploring the other dead men before deciding our next move. Alejandro Tovar and Alexis Ramirez were the two men killed at the tavern on Tuesday night. And last night, we have Ocampo, and Rodrigo Estevez."

"Which one was Estevez?" I asked.

Lily and Duncan exchanged an uncomfortable glance. Duncan spoke up. "The one with his genitals removed."

I nodded, still not able to get that visual out of my head. Something I hadn't even seen with my own eyes.

"And nothing on the other two?" I asked.

Lily shook her head. "Nothing in our system. Figure they sneaked into the country. We're sending samples to our team in Mexico to see if anything comes up in their database, but that could take a couple of days."

"I assume there are connections between these dead bodies," I said, locking eyes with Lily. Even during this official business, I felt the fire of passion raging between us.

"It's definitely a tangled web," Duncan said, taking out

his cellphone and pulling up what I presumed were notes. "We believe Estevez shot Ocampo in the head. The gun we found on his body matches the caliber of bullets we believe went through Ocampo's skull. Ninety percent match, at least, based on initial results. But that gun could have been planted. Clearly there's more going on, if Estevez ended up with his bean bag ripped off."

"Duncan!" Lily cried, a grin touching the sides of her mouth.

Duncan laughed. "Sorry. I'm trying to find any chance to lighten the mood. This is heavy shit."

I shared in the laughter. "Estevez maybe shot Ocampo. What else?"

Lily spoke this time. "Everything stopped with Ocampo, at least regarding Hamburger Stand. The business was registered under his name, all the licenses. He was operating as an LLC with only his name as the entity. The house he was living in was purchased under his name six years ago."

"Six years?!" I asked.

Duncan nodded and cut in. "Yeah, once we found that out, the floodgates opened. Everything in Hillcrest traces back to Ocampo. Hamburger Stand. His house. He also owned a bar that's no longer in business. A smoothie spot near the beach. And, finally, a car dealership."

I scratched my head. "So this operation has been running for a while now."

"Ocampo must have been the highest-ranking cartel member in Hillcrest," Lily said. "Cartels may be headquartered out of Mexico, but they set up networks all around the world. They chose Hillcrest and had Ocampo build up multiple businesses to use for money laundering. So, Ocampo runs businesses, they need employees, and that helps get work visas approved to bring over more of their team from across the border. I'd be surprised if he ever made a random hire. Everyone is placed precisely in their roles."

"Andres," I said, more to myself. I looked out to the beach where a trio of seagulls were attacking someone's open picnic basket.

"Who's Andres?" Duncan asked, shifting his weight to his other foot, eyes still scanning his cell phone.

"Andres works at the Hamburger Stand," I said. "Younger guy, late teens or early twenties. I wondered about his involvement but found it odd they'd have someone so young on the front lines."

"Family business," Duncan said. "These guys have sons and raise them to join the fun. I've seen reports of six-year-old boys dead because they were playing with fully automatic rifles. Life is nothing but another currency for these people."

Lily shook her head. "That's disgusting."

"I know," Duncan said. "And now it's here in Hillcrest. Well, has been."

"We're considering a possibility that's rather disturbing," Lily said. "Keep in mind, we have more digging to do, but if Ocampo really was the one in charge in Hillcrest, his death means people from above him are coming, or are already here."

"Most likely already here," Duncan said. "His death would have been ordered from someone above him. Yes, the cartels are full of criminals, but it's incredibly rare someone rises against the hierarchy—that only guarantees their death. And for someone to have been running things as long as Ocampo, he'd have a loyal following here in Hillcrest."

"So, we need to find out why Ocampo was murdered," I said. "If we can confirm the *why*, everything else will fall into place."

"That's a dream scenario," Lily said. "Getting the *why* isn't easy when we can't even talk to any of these people while they're alive. Dead bodies can only tell us so much. We're better off trying to follow a trail of clues and facts."

"There's a man in the hospital now," I said. "He might talk, but I wouldn't hold my breath. I did break his jaw, after all, so he might have difficulty with speech."

Duncan laughed at this. I liked him now that he had snapped out of his depressed trance from earlier in the week. "We'll try him in a few weeks when he's had some time to heal. The medic's initial thought was at least a month in the hospital. You might have crushed his larynx, but they weren't sure. If that's the case, he could be there even longer."

I gave a tight-lipped grin, not sure if he was applauding my efforts or just stating the facts.

"Well," I said, "if you two want to keep digging, I'll follow Andres home after work tonight."

Duncan shifted. "While I appreciate your help, Mr. Mendez, we can't have you just going around town beating up people for the hell of it."

I raised my hand. "No plans to confront him. I just wanna see where he lives. Who he may live with. That kind of shit. That way we can plan stakeouts and gossip and eat doughnuts."

Lily rolled her eyes and turned away, watching the last of the police officers disperse from the other end of the parking lot.

"I'm gonna hold you to that," Duncan said, playfully

pointing at me. At least, I hope it was playful. For his sake.

"Just be careful tonight, okay?" Lily said, and I saw the concern in her eyes.

I grinned and replied, "I always am."

Chapter 17

I returned to my hotel and spent the next four hours in bed trying to recover. As much as I wanted to take one of those Vicodin pills, I needed a clear head when tailing Andres later. I lay on my back and let my body do the healing. Not much progress was made in those four hours, but I at least felt better.

A gnarly purple bruise roughly the size of a compact disc spread across my abs. It hurt to laugh or draw in deep breaths, so I'd have to stay away from Comedy Central for the moment. I had no interest in eating a meal, so grabbed a bag of chips on my way out. Lay's Classic.

The night was the coolest since I'd arrived, so I slipped on my windbreaker jacket. I brought my backpack and quadruple checked to make sure the gun was in it before leaving. No way in hell I was getting caught without it again. Clouds buried the moon, making it darker than usual.

I drove across town to Hamburger Stand and parked on the curb across the street. I knew the criminal underground was on high alert following the deaths of six cartel members. Even if they handled the murders, there was a reason. These people didn't kill for the hell of it. Eyes would be on Hamburger Stand, just as they had been on Ben's house.

A pair of binoculars would have been useful, but I used my cell phone's cheap camera to zoom in and see who was working in the burger joint. Andres stood behind the counter, helping a customer with their order. The image was grainy, but I knew it was him. About five-ten, a scrawny kid with shaggy black hair. Not too many Latino boys who looked like him, although something about him seemed oddly familiar. Like I had known him in a past life.

I sent Lily a text message, letting her know I had arrived at Hamburger Stand. She had asked for regular updates throughout the night. I thought about sending her a selfie while I killed time in the car, but remembered I didn't do ridiculous shit like that. That the idea even popped into my head said a lot about Lily's impact on my common sense.

Even more tempting was the urge to grab a burger. I could smell the grilled meat lingering in the air, seeping through my rolled-down window. That would be ludicrous. I was afraid I'd taken my last step inside of Hamburger Stand. If I went in there, I'd likely be met by a dozen men with guns. And I wasn't quite ready for that. Especially in a place I had grown so fond of.

Hamburger Stand advertised their hours as nine to nine, and at exactly 8:58, Andres started cleaning the counter, strolled over to the neon OPEN sign hanging in the window, and turned it off. A couple of other men came out from the back and helped Andres sweep, mop, and put all the chairs on top of the tables. No one looked suspicious, and to the common passerby, no one would have guessed all three men inside were working for a violent and powerful drug cartel.

But I knew. Andres finally exited the building at 9:45. He stepped through the front doors and bolted them, giving them a tug with both arms to ensure they were locked in place. I watched as he strolled around the building, eyes glued to his cell phone and wearing big headphones, and disappeared into the darkness.

A minute passed, and I grew worried he had driven off in some other direction. There wasn't any type of road when I had met Ben behind the building, so I wasn't sure where the kid could have gone. He surprised me when he came pedaling around the building on a bicycle. The wheels had reflectors, and he wore a helmet with flashing lights that made his presence obvious.

This part of the job became incredibly easier than I expected. When tailing someone while driving, there was always the risk they realized they were being followed and would attempt to escape. A kid on a bike, however, had no chance of losing me. I could keep a longer distance than usual. My phone buzzed, and it was Lily reminding me to stay safe. I replied to let her know I was in pursuit and dropped the phone in the center cupholder.

Andres zoomed out of the parking lot, paying me no attention, and seemed to reach a higher gear once he got on the sidewalk. For living in such a dangerous dynamic, I was impressed with how safe the kid was. Helmet. Riding on the sidewalk instead of the middle of the street like an entitled asshole. There weren't many bicyclists in Laredo growing up, so imagine my surprise when I arrived at a college campus where these pompous fucks owned the road, walkways, and everything in between.

Apparently, everyone in Hillcrest had different places to go. I turned on my car and had to make a U-turn to follow Andres west, a new direction I hadn't explored. At least I knew we weren't going too far, considering the ocean was two miles away.

After a quarter mile, the sidewalk Andres was riding on turned into a dirt path as the main road narrowed to one lane in each direction. The shoulder was still wide enough to give him plenty of room to ride, but I was still surprised they made this poor kid do this every night. There weren't streetlights after the next quarter mile, and we were riding along in pure blackness. I stayed about two hundred feet behind the bicycle, hoping my headlights provided him with extra visibility while not being too obvious.

Andres never looked over his shoulder to see how close I was, and just kept pedaling like a crazed Tour de France participant. After the next quarter mile, Andres turned right and disappeared from my sight. I slowed down and turned onto a makeshift dirt road that strayed away from the main one. My headlights revealed a trail wide enough for one vehicle, and Andres was now three hundred feet ahead, pedaling even faster.

Shit. Maybe he saw me.

I killed my headlights and pressed down on the accelerator. The glimpse I had caught of the road showed it was mostly straight. There were some slight curves, but if I kept in the middle, I should at least stay on the road and not fall into the ditches on either side.

We were still a mile from the beach, but a stand of palm trees started decorating both sides of the road. They swayed in the evening breeze, providing a sense of relaxation.

Andres's flashing helmet continued up the road, and I had to slam on the brakes when I saw glowing lights further up. The road started an uphill ascent, ending at a mansion. It was hard to see everything through the trees, but I saw roughly seven cars parked in front. The glowing lights were coming from the massive windows. All I could see from the bottom of this hill was the top of the vaulted ceiling that was probably fifty feet high.

"This is it," I said to myself. "This is where a drug lord would live."

I grabbed my phone from the cup holder to find it only had one bar of signal. All I wanted was to open Google Maps to see where the fuck I was, but the damn thing kept spinning like the old 3G days. While it kept trying to load, I sent a new text to Lily.

Went 3/4 mile west from Hamburger Stand. Turned right onto dirt road. Big mansion at top of hill?

I assumed Lily and her team knew this city inside and out, but the mansion came as a surprise to me, especially when the rest of Hillcrest seemed like a blue-collar town. If this cartel had been making money over the past six years, they could have easily built this off-the-grid mansion. No way anyone working on Main Street could afford a place like this.

Andres was gone by now, but there was no mistaking his final destination. Or his involvement with the cartel. Why didn't these assholes give him one of the seven cars parked out front? Poor kid.

I had to get closer. My phone camera was shit, but if I could snap some shots from a distance, we could run the photos through Lily's database and see what matches came back.

I kept the headlights off and drove up the hill at a crawl. This town car kept damn near silent as long as I stayed off the gas pedal. And I only had to tap it twice to keep my momentum going—the hill wasn't too steep. I pulled aside and parked behind a palm tree that would have blocked any wandering eyes looking out the massive front window.

After killing the engine, I grabbed my gun out of my backpack and stepped out of the car. I slipped the gun into the back of my waistband. Hated doing that. Always felt like a douchebag, but sometimes I had no choice.

I approached the nearest palm tree and looked around for cameras in the vicinity. There were none I could see, but I trusted there were some along the mansion. No way a cartel didn't have their perimeter secured.

I was only twenty feet away from the nearest car. There were actually eight, and they were all parked in a single-file line leading up to the roundabout in front of the mansion's entrance. Staying low, I tiptoed toward the closest vehicle, a newer Subaru Legacy, and pulled out my cell phone to snap a picture of the California license plate.

Before I took the picture, I heard the cocking of a gun directly behind me and steel pressing into the back of my head.

A voice spoke out that sent gooseflesh across my entire body. Like a ghost calling out your name. It was entirely familiar, but different. Older. A man's voice, instead of a boy.

He said, "Hello, little brother."

Chapter 18

The sound of my brother's voice made me dizzy. Like I was having some kind of fucked up flashback. I hadn't heard his voice in twenty-six years, but his three words were instantly recognizable. Just like I could close my eyes and smell my mom cooking tortillas and green chile in the kitchen. The memories from the past always lingered somewhere in your heart and mind.

"Manny?" I said, turning my head to look over my shoulder. If this really was my brother, there was no way he would pull the trigger right now. And if it wasn't, well, I'd be dead.

The barrel of the gun trembled in his grip, and when I turned all the way around, he lowered it, rage burning behind his intense stare. I hadn't seen my older brother since he was sixteen years old, and I was twelve. But I recognized him immediately. Gone was the baby face and peach fuzz on the chin from our last encounter. Standing in front of me was a forty-two-year-old man with a full beard and a chiseled face that had some plastic work done.

But it was always the eyes that gave away a person's identity. And those were the same eyes that used to watch me through a cracked open bedroom door while I did homework on the floor.

"Why are you wasting your time learning that stuff?" my brother would ask. "We're going to work for Dad, and he'll take care of us."

I never told him I didn't want to work for Dad, even after we lost our mother. But when he asked me the night before he snuck out of our aunt's house if I wanted to join him, I never gave a response. All we found was a note he had left behind the next morning, explaining he was headed to Mexico.

"What are you doing here, Jonny?" Manny asked, his voice nearly as shaky as his hand had been. "You shouldn't be here."

"What does that mean?" I replied. "What are *you* doing here? And why did you pull a gun on me? Is this really how you wanted to greet me after all this time? Are you going to shoot me?"

The gun was now at Manny's side, but it was too dark for me to tell which kind it was. Some sort of pistol. I still sensed he could whip it back up and blast me away, but the emotions were clearly swirling for him, too. His bottom lip quivered like he was suppressing the urge to cry. And maybe he was.

"I wandered into this town," I said after he left my questions unanswered. "Was just looking for somewhere to stay with a beach."

"Are you still in the military?" he asked.

"No."

"Are you a cop now?"

"No. What's with all the questions?"

"I need to know if you're bugged," Manny said, seeming to gain more control over his voice. "Lift up your shirt."

"Are you kidding me? I'm not—"

"LIFT YOUR FUCKING SHIRT!" Manny screamed, and sure

enough, he raised the gun again.

"Okay," I said, slowly raising my hands before pulling the bottom hem of my T-shirt. "See. No wires. Just pure muscle."

"Don't be a smart ass."

"If I recall, *you* were always the smart ass," I said, shooting him a wink. "Besides, that's the second time this week I've been asked to lift my shirt up. What's with you guys?"

"Do you think this is funny?" Manny snarled.

"Funny? No. Small world. Yes. You're not the only one with questions. Why are you here? Is Dad inside that house?"

At the mention of our father, Manny lowered his gun and slipped it into a holster on his hip. It must have reminded him I was his only living relative outside of our father. Our shared bond.

"No, he never comes to the States," Manny said. "Too risky."

"Are you going to invite me in?" I asked, gesturing to the house I really wanted to see the inside of.

Manny shook his head. "Are you crazy? Everyone in there has been talking about you. Why are you snooping around Hillcrest?"

"Well, I was almost killed the night I arrived," I said. "So I wanted to see what was really going on. It's just the SEAL in me, I suppose."

"Leave Hillcrest," Manny said. "These people will kill you, and there's nothing I can do to stop them."

"Aren't you in charge?" I asked. "If you tell them to leave me alone, aren't they supposed to do that?"

"You put one of our own in the hospital. That made it personal for some of these guys. They only care about killing you or anyone close to you."

"Well, there is no one close to me," I said.

"Really? Who's the white girl, then?"

The glow from the mansion cast just enough light for me to see my brother's entire face. I'd never seen a picture of my father before Lily had shown me one from his younger days. But seeing Manny after all these years—he appeared to be the spitting image of our father.

"So you've been watching me?" I asked. "If you wanted to talk, all you had to do was reach out."

"What do you expect when you put your face right into one of our cameras?" Manny asked, frustration boiling in his voice. "*Estupido!* Everyone here works for Dad and knows who you are. When your face turned up in Javy's house, everyone knew who you were."

"And no one wanted to invite me to join the family business?" I asked, forcing a smirk. "Our father also wants me dead?"

"We know your past," Manny said. "No one will ever trust you because of your loyalty to the U.S. government."

They were wrong. I had no loyalty to the government—I had only worked for them. I hated the government as much as the next red-blooded American. My loyalty was to the country itself and to my fellow citizens. If I had to bring down a cartel single-handedly, I would. If I had to kill my own brother, it would be difficult, but I'd do it. Anything to make this world— and country—a safer place to live.

"So, what am I supposed to do?" I asked. "Just keep living like this never happened? Pretend I don't know my long-lost brother who *ditched me* two decades ago isn't living his best life in this mansion on a hill?"

"Exactly," Manny said. "And don't go back to Hamburger

Stand. Andres can't handle seeing you."

"Oh, you're friends with Andres? Way to keep a kid on your staff to run the fast-food joint. Nice touch."

"He's not my friend," Manny said. "He's my son."

"Excuse me?" I nearly choked on the air. He was my nephew. Maybe my mom was up there drawing up these crazy schemes for me to meet my nephew and save him from this road of crime he would soon be on. It wasn't too late.

"If you hurt him," Manny said, pointing a stiff finger in my face—why was everyone doing that lately?—"you'll find your body chopped in parts and spread up and down the coast of California."

I laughed and my brother recoiled. He had always been bigger than me up to the day he left. But in those years since, I outgrew him, and now stood four inches taller, with a lot more meat on my bones than him. The thought of him chopping me up into pieces almost pulled on my heartstrings. Almost.

"Why would I hurt my nephew?" I asked. "He's an innocent boy who should be as far from you as possible."

"You don't know shit about our situation."

"Does he know his mother?" I asked. "Or did you raise him to hate his mother like you did?"

"That's bullshit, and you know it!" Manny cried. His voice elevated, and I saw his fists clench into balls. "I didn't hate Mom. We just clashed a lot. Never saw eye to eye."

"Yes, because you wanted to leave her to join the cartel with our loser father."

Now Manny laughed and started pacing in circles. He was wearing a leather jacket and he kept running his fingers up and down the zipper like he was nervous. His laugh was borderline maniacal, but he calmed down and pointed at me again. "Our father is no loser. How dare you! If you only knew how much he contributed to keep you and Mom alive."

I rolled my eyes. "I don't think leaving me when I was born did anything to help my development as a person in this world."

"No, dumbass," Manny said. "Dad sent money to Mom every month. Enough to cover the bills, plus extra for other things."

"Bullshit," I said. "Mom worked every day of her life. We rarely had extra money to buy an ice-cream cone."

Manny shook his head and stopped pacing. "That's Mom's fault. The money's there. Dad used to send checks, but Mom never deposited. So he opened a bank account and sent her the details."

"She probably didn't want that dirty money," I said. "Some people have morals, remember what those were like?"

"The money's there," he reiterated. "You can take it or leave it, but it's been sitting in a savings account for at least the last thirty-five years."

"Fuck your money."

Manny growled and threw his hands in the air, turning around. He'd never been good at handling his emotions, and it appeared things hadn't changed. I supposed he handled his issues by shooting them, but he couldn't shoot his kid brother. At least, not during this first reunion.

He turned back around to face me, the darkness shadowing both of our faces. "Leave, Jonny. There are too many people in this town who want you dead. And they'll make sure it happens, especially if you keep sticking your nose in places it shouldn't be."

Manny crossed his arms and leaned against the trunk of the

car I had come to examine. His breathing grew rapid.

"Don't you think this is more than a coincidence?" I asked. "Out of all the places in the world, and we're in the same small town. Call it what you want—fate, destiny, God—it doesn't matter. But something brought us here. Maybe it was Mom."

Manny shook his head. "No, Jonny, it's none of that. It's a coincidence, and your life is in danger."

I crossed my arms to match my brother. "This can turn out different. We can be hugging it out. Swapping stories. We shared our entire childhoods together, and you just walked out on me. How do you think that made me feel?"

I'd suppressed these thoughts for more than two decades, but now the feelings were all coming back. How much I'd loved my brother. How much I hated him, too. *Still.* Resentment. Jealousy. Curiosity. Why did family relationships have to be so complicated?

"You were my world," I said, gritting my teeth. "I looked up to you. You were the only man in my life. I thought we had a sacred bond. And you left me without a second thought."

Manny had his back to the house lights, leaving his face entirely silhouetted. He kept sniffling, and I was sure he was crying. We stood in silence for the next minute when he finally spoke again. "I had a decision to make, and I made it. On my own. I'm not going to lie and say it was easy leaving, but I wouldn't change anything. We were orphans. Did you not realize that? I needed guidance, and Tia Rosa wasn't providing it. You may have not realized it because you were younger, but she was a mess when she took us in."

"Of course, I knew all this," I said. "Sure, we were orphans, but I never felt like one when you were around. When Mom died, I just assumed you and I would figure out life together.

Maybe it was wrong of me to assume you'd take care of me. Even unfair. But I would have done it if the roles were reversed."

Manny's silhouette nodded. "You were always better than me, Jonathan. You took care of Mom. Took care of yourself. You even took care of Tia Rosa, all while finishing high school. Part of me knew you were going to be just fine, and that helped my decision to leave. I'm the selfish one. Only worried about myself and my future."

I sensed he wanted to apologize, but he never did. And I knew he never would. What good would apologizing do now? It didn't change anything that had already happened. And all these years later, we were still two different people standing on opposite sides of right and wrong. Family by blood only. Just like my father I'd never met.

Headlights appeared from the bottom of the hill, turning onto the dirt road that led up to us.

"Expecting company?" I asked.

"No," Manny said, a tinge of fear in his voice. He tugged on his jacket to ensure it was covering his gun.

We watched as the headlights grew bigger and closer, eventually stopping next to my car. The lights were blinding, and my brother and I had to raise our arms to shield our eyes.

The lights flicked off, and the driver's door opened.

"Agent Duncan?" I said, instantly recognizing him by the shape of his body as he approached us, gun drawn.

"Is there a problem here?" he asked, rushing to my side. He looked my brother up and down, glaring at him. "Lily let me know where you were, and we thought it was best if I came to check on you, Mr. Mendez."

"Everything's fine," I said. "Just catching up with an old

friend. Is there a problem?"

"Not yet," Duncan said, lowering his gun.

Manny was acting too cool for my liking, but I supposed he had to. A DEA agent was standing in the driveway of his mansion, where several cartel members surely awaited inside.

"And what's your name, sir?" Duncan asked my brother.

"Manuel," he replied.

"Manuel what?" Duncan snapped back.

"Manuel Mendez," my brother said, standing tall and keeping his arms crossed.

"Mendez?" Duncan asked, more to himself. "You've got to be shitting me. Jonny, you said you weren't involved, and we believed you. You're coming back to the station with me."

"Whoa," I said. "I'm *not* involved with this sad excuse of a human being."

Manny snickered, and Duncan holstered his gun.

"You have to see things from my perspective," Duncan said. "I can't speak for Manuel, but I know you just arrived in Hillcrest, Jonny. And there are now six dead bodies since you've shown up. There haven't been six murders in this city for over a century. You may have Lily fooled, but I see right through you."

I bit my bottom lip.

"Fine," I said. "But I'm not getting in a car with you. I'll follow you to the station."

Duncan studied me. The light from the house cast over his face, and I could clearly see his thoughts spinning. "I'll follow you," he said. "You know the way. Let's go."

Duncan started back for his car.

Before I followed suit, I turned to my brother.

"You have one thing wrong, big bro," I said. "I'm not afraid of death. You can't threaten me with it. I've been running from death my entire life. I know death better than I know you. If I come back here, it won't be me getting carried out in a body bag."

I could hear the smile in Manny's voice as he replied calmly. "I love you, little bro. Stay safe out there."

Chapter 19

"What the hell were you thinking?" Duncan asked.

We drove back to the police station and gathered in his office, where Lily was waiting, her expression frantic and worried.

"I told Lily I was going to follow Andres when he left Hamburger Stand tonight," I said. "How was I supposed to know that kid was my nephew this whole time? And that he was riding his bike to *my brother*. Do you have any idea how awful that was just now? I didn't think I was ever going to see my brother again. Part of me is ready to leave Hillcrest."

"You can't do that," Lily said from her desk. They had me sit in a chair stationed between their desks. Almost like an interrogation, but more lax. I had to look to my left to see Lily, and to my right to see Duncan.

I looked left. "And why is that? I'm not obligated to be here. Hell, I'm not even under arrest. I can walk out right now and leave town. Won't even take the car you loaned me, because then you could arrest me for grand theft auto."

"That's all true, yes," Lily said. "But you offered to help us, and now there's a good opportunity in front of us."

I laughed and shook my head. "I know what you're thinking. You want to use my relationship with my brother to have me get in with the bad guys, right?"

Duncan shrugged. "Your words, not ours."

"It's not going to work," I said. "My brother and I don't exactly get along, and he just informed me everyone in that mansion wants me dead. They're not exactly rolling out a red carpet to welcome me. And to be fair, I want them dead. Leave me alone in a room with the cartel, and there will be no more cartel. And what do *you* know about my brother's involvement? You seemed to know exactly what that house was last night."

I turned my attention to Agent Duncan, who leaned back in his seat with his feet kicked up on the desk. "We know exactly who he is and what that house is used for. We've been here for two months. But we can't exactly barge into that house on a whim. Our biggest issue has been finding proof to link the drugs to anyone in particular. If we had some proof, we could get a warrant to search the house."

"It doesn't help the house is registered under a different name," Lily said, clicking rapidly on her computer. "Even if we somehow found a link, the house is registered under the name Juan Rodriguez. Custom-built property that requested permits eight years ago. There has never been a different name listed on the property, and since we can't know who actually lives there, we'd need evidence tying the *house* to drug crimes before a judge would sign a warrant."

"Juan Rodriguez?" I asked.

"Yes, do you know the name?" Lily asked, leaning forward and planting her elbows on her desk.

I laughed. "Yeah, I know multiple people with that name. Might as well look up John Smith while you're at it. I'd bet they used a fake name, but a common one, to make your search impossible."

"But they needed a social security number and other documents to prove the man's identity," Lily said. "Registered for property taxes and all that. He's a real person, but we have no idea where he is. Nothing has been attached to his social security number since registering this property."

"We think this guy's probably back in Mexico," Duncan said. "The cartel likely brought him out here, had him fill out all the paperwork for the house, then vanish so nothing else could ever be traced back to him. It's a common move for this exact reason of blocking warrants to investigate their properties."

"And you have any way around that?" I asked.

"Well, not legally, no," Duncan said, followed by a deep sigh. "We usually have to get more creative and hope we find one of the drug dealers in the act. From there, we can get warrants to tap phone lines, but still not to get into a property."

"I can go in," I said. "I don't need a warrant. Shit, I don't even need a key."

Duncan let out an exaggerated laugh. "You and what army? That's a suicide mission if you were to sneak into that house on your own. Besides, any evidence obtained illegally—which it would be, if you did this—doesn't hold up in court. It's a lose-lose."

"How confident are you this cartel is running operations out of that mansion?" I asked, burning a gaze through Duncan. I understood the rules the feds had to play within—that's why I left the CIA—but I hated the way Duncan was giving up all hope.

"Oh, we're one hundred percent certain that mansion is

hosting the cartel, and likely manufacturing their entire operation out of there. I'm sure it's all in their basement."

"A house in California with a basement?" I asked. "I thought that wasn't even possible."

"It's possible," Duncan said. He had picked up a baseball from his desk and fidgeted with it between both hands. "No laws say you can't have one. They're just incredibly expensive to have built, and they're stupid. If an earthquake hits, the cost of repairing a basement out here is often more than buying a new house."

"The blueprints filed with the city included a basement," Lily said. "Another reason we're positive it's the cartel. They have the money to build a basement, and they'd need one. Can't risk anyone with a pair of binoculars spying on them. The basement keeps their operation out of sight. One less trail of evidence."

"I still don't see why I can't go in there and handle things," I said.

"Is this guy for real?" Duncan asked Lily, his words seeming to soar over my head.

"I'm very real," I said. "And I can hang you from your underwear on the flagpole outside."

"Your tough talk doesn't work on me," Duncan said. "Lay a finger on me, and I'll have you locked up in a different state."

"Enough!" Lily shouted. "Jonny, we already explained why we can't have you go into the mansion. We're trying to create a case and need all the legitimate evidence we can get."

I nodded. "I see. And here I was thinking we were trying to stop a drug ring. Not 'create a case' where their money will help get them off. I may not get proper evidence, but I can smash in the skull of whoever is behind this."

Duncan laughed again as he swung his legs off his desk to stand up. "Well, I've heard enough. Now you're taking justice into your own hands. You're just as barbaric as the people we're trying to catch."

I clenched my jaw. Reacting how I truly wanted would only prove his point.

"Just do us a favor and stay away from that mansion," Duncan said as he shuffled toward the door, stopping and turning to face me. "It's only going to cause more headaches and could destroy everything we've been working on."

Duncan left the room without another word, leaving me alone with Lily. Normally, I'd be all about the alone time, but she was still glued to her computer screen, biting her bottom lip and rubbing her temples.

"I'm sorry," I said. "Maybe if anyone had told me my brother was here, I'd have taken a different approach. What the hell, Lily? How long did you know about this? And you were fine letting me follow my *nephew* home from work?"

Lily slammed her laptop shut and pushed it back like a frustrated child refusing to eat their peas. "First off, I had no idea Andres was Manny's son. Second, we didn't know Manny was here. This is news to us, too."

"News?" I said. "Duncan didn't seem all that shocked out there. He was glaring at Manny like he had a personal vendetta against him. I think if I wasn't right there as a witness, he might have shot him."

Lily shook her head. "Duncan would never. He's too by the book, as you've seen. The thought of taking justice into his hands deeply offends him. His partner before me was like that, and that's why he's a former partner. Killed trying to infiltrate a crack house without a warrant. Scarred Duncan for life. He hasn't said it, but I know you remind him of his old partner. Not just in your appearance, but in your approach to crime."

I stood up to turn my chair to face Lily directly and sat back down. "Well, that explains his up and down attitude toward me."

"Exactly," Lily said. "I will say, ever since he found out you're helping, he's gotten more involved. You must have set a fire under his ass."

"Glad I can help," I said.

"Are you really thinking about leaving?"

I heard the dread in her voice. She didn't want me to go, but I couldn't risk my life or her career just because we enjoyed each other's company.

I rubbed my chin. "I want to. No good will come from me sticking around. My brother...I just want to punch him in the face. Then hug him. I still remember him as my big brother, you know? Even after all the pain he's caused me, I want nothing more than to go back to how things used to be."

Lily smiled, the type used to mask pain. "I know how you feel. Sibling relationships are funny. You spend your childhood as each other's best friends. Getting through the lashings from parents together. Never speaking of that unbreakable bond you have, but still knowing it's there. Then you grow up one day and are two completely different people. Manny Mendez might have been your big brother, but that doesn't mean he still is."

"I've known that," I said, lowering my head to stare at the floor. I couldn't make eye contact with Lily. She was getting too personal. "I think seeing him has brought me that closure. I always wondered how my brother turned out in life. Part of me hoped he had never connected with our father. That maybe he settled down and raised a family in some little town in Mexico. Even if he never spoke to me again, just knowing he had a good, honest life would have brought me joy. But seeing him at that mansion tonight, where I know all those people inside have caused harm and death, just opened my eyes to the truth."

"And what truth is that?" Lily asked.

I raised my head and met her stare. "That I'm going to kill my brother."

Chapter 20

The weekend couldn't have arrived soon enough. The news of my brother and nephew not only being in the same town as me but having sold their lives to the cartel, kept me mentally off balance.

I couldn't shake the thoughts and emotions, no matter what I tried. Flipping through the channels to find a movie lasted an hour. I couldn't concentrate. Then I went to the library and was amazed at the size of the place, considering how small the town was. They were hosting an event for children, complete with a mascot of the Cat in the Hat, and story time on a round rug that stretched at least twenty feet in diameter.

I grabbed three books after browsing for thirty minutes. *It Starts with Us* by Colleen Hoover. Yes, I'm a closet CoHo fan. Leave me alone. And for balance, I picked up *Mr. Mercedes* by Stephen King, and *1984* by George Orwell. I'll read just about anything.

I checked out the books, found a quiet corner, and tried reading. But my mind kept drifting. Back to Hamburger Stand. To seeing my brother last night. Wondering what he had planned if I remained in town.

I wasn't leaving. That much I had decided. There was too much going for me to see this through to the end. I didn't want to kill my brother, but my gut told me all roads led to that eventuality. Hopefully Andres would be spared. As long as he stayed out of the way, he'd remain safe.

I packed the books into a tote bag the librarian gifted me and headed for the gym. There weren't many Saturday afternoon fitness enthusiasts at the gym, and I had the place nearly to myself. A woman ran on the treadmill, headphones on and sweat glistening every inch of her skin. A man worked with a medicine ball in the opposite corner with someone who appeared to be a physical therapist.

I went straight for the weights and did squats and bench presses until it hurt. This helped take my mind off things in the moment, but as soon as I was done, it all came rushing back. I returned to the beach that afternoon, grabbed a corn dog and French fries for lunch, and sat on the beach accepting defeat. As much as I tried to be a machine, there were times I was reminded I was merely a human being. A grown man with unchecked emotions.

This was one of those times.

I felt my mom in the ocean breeze. The steady *whoosh* of the waves was like her whispering in my ear. My mom took me to the beach once in Corpus Christi. Manny hated the beach, so we went on a weekend he was away at a football camp. I'll never forget the trip. Driving for what felt like forever. It was my first time going to the beach, so naturally, I was bouncing off the walls with anticipation.

We got little one-on-one time, seeing how cramped we were in our house. Even when my brother started high school and had activities, my mom was always working. I never knew when she came home to cook dinner, but it was always there when I got home from school, a paper plate wrapped in foil, a can of Coke in the fridge.

I was nine years old on this trip, and I remember feeling so honored that my mom spoke to me like an adult. She didn't ask how school was going, or if I liked my friends. Looking back, I suppose she also appreciated the alone time we had together and didn't want to waste a second with such trivialities.

"How are you doing, Jonathan?" she had asked me when we first arrived at the beach and claimed two chairs a few steps away from the ocean water. She never called me Jonny, because that wasn't the name she gave me.

I told her I was good, like most kids giving a one-word response. That's when she grabbed me by the shoulders.

"How are you really doing?" she asked, staring into my soul the way only a mother could. "You've been getting into fights at school. The principal called me and told me. One more and you're getting suspended."

I cried, feeling like I'd let my mom down. "I'm sorry, Ma. I never start the fights. Promise. They call me names. They tease me because of Dad. It's not fair, because I don't even know who he is."

When she smiled at me, I knew everything was going to be fine. "I know, *mijo*," she told me, wiping the tears off my cheeks. "I'm not going to point fingers or blame anyone for our circumstances. That's not how I was raised. But we have a hard life, and it's okay to accept that. What we can't do is let life beat us up. Do you understand?"

I nodded, and the tears kept coming.

She wiped them again. "Life won't always be this hard, okay? One day, you'll be grown up and making a difference in the world. You'll bring light to people's lives. I see it in you. You have determination and a hard work ethic. The only reason you haven't been suspended by your school is because your grades are the best in your class. You're smart, *mijo*. You're a kind, pure soul. Never let anyone take that from you. When you're an adult, I don't want you to worry about me. I'll be okay. Leave this life behind and never look back. Can you promise me that?"

I nodded again, crying still. I remembered this was the first time I had thought about my life without my mother. It was a sickening feeling, but the way she had spoken made it seem okay. I believed her when she told me she was going to be fine.

"I promise, Mama," I said.

I thought back to that weekend now that I stood on the beach in Hillcrest. Most of my childhood was plagued with pain and loss, but that was a shining moment that had stuck with me all these years later. I had made a promise to my mother, and it was one I'd kept to this day.

I left that life behind. Left the pain and sorrow in Laredo where it belonged. Somehow, through nearly four decades of life, fate had brought me to this little town. Brought my brother to the same place. And here we were, raised under the same circumstances by the same woman, on two entirely different tracks. Maybe if Manny had a talk like I had with my mother, he wouldn't be in a mansion concocting schemes to sell drugs to these innocent people.

But I'd never know. My brother was as closed-minded as they came. Perhaps a similar talk would have had no effect. All I could do was trust my mom's words. I was here to bring light to people's lives. That was my purpose. And if that meant pulverizing criminals with my bare hands, then so be it.

I slept better Saturday night after the beach. I needed the unplugging from the DEA and their investigation. Just me, nature, and a clear mind and conscience.

When I woke on Sunday morning, feeling refreshed for once, I scampered around my hotel room in nervous anticipation. I was going to Lily's in the afternoon for the barbecue she'd invited me to. Just us.

I had the jitters while I got ready and even took extra time to make sure my hair was perfect. No one had called this a date, but seeing how our past two outings had gone, there was no lying about how things were playing out. We'd kept our relationship professional so far, but that could change once we were relaxed on Lily's back patio, sipping lemonades and trading stories.

I liked her, and I had to remind myself during the drive over that we couldn't get too serious. It wasn't in either of our natures. Once this case ended, Lily would be back to D.C. and I'd either stay in Hillcrest or travel the country to find the next place to live. I'd toss my burner phone in the trash, and it would be like I never stepped foot in this joyous beach town. But still, I couldn't help myself.

"Live in the moment," I told myself, yet another reminder from my mother.

Lily had asked me to arrive at noon and made it clear I didn't need to bring anything. Still, I stopped at the store, disappointed to see Richard wasn't working, and bought a bottle of wine, a bag of Lily's favorite breath mints, and a small vase of various flowers.

The flowers might have come on too strong, but why not see where Lily stood? Her reaction would tell me everything.

I drove across town, following the GPS to Lily's address. I

pulled into a quaint neighborhood with about seven blocks of homes surrounding the local elementary school.

It was a perfect Sunday. Young kids played on the front lawns, older ones rode bikes and roller-skated down the sidewalks. Families were coming and going in their Sunday attire. On Lily's block, a man washed his car in the driveway, blasting Queen from his portable radio while smoking a cigar.

The neighborhood reminded me of the peaceful lives everyone deserved to have. No danger lurking around the corner. No fear of any disruptions to life. In a world where so few had access to this type of life, seeing it always kept me motivated.

I grew up in a border town riddled with violence. Hearing about the man hung from the telephone pole was only shocking because it occurred in Hillcrest. I saw that happen three times throughout my childhood. We often fell asleep to a barrage of gunfire taking place across the border. Fully automatic guns blasting were the crickets of our nights. Screams and shrieks of desperation. Rarely any sirens.

Sure, we had our issues in Laredo, but nothing compared to what was going on across the border. In comparison, we lived in paradise less than a mile away from hell.

I pulled up to Lily's house and parked along the sidewalk. She had a fenced-off yard with a green lawn split by a paved walkway down the center. Flower beds decorated both sides of the path, and a jacaranda tree stood towering on the right-hand side. Its branches were dotted with purple, as the tree had just started its spring-time blossom.

I stepped out of the car and drew in a deep breath before circling to the passenger side to grab the things I had purchased at the store. I held the flowers in one hand, the wine bottle in the other, and tucked the bag of peppermint candies under my arm.

Lily gave me no chance to psych myself up and opened her door, stepping onto the landing of the porch.

"I said you didn't need to bring anything," she shouted with a grin. "Need a hand?"

"I got it," I said, crouching down to open the latch on the gate and start up the pathway. "I wouldn't dare show up empty-handed. My mom would whoop my ass from the heavens."

Lily laughed and stepped aside to let me enter her home, rubbing her hand up and down my back as I passed.

"This is all for you," I said, first handing her the flowers.

She wasted no time grabbing them and sticking her nose in the assortment to take a deep whiff.

"Why, thank you," she said, batting her eyelashes. "Let me get a vase."

Lily spun around, and I followed her into the kitchen, where she had a charcuterie board on the island counter, complete with cubed cheeses, rolled deli meats, grapes, olives, and crackers.

"What's that smell?" I asked as Lily searched underneath the sink for a vase. "It's incredible."

"Cookies in the oven," she said, standing back up and transferring the flowers to the vase. "Can't have a barbecue and no dessert."

"I should have worn my stretchy pants today," I said. "Didn't realize it was going to be an all-day feast."

Lily giggled and brushed back her hair as she leaned against the counter on one arm, staring at the other items in my possession.

"Like the flowers?" I asked.

"They're beautiful," she said, a slight blush touching her cheeks.

Jackpot.

I raised the wine. "Got us a bottle to enjoy with our lunch. And these." I handed over the bag of peppermints, and her eyes lit up.

"You shouldn't have," she said, mouth hanging open. Apparently, these candies were better than money for Lily. She took the bag and hugged it tight against her bosom, a childlike grin stuck on her face.

"It's the least I can do," I said, returning a smile. "You've clearly put a lot of work into today already."

"It's nothing, really. I love hosting and never get the chance. I tried something like this with Duncan, and it was a dud. He only ate the cheese and drank all the beer."

"I'm not picky, and I'll happily eat whatever you put in front of me," I said.

"Good to know," she said, placing the bag of mints next to the bottle of wine on the counter. "It's a beautiful day. Care to sit out back?"

"Absolutely."

I followed Lily through the house, passing a living room with a comfy-looking sofa facing a TV mounted to the wall. A bookshelf stood in the corner with a small selection I was eager to check out. You can tell a lot about a person by the books they keep on their shelf. Sometimes, everything you need to know.

But Lily was on a mission and marched forward, sliding the screen door open. She had a wooden patio overlooking a small backyard xeriscaped with an assortment of rocks, gravel, and wood chips. On the patio stood a grill, fire pit, and patio chairs surrounding a small table for two.

A jug of iced tea waited on the table between two glasses. We sat down, and she poured our drinks.

"How are you doing?" she asked, sliding my glass over. "I'm sure this whole thing with your brother hasn't been easy."

I grabbed my glass but didn't take a drink. "I was a mess yesterday. Very conflicted. But there's nothing I can do about it. My brother is here. He's a bad man. And that's all there is to it."

Lily took a sip of her tea and sucked air through her teeth. "You can't dismiss it so easily, Jonny. It's complicated. And that's an understatement."

"Complicated for who? You?" I asked, shifting in my seat.

"No, not me. Just for the situation. We suspected your brother was part of this cartel, but his presence in Hillcrest at the same time as you was not something we expected. Duncan is insistent on not trusting you. Still thinks you're involved somehow."

I laughed. "Of course he does."

Lily rolled her eyes. "Of course. I spent time calling your past officers from the SEALs and directors from the CIA. They all swear by your loyalty to the country. Not a single person I talked to thought it was possible you would be tied up in any type of organized crime. Especially from a foreign country."

"Well, that's promising," I said, finally taking my first drink of iced tea.

"Yeah, but it still wasn't enough," Lily said. "Duncan is out there thinking up reasons to arrest you. He really wants to question you."

"Then he can come ask me questions any time," I said. "I'm

an open book."

Lily shook her head. "He's not going to do that. If I thought he could remain civil, I would have invited him here today, just so he can ask his questions and get it out of his system. But my trust is low right now. He seems more concerned about you than our actual case."

I shrugged. "I guess I can understand his concern. It's been made very clear I'm the source of death and destruction in this town since I showed up last week. Not like I didn't almost get shot at the tavern."

"I believe you," Lily said, firm and leaving no room for discussion. "It's an absurd long shot you and your brother ended up in the same city at the same time. But people win the lottery, right? Against all the odds, it happens over and over."

I never thought of it that way, and she had a point. Although, I didn't feel much like a lottery winner.

"Okay," I said. "You're right about my brother adding a level of complication, but I've already moved on. And I accept I may have to do things I don't want to. But I'll still do them. Collateral damage, right? I've killed innocent people, but only because they were standing next to some of the most dangerous men in the world."

"Well, how innocent could they really have been if they were in the same rooms as those dangerous men?" Lily asked.

"That's not for me to judge. You'd be surprised how naïve some people are. My point is you don't need to worry about me. If I get the chance to bring down this cartel and make Hillcrest a safe place again, I'll do it. Makes no difference to me who impedes that."

Lily pursed her lips and nodded slowly.

Her phone chimed, and she pulled it out of her pocket to place it on the table without looking at it. "Doorbell sensing motion. Probably the Amazon guy—I'm expecting a package."

"Do you want me to get it?" I asked, pushing back my seat.

"No, it's fine."

"It's really no trouble," I said, standing up. "Lots of porch pirates out there."

Lily grinned. "Okay, fine. You go grab the package, and I'll bring out the charcuterie board so we can actually enjoy it."

I strolled into the house, pausing for a moment in the kitchen to breathe in the scent of baked cookies. Lily was spoiling me today. Glad I stopped at the store, or I'd feel like a total chump.

Lily came in behind me, humming a tune under her breath as she checked on the cookies, pulling open the oven door to let the heavenly smell grow even stronger.

I went to the front door and pulled it open, spotting the object on the other side of the screen door. It was a small package left on the doorstep, so I had to crouch to pick it up after opening the screen door.

I brought the box into the kitchen, finding it lacked any sort of shipping label.

"You said this was from Amazon?" I asked, placing it gently on the countertop. "It has no label."

Lily had pulled out the tray of cookies and was examining them on the stovetop. She turned around with a frown, eyes beaming on the box. "Yeah, I ordered a new coffee tumbler. Was supposed to arrive today."

She opened a drawer next to the sink and pulled out a pair of scissors, shuffling over to the box. After a quick examination and more confusion, she shrugged and stuck the scissors into the taped crease, gliding the blade down to cut it open.

I was looking around the kitchen, admiring the homey decor, like the picture of sizzling bacon and eggs hanging on the far wall above the kitchen table.

Lily shrieked at the top of her lungs as she jumped back from the box. She crashed into the counter behind her, pointing a trembling finger at the box.

My mind kicked into high alert, and the adrenaline started flowing. I took one step toward the box and lifted the flaps to peek inside.

Looking back at me was a severed hand.

Chapter 21

Finding a severed hand in a box was a sure way to kill any romantic vibes. Within fifteen minutes, Hillcrest police and Agent Duncan arrived at Lily's home.

Duncan had been the first to arrive and wasted no time shouting accusations at me.

He walked in, took one look around, and stomped toward me with his finger pointed out, which he jammed into my chest.

"What the fuck is this game you're playing, Mendez?" he snarled, spit flying from his lips and decorating my face. I let it slide. Feeling how weak his finger was made me realize I could break his forearm with little effort. "I know you're involved, and I'll be damned when I find out how. Can't wait to lock your ass up."

I only grinned in response. This poor man was wasting his time with me, and perhaps I needed to lie low. For Lily's sake. The last thing she needed was Duncan calling their boss to report her for involving a 'person of interest,' as he would undoubtedly frame it.

"Enough, Duncan!" Lily shouted.

She had regained her composure, and even apologized for her initial reaction to seeing the severed hand.

"That's nothing to apologize for," I told her. "Your job title doesn't make you immune to being human. Why would you have expected to find a hand in that box?"

Duncan had slipped on his rubber gloves and took the box outside to the backyard, claiming he didn't want to examine it in Lily's kitchen and didn't dare cause a scene in the front yard for all the neighbors to see.

Without skipping a beat, Lily fished out a pair of her own gloves from under the sink and joined Duncan.

I wasn't sure what to do. I had no background in forensics and could offer no help with the hand. Then I saw Lily's phone on the counter and picked it up, just as four police officers knocked on the front screen door and let themselves in, led by Officer Matthews.

"What the hell are you doing here?" he asked me, stopping and crossing his arms.

The other officers stopped in their tracks, and I recognized Officer Collins from the night at the tavern.

"Good afternoon, Chief. I was just here having a barbecue with Lily," I said, raising my hands in the *don't shoot me* position.

Matthews snorted. "Barbecue, huh?"

He walked past me, sure to brush his shoulder against mine, and his team of three officers trailed behind him in single file outside, where Duncan and Lily hovered over the boxed hand.

Lily's phone was locked, requiring a fingerprint to allow me access. I went outside to find Lily and Duncan standing to the side while the officers took turns looking into the box. This was surely out of their comfort zone for a town where the worst crimes were adolescents shoplifting.

Lily looked over, saw me, then shuffled over. Duncan

glowered at me while remaining in his position.

"I'm sure this isn't what you had in mind for our barbecue today," Lily said, forcing a grin like she had just bitten into a piece of sour fruit.

"Do you not have chopped off hands at all your gatherings?" I asked. "I thought that was the norm."

Lily laughed, perhaps too hard, as two officers look over their shoulders at us.

"Hey," I said. "I was trying to get in to your cell phone. Want to check out what the doorbell camera picked up?"

Lily's face lit up. "Perfect! Yes."

She snatched the phone out of my hand, pressed her thumb onto the sensor, and immediately scrolled through her apps until finding the one linked to her doorbell.

"Come look, everyone!" Lily shouted to the rest. "Pulling up the doorbell camera."

Seconds later, the four police officers and Duncan huddled around me and Lily. Duncan stood as far away from me as he could in the confined space. I smelled Matthews's bubble gum as he chomped like an anxious goat.

We all stuck our heads over Lily's phone, watching the circle spinning to show the video was loading for a few seconds before it gave way to the recorded footage.

A figure dressed in all black walked up from the sidewalk, wearing a balaclava that covered their entire face except for the eyes. The person strolled up the pathway with the calmness of a neighbor dropping off a cup of sugar. They held the box in both hands in front of their torso, bent down on one knee to place the package neatly on Lily's doormat, then turned away to run down the pathway and out of sight.

"God dammit!" Matthews cried. "That's no help."

"Not immediately," Duncan said, frowning at the screen. "But we can get forensics to look. They'll be able to tell us their height, weight, and shoe size within reason. Slim chance they can pull anything from the eyeballs and compare to optical records, but it's worth a shot."

Lily nodded. "Yep. You take care of that, and I'll ask my neighbors if they have any security cameras we can look at. Hopefully pick up which way this person went. Possible they had a getaway car parked out of the camera's view."

"Let's get to it," Duncan said, his voice overcome with enthusiasm.

The cops looked around at each other before settling their gazes upon their chief.

Matthews pursed his lips and drew a heavy sigh. "Okay, men. Let's assist the DEA however they need. Collins and Richards, why don't you two canvass the block and ask the neighbors for any footage their cameras might have picked up."

Officer Collins and the chubby man who was Richards both nodded their heads and hurried back into the house.

"Billingsley," Matthews said to the remaining officer, a muscular man with red skin from too much time on the beach. "Let's you and I go outside and see what we can find. Tire marks, shoe prints. Anything like that."

Matthews was an amateur, but I couldn't call him out, especially in front of another cop. He should have been on the phone with the city to see if any traffic cameras picked up anything of value. Tire tracks and shoe prints would only take him so far in an investigation like this. A desperate reach to seem busy and important.

Matthews looked me dead in the eye. "And why don't you

get the fuck out of my city already!"

He left me no chance to respond, turning and following behind Officer Billingsley to do their busy work.

Agent Duncan chuckled at the remark.

"Something funny?" I asked, blinking rapidly at Duncan.

The asshole shook his head, eyes boring into my soul. "Nothing funny about a hand in a box, is there, big guy?"

Now I chuckled, mockingly. "If you got something to say, just come out and say it."

"Stop it, you two!" Lily cried. She had been scrolling on her cell phone and abruptly stuffed it into her pocket to give us her full attention.

"I'll stop when this Sasquatch is behind bars where he belongs," Duncan said.

Ouch. I thought we were becoming friends after our previous encounter, but clearly that was all a front.

"Duncan!" Lily shouted. "What has gotten into you?!"

"It's fine, Lily," I said, raising a hand. "Agent Duncan, why don't we start over? Lily let me know you have some questions for me. Let's hear them."

"Really, Sutton?" Duncan said, looking at his partner with his jaw twisted in rage. "You can't just go around spilling sensitive information to whoever you're sleeping with for the week."

"Fuck you," Lily said, and I could tell she wanted to slap the shit out of him. Maybe we could both get in on the action. "I haven't told Jonny a single bit of sensitive information. You complaining about him like a middle school girl isn't exactly top-secret stuff."

"You think I'm involved because of my brother," I said to Duncan. "But I can promise you I'm not. I've already come to peace with the fact I may have to kill my only living family."

"Don't forget about your father," Duncan said with a smirk, crossing his arms.

I laughed again. This time it was full of anger. "Lily was right. Fuck you. If I knew you weren't a coward who would throw me in jail, I'd punch a hole right through that smug little face of yours. See how that holds up in divorce court."

Hey, he wanted to get personal with me, so I threw the best emotional punch I could.

Duncan's jaw dropped, his eyes blazing with fury as he turned and looked at Lily.

"You bitch," he whispered. "I can't believe you."

Lily's face turned red. "Duncan, I'm sorry. I shouldn't have spoken to Jonny about your personal life. But I've been so frustrated because it feels like I've been doing all the work while you lounge around."

Duncan shook his head, mouth still hanging open. "Un-fucking-believable," he said. "You two can finish this case. Apparently, I'm just a guy standing on the sidelines."

He stomped away toward the door.

"Duncan!" Lily shouted, but he didn't stop, continuing through the house and slamming the front door with author-ity. She turned to me, bottom lip trembling. "Why did you say that to him?"

My heart immediately sank to my knees. I had no intention of upsetting Lily, but here we were. Alone again, and now she was pissed off.

"Lily, I—"

"Save it, Jonny," she cut me off. "You two have been at each other's throats, and it's making my life *hell*. All I wanted was some help on this case, and you're both just bringing more drama to it."

Lily balled her fists and turned around. She walked to the edge of her patio and looked out across the backyard, taking deep breaths.

I gave her a minute, standing awkwardly behind her while she cooled down. Her emotions were all over the place, and I couldn't blame her.

I shuffled up behind and placed my hands on her shoulders. "Lily, I'm sorry. I should have kept my mouth shut. I usually can, but he got under my skin, and I lost control. It won't happen again."

Her shoulders slouched back, leaning into my grasp like she wanted them there. She even took a step back, and her alluring scent drove me mad. "I know you're a good man, Jonny. I've put in the work of finding out the truth, and all those people raved about you. The CIA would welcome you back with open arms. The SEALs would have loved to have you back if it wasn't for the hearing loss you suffered."

I grinned. She really had done her homework on me. "I can still hear fine—it's just one ear that won't pass a test. That's why we have two, right?"

Lily turned around, looking at me with those bright blue eyes, blonde hair swaying in the gentle breeze. I wanted to pull her in and plant my lips on hers, but our signals were so crossed up at the moment. I couldn't risk it.

"Jonny, I read your entire file," she said. "You've done disturbing things to evil people. I get that was your job. Your duty. But how you came out of all that so...normal. I'm not sure I could look myself in the mirror if I did half the stuff you have."

"I've always seen it as my destiny," I said. "To protect the world. I started out young, having to protect myself. Bullies and all that. Kids can be real assholes when you come from a family background as twisted as mine. Once I hit puberty and grew bigger than anyone else around me, I started protecting the little guys who got picked on. Because I remembered what it was like." I shrugged. "I've kept that same approach to everything in life. It would be much easier for me to leave Hillcrest, but I see this small town as the little guy being picked on by the bully cartel. And I can't just walk away from that."

A smile touched Lily's lips. Silence hung between us, our eyes studying each other. She stared at my lips, and I looked right back at hers. It was like a lightning bolt had gone off between our faces, but I still couldn't make the first move. Not with a man's chopped off hand as the highlight of the day.

We cleared our throats awkwardly at the same time, causing us both to laugh.

"So, what are you doing next?" she asked, eyes still locked on mine.

"I'm gonna do some digging," I said. "Something's not right with this police force, and I want to find out. I'll be lying low for the next couple of days. You need to patch things up with Duncan, and you can't do that if I'm always lurking around the corner. I'll be around, but you won't see me."

"But I *want* to see you," she said, reaching out and grabbing me by the wrist. "I enjoy spending time with you. You keep me grounded. And sane."

My throat pooled with saliva I had to gulp down. "And I want to see you. But this is for the best. You're going to be busy this week after that package you received today. How about we plan to meet Wednesday night at the diner? Dinner at seven?"

Lily sighed, then nodded, taking a step back. "Fine. That's fair. I'll see you Wednesday night then."

"You going to be okay around here?" I asked.

Lily let out a nervous laugh. "You mean with the cartel knowing who I am and where I'm living? I'll make sure the police keep a patrol car out front around the clock now. And if they don't, I guess I'll sleep at the station."

"Keep a gun on your nightstand, even if there is a police presence parked out front."

"I always do."

I nodded to her and pivoted to leave the house. When I looked back, she was staring at me with an affectionate grin.

Next time I saw Lily, I was going to kiss her.

Chapter 22

I kept Lily's spare pistol on my nightstand while I slept. If they knew where she lived, they certainly knew where I was staying. I still didn't think Manny had any reason to kill me. He couldn't erase our bond or past because of my mere presence in Hillcrest. As long as the cartel thought I was keeping to myself, and no longer snooping around their properties, they should leave me alone.

And if they didn't, well, that would be their problem.

So I kept to myself on Monday. After a full night of sleep, my body woke naturally at 6:15 a.m., and I dressed to head for the gym. More weights and cardio for me. A showdown was coming, and I needed to be ready. One thing my drill sergeant in the SEALs had so gracefully screamed into our ears during boot camp was the importance of staying ready. The bastard even incorporated these drills into our down time.

Eating dinner and watching whatever sports game was on TV? Not on his watch. He'd blast into the dining hall, face red, and blow his whistle, demanding we drop what we were doing to go on a four-mile run.

Sergeant Leipsitz was his name. He was the stuff of nightmares. A mean old grump whose job was to drive all SEAL recruits into quitting. They didn't care about having a certain number of recruits make it through to the end. They only wanted the best to be the last ones standing. And Sergeant Leipsitz was the perfect man to make trained killers cry for their mommies.

Yeah, we called him Sergeant "Lip Shits" behind his back, but only because we feared him. If he ever heard one of us say that nickname, the vein in his forehead would have most certainly burst.

"Always be ready," was his motto, and one that I've lived by to this day. Evil rarely waited for a convenient time to strike. I fell into that mental state of readiness while I was at the gym on Monday morning. Gun in my backpack. Eyes watching every single person who walked in and out of the building. Every passerby out for a stroll down the sidewalks outside. When I walked into a room, I located all entries and exits. I knew where every person in said room was standing and what they were doing.

It's a shitty way to live life, and that's why I was grateful to have developed the ability to turn it on and off like a switch. As long as I remained in Hillcrest, I'd have to remain on. Sleep with one eye open and be ready to pounce.

After the gym, I went to a coffee shop down the street. Six people inside, not counting the staff. Three had headphones on and were focused on their open laptops. Gen Z hard at "work." The other three appeared to be friends. They sat at one table together, laughing and swapping stories.

The coast was clear for me to grab a table away from the window, in the corner nearest the restrooms. Perfect spot to monitor the room and do my business on my cell phone.

Without a computer or Lily, I started my research on Hillcrest's police department by visiting their shitty website.

The top banner scrolled through photos of the police at community events. Posing for pictures, big smiles on their faces, no signs of corruption. Further down the page was an announcement they were hiring entry level officers, along with a scheduled Drug Take Back Event. Scrolling down the page highlighted the community outreach programs and projects the department was involved in. And the last item at the bottom of the page was an embedded video for active shooter training. Good God, America, do better.

It took me a while to find a menu on this garbled interface, and when I did, it had few options. I clicked on the "About Us" link and watched as it loaded a new page with Chief Matthews's official portrait at the top.

The photo was taken years ago, judging by his youthful countenance that I had yet to see in real life. His teeth were obnoxiously white, and I assumed he used some of those whitening strips to counter his smoking habit back in the day. Next to his portrait was a quote from the man himself.

Thank you for visiting the Hillcrest Police Department website. It is my honor and privilege to lead the sworn men and women of our police force to protect and serve our community. As a native of Hillcrest, I understand the struggles we face as a small town in a big state. Most crimes come from outside forces, and we must remain vigilant in keeping our town safe.

I live with my dog, Bravo, and you can often find me visiting the local businesses in downtown Hillcrest. If you see me, don't be afraid to say hello!

Well, that's not at all the type of tone I expected to hear from Matthews. To the citizens, he was a man of the people. One of their own. To a passerby, he was a calming presence in the local community. Reliable. And of course he had to mention his dog. People eat that shit up.

His portrait complemented the quick note. American flag on the left, wide grin, and lots of ribbons and pins on his dark blue uniform. If I was the cartel, this would be the guy I wanted on my side. Get someone who the community adored, and there was no limit to what they could get away with.

The website was a dead end beyond that. It had pages of community meetings, links to apply for weapons permits, press releases, and general contact information. I went to the press page, curious to find where local news came from, and I stumbled across links to the *Hillcrest Daily*, a newspaper still in operation today.

I visited their site and found it much more modernized. There was a link to register to receive physical newspapers. I had no idea that was still a thing. Otherwise, the news was freely accessible on the website.

They offered a search bar at the top of the site, so I typed in *Police Chief.*

It returned two hundred and fifty-five results. Eleven pages worth of articles, most of the headlines talking about the city council, Democrats and Republicans, and obituaries. So, not at all what I was looking for. This was my reminder of why I avoided technology. It was supposed to make our lives easier, yet around every corner were ten levels of frustration waiting.

I scrolled, hoping something would give. After five minutes, and on the tenth page of results, I saw what I wanted.

The headline read: *HILLCREST SAYS GOODBYE TO BELOVED POLICE CHIEF.*

The article was dated November seventeenth, a little over four months ago. I clicked on it and read.

Beloved Hillcrest Chief of Police, David Samuels, announced his retirement at a surprise press conference last night with the city council and members of the media in attendance. After forty-two years of service, Chief Samuels and his wife Ruth will move to Arizona. The chief was somber in his announcement but seemed optimistic about the days ahead on the golf course.

"It has been the honor of my lifetime to serve the community of Hillcrest for more than four decades," the chief said. "I started here as a young man and rose through the ranks with hard work and dedication. I owe a lifetime of gratitude to all my fellow officers I've worked alongside over the years. Without you, I'm just a man in a uniform. While it's hard for me and Ruth to say goodbye to the town we love, life is taking us on a new adventure to spend the remainder of our days. I give thanks to God and the fine people of Hillcrest for allowing me to live this incredible dream of a lifetime."

Chief Samuels had prior announced plans to remain in his position for another two years. He did not share any details regarding his sudden change of heart and will leave Hillcrest with its lowest crime rate in the town's history. Longtime officer and native, Russell Matthews, will step into the chief's role on an interim basis. Mayor Tony Reece will make the final decision on whether to keep Officer Matthews in the role or appoint another candidate.

The Hillcrest Police Department has stated they expect no interruptions to their daily operations during this transition period.

Beside the article was a picture of Chief Samuels. He had white hair and a matching handle-bar mustache, a stern expression for his official portrait.

"Why did you leave?" I asked my screen. "Lowest crime rate. Beloved. You had it made. What would make you give it all up?"

As Lily had said, and was confirmed by the article, there was no mention of family in Arizona. It would have been one thing if he and his wife wanted to spend more time near their kids or grandkids, but that wasn't the case. If crime was spiraling out of control, that might have prompted him to step away. But he didn't seem like a quitter, either.

From my experience, there were only two reasons people abruptly left their lives behind. An opportunity to make drastically more money or to flee a dangerous situation.

I read more news articles from the same date, and there were zero signs of trouble in Hillcrest at the time of the chief's retirement.

A boy from the middle school was chosen to spend a day at the state capitol in Sacramento. The city council lifted an age-old law banning drinking alcohol on your front lawn. A local mother published a children's book.

I looked through six pages of articles and not a single one had anything negative to say.

Samuels definitely didn't leave because of danger. And that left money.

I couldn't jump to conclusions, especially about a man I'd never met. But common sense could do wonders. And it was the move to Arizona that made me question the cartel's involvement with the chief's sudden retirement. He had already earned a pension that would have paid him comfortably for the rest of his life. If he'd worked in Hillcrest for forty years, it was likely his house was paid off. That left him with low-maintenance bills and a steady stream of cash.

Again. Why leave it?

I clicked back to the page with Matthews's fake smile looking at me. In hindsight, he had the most to gain from the chief's retirement. But did he know that at the time? Had the chief told him he'd get the role once he stepped down? There were too many variables, and Matthews wasn't exactly on speaking terms with me.

I gazed at his picture, looking into his eyes.

"What are you hiding?"

Chapter 23

I spent the rest of Monday in deep thought. Chief Samuels to Officer Matthews. How did Mayor Reece factor into all this? I wanted nothing more than to call Chief Samuels and ask him some questions. With my history in the CIA, I knew how to make those calls sound official.

But with his generic name, and not even knowing which city he moved to in Arizona, it was impossible for me to find his information. I still had friends at the CIA who told me to call them any time I needed something, but I couldn't bring myself to do it. Those phone calls would inevitably lead to them asking me to come back. And if they knew where I was, I'd never live with myself. Too much work went into a life off the grid, and I wasn't about to throw it away for a phone call that might not even lead anywhere useful.

I stayed at the coffee shop until noon, then headed to the beach to continue the browsing on my phone. Fortunately, the *Hillcrest Daily* was the only news source in town, so I spent a majority of my time on their site. Scrolling, clicking, reading. I hated this part of the process, but sometimes it was necessary.

I found it strange there had been no mention of the dead bodies I had visited at the morgue.

There was an article, albeit vague, that mentioned the shots fired outside Ocean Wave Tavern last week. The victims were not identified, no interviews with witnesses were included, and it mentioned they had a "person of interest" in custody. I could only assume I was that person.

But no mention of dead bodies hanging from telephone poles, dismembered hands, or missing genitalia. It seemed there was only one news reporter, however, and it would be impossible for him to know every single thing happening in town without tips from the citizens—hence, the tavern shootout.

But did that mean the police department was also not sharing information? Could the DEA have prevented them from sharing any details? I lost track of how many times, while in the CIA, I befriended members of the press with the goal of having them *not* publish certain articles—or at least, delay them—while working a case.

I'm all for a free press, but when you're undercover trying to catch a terrorist, it's better to not have members of the public snooping around and trying to play the hero.

By Tuesday morning, I wanted desperately to call Lily to see if she could gather any information about Chief Samuels. But I had promised to keep my distance.

I hoped she could convince Duncan not to view me as a suspect. If he and I could get on the same page, there was no saying what the three of us could accomplish. I regretted attacking his personal life. That was low. Not sure how far an apology would go, but I'd give him one the next time we met.

For now, I had another day ahead with no plans.

I was running low on snacks in my hotel, so I drove back to Fresh Valley Grocers after having my continental breakfast.

I mostly wanted to see Richard, and to my delight, he was posted in his same position at the customer service counter.

There was no line, and he was distracted by something on his computer screen, so I hurried over to the counter and planted my elbows on it.

Richard cocked an eyebrow before looking at me. His hard expression softened the moment he looked up and recognized me. "Mr. Navy SEAL," he said. "What brings you back here, young man?"

"Good morning, sir," I said, nodding to the old man. "You told me to reach out if I ever needed something."

"I sure did," he said, crossing his arms and taking a step back from the counter. I could tell he was intrigued by the elevated pitch in his voice. "What do you have for me?"

I leaned in. "Can we speak in private?"

Richard licked his lips while sliding up his shirt sleeve to check his watch. I caught another glimpse of his Semper Fi tattoos. "Okay, I can step outside for about ten minutes."

He reached down below the counter and brought up a sign that read, *BE BACK SOON! THANK YOU FOR YOUR BUSINESS!*

Richard slid the sign onto the counter and took off his work apron, tossing it on a round stool I had yet to see him sit on. He took labored steps out from behind the counter, starting for the grocery store's main exit.

He didn't walk with a limp, but a slight hitch in his stride.

I followed him to the bench I had sat on after buying my burner phone from him last week. He sat down first and reached into his shirt pocket for a pack of cigarettes.

"Smoke?" he asked me, stuffing a cigarette in his mouth and firing up the tip with a lighter.

"No, thank you, sir," I said. "I don't smoke."

He nodded like he expected my response and returned the pack to his pocket, taking a long first drag of his fresh cancer stick. "So, what can I help you with, young man?"

I sat next to him, leaning back so I could better make eye contact with him. "Soldier to soldier, I'm gonna cut right to the shit," I said.

This earned a grin from Richard, who nodded for me to continue.

"There's a drug cartel operating in Hillcrest," I said. "And they've been here for several years, although we're not sure how long they've actually been selling drugs. At the least, they've been preparing multiple businesses to launder money through and put their people in place."

Richard nodded slowly, taking puffs from his cigarette and blowing smoke clouds into the air. "So that explains why the DEA is here."

"How did you know that?"

Richard chuckled. "Two of them, right? Guy and a lady. I saw them come in together a few months ago. The guy wanted to buy chewing tobacco, so had to come see me at my counter. When I asked for his ID, I saw the DEA badge in his wallet. I just assumed the girl worked with him because she had that look."

"What kind of look?" I asked.

"The look any of the feds have," Richard said. "Like they have a stick up their ass. They hate smiling. So serious. Now, don't get me wrong, I'm the same way, but I'm a grumpy old man."

I laughed. "I think you've been nothing but pleasant."

"Only to you," Richard said, hitting the cigarette harder as it neared its end. "We're on the same team. Not like all the other hippie dippies that live around here. Any who, what do you know about this cartel?"

"Not much," I said. "We're following up on leads but getting nowhere. I was wondering what you could tell me about Chief Samuels."

Richard finished his cigarette and flicked the butt into the distance. His eyebrows touched the top of his forehead. "Samuels? I haven't heard that old goat's name in a bit. Bastard left us to move to Arizona. I'm sure he's cooking down there."

"So, you knew him?" I asked, turning to face Richard straight on.

"Of course I knew him," Richard said, cracking a subtle smile. "He asked me at least once a month if I'd come work on his police force. They always try to get us ex-military guys. And I told him every month that I wasn't a cop. My background in the Marines got nothing to do with police work."

"Do you have his cell phone number?" I asked. "I'd love to ask him a couple of questions."

Richard scrunched his face as he looked me over. Apparently, I crossed a line he wasn't expecting. He chewed on his bottom lip as he considered my request, then finally nodded. "Okay. I guess it won't hurt, since he's no longer the chief. Just an old, retired bat with nothing else to do."

Richard reached into his pants pocket to pull out a cell phone in a shaky hand. I watched him scroll through his list of contacts with one finger. He found it and read off the phone number to me, and I entered it into my phone.

"I really appreciate it," I said.

"My pleasure, young man. Now, you're not saying old

Samuels is involved with this somehow?"

I shook my head. "Not in the slightest," I lied. Although, getting paid off to leave town wasn't entirely *uninvolved*, either. "I just have some questions about things that happened before he stepped down from his position."

"Matthews giving you a hard time?" Richard asked, grinning.

"How did you know?"

"He hates outsiders. I know him well enough, too. Always rambling about outsiders destroying Hillcrest. Perhaps not the most stable man for the job, but no one can question his loyalty to the town."

"So, you don't think there's a chance he could be involved with the cartel?" I asked.

Richard wasted no time shaking his head viciously from side to side. "Heavens no! I'd have him at the bottom of the list of possible dirty cops. I get his personality isn't as attractive as Samuels's was, but that doesn't make Matthews a crooked cop. He's stuck in his ways and has no interest in hearing outside opinions."

That all tracked with the man I'd met.

"I'll take your word for it," I said. "Knowing that, I can vouch for his hatred of outsiders."

Richard cackled and slapped his knees before standing up. "I need to get back to living the dream. Come by and see me if you need anything else, okay? I'll keep an eye out for anyone suspicious. Good to know the cartel is here. Maybe I'll start carrying when I leave the house."

"I appreciate the help, sir," I said, standing up and offering my hand to shake. He grabbed it firmly.

"My pleasure, young man. Don't go getting into too much

trouble out there."

Richard strolled back into the grocery store, and I immediately pulled my phone back out and dialed Chief Samuels.

It rang three times before an older man answered. "Hello?" he said, the sound of a blowing fan strong in the background.

"Hi, is this Chief Samuels from Hillcrest?" I asked, pausing to hear the man's breathing grow a little heavier.

"This is," he said. "May I ask who's calling?"

"Hi, Chief, my name is Jonny Mendez. I'm a friend of Richard."

I didn't have Richard's last name, and could only hope Samuels knew who the hell I was talking about.

"Oh, shit," Samuels said. "Don't tell me Richard is gone."

"No, no," I said. "Nothing like that. He's alive and well."

"Good," Samuels said. "I always told him if he goes before me, I'll visit his body and use it as a punching bag."

Samuels laughed, a sound similar to the one Richard had let out.

"What can I do for you?" Samuels asked, and I sat back on the bench.

"Well, Chief, I'm working alongside the DEA in Hillcrest, and we're investigating a possible drug cartel in operation."

"Is that right?" Samuels said, and I immediately sensed the shift in his voice. That tone a child used on their parents when they knew they were in trouble and trying their best to lie their way to freedom. It was an odd mixture of confidence and hope.

"Yes, sir," I said, keeping my voice the same. Casual. I needed to play dumb if I wanted any information from Samuels. If I implied I knew more than I should, he might shut down and refuse to talk. "We're in the early phases of the investigation and wanted to pick your brain about anything that might have been happening around Hillcrest before you moved away."

There was a brief pause, followed by some sort of clatter on the other end of the line. "Nothing is coming to mind," he finally said. "I left with the lowest crime rate in Hillcrest's history. Now, I won't lie to you and make that seem like a big deal. We always had a low crime rate as long as I was chief, but that is the fact. There definitely wasn't anything like a drug cartel operating in town."

"That's part of what we're hoping to figure out," I said. "We don't know *when* these people arrived, or what they might have been working on behind the scenes. Cartels are typically large operations. Did you never notice a large influx of new residents, or any new businesses, within the last five years?"

"Hmmm," Samuels said, and I knew from the sound he was full of shit. This was all an act. He was probably running around his Arizona house, gathering up the cash they had paid him off with, and planning to get the hell out of town until this investigation died down. "There's been an increase in the number of illegals moving into Hillcrest that I'm sure is still going on. Funnily enough, that never correlated to a higher crime rate. And that started many years ago. Most of those folks kept to themselves. Never caused a ruckus."

"Interesting," I said, then left a long pause to drive the old chief crazy. I held my silence for twenty seconds when he finally caved.

"What's interesting?" he asked, and I heard a slight panic in his voice.

"We don't have all the details—far from it—but we believe the cartel is based out of Mexico. So an increase in the Mexican population could definitely align with the early stages of a forming cartel. But if they're undocumented, we don't have a way to track these people down."

"Few of them actually live in Hillcrest," Samuels said. "Lots commute into town from nearby."

"I see." I couldn't recall being on a phone call where the other person was so poor at lying. That told me Samuels had no interest in being involved with the criminal underworld.

"One last question, sir," I said. "And I'll let you get back to your day."

"Okay, what's that?" he replied, his voice dripping with relief. He actually thought I was going to let him off the hook.

"How much money did these guys pay you to retire early?"

Chapter 24

Samuels hung up after I asked that last question, which couldn't have been more of an admission of guilt.

It was fine. I had only made that call to confirm what I already suspected. Samuels would never share any details. The cartel had certainly threatened his life if he ever let anything slip. That was just standard business practice for these friendly thugs.

Now was the hard part.

If the cartel paid Samuels to leave, that meant they couldn't influence him enough to remain in power while also working for them. They wouldn't have made such a hefty investment without getting some type of control back. They would have needed to implement an insider after sending the chief away.

I trusted Richard and his sense of judgment. We military guys weren't perfect, but most men and women I'd worked with throughout my career had a strong sense of reading people. If Richard felt so strongly about Matthews being a straight arrow, then who did that leave for the cartel to put into a position of power?

The mayor had the ultimate say over who held the position of police chief. But that would mean the cartel would have been fine with Matthews being in charge. And that meant

Matthews was easy to influence, or the cartel had zero fear of him actually catching them.

And after seeing him in action at Lily's house on Sunday, I'd call his basic detective skills subpar at best. Sometimes you just needed an incapable person in power to get away with whatever you wanted. Like a substitute teacher who didn't really care if you passed notes behind their back.

Matthews may have cared about his town, might even be willing to die for it, but none of that meant he was actually qualified to be its police chief.

Still, something about Matthews tugged at me the wrong way. I needed to follow him and planned to do exactly that tonight. If I was to meet with Lily tomorrow night, I needed something concrete to offer her after two days.

I grabbed lunch at a sandwich shop on Main Street. An Italian on wheat with extra salami. After scarfing that down, I attempted to search for any public information on Matthews, but none was available aside from the interviews he'd given to the *Hillcrest Daily*. No phone number. No address.

I expected as much. No town, even one as safe as Hillcrest, could risk having citizens go knocking on the police chief's door for the hell of it. I was sure Lily could get me the info I needed, but I knew she'd be opposed to me snooping around the local police. Especially with her already on thin ice with Duncan.

I was on my own until we met for dinner tomorrow.

Sitting outside the police station wasn't an option, so I killed the afternoon by staying in the area. Visited a hidden gem called Bill's Books, a local shop with everything from new releases to used classics. I already had my haul from the library, so bought nothing, but enjoyed an hour browsing books and breathing in the exquisite scent of paradise.

I later found a park and sat on a bench, watching kids walk home from school later that afternoon. I thought back to Dominic Evans from that news story, and remembered why it was important I stay in town. Dominic wouldn't be the last victim. Not until this operation came crumbling down.

Some of the high school kids kicked around a soccer ball while crossing through the park. Others found not-so-hidden places among the trees to make out and feel each other up. Another girl sat on the nearest bench fifteen feet away from me, opening her chemistry book on her lap and jotting notes on a tablet.

I felt it all at that moment. What life in Hillcrest was like. Peaceful, hard-working people. Normal, everyday life. The perfect target for a group of crooks to come spread their trash among the community. All in the name of making a dollar.

I hated money. I supposed that was easy to do growing up with little of it. My years with the SEALs and CIA allowed me to grow a rather comfortable savings account. They paid me way more than I ever needed. Just under six figures from the SEALs, and I've calculated I only required around thirty thousand to live my lifestyle as a drifter. And even that was a stretch for splurging on nice things like hotels with air conditioning and cable TV.

My mom had always taught us to live within our means. Imagine my surprise at seeing my brother coming out of some fancy mansion in the middle of nowhere. If he had earned his money legitimately, I'd have no issue with him losing sight of our mother's financial values. But I knew where his money came from.

Fuck him.

You'd never catch me dead living in a mansion. Or buying fancy cars. I loved a good steak and knew I could find one reasonably priced at a local diner like Jo's, rather than dropping seventy on a slab of meat from an upscale steakhouse. It was all bullshit, really, and my mother had helped me see through that. That all set me up for my life on the road.

It never stressed me out. I kept cash in a safe deposit box in Laredo and usually had to stop there a few times a year to pick some up. If I was too far, I'd just find some odd job, usually manual labor to help keep fit, and earn money that way.

Maybe doing that here could get me in tighter with the undocumented community, and I could get a unique insight. But time was running short. We all sensed it. Lily had her back on the ropes. Dead bodies were turning up. It was time for action, not fucking around.

One of the soccer players kicked the ball wildly, and it rolled toward me. I got up, jogged a few feet ahead, and drilled it back to them thirty yards away.

"Thanks, mister!" the kid shouted, waving.

I waved back and smiled. I couldn't remember the last time I'd kicked a soccer ball. My brother and I played all the time when we were kids. Hell, we played everything from baseball, basketball, soccer to American football. But Manny had a natural gift for soccer. He should have been in college playing on a full ride instead of doing the cartel's dirty work all those years ago. Such a dumbass.

It still ate me alive, knowing what he had become. I'd never fault him for wanting to find our father, and even getting to know him better. He had actual memories with our father that I did not as an infant. But to disown me and pretend I never existed while working his way up the cartel corporate ladder still pissed me off beyond belief.

When you lose a parent early in life, you develop a sense of urgency to make them proud in the heavens above. My mother's death left a hole in my soul that has been impossible to fill. She was always positive and wanted to spread kindness around the world. My years in the SEALs chased that same thing, albeit through a completely different approach.

Killing terrorists and criminals gave me the best of both worlds. It allowed me an avenue to let out my aggression from feeling abandoned early in life, all while making the world a better place. I didn't spread kindness, not when I was slitting a man's throat, but I removed negative energy from our universe. And that was good enough in my book.

The nostalgia was getting the best of me, and I had to leave my bench and get the soccer ball out of my sight. The littlest things could spark so many memories, it was impossible to keep any type of focus.

I had to tail Chief Matthews tonight. No excuses. If I could at least get an understanding of his life outside of the police station, I could either cross him off my mental list of suspects or pursue him further.

I grabbed my backpack and left the park, starting back to my car, when my cell phone buzzed in my pocket. An incoming call.

I snatched it out, and my heart immediately raced when I saw Lily's number. *She* was calling *me*. Earlier than we had agreed.

"Hello?" I said, licking my lips in giddy anticipation.

"Jonny," she said, her voice low and disturbed. "Where are you?"

My excitement faded as quickly as it had arrived. She wasn't calling to ask me to dinner a day early.

"I'm at some park," I said, looking around for a sign now that I had reached the outer perimeter. "Seaside Park. Why?"

"And you've been there for a while?" she asked, her tone growing more grave by the second.

"Yes, I've been out on the town all day, actually."

"Okay, good. At least you'll be cleared."

"Cleared? What's going on, Lily?"

She paused, then spoke in an even lower voice. "Matthews is dead."

Chapter 25

I guessed I wouldn't be following Matthews around tonight, after all.

My first instinct was to head down to the police station. The officers would be in a mournful panic. Lily was shaken up. Things were hitting too close to home now, especially for her. She gave me no details, but I still assumed this was tied to the cartel.

Lily insisted I stay away from the station. Emotions and tensions were high. And she had no idea how the other officers would react to my presence at such a vulnerable moment.

Mayor Reece was planning to deliver an official statement at an impromptu press conference outside of city hall at the top of the hour. This would be my first chance to see him in action.

I returned to my car, unzipped my backpack, and confirmed my gun was loaded. It felt like something could happen at any moment. When a small town's police chief is killed on the job—as I assumed was the case—the citizens tend to hide inside until life feels normal again. If it's not safe for the chief of police to roam around town, then why should they?

I drove back across Hillcrest. City hall was in the same neighborhood as the police station, so I had to pass Hamburger Stand on my way, where business continued as usual.

Still had a hard time knowing my nephew was in there working for the bad guys.

The press conference was to begin at five o'clock. I pulled up to a mob of people already formed at 4:40. About three hundred, if I had to guess. Parking was already impossible to find along Hillcrest Avenue, so I had to drive a couple of blocks away and walk over.

Several others were doing the same, as we parked in a quiet neighborhood and made our way to city hall. By the time I joined the crowd, it had already swelled to four hundred people.

Some people were sobbing, tears streaming down their faces. Most others were talking in hushed tones to each other, speculating about what had happened. News spread fast in this town, apparently.

I wanted a good view of the mayor, so pushed my way toward the front of the crowd. There were fences in place to serve as barriers, a handful of police officers standing with their arms crossed, assault rifles held at the ready. All were wearing sunglasses, likely to hide their sorrow or fear.

I recognized a heavyset man standing in the front row, his belly pressed up against the barrier.

Theo Rambis, the reporter from the *Hillcrest Daily* who had written at least eighty percent of the articles I'd read over the past couple of days. With his sheer volume of published articles, he was the main reporter in town. His front row spot for the press conference only confirmed that.

I wanted to talk to him but wasn't even sure what to say. What if he knew I was the person of interest they had arrested after the shooting at the tavern? The last thing I needed was my face or name to show up in a local paper. And when the people were on edge and desperate to hang blame on anyone. Forget it.

I kept my distance and let the dozens of people fill the space between him and me. My size wasn't helping my cause, so I slouched low, trying to get level with the average height of everyone else in the audience.

The people directly around me were in heavy tears, saying things like "I can't believe he's really gone" and "What's happening to our city?"

That last question caught my attention, and I immediately started beating myself up for not getting closer to the locals. Sure, I'd met and conversed with people like Richard and Jo, and even my good friend Ted at the bar. But I had no sense of how the general population was feeling about things.

My travels around the country have taught me that cities are like humans. They all react to scenarios and tragedies differently.

With something like a drug epidemic plaguing a town, some would react with activism. People marching and toting signs to demand the local government get the matter under control. Some would go as far as rounding up any citizens who wanted to help on a special task force to hunt down the criminals behind the issue. And others pretended the issue didn't exist. Swept it under the rug like a dirty secret no one should talk about. I sensed Hillcrest was the latter type, considering how regular day-to-day life had seemed. No protests. No task forces.

But when something as tragic as the police chief getting killed happened, the floodgates collapsed, and everything came pouring down. Police chief dead. Teenagers dying or in the hospital because of drug overdoses. The quieter towns were content with leaving the authorities to resolve such a matter, even one as depraved as drugs spreading among the youth. But when the authorities were in danger, where were people to turn?

Desperation.

And desperate people took matters into their own hands. Rules didn't apply in desperate times. A dead police chief could lead to anarchy in some small towns. I'd seen it, and it was frightening.

The last thing Hillcrest needed was a group of people like, say, Ted and his friends, rising to the occasion to deliver justice for the chief. Whenever some bozo with a gun got involved, innocent people died. Every time.

I was snapped out of my thoughts as the crowd fell silent. We all watched Mayor Reece stroll from the entrance of city hall and make his way toward the podium they had set up on the top landing of the stone steps leading to the building.

The mayor stood at average height. Jet black hair slicked to the side with too much product that made it glimmer in the sunlight. He shook hands with a procession of police officers lined up along his pathway toward the podium. His face appeared stiff, like he had Botox done. No wrinkles. Obnoxiously white teeth. And he wore eyeliner that drew attention away from the rest of his counterfeit face. The guy looked like he belonged in Los Angeles, not Hillcrest.

He reached the podium with a somber expression and slipped his hand into his suit jacket to pull out a stack of note cards. I caught the slightest tremble of his hands as he placed the cards on the podium. Public speaking still made him nervous.

Two officers with AR-15s stepped within arm's reach of the corners of the podium, scanning the crowd. Ready for someone foolish enough to make another move on a public figure.

Mayor Reece tapped the microphone with a stiff index finger and cleared his throat.

"Hello, fellow residents of Hillcrest," he said, his voice strong as it boomed through the speakers set up along the sides of the steps. "For those of you not familiar, I am Mayor Tony Reece, and I come to you with a heavy heart and terrible news. Hillcrest has lost one of its finest today. Chief Russell Matthews."

Sobs broke out at the mention of the name, and the mayor took a step back and wiped at his eyes.

He returned to the podium. "I have been mayor of this fine town for only two years now, and I owe so much gratitude to Chief Matthews. He was one of the first people I met while I was campaigning for mayor. He believed in me. Russ was a native of Hillcrest. Attended elementary, middle, and high school right here in town. He was a track star for Hillcrest High and still holds a handful of records. He joined the police academy straight out of high school and never looked back. When I think of someone who loved Hillcrest more than themselves, I think of Chief Matthews.

"He was a staple of our community, and nothing brought him more joy than the opportunity to serve his hometown. I once asked him if he ever had plans of settling down and getting married, and he told me Hillcrest was his one true love. Putting on the uniform was much more than a job for Russell Matthews. It was his calling. He was Hillcrest, and Hillcrest was him. As mayor, I'm aware of complaints filed against all of our public servants. I've never received one regarding Chief Matthews.

"When Chief Samuels retired, and Russ took the job on an interim basis, I had no doubt he was going to stay in that role. I actually spoke with him on his first morning and told him not to stress about job security. The position was his, as long as he wanted. He sounded like an excited kid ready for the first day of school and told me his whole life led to this moment. He wanted to be the chief of police until his final breath."

Mayor Reece stepped back again and wiped tears from his eyes. He reached to a lower shelf on the podium and pulled out a water bottle. It felt like he was already delivering a eulogy, judging by the crowd's sorrow. I wished I had known the good man everyone else seemed to remember, but he never gave me the chance. He saw me as a threat to his hometown, jumping to conclusions that weren't true.

The mayor returned to his speech. "It's not going to be easy moving forward, but we must. It's what Chief Matthews would expect of us. His death will not be in vain, and I have signed a proclamation marking today Russell Matthews Day to honor one of the finest people to come from Hillcrest. We have lots of work ahead to make sure justice is delivered to whoever is behind this senseless murder. I have faith in our police force to work tirelessly until this matter is resolved. It's the least we can do to honor our fallen hero.

"Thank you all, and God bless Hillcrest."

Mayor Reece stepped back from the podium, and chatter immediately broke out. People hurled questions toward the mayor, pressing forward against the barrier. Theo Rambis shouted something while jotting on a notepad, but I couldn't make out his words through all the commotion.

The mayor was not taking questions and was whisked away back into city hall. They surely didn't want him standing exposed to the public any longer than necessary. Not until they found Matthews's killer.

The emotions among the crowd were electric. I felt the anguish. And the fury. The people came to the press conference for answers and left with a tribute. Was it safe to go about life as normal? The desperation loomed, so I pushed my way to the back of the crowd, where I found Agent Duncan with his arms crossed, leaning against the hood of his car parked in the middle of the street that had now been barricaded at both ends.

I approached him, and he looked me up and down with little emotion on his face.

"Fancy seeing you here," he said, pursing his lips.

"Look, Duncan," I said. "I want to apologize for how I left things on Sunday. Lily told me your personal matters while venting. I had no right to throw any of that back in your face. My emotions got the best of me. Please don't hold any of that against Lily."

Duncan stood up and uncrossed his arms to place his hands on his hips. "Not many people have the stones to apologize these days," he said. "I'm impressed."

"I've never had an issue owning up to my faults," I said. "You're here under stressful circumstances, both personally and professionally. You don't need some asshole like me making matters worse. To be fair, I only want to help."

Duncan nodded, puffing out his chest like it was supposed to intimidate me. Poor guy. "I don't support these unorthodox methods Lily tries. To me, asking a citizen for help is utter lunacy."

"I'm not just—"

Duncan shot up a finger to interrupt me. "But I understand your background. You're not just some Joe Blow off the street. You have skills that could actually help us."

"What are you getting at?"

"I'm not entirely sure yet. Haven't thought things through. This murder is throwing a wrench into our plans. The FBI might get involved, although that shouldn't have a direct impact on our case."

"Unless they find the cartel is behind the murder."

Duncan nodded slowly, biting his bottom lip. "Of course. Which I believe they were. They've been behind anything bad that happens in this town. Those dead men at the morgue. Chief Matthews. The hand at Lily's house. It's getting dangerous out here. Wouldn't be surprised if some of them are in this crowd right now, scouting other potential targets. See, I've studied cartels for more than a decade and they're mostly all the same. If they can't operate in peace, they cause mayhem to mask their activities."

"Killing the chief of police is certainly mayhem," I said, enjoying the insights Duncan was finally comfortable enough to share with me.

"Exactly. Now the police force will be spread thin. Their efforts shift to solving this murder, as they should. But they don't have qualified detectives. Not for something of this magnitude. That's where the FBI will need to step in."

"What about you and Lily?" I asked, only really caring about Lily.

Duncan licked his lips, staring at the ground as the crowd dispersed around us. "Well, Lily had a police presence outside her home after the events on Sunday, but I highly doubt they'll be able to keep an officer sitting in a car all day. I've reached out to our boss in D.C. to request more resources. We'll see what happens."

Duncan shrugged, as if he had done everything he could. And perhaps that was true. Considering he was a man who played by the book, I didn't expect him to take matters into his own hands. Or ask me his next question.

"Personally," Duncan continued, "I think we need to wrap up our case and get out of Hillcrest. It's getting too dangerous for either of us to still be here, especially with the cartel knowing where Lily lives, and probably me, too."

"So what will that require?"

Duncan looked up at me with a slight grin. "What do you think of meeting with your brother?"

Chapter 26

I returned to my hotel room and lay in bed for the rest of the night. I had no interest in food or following anyone around town.

My idea of bringing a swift end to the cartel's operation would be to barge into that hidden mansion with guns blazing and firing every round until I was the last one breathing.

Duncan's idea was to orchestrate a truce between Manny and the town of Hillcrest, using me as the pawn to make it all happen.

He must have had a look at my file, or maybe Lily shared info as a peace offering. I had extensive experience as a negotiator for the CIA and knew all the methods to deploy depending on the situation. I've led the release of hostages all around the world, and in a way, Hillcrest was being held hostage by this cartel.

I hadn't agreed to Duncan's suggestion, telling him I would need some time to think about it. Asking me to serve as the middleman between Hillcrest and Manny made little sense to me. I didn't know either party all that well. The Manny Mendez I knew was not the same person holed up in the confines of a hillside mansion. I knew a teenaged version and only had harsh judgment toward the adult version he had become.

I fell asleep around ten o'clock that night, the TV showing old reruns of *The Office*. It was usually good for a night of laughter, but I was in no such mood.

When I woke Wednesday morning at seven, my sheets were half hanging off the edge of the bed, half wrapped around one leg. It was a rough night of sleep, and I felt it in my groggy head. I didn't feel rested in the slightest and knew a long day waited ahead. At least dinner with Lily was still on the docket.

I hated starting a day feeling exhausted but had no choice but to power through.

I took a quick shower and headed down with my backpack to grab a glass of juice before going out. Normally, I'd eat breakfast in the dining room but needed something extra, considering how I felt.

The diner would suffice, and I didn't mind eating there twice today. Jo had enough of a variety that you could eat there ten meals out of the week and have a unique experience each time.

But those hash browns and bacon were calling me, tempting me with the pick-me-up I desperately needed.

I slammed the juice and left the hotel. It was a cloudy morning, as had been the norm. The skies rarely opened until noon, raising the temperature and teasing everyone to spend time on the beach.

The morning wind blew east, draping the scent of saltwater across the town like a blanket. I drove with the windows down, happy to let the wind whip around as I reached a higher speed. It helped me feel more alert, which was good. I was going to need it.

Jo's Diner was fairly busy when I pulled into the parking

lot. Lots of folks dressed in business attire cramped inside, steaming mugs of coffee next to their plates of breakfast foods.

Jo kept a bell that jingled each time the front door opened, and it seemed like every head turned to look at me when I stepped through. I grinned awkwardly and nodded toward whoever was brave enough to make eye contact.

The chatter inside hummed as Jo scooted out from the kitchen, smiling and waving when she saw me. She strolled over and grabbed a menu from the host stand.

"Just you this morning, dear?" she asked, grabbing a set of silverware to pair with my menu.

"Yes, ma'am," I replied, scanning the dining area.

"I can get you a seat at the bar, if you don't mind," she said. "Leaves a table open in case any groups come in."

"Fine with me. Thank you."

I followed her straight back to the vintage-style bar, complete with a low countertop and swivel barstools drilled into the floor. I took my seat and enjoyed a view straight into the kitchen. An older Latino man tended to the stovetop with sizzling meats and eggs cooking. He reminded me of pictures I'd seen of my grandfather, with his slicked-back white hair, matching thin mustache, and thick-framed glasses.

The angelic voice of Vicente Fernandez poured out from a speaker in the kitchen, and it may as well have punched me in the heart. Tight pressure squeezed the front of my chest. All the blood rushed to my eyeballs.

Hearing Vicente Fernandez always put my emotions in the spin cycle. My mom listened to him on an old record player in the living room every weekend. She'd dance by herself. Sometimes she let me or Manny join, but when the music played, it was like my mom was transported to another world. Probably to Guadalajara where she imagined Chente himself serenading her.

Music had a unique of way of taking me back to a certain memory in life. Any Vicente song took me back to my mom, just like hearing Snoop Dogg's "Drop It Like It's Hot" always dumped me right back in my senior year of high school, driving myself to school without a care in the world.

I watched the cook whistle along to the tune and had to bury my face in the menu to regain some composure. Jo startled me from behind by clapping a hand on my back as she came around the counter to take my order.

"Sorry, dear," she said. "Is everything okay?"

"Yes, sorry," I said, not sure what I was apologizing for. "Just have a lot on my mind."

"Well, maybe some breakfast will help clear your thoughts."

"I'm planning on it."

I placed my order of two eggs, over-easy, with hash browns and extra bacon. Stress was trying to take over me, but when was the last time someone eating bacon was stressed out? Impossible combination.

Jo disappeared into the back, leaving me with a cup of coffee I had no interest in drinking. A few people started leaving the diner to start their days, and when I looked to my right, I nearly fell off my stool.

At the end of the bar, sitting at a table around the corner wall, were Agent Duncan, Mayor Reece, and Theo Rambis.

"What the fuck?" I whispered to myself. The mayor, a DEA agent, and the town's main reporter were gathered for breakfast the morning after the chief of police was shot dead.

Seeing Theo reminded me I had no idea what actually happened to Chief Matthews, so I pulled out my cellphone and went to the website for the *Hillcrest Daily.*

The home page was completely overtaken by a blown-up version of Matthews's official portrait. *CHIEF MATTHEWS DEAD,* the headline shouted.

I tapped on the article and read the new page that loaded, written by the one and only Theo Rambis. Chief Matthews was shot on his front porch shortly after his lunch break. He often liked to drive home for lunch to check on his dog and eat his meal in peace. There were no witnesses to the shooting, but early conclusions believe just the one shot was fired from twenty feet away, the distance between the sidewalk and the front door.

One shot square in the back of the head while Matthews was turned around to lock his front door. A next-door neighbor saw the chief's body splayed out on the front porch and rushed over to find him dead.

Anyone who only needed one chance to land a perfect head shot was a professional. I could do it, but knowing someone else in Hillcrest had the same capability made me uneasy.

It was a straightforward assassination that made me wonder if the chief was actually making progress on the drug case. Either that, or the cartel needed a distraction, like Duncan had mentioned.

I pulled out my cell phone and sent a text to Lily.

Duncan and mayor at diner. With Theo Rambis. Do you know about this?

Seven barstools separated me from their table, so I scooted down one, planning to get as close as I could. All three men were leaning in to the center of the table, speaking in hushed tones. The diner was much too loud for me to have any chance of hearing them.

My phone buzzed with a response from Lily.

Yes. Me or Duncan usually met with Matthews once a week. Mayor now involved. Not sure about Rambis.

Okay, so only part of this meeting was expected. I supposed the mayor might want certain details left out of the news to protect the investigation. If that was the case, why meet in a public place? If there were sensitive matters to be contained, they should have met behind closed doors.

I shifted down one more seat, delighted I was the only one at the bar. It paid to be a loner sometimes.

Jo returned with my plate of breakfast and looked puzzled as she studied the empty seat I had abandoned. She frowned, then shook her head and slid the plate toward me. "Anything else, dear?" she asked, grabbing a bottle of ketchup from beneath the counter and putting it in front of me.

"I'm all set. Thank you." I flashed a grin, and she hurried away to tend to another table. The three men continued talking, so I slid down another stool. The wall at the end of the bar was just tall enough to keep me out of sight from them so long as I stayed crouched just low enough. I thought I looked natural, like a tall man trying to lower himself toward his plate to eat, so I did that and stuck a slice of bacon into my mouth.

I was too distracted to enjoy the flavor, but somewhere in my brain, the endorphins were doing cartwheels. Even with the dining room clearing out, it was too loud for me to hear their conversation. Between the conversations of others, Vicente and his listener belting out from the kitchen, and the clatter of dishes and silverware, I just wanted to jump on the bar and tell everyone to shut the hell up.

Instead, I slid down another seat and brought my plate with me. I was now four empty stools away from the wall at the end and craned my neck for a better chance of hearing.

Still nothing, and now I was getting pissed.

"Is everything okay?" Jo asked, sliding up from nowhere to stand on the opposite side of the bar. She crossed her arms and looked from me to the table and back, one eyebrow cocked as she demanded an answer.

"Yes," I said in a low voice and waved her to come closer. She leaned in. "Do you know why those three are here?"

Jo stood back and raised her other eyebrow. "They come here at least twice a week for breakfast. Well, I should say, Chief Matthews was normally part of that group. Looks like they've replaced him with the mayor."

This put me at ease. Somewhat.

Jo leaned in again. "That other guy works with Lily, that cute blonde you're interested in, right?"

The words caught me off guard, and I forgot all about the three men as I swung my gaze back to Jo, who stood there with a crooked smile. "I'm not interested...I'm just—"

"No offense, but you're lying, dear," Jo said, thankfully cutting off my blubbering self. "You think I can't recognize when someone is lovestruck? I run a diner in a small town. I can read people like a book. And you got it bad. I saw the way you looked at Lily the other day, and I don't blame you. She's cute. Independent. And just the sweetest little thing."

"The other guy does work with her," I said, desperately wanting to change the subject. Why were we even talking about my love life right now?

"Hmm," Jo said. "Something's going on around here, and

I don't know what. That cutie of yours told me she's here to work on a case of some sort. But I didn't ask for details. That's a bit out of my pay range."

She chuckled. I didn't want to waste the opportunity. Jo probably knew more about the happenings in Hillcrest than the police department and could possibly share some useful information. A diner was a safe space. Both the good guys and bad guys would spend time here to relax and unplug. Enjoy a meal.

"Can I ask you something?" I said, and Jo quickly nodded, leaning in closer. "There *is* something going on in Hillcrest. I'm not part of the investigation, at least not in an official way, but I'm trying to piece things together. Have you seen any increase in Latin men in town over the past few months?"

Jo stepped back and pursed her lips. I saw the dials turning in her mind. "Yes," she said. "Now that you mention it, I've had some regulars come in here almost every day. Sometimes it's a couple of men, other times it's been about fifteen of them. They're bilingual, most of them. Speaking Spanish to each other, but English to me."

"Do they come at the same time each day?" I asked.

Jo nodded slowly, going through her memory to get the details. "Yes. They actually come during off hours. Between two and four in the afternoon. Sometimes after nine o'clock at night. They've never been here during the busy times. Should I be worried about them?"

Jo raised an eyebrow. She was jumping to conclusions of her own already.

"No," I blurted. "We're still trying to piece things together, but I can't imagine they pose a threat to you or your diner. They want to fly under the radar and not be noticed. I imagine that's why they come at such odd hours."

Jo slapped her hand to her forehead. "I always thought they worked together and had funky shifts."

"Do they tip well?" I asked.

"They usually tip me thirty percent, so I have no complaints. Not sure about the times they come at night. I've only heard about them from the girl who covers the night shift. Never asked what they tip her."

"Would you mind if I hid out somewhere in the back this afternoon?" I asked. "Just so I can observe them from a distance."

Jo considered this, biting the inside of her lip. "Okay. If you think it's necessary."

"I do. And I'll be coming back here for dinner tonight...with my friend."

Jo's lips spread into a grin. "A second date? Look at you go!"

I couldn't tell if she was patronizing me or genuinely excited. It didn't matter. She was letting me hide out to watch these cartel guys have their not-so-secret lunch in the diner.

Jo reached into her apron pocket and pulled out a handful of the peppermint candies. She put them in front of my plate and said, "These always make her smile."

I scooped up the candies and quickly put them in the front pouch of my backpack. "Thank you, Jo," I said with a grin. "I'll see you later."

She nodded and knocked on the countertop before disappearing back into the kitchen.

I returned to my breakfast and was soon reminded why I was closer to the end of the bar.

A voice called over the wall. "Hey, Jonny! What are you

doing here?”

Chapter 27

Agent Duncan was standing up and looking over the wall at me. He shot me a quick smile before returning to his stern expression.

"Hello, Agent Duncan," I said, promptly returning my attention to my plate. I didn't want him to think I was eavesdropping, so I acted like I was just going about my business.

"Funny finding you here," Duncan said. "We were just talking about you. Why don't you come over and have a chat?"

I didn't like the laxness in his voice. Like we were buddies who just ran into each and wanted to grab a beer. I looked down at my plate.

"Bring your breakfast over," Duncan said. "We have room."

I heard the other two men moving things around on the table to clear space for me.

"Alright," I said, standing up to first throw my backpack over my shoulder before taking my plate and coffee mug to the table I'd been trying to spy on.

"Good to see you," Duncan said as I passed him, clapping me on the back.

I wasn't sure if he was trying to sweet talk me into agreeing to his proposal or if he was just acting like a douchebag because we were with the mayor.

The open seat was between Theo Rambis and Agent Duncan, so I sat down facing the mayor of Hillcrest.

Duncan sat down. "Jonny, I'd like you to meet Theo Rambis, editor of the *Hillcrest Daily*. And Mayor Reece."

Theo stuck out a hand, and I shook it, finding it warm and clammy. I then shook the mayor's hand. "I was at your speech yesterday, mayor. You did an excellent job."

He waved me off. "I appreciate that, but I wasn't trying to deliver a professional speech. Just remembering a good friend."

"Speaking from the heart is sometimes the best way to go," I said. "Unfortunately, I didn't have any emotional connection to Chief Matthews—I just got into town—but it looks like everyone else was touched by your words."

"Thank you," the mayor said, nodding at me appreciatively.

"So, you said you were talking about me?" I asked Duncan, not having the patience for small talk. Not if my name was in their mouths.

"Yes," Duncan said, shifting in his seat. His ass-kissing voice gave way to a more professional one. "First off, Jonny, everyone at this table knows what's going on in that mansion you were at the other night."

"Hold on a second," I said. "You're making it sound like I was hanging out with those guys. I was only in the driveway trying to see what I could find. Was actually about to take down some license plate numbers before they confronted me."

"They?" Duncan asked. "You mean your brother?"

The other two looked at me like they were expecting a reaction. I wasn't sure what Duncan was trying to accomplish, so I played it off.

"That man is only my brother by blood," I said. "I don't know him any more than I know Mayor Reece." I took a bite of eggs.

"Jonny," Mayor Reece said, "Agent Duncan told me about his plan to have you meet with your brother. Now, it was all his idea, but I'm on board. We need these thugs out of Hillcrest. Sooner than later. I'm taking calls from the governor and the FBI. They want to know what the hell is going on in our small corner of the world. We've assured them the DEA is on top of it, but if one more public official gets killed, our town is going to be crawling with feds. The people here can't handle that. Our economy would collapse."

I swallowed my eggs and cleared my throat, turning my attention to Duncan. "You mentioned this idea, but I'm still not sure what you want me to do. Sit down with my brother, then what? Ask him nicely to leave. Take his crime ring to some other town?"

"That's a start," Duncan said.

"We have emergency funds we can use," Mayor Reece said. "We can offer them payment to leave Hillcrest."

I scratched my head. The temperature seemed to rise in the diner. Theo Rambis leaned back in his seat with his hands folded over his gut. His notepad was on the table, but he didn't touch it. Not now. This was not the sort of back alley shady dealings that made it into the headlines.

"I don't understand," I said. "What does this approach solve? The DEA would still have to follow these guys to the next town. This does nothing to help your case, except to drag it out. And why would you want to negotiate with the cartel? These aren't exactly people who stay true to their word."

"We want a peaceful resolution," the mayor said, blinking rapidly. He interlocked his fingers and rested his hands on the table. "We don't want the drama that comes with arresting cartel members. Arrest a handful, then our police station becomes a target. Not just that, but also our officers, judges, district attorneys, and so on. Arrest them all, and we're looking at an even higher risk of all of that happening."

"We've done some snooping around this cartel," Duncan said. "We know things they've done in other small towns. They've burned down courthouses. Murdered judges and mayors in broad daylight."

Mayor Reece shuddered at this comment.

"I understand all that," I said. "But I still don't see what asking them to leave achieves? They'll go to a different town and do these terrible things there. Seems like Hillcrest wants to pawn off this issue to the next taker. Why aren't we discussing a way to end their operation? Fear is no way to approach this."

The mayor and Duncan exchanged a glance.

Duncan spoke next. "We don't expect them to agree to our terms. But that's why we want you taking the lead on this. How do you feel about killing your brother?"

I shook my head. Did these assholes really just ask me that? I already planned to do this, but them requesting gave me a brief hesitation. "You've got to be fucking kidding me."

Duncan stuck out a hand, gesturing me to calm down. "Hold on, Jonny. I understand how absurd that question is. Let me back up. Manuel Mendez is the highest-ranking member of this cartel currently in the United States. There are only two people ranked above him in the overall organization. Your father being the top dog. Hear me out. If we can kill Manny, that's like cutting the head off the chicken. Once he's out of the picture, we can pick off everyone else. Throw the ones in jail who don't put up a fight and kill the ones that do."

"This seems a little out of the box for you, Agent," I said, growing nauseous. They were going to pressure me into this twisted scheme. I could always agree and flee. They expected my help like I owed them something. Fuck these guys. "Does your boss know what you're scheming up out here?"

Duncan laughed. "My boss has given me free rein on this one. This cartel has been on our watch list for several years. It's time to bring an end to them."

"But you just said you want to ask them to leave. Like they're a fucking door-to-door salesman."

Duncan's mouth twisted into an awkward grin. "That's just our front. They're not leaving, even if we offered them a million dollars. They're comfortable here. Have a solid system in place. We need *you*, Jonny. Your brother will never agree to meet with us. But he will with you. He might even meet with you alone, which is what we're counting on. If you have Manuel Mendez alone in a room, you can end his life and bring down this cartel that has harmed countless communities across North America."

"Funny," I said, crossing my arms and leaning back. I'd lost my appetite and wouldn't be finishing my tasty breakfast. Fuck these guys. Secluded booth in the diner like they ran the damn place. Coming during peak hours so no one could overhear their shady conversations. "A week ago, you wanted me behind bars because you thought I was involved with these assholes. Then you wanted me to leave town so you can continue to fuck up this case on your own. Now that you see my blood connection as a weapon, you want me to stay, and you're willing to offer me as a sacrifice to my own brother. I don't use these words lightly, Agent Duncan, but you can go right ahead and fuck yourself."

Theo chortled at this comment, and promptly took a long drink from his coffee mug.

The mayor and Duncan both seemed unfazed.

"Jonny," Mayor Reece said, "we wouldn't have come to you if we didn't trust you. Now, I can't speak to your experiences with Agent Duncan, but I can't even begin to speculate the long shot odds of you ending up in Hillcrest at the same time as your brother and his cartel, but this presents us with a unique opportunity. Even if you and your brother have fallen out of touch, we still believe he trusts you enough to meet with you. In private. He might have a reputation as a stone-cold killer, but he's still human. We want to leverage his emotions and get him in a room with you. We'll make all the arrangements. Where to meet. Body armor. We'll have officers hidden in the distance in case you need backup. But we know you won't. You don't even need a weapon to kill your brother, but we'll still provide you with whatever you need. You can end this, Jonny. Once and for all."

He made a compelling point. I'd been struggling to come to terms with why I ended up in Hillcrest at the same time as my long-lost brother. Of all the small towns I could have stopped in. I just had to have a beach.

"This isn't a decision I can just make on the spot," I said. "I still don't know if I trust any of this. I'm not employed by either of you or anyone you work for. Seems like you're using me to do your dirty work."

The mayor shook his head. "We want to use your expertise. Agent Duncan shared your record with me. All those secret operations. Stealth missions. Assassinations. And that's not even including your time with the CIA where you worked undercover for years." Mayor Reece shifted in his seat and leaned forward, planting his elbows on the table and balling his fists together below his chin. "We can make the calls and go through the proper channels to get a full team of agents out here. And it will require about thirty for a raid on the mansion. That takes time. And paperwork. But more importantly, it adds risk. The cartel may have eyes in the town—most likely, in fact. They'll see the feds' presence and make plans of their own. If we barge into a mansion with thirty agents, some of them may get killed. But if we can get just you and your brother alone in a room, and you take care of business..." The mayor leaned back and tossed his hands up, making a gesture that said *this is all common sense.*

"No risk," Agent Duncan said. "No fuss. This cartel can vanish overnight with your help, Jonny. Plus, there is a hundred-thousand-dollar reward for anyone who helps lead to the capture of the top-ranked members of the Eldorado Cartel. I can see that you receive that money."

I never took a job for money. That would make me a hit man, and that's not what I was in this for.

"Take your time, Jonny," the mayor said. "But not too much. We need to move quickly with whatever our next decision will be."

I looked at Theo on my right. "You've been awfully quiet."

Theo shrugged. "I've got nothing to contribute to this conversation. Just here to understand the timeline of events, so I can prepare my schedule."

"Mr. Rambis is the best reporter in town," the mayor said. "He's the editor of the paper, sure, but his work is flawless.

We like to keep him in the loop and make sure he has all the correct details. Everyone in town believes everything he writes. He's earned that reputation. It would be a shame if a story leaked about the cartel being in town and its leader being your own brother. Might make people re-consider what exactly happened that night you were at the tavern."

I shook my head. "All you politicians are the same. Crooked pieces of shit."

The mayor studied his fingernails, refusing eye contact with me. He finally looked up, staring at me with a *don't fuck with me* look on his face. "So, Jonny, do we have a deal?"

I stood up and tossed a ten on the table to cover my breakfast. "You didn't need to blackmail me, asshole. I'll do it."

Chapter 28

I left the diner in a fury. All I wanted was to leave Hillcrest and never come anywhere near this town again. But I couldn't leave Lily to fend off the cartel on her own. This past meeting only proved how incapable her partner was. Duncan's desperation was leading him to make questionable decisions. I wouldn't exactly call the mayor corrupt, but he was walking a fine line.

I was ready to agree to the mayor's terms, but his last threat left a sour taste in my mouth. This all needed to end. For my sake. For Lily's. And for Hillcrest.

Duncan told me he'd be in touch tomorrow regarding how this plan would unfold. I reluctantly gave him my burner phone number and refused to tell him where I was staying. I didn't want to deal with the fees for repairing the drywall in my hotel room if he showed up at my door and I smashed his head through the wall.

Not this time.

I hated not having control over a situation, and this ordeal made me feel like I was following orders. And not from people I had a shred of respect for.

With my breakfast a failure, I returned to the gym and lifted weights for an hour. I squatted until it felt like my thighs would burst. Bench pressed until the veins popped out of my arms and chest. I was awake now. As much as I thought about having to kill my brother, I also thought about Duncan and the mayor behind bars for leveraging me as a pawn in their sick game.

This would all be easier if neither of them were in the picture, but Mayor Reece was right. If another public official went missing or wound up dead, Hillcrest would become home to federal agents patrolling every damn street corner.

Dealing with them would have to wait. And for now, I'd play along. I once convinced a leader of a Southside Chicago gang that I was on his side. Doing the same to these jackasses wouldn't be difficult.

I showered off at the gym and went down the street to a sandwich shop for my second attempt at eating. This time went more smoothly, as I scarfed down an Italian on wheat bread in about two minutes. For the first time today, I felt like me, and headed back to the diner so I could get into position before any of the cartel showed up for lunch.

It was 1:45 when I passed through the entrance, and Jo was right. The place was empty. Not a single patron inside.

Jo poked her head out from the back and waved me over to join her. I strolled past the bar where I had sat hours earlier, and she greeted me with a warm smile.

"I saw you finally got to talk to your friends this morning," she said.

"Not my friends," I replied. "Far from it. I'd be hesitant about who you trust in this city right now. Whatever is going on might be bigger than anyone realizes."

"I keep a shotgun cocked and ready in the back," she said, still grinning, unbothered by anything I just said. "And I'm not afraid to use it. Come."

She pivoted and led me down the walkway through the kitchen. The cook from earlier was nowhere to be seen. No music blared from the speakers. Instead, I heard the hum of voices talking from a TV as we reached a swinging door in the back. To the left was a short hall that led to an emergency exit out the back of the diner.

"Be careful on the kitchen floor," Jo said. "It's slippery if you're not wearing the proper shoes."

This I already knew from my brief stint working as a busboy at a local Mexican restaurant during my freshman year of college. I only lasted a month at that job before I quit. Coming home and smelling like a kitchen every day had driven me nuts.

We stepped into the back room that served as Jo's makeshift office. She had a desk with a monitor, keyboard, and mouse—the old desktop computer plopped on the floor like the ancient relic it was. A basket full of torn-open envelopes sat on the corner of the desk. A television stand was in the opposite corner of the room, a basic eighteen-inch TV showing a local news station as they yapped about the splendid weather in southern California.

"This will be the perfect place for you to hide out," Jo said. "I'll try to seat them at the table you can see directly from the window."

She pointed to the circular window on the door, and I turned around to look through it. At the end of the short path we'd just walked down was a rectangular table that could fit up to eight people.

"Perfect," I said.

"If you want to get closer," she said, opening a closet door to the left of her desk, "I have aprons and hairnets, so you can pose as a cook. Just put them on and step on out to join me in the kitchen. Julio doesn't come back until the dinner rush around 4:30, so I just run things myself until then. Remember, though, watch your step in the kitchen."

"Got it."

"Is there anything else you need from me?" she asked, leaning on the edge of her desk.

I pulled off my backpack and slung it over the chair. "I believe I'm all set. Like I mentioned, you have nothing to worry about. This is strictly observational. I just want to see who all is meeting here, maybe snap some pictures."

Jo tossed her hands up. "The less I know, the better. I'll just go about my business as usual."

"Works for me," I said, craning my neck to look through the window. "Before anyone gets here, I was wondering what you can tell me about Theo Rambis. He was here this morning and said almost nothing during the conversation."

"Oh, Theo," Jo said with a faint laugh. "I've known Theo since he was a little boy. He and his family used to come in here every weekend for breakfast after church. He's a good man but grew up to be quite the introvert. Has a hard time communicating verbally. I suppose that's why he's a writer."

"Do you think he'd get caught up in any sketchiness?" I asked, watching as Jo's face scrunched into deep thought.

"I'd say it's possible, but not likely. He once got caught smoking a cigarette in high school. His mama whooped his ass right out on Main Street. That's the extent I know of him doing anything slightly wrong. But then again, the boy's hard to read. A closed book. I have no idea what he's thinking half the time. He's a Hillcrest boy through and through. His family has been here for generations. No Rambis has ever left Hillcrest, except for attending college. But they always come back."

Theo Rambis had an unwavering loyalty to his hometown. The type that gets drilled into your head as a kid.

"Would you say he's morally sound?" I asked.

"To me, good people do the right thing when no one is watching," Jo said. "I once saw him help a wounded bird from across the park. He didn't know I was there. That might seem like a silly thing to say, or even remember, but it counts in my book."

I nodded. It counted in mine, too.

The bell jingled from the front door, Jo and I instantly locking eyes. She shuffled over to the door. "Right on time," she said. "It's them. Let me get them settled."

Jo pushed through the door, and I heard her greeting the group of men as I crouched low, poking my head up just enough to see through the window.

Four men stood around the host stand, the one in front nodding and waving to Jo, who was gathering menus and silverware. As promised, she sat them at the table in clear view.

Two of the men I recognized. They were with the group sitting at that corner table in the tavern the night I arrived. They were the ones who had gotten away and left their friends to die in the parking lot.

Fucking scum bags.

My heart raced upon seeing them. These men were definitely part of the Eldorado cartel. They worked for my brother. Flashy jewelry graced their necks and fingers. They looked genuinely happy as they sat down.

I was right. The diner was their safe space. No worries. No threats of being shot. The diner allowed them to be regular people out for a meal with friends. They laughed and conversed. A random person wandering into the diner would think nothing of the men at the table.

But they came at two o'clock for a reason. If they came when everyone else in town was here, people would recognize them. And their operation couldn't handle that. Apparently, they were fine with Jo knowing them, because she was still at their table, laughing along as she took their drinks orders.

Even to Jo, these were just some new regulars. Until I had to come and make her all paranoid.

She was playing her part to perfection, making me feel even more like an insignificant fly on the wall.

Jo shuffled back into the kitchen and prepared a tray of drinks. Two waters and two sodas. She delivered their drinks and took their orders without using a notepad. That always impressed me. I could barely remember what I had for dinner last night.

She went straight for the kitchen, paying me no attention while firing up the stove.

This was my chance. The men at the table were minding their business, not a care in the world. I pulled my cell phone out of my pocket and raised it up to the window. The camera kept focusing on the window and blurred out everything in the background. I tapped on the screen to adjust the focus, but it kept reverting to the damn window.

Fucking technology.

I took a step back from the door to try a different angle, and it still didn't work. If only I could throw the phone down and stomp on it. That would make me feel better, but I needed the damn thing still.

"Well, what the fuck?" I said under my breath, stepping back toward the door so it was inches from my face. I took another look through the window and saw the men focused on the one sitting on the right from my angle. He was talking, gesturing with his hands, and seemed to have the rest of the table engaged. "Fuck it."

I pushed open the door about three inches and dropped to a knee, sticking out my hand holding the cell phone. I reached around the door, mentally positioning the phone to get a clear shot of the table, but having no clue if I actually was. When I pressed my thumb on the button to snap the picture, a man's voice shouted.

"Hey! Ma'am! There's someone in the back!"

Oh shit.

I whipped my arm inside the door and backed away, grabbing my backpack from the chair and rushing into the closet. A handful of white aprons hanging from a hook on the back wall greeted me, and I closed the door quickly and quietly.

The commotion grew louder. I could hear it even from inside the closet. The voices carried closer to the office door. Right outside of it now.

"I promise you no one else is here," Jo said.

"Ma'am," the man said, nearly panting. "I'm telling you. I just saw this door open and someone sticking a phone out of it. Looked like they were trying to take pictures."

I fumbled through my backpack in the dark closet and fished out the Glock 48. The last thing I wanted to do was fire it. Then Jo would have to shut down for a few weeks while the bodies were cleared out and the diner underwent a thorough cleaning to get the blood splatters off the walls and ceiling.

This was entirely my fault. Jo trusted me out of the kindness of her heart. I assured her she was in no danger, but I knew better. There was no such thing as true safety when you lived in the same town as the cartel.

"Taking pictures?" Jo said. "You must be mistaken."

"I'm telling you," the man pleaded, and now the others were chirping at Jo, too. I worried what they might do to Jo if I didn't get involved soon.

They were blocking the pathway to the emergency exit. I'd have to fight them within this office. And if they were each packing a gun, I'd have no chance.

"Miss," another man's voice cried out. "I saw it, too. Someone is hiding in this back room. We need to look around."

"The hell you do!" Jo shouted back. "This is my diner, and it's none of your concern."

Silence.

Then the sound of a slap across Jo's face. She whimpered.

"Get the fuck out of our way and let us look," the first man said, followed by the shuffling of multiple feet entering the office.

Jo was no longer putting up a fight. She was either knocked out on the floor or had already run out of the diner. Either way, she was incredible and bought me just enough time to prepare for the pending encounter.

I drew in a deep breath. It always helped me focus and keep my heart rate at bay. Whether I was lining up a long-distance shot with a rifle or preparing to take up fists with a group of crooks, controlled breathing always readied every part of my body.

My Glock was ready to fire. I kept my guns that way after

learning the world doesn't wait for you to take off the safety. I dropped to one knee, knowing whoever opened the closet door would look straight ahead before looking down. Every second mattered.

When I kneeled, however, my foot brushed against something hard lying across the floor. I felt around and grabbed hold of Jo's shotgun.

Okay. This was good.

The sound of a shotgun was much more terrifying than most firearms. Intimidating. Made people flee the scene. I didn't expect any of these men to run, but once they heard the shotgun, their minds would be thrown into disarray.

"Check under the desk," a voice said in a low tone. They were sweeping the office.

Jo said the shotgun was cocked and ready, and I could only trust her. I felt around in the dark and everything seemed ready to blast. And it was a pump action, so I could fire off five shots in fairly rapid succession.

"Show yourself, and you won't get hurt," the man called out.

That was a fucking lie.

I returned to my position, now with the shotgun instead. I stuck my Glock into the back of my waistband and pulled an apron off the hook above my head.

The footsteps grew closer, and I saw the shadow in the crack between the bottom of the door and the floor. Someone was standing just on the other side.

I balled up the apron with my left hand just as the doorknob turned.

When the door swung open, I threw the apron up toward the man's face. He let out a panicked shriek as the apron expanded and got tangled around his face. He tumbled backward, blinded by the white cloth.

All four men were indeed in the office. The tumbling man scampered backwards into another, so I looked left and fired the shotgun at the man standing in front of Jo's desk.

His head exploded. Shards of skull fragments and chunks of brain splattered the ceiling instantly.

Sorry, Jo, but your shotgun is bad ass. I might ask to keep it.

Another man stood by the door to the kitchen, jaw hanging open as he watched what remained of his friend's body fall face-first—well, shoulder first?—onto Jo's desk.

I pulled back the fore-end to ready the next round and fired a second time.

This one caught the man square in the chest. Less of a mess to clean up. He dropped like a sack of potatoes without so much as a whine.

The man who had been dealing with the apron finally got it off his head and bolted straight at me. His mouth was snarled like a pissed-off dog; his teeth bared, and a trail of drool ran from his lips down both cheeks.

Poor guy was having a rough moment.

He lunged through the air before I could get the next shot ready and knocked the shotgun out of my grip. We rolled back into the closet, so I pulled him into me, twisting his body around so I could wrap my arm around his throat.

I stood, and he came with me.

His friend held a black pistol, pointing it at us. I kept the man in front of me as a shield and realized I needed to keep him alive.

"Let him go!" the other man shouted. Thick accent from

south of the border. Heard plenty like it in Laredo all my life. He was dressed in black jeans and a leather jacket. The gold chains around his neck were freckled with blood. "Let him go or I'll blast your fucking brains out!"

The man in my chokehold gasped for air, and I gave him just enough to stay relevant to my cause.

"There's been enough brain blasting today," I said. "Leave the building, and I'll let your friend here go. Wouldn't be the first time you guys have left one of your own behind to die, so don't act like his life matters to you."

"LET HIM GO!" the man screamed at the top of his lungs.

I could have reached for the Glock in my waistband, but any sudden movement would have surely made this scared little shit pull the trigger.

Instead, I released my hold around the guy's neck and shoved his body forward as hard as I could. He was mostly deadweight by now and collided with his companion once again.

They both crashed into the wall, and the man with the gun dropped it on his way down. The one I was choking was first to scramble back to his feet. I took two steps toward him, reared back a fist, and powered it through his face. A nasty crunch from my knuckles connecting with his cheek, shattering it in several places.

He screamed, blood shooting out of his nose, as his hands clasped over his face. The poor guy jumped and spun, cursing the heavens in both English and Spanish. He still wouldn't go down, so I grabbed him from the back of his head, getting a tight grip in his thick, greasy hair, and slammed his head into the wall.

His noises ended abruptly as he dropped to the floor in slow motion, leaving a smeared trail of blood during his descent along the fractured drywall.

The guy who had dropped his pistol looked a bit dazed as he sat on the floor with his back against the wall. He may have bonked his head already. But his brown eyes widened when he saw his pistol just out of arm's reach. He licked his lips and lunged from his seated position toward the gun.

I stomped on his wrist just as his fingers grazed the pistol's handle. I pressed down with my heel and twisted like I was squashing a bug.

The man shrieked and swung his free hand around to plant a lackluster punch on my thigh. I stepped off his wrist and reached down to grab him by the shirt, pulling him up eye level with me as I pressed his back into the wall. His panting breath smelled of onions and fear. He was the only man from the cartel who did not have some sort of facial hair, making him appear in his early twenties.

"Are you working for Manny Mendez?" I asked, not worried about apologizing for the spit that flew out of my lips and landed on his face.

The man was holding on to both of my forearms to support himself. If he let go, it would just be my grip around his shirt collar. One of his gold chains had broken and fell to the floor. He kicked his feet, but the blows felt nothing more than annoying mosquitos buzzing around my shins.

"Who do you work for?!" I snarled. "Tell me or end up like the rest of your asshole friends."

I jammed him harder into the wall, and he let out a desperate gasp for breath.

"Yes. Manny Mendez! Your brother! Now put me down."

The hell I would.

Instead, I laughed.

"You can tell Manny that if he wants his men to stop dying while I'm around, he needs to agree to meet with me. In private. Do you understand?"

The man nodded, breathing harder.

"Can you deliver him that message for me, or do I need to write it on a note and shove it up your ass?"

He nodded weakly, only making guttural sounds.

My hands had found their way around his neck, and I might have been squeezing a bit too hard.

Oops.

I released the man, and he collapsed to the floor, still gasping like he had just been saved from drowning. I picked up his pistol—a compact Beretta APX—and stuffed it into my waistband next to the Glock.

"Get the fuck out of here," I said. "If I see you again, it'll be the last time."

The man jumped up on wobbly legs and bolted out of the office without another word. I didn't know what Agent Duncan had in mind for this meeting with my brother, but I'd at least sent out the first invitation.

It was now up to Manny if he wanted to accept it.

Chapter 29

I called Lily to tell her we wouldn't be meeting at the diner tonight. She didn't answer, so I called the police station to let them know what had happened.

They were already aware, as Jo had called them upon fleeing the diner. I still hadn't seen her return and didn't blame her. Her place of business was in shambles. Well, at least the office portion was. The dining area and kitchen were untouched by any of the damage, save for a pair of bloody footprints that trailed out through the front door. Nothing some bleach wouldn't cure.

But we fucked up her office pretty good.

Dead bodies. Blood and brain splatters. And so much damage to the walls.

I waited in the office until the police arrived five minutes later. They immediately put up yellow tape to block off the crime scene.

Officer Collins was first to enter the office. He looked from the two dead bodies to the stains on the walls and ceiling, then back to me. "You took on these four guys by yourself?" he asked, as two other officers entered behind him. Richards and Billingsley, if I remembered correctly, from Sunday afternoon at Lily's house.

One of them stood mortified in the doorway. The other clutched his stomach and bolted out of the room.

"I did," I said, offering a smile I wasn't sure was appropriate.

Collins pinched his tongue between his lips and looked around, nodding. "Impressive. Just so we're clear, I don't have any bad blood toward you like..." he trailed off.

Like Matthews did.

The topic of Matthews was still too fresh.

"Thank you, sir," I said. "I'm not here to step on anyone's toes. But my options were to either kill these men or get killed myself."

"They're all dead?" Collins asked.

"I don't think that one is," I said, nodding to the man whose head I had smashed into the wall. "He's out cold. The other two are very dead."

Collins chuckled at this statement. "Cartel, I'm assuming?"

I nodded. "All four of them were. One got away. Don't think he'll be back around, either."

"Very good. Richards, make some calls to get all hands on deck. We're in for a long night of bagging evidence."

Richards. I knew it.

Richards nodded and spun out of the office a little too eagerly, pulling out his cell phone and pressing it against his ear.

"And you're in the clear, Mr. Mendez," Collins said. "Jo told us everything that happened. Says she has camera footage that will confirm it, too."

I looked around, and sure enough, a camera was mounted in the corner above the closet. I assumed Jo had more throughout the diner, so they'd have no issue piecing together what exactly happened. For once, I caught a break and wouldn't have to spend an evening in jail for self-defense.

After giving an official statement for the record, Collins jotted down my comments in a notepad and looked up at me with a forced grin.

"I take it you'll be staying in Hillcrest, right?" he asked.

I nodded. "Yes, sir. Still have some matters to tend to. Speaking of, why aren't the DEA agents here?"

Collins shrugged. "We told them what happened. Looked like they were in the middle of a rather intense conversation with someone on the phone. Not sure when they'll make it down here."

I pulled out my phone to check the time. Only 2:45. Apparently, time didn't fly when you were killing bad guys.

"I see," I said. "Must be why Lily didn't answer. Are you fine if I head back to my hotel? I'd like to get cleaned off."

I stuck out my arms to show the speckles of blood decorating my skin, none of it my own.

"That'll be fine," Collins said, so I made my way to exit the office.

"Mendez," Collins said when I reached the doorway. I stopped and turned back around. Collins's gaze lingered at his feet before coming back up to me.

"Yes, sir?"

"Thank you. We don't know how big this crime ring is, but they're down two members now. You didn't need to do any of this, but you're still here helping. And we owe you some thanks."

Officer Collins was one of the good ones.

I nodded appreciatively and left the diner to return to my hotel. I sent a text message to Lily, asking her to call me as soon as possible.

When I walked through the hotel lobby ten minutes later, I received more than a handful of curious gazes from everyone I strode by. I'm sure I looked like some crazed lunatic. And maybe I was. But I hadn't done anything tonight that I wouldn't do again if the situation called for it.

I washed off in the shower, blasting the heat and steam. The blood swirled around the drain before its scarlet trail disappeared into the void. To my delight, I only had one scratch on my back. Must have happened when the apron dude and I rolled into the closet. One against four and I barely needed a Band-Aid. I'd like to say we had a fair match, but clearly I had the upper hand. None of those guys knew shit about fighting and never had a chance.

Part of me wanted to feel bad for them. But fuck 'em.

I got out of the shower and turned on the TV to watch the news while I dried off and got dressed. A news anchor spoke in a concerned tone while explaining there had been some sort of a shootout at Jo's Diner. This was the local station that I'd seen show everything from news segments, city council voting, and plenty of infomercials during the wee hours of the night.

But it was the middle of the day, and the anchor, a woman by the name of Sarah Potter, looked sick while delivering the story.

"This is a developing story," she said, as the feed switched to a camera positioned across the street from the diner, where half a dozen police cars lined the block, all flashing their lights. Yellow tape circled the entrance as small huddles of officers chatted outside the building. "All we know at this time is that shots were fired. The diner's owner, Jo Ellen Walker, ran out of her business after being assaulted by a group of men who were dining in. We don't yet know who the men were, or who may have been injured."

Her voice faded into background noise as I focused on the screen. I saw Agent Duncan let himself under the tape and disappear into the diner. But still no Lily.

I pulled out my phone and sent her another text message.

Is everything okay?

The news changed stories and flashed the image of a teenage boy on the screen. My heart raced at seeing his grinning face.

"In other news," Sarah said, a more upbeat inflection in her voice. "Local teen Dominic Evans has woken from his coma. Doctors expect him to make a full recovery physically, and he is still being evaluated for any brain damage that may have been suffered."

The screen cut to a middle-aged woman with tears in her eyes. A graphic showed her name as Michelle Evans, Dominic's mother.

"We're beyond grateful our sweet Dom woke up today," she said in a strained voice. I could tell she'd been crying for at least the last two weeks, and probably had little to no sleep, judging from the heavy bags under her bloodshot eyes. "He's been very much himself and is itching to get on the basketball court. The doctor said if everything clears with his mental evaluation, he can be back on the court in two weeks." She paused and broke into hysterical sobs. "I just feel like God has given us a second chance with my baby boy, and I don't want to waste it. No one should. My message to all the parents in Hillcrest is to get more involved in your kids' lives. Ask them the uncomfortable questions, because if you don't, it could end up being too late. We have a problem in our town, and it's not going away."

I clicked off the TV. Dominic Evans would have answers. I needed to speak with him.

My phone buzzed, and it was a response from Lily.

Dinner at Carlo's. Same time?

That left me three hours until dinner.

I replied, *See you there.*

I knew Lily was under plenty of stress, but I couldn't understand why she hadn't shown up to the mayor's press conference after Matthews's death, and now the crime scene at the diner. Maybe she was on to something else and gave that all of her attention. She may have even wanted to take advantage of Duncan being occupied. She had mentioned he was more of a burden than a help in this case.

Send him to deal with the busy work while she made actual progress.

I grabbed my backpack, now equipped with two guns. The Glock 48 and my new Beretta. It was kind of girly for my liking, but I'd take whatever reinforcements I could get at this point.

Before dinner, I needed to stop at the hospital to ask Dominic Evans some questions.

Chapter 30

Hillcrest only had one hospital. It stood two levels with an attached parking garage. It was on the south side of town, so the drive took me about fifteen minutes, mostly because of the downtown area having several roads blocked off during the investigation at the diner. I was supposed to cut through the heart of town and save about five minutes, but this was my fault.

I just couldn't help myself when it came to bringing imme-diate justice to the low-life scum of the earth.

At 4:32, I stepped into the hospital lobby, which doubled as the emergency room waiting area. There were a handful of people waiting patiently, eyes glued to the TVs covering the unfolding scene at Jo's Diner. If these people only knew I was the one responsible for the two deaths that were now being reported by Sarah Potter.

I strolled up to the front desk, where a twenty-something nurse in light green scrubs blew a bubble of gum while clicking furiously on her computer.

She stopped and took her time looking at me from the bottom up. I supposed she hadn't encountered too many people of my size.

"Good evening, sir," she said politely enough. "How can I

help you?"

"Yes," I said. "I was hoping you can point me to the room of Dominic Evans."

She frowned immediately and looked me over a second time. "Are you a relative?" she asked, already doubting me if I said yes.

"I'm not," I said. "But I am a friend of the family. Do you know Dominic's mom? Michelle? She and I go way back. She told me about Dom last week, but I haven't been able to get up here—I live in L.A. I was already driving up to surprise her when I heard the news that Dom woke up. Such a miracle. But now this can be an even more joyous celebration for us."

I felt like I was rambling too much. Lying was one thing that ate away at my soul, but sometimes I had to do it for the greater good. I'd repent for this later.

The nurse chomped her gum in a way that reminded me of Chief Matthews, although the way she did it was more annoying and less assholey.

She kept studying me, trying to find a reason to call me out for lying, but coming up short.

"Okay," she said. "Room 208 upstairs. Just take the elevator at the end of the hallway and it should be one of the first doors on your right when you get to the second floor."

"Thank you," I said. "I can't wait to surprise the family."

She said nothing more as I spun away and started down the hallway. I passed several examination rooms with their doors closed and was practically jogging by the time I reached the elevator and pushed the call button.

The doors parted immediately, and I stepped in, pressing the button for the second floor. After the brief ascent, the doors opened, and a group of doctors and nurses stepped aside to let me pass before piling in. Behind all of them, however, was a familiar face who almost bumped into me because he was too focused on his notepad.

"Theo," I said, startling him into looking up at me like he had been doing something wrong. "What are you doing here?"

"Mr. Mendez," he said, and I couldn't tell if it was panic or excitement in his voice. Jo had said this man was impossible to read. He tucked his notepad into his breast pocket. "I was just here trying to get a quote from the Evans family. They were in no mood to talk and rushed me out of the room. Said Dominic was sleeping."

"Surprised you're here instead of down at the diner," I said. "Because that's a breaking news story."

Theo shrugged. "If I could be in two places at once. That's the bad part of being the only reporter in town. If two stories break, I have to pick one to focus on. Looks like I chose wrong today. Now, the big question is, what are *you* doing here? You killed two cartel men and show up at the hospital an hour later? Coming back for unfinished business? There are now two of those men on this floor, all thanks to you."

The guy I destroyed at the beach must have still been here. His friend who met the inside of Jo's drywall had likely arrived not too long ago.

"I came to speak to Dominic Evans," I said, and this made Theo whip his head up to me.

"What on earth for?" he asked, voice cracking slightly. He took a step back, no longer interested in returning to the elevator.

"To know where he got the drugs that almost killed him," I said.

"Well, they came from the cartel, didn't they?" Theo asked. "We never had a drug issue until these guys arrived in town."

"Sure," I said. "It's obviously the cartel. I don't need to talk to Dominic to know that. I *need* to know who specifically gave him those drugs. That way, I can trace it back to the source. I'll likely take down everyone who was involved along the way. He could have gotten the drugs from a kid at school. Most likely, in fact. I doubt Dominic ever wandered into Ted's Place looking to score. But where did the friends get it? And so on. I presume my quest will lead me back to the cartel, but I get the sense there are other people involved."

"Other people like who?" Theo asked, and I could hear the desperation in his voice. Even without his notepad, he was still taking notes in his head. This was too juicy for a local reporter to pass on.

I shrugged. "Who knows? Whenever the chief of police gets murdered, that means he pissed off the wrong person."

"You're saying Chief Matthews was involved?"

"No, I'm not saying that. I'm saying his death wasn't some random drive-by shooting. If the cartel has the presence in Hillcrest that we believe, then they saw a reason fit enough to kill the police chief. They don't do shit like that for the fun of it. Every move is deliberate."

Theo rubbed his forehead that had broken out in a light sweat. "This is like a movie. Drugs. Government insiders. I don't know what to think."

"You don't have to think anything," I said. "This is all speculation until there is actual proof. And I'm trying to find that proof. Now if you'll excuse me, Theo, I'd like to speak to Dominic, or at least his family."

I took a step, and Theo whipped out his hand to grab my

arm. I was surprised at the speed of his motion. Almost catlike. "I'm telling you, Jonny, don't go back there. The family is a mess right now. They're happy, then they're crying. Then they're fighting. This whole thing has put a strain on the parents. They're at each other's throats daily, trying to place blame. I'm not sure a stranger poking around and asking questions is the best idea right now."

"But it's fine when you show up?"

Theo raised his hands. "I'm no stranger. I've known the Evans family for over ten years. Who do you think covers the basketball games in this town? I like to think I play a small part in Dominic having college scouts attend his games."

"I see. Well, if you know the family that well, I'll take your word for it. Let's go."

I sensed Theo had planned to put up a fight to keep me from going into that room, so I pivoted back around and pressed the button to call the elevator back down. Two could play this game.

The elevator opened up, and we stepped in, riding back down in silence and crossing through the emergency room waiting area without a word.

When we stepped outside, Theo said, "I appreciate you respecting the family's wishes, Jonny. Not everyone is so courteous these days, especially with a high-profile case like this. If you'd like, I can speak to Dom's parents and arrange a time for you to meet with them. When they're up to it, of course."

"That would be ideal," I said, clapping Theo on the back. If you wanted someone to believe you were going along with their shenanigans, you might as well sell it. "I appreciate it, Theo. Glad to know you're willing to help with the investigation. I'll look forward to your call. The sooner we can arrange that meeting, the better."

"Will do, Jonny," Theo said, and he offered his sweaty hand for me to shake.

We parted ways in the parking lot, and I reached my car first, pulling out of the lot without a moment's hesitation. I kept my eyes on the rear-view mirror and watched as Theo pulled out behind me and took an immediate right turn.

I flipped a bitch and raced back to the hospital. Theo was skittish and lacked any confidence in his ability to lie. He avoided eye contact and was sweating profusely by the time we parted.

Theo Rambis was full of shit, and I was going back into that hospital to find out why.

Chapter 31

Knowing where I was going now, I marched through the lobby and hallway like a man on a hellbent mission.

It didn't bother me when professional criminals lied to my face. It was part of the territory. No one wanted to admit the truth, even with a gun pressed against their forehead. But for someone to lie to me with no skill whatsoever offended me beyond belief.

And I was hard to offend. It didn't even bother me when Ted and his drunk buddy had called me Bean Boy. I loved a good joke. Racial, sexual, it didn't matter. The more politically incorrect, the better. I was an older Millennial, only a few years from being Gen X. We grew up with *Beavis and Butthead* and *South Park.* I remember when all jokes were fair. Before the world turned people into a soft pile of sensitive Sallys.

But Theo lying to me pissed me off more than anything since I'd arrived. I now wanted to solve this case tonight, just to prove a point to the little shithead.

I reached the second floor and headed straight for Dominic's room. When I stepped in, Dominic was wide awake, talking with his parents, who were sitting next to him in two chairs. Michelle was holding her son's hand while Dominic spoke.

I recognized him immediately from the yearbook picture that had been floating around the news coverage. His sandy, spiked hair lay matted down with a couple of clumps standing upright.

The conversation ended the moment I strolled in, all three pairs of eyes immediately looking me over.

"Is there something we can help you with?" the father asked, standing up. His joints creaked as he rose to his feet. His face was sunken, cheek bones protruding beneath the black bags under his eyes. He looked like he hadn't eaten since the start of Dom's coma.

"Hello Mr. and Mrs. Evans," I said. "Dominic. My name is Jonny Mendez, and I'm working with the DEA to bust the drug ring spreading across Hillcrest. I was hoping to have a few words."

Mr. Evans exchanged a glance with his wife while Dominic kept staring at me.

"Come in, Mr. Mendez," Michelle said, also standing up. She released her hand from Dominic's and extended it my way. She looked tired, as I had just seen on the TV not long ago. But she seemed like a burden had been taken off her shoulders. She brushed back her graying brown hair and offered a small grin. "My name is Michelle, and this is my husband, Charles."

I stepped in all the way and extended my hand across Dominic's bed, shaking with both Michelle and Charles. "A pleasure to meet you," I said.

"Apologies, Mr. Mendez," Michelle said. "But we weren't expecting any company today. We usually get a call to alert when someone is on the way."

"No need for apologies," I said. "And I don't want to take much of your time. I'm sure you have lots of catching up to do."

"You said you were with the DEA?" Charles asked, sitting back down and folding his hands on his lap.

"Yes, sir."

"We haven't heard from you guys since Dom first went into his coma. Some blonde lady and a grumpy man spoke with us and assured us they would get to the bottom of this."

Charles spoke with a mixture of disgust and sorrow in his voice.

"It takes time, Mr. Evans, and I assure you, our team is working around the clock. We're making progress I can't exactly share details about, but that's why I'm here. Do you mind if I ask Dominic some questions?"

"Do you feel up to it, Dom?" Michelle asked her son.

His bed was already in the elevated position, so he adjusted his body to sit more upright. "Yes," he said, voice clear and focused.

Not a damn thing Theo had told me appeared to be true so far. Michelle and Charles were now holding hands, stroking the inside of each other's wrists. Dom had definitely not just woken up.

"Go ahead, Mr. Mendez," Michelle said.

I cleared my throat. "First off, we're glad you're back with us, Dominic. Everyone in town has been praying for your recovery, and it sounds like those prayers were answered."

"Thank you," Dominic said, cracking a smile.

"Now, like I mentioned, we've made some progress in our investigation. We have some suspects, but I need to work backwards to see if the paths cross. Can you tell me who you got the drugs from?"

Dominic looked at his mother, the smile wiped away.

"Really?" Charles said, releasing his grip from Michelle's hand. "All that progress and you come in here asking the same question everyone else has asked hundreds of times? This entire process has left me with zero faith in our justice system."

"Mr. Evans, I'm new to this case," I said, dreading that I already needed to lie again. "Just got here yesterday. I specialize in interrogating suspects, and that's why I'm here. I just need the complete picture before I can proceed with that portion of my job. Nothing in my files shows this being discussed already."

Michelle nodded. "It's fine, Charlie. Mr. Mendez, we have answered that question several times to the local police."

"Ah," I said. "Well, that explains why I don't know. Funnily enough, the police don't share their reports with the DEA, and vice versa. And if you haven't met with anyone from the DEA since the start of the coma, that's why we don't have that detail."

Charles couldn't wipe the frown off his face, glaring at me like he didn't believe a damn word I said. I wasn't sure how much of what I said was true. But no one had asked to see any credentials, so they must have trusted me enough.

"The kid's name was Andy," Michelle said. "That's all we know."

She looked at Dominic, who nodded in agreement. "I met him at a party. Andy. He didn't go to our school. Said he was a friend of a friend. Offered me a pill, saying it would relax me and allow me to have a better time. I don't drink like the other kids, so I thought trying the pill would let me achieve some sort of high. I took it, and that was the last thing I remember before waking up today."

"And what did this Andy person look like?" I asked.

Dominic drew in a deep breath. "Hispanic. Probably just a little older than us seniors. I saw him talking to just about everyone at the party, so I'm not sure who he came with."

"Did you see anyone else taking pills from him?"

Dominic shook his head. "Not that I saw. But like I said, he was talking to everyone. And with me, he was discreet. Bumped into me in the hallway after I came out of the bathroom. We were the only two in the hallway, and he was speaking quietly."

"Had you seen him at other parties before?" Some pieces were coming together for me, and I was growing queasy at the unfolding realization.

"Not that I remember," Dominic said, suddenly looking down like shame had just struck him on the back of the head. "This was also my first party with no adults present."

I had apparently struck a nerve with Dominic having to relay this last bit, so I changed the subject. "I think I've heard enough about that, Dominic. Thank you for sharing. This helps tremendously."

"Thank you, Mr. Mendez," he said. "I hope it helps stop whatever is going on. I'd hate for this to happen to any of my classmates. They may not get so lucky and wake up like I did."

"We're working tirelessly," I said. "And I can guarantee you I won't be leaving Hillcrest until this matter is resolved." I turned to his parents. "I have a question for you two if you're comfortable answering."

"Sure," Charles said, sounding more at ease.

"Theo Rambis was just here trying to get a quote from you," I said. "I'm just curious what type of questions he asked you."

Charles and Michelle looked at each other, confused.

"I'm sorry," Michelle said. "Theo who? No one has visited us today besides Sarah Potter from the news station. Set up her cameras and stuff in the family waiting room down the hallway. But she's been gone for a few hours now."

"Theo Rambis," I repeated. "He's the editor for the *Hillcrest Daily*."

Recognition flickered through both of them.

"Oh, Theo Rambis," Charles said. "The reporter, Michelle."

Michelle nodded. "We know who that is, but he hasn't been here."

"And you've been in this room all day?" I asked.

"At least one of us has," Charles said. "I stayed back while Michelle did that interview with the news lady. Didn't want her to. It's no one's business what's going on with Dom. But she insisted."

He didn't sound too angry at this. More like he had accepted defeat and had to concede to his wife's wishes. Again, no intense bickering or being at each other's throats like Theo had suggested.

"Interesting," I said. "I passed him when I came in and just assumed he was here to interview you. Must have been here for someone else."

"Definitely wasn't in here," Michelle confirmed again.

"Do you know Theo at all? You must, if he covers the basketball games."

"I can't say we know him too well," Charles said. "We *see* him at all the games. He'll sometimes get a quote from Dominic after a win, but I'd say we've probably spoken to the man two or three times in total."

What the actual fuck?

Perhaps Theo was a better liar than I gave him credit for. His first lie was weak, but I let him think it had gotten me out of the hospital. But there were more layers to it. He now had me standing in this hospital making a fool of myself. But why would he have made up the entire story about the Evans family knowing him? What did he gain from that?

"I see," I said. "On that note, I should go back to the office. Thank you all for your time today."

I hurried out of the hospital room, not giving them a chance to respond. I felt like I had done something wrong and didn't need them calling me out.

Fuck you, Theo Rambis.

I wasn't supposed to be leaving the hospital with more questions than when I arrived, but that was exactly what happened. Thoughts swirled around my head as I took the elevator down and dashed out of the building.

Theo. Andy the drug dealer. Theo lying about why he was in the hospital. Was he just trying to sneak a picture? See Dominic for himself? He was no friend of the family, which means his fabricated story had only one purpose.

To keep me away from Dominic.

And if he wanted me away, that could only mean Theo had something to hide.

I only had two hours until dinner now and couldn't pursue Theo until later. But there was something about him. I couldn't make the leap and assume he was involved with the cartel. His personality suggested otherwise. Those men would chew him up like a stick of gum and spit him out when they were done.

But he *was* hiding something. And I'd be damned if I didn't find out what.

Chapter 32

It didn't take long for me to figure out who Andy the drug dealer was. Could he even be called a drug dealer if he was handing out pills for free?

I knew the practice. Give these kids a sample, and if they liked the way it made them feel, then they became repeat customers. A loss leader, as it's known in the business world.

I didn't think the Evans clan was fluent in two languages. But I was. Once Dominic told me the drug dealer was a Hispanic man slightly older than him, that narrowed the pool of suspects to one person.

My nephew.

Andres is the Spanish version of the name Andrew. Andy is commonly a shortened nickname for Andrew.

It was the perfect scheme, and I understood that was Andres's actual purpose for being in Hillcrest. He wasn't running the front at the Hamburger Stand. No. His job was to get in with the high schoolers and get them hooked on the pills. Customer acquisition.

The thought made my blood boil. My nephew may have already been too far gone if he was involved at this level. As much as I wanted to save everyone, sometimes I had to let them go down their own paths of destruction.

This added an obstacle. My plan was to follow the trail and beat up everyone along the way to the top of the cartel. But I couldn't do that to my nephew, even if I'd never formally met the kid. He had my mom's blood—*my* blood—pumping in his veins. I couldn't discount that simple fact. Plus, if I harmed him, or took him hostage, I'd have the entire cartel on my case.

I needed to skip Andres in the hierarchy and find out who was also taking direct orders from my brother. I also needed to learn what the fuck Theo Rambis was up to lurking around the hospital for no apparent reason.

But that all had to wait. I sat in the park again to think this through. The same bench was open from last time, so I happily took it like the creature of habit I am.

A flock of geese scattered about the grass, honking their conversations among each other, dropping shit for the rest of us to navigate around later. My mind had fallen into my past, urging me to remember my brother for who he had been instead of who he became. I supposed my subconscious was trying to talk me out of killing my brother. Or preparing me for it.

After an hour at the park, I went back to my room to freshen up. Splash water on my face, reapply deodorant, mouthwash. The full service.

I was done waiting for anyone to apply labels. Tonight's dinner was a date. Hopefully I could brighten up Lily's week and we could seal a delightful evening with a kiss goodnight.

I drove to Carlo's and parked around the corner of the block. Downtown was quiet, even for a Wednesday afternoon. With all the drama unfolding at the diner, I supposed people weren't in the mood to go out to dinner. The public would start piecing together their own conclusions. Some would start theories and rumors. We had to end this shit quickly, before matters got even more out of hand.

I checked the *Hillcrest Daily* website and found nothing beyond the same headlines about two men being shot to death at Jo's Diner. Still no word on the victims' names. With Mayor Reece already aware the cartel was in town, he might have been ordering Theo—and Sarah—to withhold certain details. Of course, that wasn't something he could actually enforce, but if they had strong enough personal relationships outside of the public eye, there was no extent to which the favors could go to one another.

I waited outside of Carlo's, leaning against the brick exterior and planting one foot against the wall. I peeked through the entrance and saw a handful of tables filled with people. A slow night indeed.

Lily's car appeared from the north end of the road. She crept past the restaurant and parked at a meter forty feet away. I strode over, reaching into my backpack's front zipper where I kept change and fed several coins into the machine until it showed two hours.

Lily got out of her car, hair frazzled. Her puffy eyes were red like she had just cried for an hour straight.

My stomach immediately sank. This no longer felt like a date. Lily was going through some shit, and I needed to be there for her.

"Lily, what's wrong?" I asked as she circled around the car to greet me on the sidewalk. She looked me in the eye, then threw her arms around my shoulders for a hug. I squeezed her back, feeling her heart beating against my chest.

She pulled back, sniffling and wiping her nose. "Everything

is wrong, Jonny. Every damn thing."

"Should we not go inside?" I asked, ready to take Lily wherever she wanted.

"Oh, we're going inside," she said, wiping at her eyes, pressing into the swollen flesh like that would help. "I haven't eaten since breakfast and am starving. We have a lot to talk about, and a glass of wine would be great."

I nodded. "Okay. Wine it is. Let's go."

She didn't wait for me and spun around on her heels to head into the restaurant. Lily wore jeans and a baggy windbreaker over a solid T-shirt. A date was the furthest thing from her mind, but it was obvious so much more was on her mind.

We went into Carlo's, and the host seated us within seconds. This time, we had a window table overlooking Main Street.

Lily promptly grabbed her glass of water that had already been served and chugged it like she just finished a week-long journey through the desert. When someone was in a bad mood, I kept a hands-off approach until understanding what they wanted. I remained silent as a server brought us a basket of bread, and Lily scarfed two slices without a peep. She seemed to have the crying under control, and her eyes were looking better compared to when she had pulled up.

She had news to deliver. Bad news. I could always sense that shift in the universe right before someone was going to tell me something I didn't want to hear. When my aunt told me my brother had run away—granted, I had an idea. Later, I sensed it before the doctors told me my aunt had passed away on the operating table. And when the Navy doctors told me I could no longer be a SEAL because of my failed hearing test.

All three instances were preceded by a heavy weight draped over my shoulders. Like a fifty-pound blanket I couldn't remove. The feeling returned tonight at our window-side table in Carlo's.

Lily kept her gaze down at the menu. She hadn't made eye contact since we sat down. I didn't quite feel like she was mad at me, but I wasn't sure. Did I cross a line by killing those two men today? I had little choice. But maybe the complete story had not been relayed to Lily.

Our server came over, a young man with too much perkiness for the situation. "Good evening, you two!" he said, clapping his hands together, a wide grin revealing pearly whites. "Can I start you off with any drinks?"

"A bottle of your finest red wine," I said, not giving Lily a chance to speak. Not that she would. She still hadn't looked up.

"Absolutely, sir," the server said. "And I'll bring a fresh water for the lady. Any appetizers catching your eye tonight?"

"Not at the moment," I said. "Just the wine would be nice."

"You got it!"

The guy actually gave me a thumbs up before walking away. Under different circumstances, we'd probably be laughing up a storm over our spirited server. Instead, we sat in silence.

After another minute, Lily finally looked up, her sky-blue eyes studying my face.

"Jonny," she finally said, her voice distraught. She shook her head, and her eyes welled up with tears again.

I extended my hand across the table, palm up and open, and gestured for her to place her hand in mine. "Just tell me, Lily."

She pulled her hand up from beneath the table and caressed my wrist before wrapping her fingers tightly around mine. The grip was intense, like she never wanted to let go.

"It's all over, Jonny," she said.

"What's over?" I asked, growing nauseous. Surely she couldn't have meant us. We hadn't even started anything to be over.

"They're pulling me off this case and sending me back to D.C."

Lily let those words linger, and I frowned as the reality settled in.

"Are you shitting me?" I asked, squeezing her hand back.

Lily shook her head. "I wish. I was on the phone all afternoon with the D.C. office. It all ended with a call from the deputy director telling me they have to shake things up because no progress is being made."

"But that's not true."

"I know. Lots of progress has been made. They just want to see more, I guess."

The server returned with our bottle and saw we were deep in an intense conversation. He kept quiet while pouring wine into our glasses and left without a word.

"Did Duncan have something to do with this?" I asked.

"I honestly have no idea," she said. "I saw Duncan this morning. Everything was fine between us. He was gone for lunch when the phone calls started, and I haven't seen him since. I texted him, asking if he knew about any of this. He claims he did not. Then I called him after they officially pulled me off the case. He didn't answer, but now I see there was a lot going on. I'm not even allowed to go near the diner right now."

"This is bullshit," I said. "Do you want me to make some calls? I still have lots of contacts in the CIA."

Lily shook her head. "You and I both know that won't fix

anything. The DEA doesn't give a damn what the CIA says to them. Unless you know the president, I'm not sure there's anything that can be done."

Unfortunately, I had not met the current president. That had been a perk of being one of the best special ops agents in the SEALS and CIA. Recognition dinners at the White House. The food was out of this world.

"When do you have to leave?" I asked.

"Tonight," Lily said sternly. I could feel her rage emitting from across the table. "They booked me a red-eye. I'll head to the airport from here. Sorry, Jonny. I thought we'd have more time together."

I loosened my grip and brushed my thumb along the inside of her wrist. "You have nothing to apologize for. This isn't your fault. This is a conspiracy, if anything. If they wanted to shake things up, why does Duncan get to stay?"

Lily shrugged. "He has seniority over me. They'll be sending a new agent for him to work with until the conclusion. Someone more seasoned. Whatever the hell that means."

"Seniority? What a crock of shit! There's nothing you can do?"

Lily shook her head. She seemed relieved now that she had shared this information, but still plenty distraught. "My direct supervisor called me first, letting me know this was likely going to happen. Then we got on the phone with his supervisor. I told them everything that had been going on with Duncan since we arrived here. He's been lazy. Checked out. Zero focus on our case. I spent an hour going through my files and notes, sharing every bit of progress we've made."

"Did you tell them about me?" I asked.

"Of course not. If they knew I had you helping us out, they'd have you removed from Hillcrest. That's the only reason I believe Duncan wasn't involved with any of this. Because if he had been, he would have mentioned you. We both know he'd jump on any chance to see you tossed out of town."

I nodded. "Maybe. He might see my value now, but I'm not entirely sure."

"How do you mean?"

"That morning at the diner, Duncan called me over to the table with him, the mayor, and Theo Rambis. They want me to meet with my brother. In private. And they want me to kill him."

"Jonny!" Lily cried, slapping the top of the table. "You can't do that. Way too risky. They're only using you. That's completely dirty, and I'm appalled Duncan even suggested such a thing."

"That may be so," I said, watching Lily take a sip of wine. "But I'm not against it. Manny has the most power of anyone in Hillcrest right now. If he's gone, the others will flee. That's just how these things go. I've seen it before with terrorist organizations, mafias, you name it."

"He's your brother, Jonny," Lily said, softening her tone. She was done crying, and compassion returned to her eyes. She allowed a soft grin and reached out for my hand again. "You may think you're talking yourself into this need to kill him, and I'm sure you have a lot of personal reasons to justify it. But when it comes time to do the deed, it's not going to be as simple as you think."

My body was stiff with tension. "What makes you think that?"

"Because you're a good man, Jonny," Lily said, and with those words, combined with her fingers dancing along my forearm, the electricity between us returned like a sudden bolt of lightning. "I know you have a reputation to maintain and a facade to uphold as a big, bad, tough guy. But you're genuine. You care about people. Just because your brother became a criminal doesn't erase the good times you shared with him. That will all come crashing down when you see him again."

My throat was nearly clenched shut. Was I about to cry? I snatched my glass of water and took a long swig. "I've killed people I didn't want to kill. It's part of the job, and I understand. You're right. I'll always have a spot in my heart for my brother. Nothing can take that away. But he's an evil man. He's corrupted my nephew. Poor kid never had a shot at a good life. Sometimes you just have to remove evil from the world and move on with your life. It's not like my brother has tried to reach out to me after all these years. He abandoned me, and now I'm comfortable being alone. It's his own fault I've already grieved losing him. That just leaves one thing left for him and me."

Lily sighed, still playing with my arm. "I just wish I could be here for you, Jonny. To comfort you afterwards."

"I know," I said, and our server returned to take our food orders. Lily ordered a seafood platter, and I asked for a bowl of fettucine alfredo with extra chicken. Once we were alone again, I said, "I need whatever information you can give me about Theo Rambis."

"Theo? What's he got to do with any of this?"

I told her about our encounter at the hospital and the lies he told to get me out of the building.

"Interesting," she said. "We don't really have anything about him. He's never been mentioned as a suspect. I can get you his home address and phone number, though."

"That's perfect," I said. "I'm not convinced he's tied up with any of this, but something feels out of place. I just want to check it out."

"So many loose ends in this case," Lily said, drinking more wine. "All these dead bodies belong to the cartel. I've been pushing that fact on Duncan, but he's refusing to accept it until we have sufficient proof. If he were to agree to that, he'd be able to get more resources out here. His closed-mindedness is going to get more people killed. Hopefully, none of the future victims are innocent bystanders."

Our food came ten minutes later, and we allowed the conversation around the case to fizzle away. Dinner flew by, knowing Lily would be off to the airport as soon as we finished. Why did the clock do things like that? We talked about our favorite parts of Hillcrest.

Lily would miss Carlo's and Jo's Diner. I promised to thank Jo on Lily's behalf for all she had done. And that reminded me of the breath mints I had in the backpack from breakfast that morning. My bag was on the back of my seat, so I twisted around to retrieve them and plopped a pile of fifteen mints in front of Lily's plate.

Her mouth widened into a grin immediately, and she pulled the pile in towards her. "You sure know the way to my heart," she said.

"If only," I replied, and a palpable sense of dread lingered between us.

No food remained on our plates. The wine bottle had been emptied. And the soft Italian jazz playing through the speakers teased us with a romance that would never be. It always held true in my life. If someone got close to me, I could guarantee they'd get taken away.

We had a genuine connection, so naturally it was time for Lily to go.

She paid the check, more out of spite toward the DEA. "These assholes can cover our dinner tonight!"

Lily popped a peppermint candy into her mouth, slipped the remaining pile into her jacket pocket, and grabbed another handful on our way out of the restaurant. If TSA had rules against flying with the round red-and-white candies, Lily would get sent to prison in a heartbeat.

The night had turned cloudy, blocking out the moon and making it much darker than usual. A chilly breeze rushed along Main Street, kicking up swirls of dust and debris. We walked hand in hand toward Lily's car.

"Do I need to give your gun back now?" I asked.

Lily laughed. "No. You need it more than me. Just keep it, and I'll have the DEA get me a new backup. I'll tell them I forgot to pack it since they made me leave in such a rush."

"Those assholes," I said, earning a smile from Lily. "Won't you get in trouble for leaving a firearm behind?"

Lily shrugged. "A reprimand, sure. That's not anywhere near as bad as getting pulled off a case. What a slap in the face."

She seemed happy as she moved in front of me when we reached her car parked along the curb. She put her hands on my chest and looked up into my eyes. Our gazes locked, and it felt like we were the only two people in the world at that moment.

Lily gulped, then stood on her tiptoes, her face inches from mine. I lowered my head, and our lips met.

It was everything I imagined. The peppermint from her

candy had that icy sting as I breathed her in. Our lips parted and our tongues found each other. When she swirled hers against the roof of my mouth, the mint she had still been working on slipped into my mouth.

Lily pulled back, laughing as she raised a hand to cover her face. "Oh my God, that's embarrassing!"

I chuckled back, sucking on the half-dissolved mint now. It helped get the garlic and wine off my breath instantly. "Still tastes good," I said. "Don't worry about it."

"This has never happened," she said, still embarrassed.

"You often kiss men with a mint in your mouth?"

She giggled. "Not often, but I can't say I've never done it."

"I think you have a problem, Lily. Is there a Peppermints Anonymous I can sign you up for? I'll drive you to all the meetings if you need."

Lily clutched her stomach and howled with laughter. We both needed that.

When the laughing stopped, the moment we'd been dreading finally came.

She gave me one final peck on the lips. "It's time for me to go. I'll never forget you, Jonny Mendez."

"You don't want to stay in touch?" I asked.

She shook her head. "You and I both know we're not the type of people to entertain a long-distance relationship. This will just be a moment we shared in passing. I'll miss you."

She was right.

"Me too," I said. "Be safe out there."

We hugged, and I watched Lily get back into her car, start the engine, and drive away.

She didn't look at me again. It would have been too hard for both of us.

Just like that, Lily was gone, and I had to navigate the rest of this case as I knew best.

Alone.

Chapter 33

I woke the next morning much later than I had planned to sleep. After Lily drove off, my energy was shot. I had no interest in tailing anyone late in the night and just wanted to sleep off my emotions.

And it worked.

Of course, part of me still longed for Lily. I could still taste the faintest trace of the breath mint. Her hands on my chest. Her lips against mine.

Fuck the bureaucracy.

All that aside, I was well rested. The rain had started shortly after I climbed into bed and was still going. The steady white noise it provided kept me relaxed during the night, and I slept like a rock.

Starting the morning off with pure determination in my heart was never a bad thing. I showered quickly, not from being in a rush, but from having too much eagerness to do the next thing. I called these instances "productivity highs," and I never wasted them. Today, I had every intent of entering Theo Rambis's home. Lily had graciously texted me his address shortly after we had parted.

That man was hiding something, and every instinct in my body was on fire, knowing he was somehow tied to all this.

He knew the mayor, Agent Duncan, and had kept particular headlines out of the public view. Being a journalist, I could only assume he had a thirst for information. Even if he wasn't publishing every little detail, he at least knew them. If I could catch him off guard at home, I could push him into giving me valuable information.

I turned on the TV while I finished getting ready, curious to see what the local news station had to say.

Dominic was still in the headlines scrolling across the bottom. The weather segment was currently on, an older man explaining how the current rainstorm was expected to last well into the night. The next four days would have lots of rain on and off, so cancel those beach plans.

The beach was the furthest thing from my mind.

After combing my hair, I grabbed my backpack, still with the Glock and Beretta inside, and headed for the door. I'd grab breakfast downstairs before heading out. I needed to see where Theo lived and get a feel for his property. Did he have back doors or windows I could try to slip through? How close were his neighbors? Details like this determined when I could enter his home with the best odds of not being caught.

And this time around, I had to be extra cautious. If Theo called the cops and they caught me, my time in Hillcrest was over. Hell, being a sitting duck in a jail cell in a town where several cartel members wanted me dead could mean my time in this life was over. Every case I'd ever worked on seemed to reach this point of no return. No mistakes, as one simple error could spiral into failure or death.

I'd understood from an early age there was no such thing as perfection. Or luck. All you can do is put yourself in the best possible position for success. But perfection was like the devil in your conscience, always whispering and tempting. And now I was putting an extra layer of pressure on myself to see this through.

For Lily.

She'd put enough time and energy into this case to see it end. Even though the DEA had sent her back to D.C., I knew she'd still check on the progress.

I slipped on my windbreaker jacket as I reached my door, then pulled it open.

Something caught my attention on the floor just before I stepped out. My heart raced when I saw it, and my subconscious immediately tried convincing me it was anything else.

But I knew what it was. And what it meant.

I squatted down for closer examination and grew nauseous once I confirmed the lone object was a red and white peppermint candy.

Fuck.

Lily wouldn't have come all this way to leave some romantic gesture before heading to the airport. She would have knocked and wanted to talk one more time.

The cartel liked to play mind games, and this was their next move in this chess match. They'd been watching long enough to know Lily was obsessed with these candies. Had they seen me give her that pile in the restaurant last night? There was no saying who in this town hadn't been paid off by the cartel to help their cause.

They had Lily, and they were using her as bait to lure me. They could have left the candy at Agent Duncan's place, or even the police station, but they chose me.

I wondered if asking to move rooms would be worth my while but decided it didn't matter. No one in this town had a clue which room was mine, not even Lily, yet they still found me.

I picked up the candy and returned inside my room, tossing the mint into my backpack and pulling out the cell phone.

I tried Lily's number first, but it went straight to voicemail. They probably tossed her phone into a ditch or down a sewage drain.

Lucky for me, Lily's voicemail had been set for this case still, and she left Duncan's phone number as a second point of contact.

I hung up and dialed him.

"Agent Duncan," he answered, sounding focused on something else. I heard the clatter of a keyboard in the background.

"Duncan," I said. "It's Jonny."

The keyboard stopped promptly. "Jonny? Why are you calling?"

"They have Lily."

"Who has Lily?"

"God dammit, Duncan, now's not the time. The cartel has Lily."

"Whoa, big guy, slow down," Duncan said, with something that sounded like a weak laugh. "That's a pretty big accusation. Besides, Lily flew home last night. Did she not tell you what happened?"

I couldn't tell if there was a sick satisfaction in his voice. I thought there was, but I was also ready to throw this man off a bridge. That feeling always made it difficult to make a fair judgment.

"She told me everything, asshole," I said. I didn't care what Lily said about Duncan. She shouldn't have ruled out his involvement so quickly. I didn't trust the guy. "I'm well aware she was supposed to be on a flight back east last night, but she never got on that plane. She's still in Hillcrest, and I'm willing to bet she's in that mansion. I swear to God, if they hurt her, I'm going to burn this city to the fucking ground."

"Jonny, take a breath," Duncan said with a chuckle. Why was he taking this so calmly? "How do you know they have her? Let's start there."

"They left a breath mint outside my door. The kind she was always eating."

Duncan let out a full on laugh now. "A breath mint? Jonny, if an agent was in trouble, I'd have no issue getting additional resources out here. But no one is going to sign off that request because of a breath mint. That's not exactly proof of anything. How do you know the mint didn't fall out of your pockets when you took out your room key?"

"I didn't have any of those damn candies on me last night," I said through gritted teeth. If I could just reach through the phone and squeeze this weasel's throat, I'd get a whole ten seconds of satisfaction. "I gave the last of the candies I had to Lily. They've been watching her. That's the only way they could know about the candies."

"And they know where you're staying, too, I suppose," Duncan said mockingly. "Even I know you're staying at those suites on the north side of town. This isn't enough, Jonny."

The phone was shaking in my hand. If I squeezed any harder, it might have exploded. It had happened before, so I needed to keep my emotions in check.

I lowered my voice and said, "If you're not going to do anything, then I will. And if I get involved, I don't want to hear any bullshit from you about how many dead bodies there are. Because there will be many. I promise."

Duncan sighed. "Okay, Jonny, I can look into it. Let me start by making some calls to see if Lily boarded the plane last night. If I get confirmation she did, will you let this go?"

"I'll feel better about it, but not entirely until I hear from her directly."

"Fair enough. Give me twenty minutes. Can I call you back on this number?"

"Yes, I'll keep the phone next to me."

"Good. And Jonny, don't go doing anything stupid. Okay?"

I swallowed hard, my throat having tensed up. "Just call me right away."

I hung up and opened the search bar on my phone. The airlines would have no way of lying about a customer being on board or not. I fully expected Duncan to call back with word that Lily had not boarded the plane, but I desperately wanted the opposite to be true.

I couldn't sit around for twenty minutes, not under these circumstances. In the search bar I typed, *HUNTING STORE NEAR ME.*

The results came up, and I bolted out of the hotel building.

Chapter 34

I arrived at Big Ed's Outdoor and Hunting store ten minutes later. The rain had softened, but still came down steadily. The shop opened at ten o'clock, and it appeared I was the first customer of the day when I strolled through the entrance.

To my right were a handful of tents on display, along with a wall of fishing poles. To my left were racks of clothing. Camouflage. I sifted through the racks until I found pants and a jacket of the darker green variety.

A long hallway stretched to the back of the store, where a glass counter held smaller guns. Rifles were mounted to the wall below the head of an elk watching over the shop. I passed sleeping bags, thermal clothing, portable grills, and first-aid kits while whisking to the back of the store. I spotted a rack with camouflage makeup kits and took one to match my new attire.

I proceeded to the back counter, where I was greeted by a heavyset man with a thick brown beard. He had long, scraggly hair, and what appeared to be breadcrumbs in his beard.

"Morning, sir," he said in a deep baritone. "Anything I can help you with?"

He eyed the clothes and makeup in my hands.

"Good morning," I said. "I was hoping to look at your

hunting knives."

"Certainly. This way."

He turned and started along behind the counter. We passed all the guns and reached a small counter full of knives. At least twenty in total on display. Orange price tags were stuck to the handle of each, the prices ranging from fifteen to four hundred dollars.

I spotted a thirty-dollar all-black folding knife. It was beautiful and would get the job done.

"I want that one," I said, pointing at it through the case.

The man nodded. "That's a popular knife. Kershaw Shuffle. The grip fits naturally into the hand, probably better than most of the others. You got a hunting trip coming up?"

I knew why he was asking this question. It wasn't anywhere near hunting season. Fortunately, I knew that because I met a group of guys in basic training for the SEALs who were obsessed with hunting. They had sought permission to leave for three days for a quick hunting trip and returned with an elk.

My life was filled with enough killing that I never felt the urge to take it out on any animals.

"No hunting trip," I said, dropping my clothes on the countertop and crossing my arms. "I'm taking a camping trip deep into the woods, though, and want to be prepared. You never know."

The man cracked a grin that revealed teeth stained brown from excessive tobacco chewing. I could smell the minty scent when he spoke. He trusted me now. I wasn't just some asshole with a fabricated story about why I needed this gear in the middle of March. "Don't need any guns or ammo?" he asked, his inner salesman waking up.

Shit, good call.

"Actually, I could use some ammo. I have a Glock 48."

"Nine mil?"

"Yes, sir. I'll just need fifty rounds."

I had to stay within my limited budget.

"Let me grab your knife and ammo from the back," he said, turning around and disappearing through a curtain hanging over a doorway.

My phone buzzed, and I immediately whipped it out of my pocket to answer.

"Duncan," I said. "What did you find out?"

Duncan sighed. "You're right, Jonny. Lily never boarded that flight last night. We've located her cell phone and found the coordinates lead to a field just outside of town. A team is headed out to check the area, but I think they just dumped her phone."

"Fuck," I said, dreading this moment. "How could this happen? Was she supposed to drive straight to the airport?"

"That was the plan," Duncan said, and I heard the concern slipping into his voice. He realized this case had gotten a lot more serious. Perhaps he should have been putting in more effort from the start.

"Duncan, who all knew about Lily needing to leave last night?" I asked in as stern a voice as I could muster. "From Hillcrest?"

I heard his heavy breathing through the phone. "Shit, Jonny, everyone around the police station knew. They heard Lily shouting into the phone earlier in the day. Saw her crying. Walking out of the station with a box of her stuff like she had just been fired."

"How do you know all this?" I asked. "Weren't you at the

diner all afternoon?"

"Rambis told me everything. Not sure if he was there or had a source. I was there during the morning, though." Duncan lowered his voice. "I couldn't hang around. Our boss called me the night before and let me know what was going to happen to Lily. I couldn't bear the thought of watching her suffer through all that."

Rambis? That fuck.

"So you left her out to dry on her own. What an incredible friend and partner you are. No wonder she had nothing but bad things to say about you."

Duncan sighed. "I deserve that. But that doesn't matter right now, Jonny. We need to rescue her."

"We? Didn't you say you would have a full team out here if Lily was missing?"

"Yes, and they're on the way, but they don't just make moves based on instinct. They want proof of her location before raiding a place."

"How the hell can we prove she's in that mansion?"

"I'm afraid we can't. Unless we get lucky and snap a picture of Lily standing at the window. We haven't found any evidence this entire time linking the drug crimes back to that mansion. That's why progress has been stalled."

"God dammit, Duncan, we know she's in there. We know who those people are and what they're doing. This has got to be the biggest crock of shit I've ever heard."

"And I agree completely," Duncan said calmly. "But I have to keep the future trial in mind. Evidence is not valid if it's obtained illegally. You know that. And this cartel has done excellent work covering up their tracks. We can't make a move because of it."

"What a fucking joke," I said through gritted teeth. "We can't send a team of federal agents to rescue one of their own because it might damage a future case for some asshole criminals? Sounds like the priorities are totally fucked."

"You're right, Jonny. *We* can't. But you can."

"That's a suicide mission," I said. "They'll be ready and waiting for me. That's why they left the candy outside my door. They want me there, and it's not to have some margaritas."

"That may be so," Duncan said. "But they have Lily, Jonny. If I go with you, do you think we can make it work?"

"Two against the cartel is better than one," I said. "It increases our chances of saving Lily, but we'll still both have an even better chance of ending up dead in that mansion."

"Then so be it," Duncan said. "My life is a mess. I have nothing to lose. Might as well try to save my friend. She'd do the same thing for me. I have no doubt about that."

"Meet me at the bottom of that long driveway leading up to the mansion. We'll need to approach on foot. Tonight, at sundown. Don't be late."

"You want to waste the whole day?" Duncan asked. "Think about what can happen to Lily over the next few hours."

"They're not going to hurt her. They want *me*. I have matters to tend to."

"What could possibly be more important than this?"

"I'm going to make Theo Rambis squeal like the pig he is."

"Rambis? But—"

"I gotta go," I said, and ended the call.

The bearded man stepped out from the back room with two boxes in hand. One with my new knife, the other with the ammo.

"Anything else I can get you today?" he asked.

"No, sir," I said, pulling out my wallet to grab a wad of cash and passport. A sign next to the register said, WE I.D. ALL TRANSACTIONS!

"Good luck with your trip into the wild," he said, scanning my passport while collecting the cash and handing back change. "Every young man should spend some time in the wilderness. You can learn a lot about the world that way, but even more about yourself. No technology, no distractions. Just you and God's given Earth."

"I agree, and am very much looking forward to it."

He bagged up all my stuff and sent me on my way. I hadn't completely lied to this man who held his gaze on me while I strolled out of the store.

I was going into the woods later that night, and I needed to blend in. The camouflage clothing and facepaint would make sure no one saw me.

But I had lied about one thing.

I was absolutely going hunting.

Chapter 35

I pulled up to Theo Rambis's house twenty minutes later. He lived in a small ranch-style home a couple miles east of downtown, with a gated front yard with tall grass that hadn't been cut in at least two months. Fallen leaves still peppered the lawn from the prior autumn.

A short driveway ran along the side of the house and into the backyard. The homes on this block were practically on top of each other. Only three feet separated Theo's driveway from the yard next door.

The house was a soft yellow with a wind chime dangling from the corner gutter. Theo had no front porch, only a slab of concrete serving as a step into his residence. The front door was dead center, splitting the house down the middle. It couldn't have been more than the basics for a single man—kitchen, bathroom, bedroom, and maybe a tight living room.

Realtors would call this place "cozy" to make it more appealing. I'd lived in plenty of houses like this during my travels around the world, and they were far from cozy. Then again, I was six-and-a-half feet tall, and always struggled to find a bed where my feet didn't hang over the edge.

Cozy my ass.

A car was parked at the back of the driveway, suggesting

Theo entered and exited his house from the backdoor.

I drove a couple of houses down the block to park along the curb, hoping no nosy Karens were watching out their windows. The neighborhood was quiet when I stepped out. It was the middle of the workday in a blue-collar town, so I presumed most people were at work. Although, I've heard many people work from home these days. Wild. I was a homebody, sure, but I couldn't imagine sitting in the same place all day and night for weeks at a time. Maybe that was just the SEAL in me.

I regretted not buying a holster for my gun while I was at the store. They just made life easier. Instead, I tucked the Glock into the back of my waistband again like some wannabe gangster. I'd be fine. I was on a mission once in the Middle East and lost my holster somewhere on the journey. With too many layers on, I couldn't even reach around the back of my waist and had to stuff the pistol inside my boot while trudging through the desert. *That* shit was difficult.

I shuffled down the sidewalk and looked around when I reached the edge of Theo's driveway. Houses to my left, right, and across the street. Not a single person visible through any of the windows, including Theo's.

I started up the driveway, the thought of Lily trapped in that mansion with all those criminals eating away at the back of my mind. I'd seen plenty of scenarios that proved why men couldn't be trusted alone with women. And in this case, *several* men were keeping company with one woman.

My blood boiled. I'd kill every one of these motherfuckers for putting Lily through this. I had to move quickly while the sun was out, because once it went down, I was meeting Duncan at the mansion.

I felt no fear of how the events might unfold later. I

understood I was more likely to end up dead than alive, but I'd overcome those odds plenty of times before. An angel had my back. Not sure if that was my mother or other ancestors, but they never let anything truly awful happen to me.

I reached the back of the house and saw another miniature lawn, except this one had more weeds than grass, which also hadn't been trimmed since around Christmas time. A lone palm tree swayed along the back fence, towering over the yard and the rear neighbor's manicured lawn.

To my left was another concrete slab leading up to the door. The screen door hung lopsided and creaked as I pulled it open.

I knocked aggressively on the main door. It had no windows and lots of chipped areas along the surface. A single coat of paint would make it look good as new, but clearly Theo gave zero shits about the appearance of his property.

I stood there for a minute and knocked again. When another minute passed, I tried the doorknob and found the door unlocked. I didn't *want* to break and enter, especially into the home of this strange man who apparently had some pull in Hillcrest, but he left me no choice by not answering.

Theo already knew my role in this case, so it wasn't like I could make up lies saying I was here on official business. I just needed to talk to the guy.

I stepped through the door and into a kitchen that smelled strongly of bacon. Sure enough, I spotted a skillet full of grease on the stovetop. But no bacon. Dammit.

Dirty dishes piled high out of the sink, chunks of food stuck to the plates and silverware. A mountain of empty milk cartons and cereal boxes toppled out of the garbage bin.

I never understood how people lived like this. My mother would whoop my ass if I so much as left a dirty spoon in the sink. She relied on us to keep the house clean while she was working double shifts cleaning other people's homes, and we took that shit seriously.

A measly two-seater table was flushed against the wall, a chaotic pile of magazines and mail in the space where Theo clearly never sat. I took a peek. Playboys, Maxim, Hustler. Something told me those pages might be sticky, so I moved on to the letters. Past due bills, spam, fast food coupons. Not a damn thing worth a second look.

I continued through the kitchen and stepped into a short hallway that led to the front door. Three doors were in the hall, all closed.

Why would someone who lived alone keep all their doors closed? I pulled out my Glock, sensing something not quite right. Theo could have seen me through the window and was hiding. But why would he feel the need? I'd never made a threat against him, and we left the hospital on cordial terms.

"Theo, are you home?" I called out, receiving only my echo in response. "I have some questions I thought you might have answers to."

Silence. And it was deafening.

His car was here, and I highly doubted he had two. It was possible he was out at a neighbor's house, or perhaps someone had picked him up for a ride somewhere, but I didn't believe any of that.

I felt someone else's presence in this house.

The end of the hallway was half foyer, half living room. All Theo had was a recliner parked in front of a forty-two-inch TV. A dinner tray stood next to the recliner with a half-eaten doughnut and its crumbs scattered about.

I turned back around and started down the hall. I pushed

open the lone door on the right and found the bathroom. All I needed was a glimpse of the tiny hairs speckled all over the sink to close the door again.

I pivoted around and opened the door behind me.

An office.

I stepped in and saw a computer desk with an opened laptop. It was turned on and humming gently. I hurried to the laptop and saw several tabs open on the internet browser. The page on display was the *Hillcrest Daily* site, showing an article stamped with today's date about a school funding bill to be debated by city council. Theo had just been here.

His notepad lay on the desk next to the laptop, and I read the messy handwriting.

My name was scribbled across the top.

Jonny Mendez. Age 38. Hispanic.

Murdered man at beach shop.

Got into fight at store. Jonny fired gun and hid in back, waiting to kill the other man.

Victim died in hospital after several days.

Suffered from organ damage due to punches from Mendez?

Use name of Omar Jimenez for victim.

JM wanted for murder.

"What the fuck?" I whispered.

I never killed that man at the beach. He was still in the hospital, alive and breathing well for all I knew.

There was a line drawn under these notes to separate a different set of words.

Wait for HD to give green light to publish.

Victim will die on Thursday.

Today was Thursday, and suddenly my skin crawled. They were going to frame me for murder at the hospital, and this asshole planned to publish an article about it?

And who the fuck was HD? The head? Head of the cartel? Head of the police department?

Fuck.

I had to save my name, but had no idea where to go.

If Theo saw me, could he have run out the backdoor and gone into hiding? How urgent was it for him to get this fake article published? And who would believe him?

The answer to that question made me sick. Everyone in Hillcrest believed him. If the man I had beaten at the beach shop was still in the hospital and had a scheduled death, that meant someone else was going to kill him today. And they were going to make it look like I did it. That meant it could be either the cartel or the police department. The cartel would have no issues carrying out a planned murder and making it look like someone else had done it. But the police would be the ones to tie it back to me, and who knows what false evidence might have been planted to frame me?

If Lily wasn't trapped in that mansion, I'd be flying out of Hillcrest without a second thought. But I couldn't just run from all of this. Not now.

As badly as I wanted to grab the notepad, I couldn't risk putting my fingerprints anywhere in this house, especially if they were trying to frame me. I'd already touched the doorknob to enter the house and regretted not slipping on a pair of gloves. To be fair, I wasn't expecting any of this. Just a friendly conversation with Theo.

Besides, taking the notepad wouldn't stop the article from being published. Someone wanted me out of the way, which meant I was getting too close to the cartel. The laptop was the source of my problems, and even stealing that couldn't guarantee anything, although it could delay matters.

None of that mattered, however, when I heard the click of a pistol from behind me. I spun around and saw Theo Rambis pointing his gun at my face.

Chapter 36

"Put the gun down," Theo said in a surprisingly calm voice. He thought he was in control of the situation.

I tightened my grip on the Glock, which was hanging at my side. Theo's shot was lined up perfectly to connect with my nose, so any sudden movement would spell the end of my life.

"PUT THE FUCKING GUN DOWN!" Theo screamed. His double chin jiggled as he gritted his teeth. A pink tint spread across his face, and Theo licked his lips like some crazed animal ready to pounce on its prey.

"Theo," I said. "I think there's a misunderstanding. Why don't we both put our guns down and talk this out?"

"Do you think I'm an idiot?" he asked, eyes focusing more intensely, his chubby index finger tightening around the trigger.

"Do you really want me to answer that?"

"Shut the fuck up, and drop the gun!" he shouted again, his face almost purple now.

I wasn't sure if he was enraged or nervous. Put a man in this position who wasn't used to killing, and they often folded under the pressure. I doubted Theo had ever so much as harmed a mosquito. Had even saved a wounded bird, according to Jo.

"Okay, okay," I said, slowly raising my free hand to prove my cooperation. "I'm going to place my gun on your desk and step away from it."

"No shit!" Theo snarled. "Any other movement, and I pull this."

His voice had the slightest quaver I picked up on. He was nervous. I could talk him off this ledge.

"Relax, Theo," I said, keeping my Glock pointed to the floor as I moved my arm like molasses toward the desk. It clattered when I dropped it on top of the notepad, then I took three slow steps backwards, both arms still raised.

"Good," Theo said. "So you do know how to listen."

I didn't know what that was supposed to mean.

"Why are you doing this, Theo?" I asked. "I came here to talk to you, and you greet me by pulling a gun."

"You broke into my house," he replied, eyes still blazed with fury. "Did you want me to come give you a hug instead?"

"I'd definitely prefer that."

"Your smart-ass comments don't work here. You can't charm your way out of this."

Theo took a step closer. Rookie mistake.

I had nothing within arm's reach, but with another two inches, I could reach out and smack the pistol out of his hand. Theo was rocking a Ruger nine millimeter. Good gun for home protection.

I twisted my feet an inch forward, a subtle movement Theo didn't notice.

"Let's talk, Theo," I said. "You're clearly caught up in all of this drama with the cartel. Let me help you."

Theo laughed. Sweat streamed from his forehead and down his cheeks. "You can't save me. And you don't know shit!"

"Why did you lie to me at the hospital? I went back and talked to the Evans family. They said you never spoke with them. They hardly knew who you were."

"You did *what*?!" Theo shouted. He waved the gun, as if it was supposed to scare me. If he only knew how many times I've stared down the barrel of another man's gun. I was practically numb to the sensation. "You son of a bitch."

"What's the matter?" I asked. "Worried my presence at the hospital was going to throw off the bullshit story you're writing about me? Tell me, how are you going to do it?"

"Do what?"

"Kill that cartel thug in the hospital. That's the only reason you could have been there, now that we know you weren't actually there to speak with the Evans family."

I saw fear replace the anger in Theo's eyes. That was neither good nor bad for me. Fear could push a man to the edge just as well as anger. I called him out on his bullshit, and he didn't know what to say.

"I...uh," Theo stammered.

"Let me help you, Theo. I've dealt with guys like this before."

Theo shook his head. "No. If I turn my back on them, they'll kill me. Even if I go into hiding, they'll find me and snap me like a twig. I've seen them do it."

"You can leave Hillcrest right now," I said. "They'll never expect it. How long would it be until they notice you're gone? Four hours? Eight?"

Theo pursed his lips as thoughts swam behind his eyes. He shook his head again, but tears started streaming down his face. "I can't do it, Mendez. You don't understand."

"And what is shooting me going to achieve for you?" I asked.

"You and I both know these guys don't give a shit about your life. They just want you to do this dirty work for them. They'll still kill you the second you turn your back on them. Do you really want to live the rest of your life having a blind loyalty to these guys?"

The gun trembled in Theo's hand, and I didn't know if he was getting closer to putting it down or pulling the trigger. An invisible clock ticked away in my head. We couldn't stand here all night. Something had to give. I twisted my feet forward again, about another inch.

My vision pulsed, creating a tunnel on the Ruger still pointed at my face. I thought I could whip it out of his grip, but still risked the trigger getting pulled. That would land a bullet in my shoulder or arm.

"When you work for the cartel," I said, "all you're ever really doing is delaying the inevitable. You're an outsider to them. Can't you see that? They want you for your influence in Hillcrest and nothing more. Are you really going to compromise your journalistic career to publish a frame job about me?"

"They paid me fifty-thousand dollars," Theo whispered. "That's more than I make in a year. They're going to pay me another fifty after the article is published and you're locked in prison."

The cartel loved to prey on the financially vulnerable. The money was pennies to them, but life-changing for the people they tried to corrupt. I once dealt with an Irish mob in New York City who was paying a high school boy fifty dollars a day to deliver packages to a remote location. The kid would swing by the back alley of their front—a pub—collect one or two packages on his bicycle, and ride a mile away, where they instructed him to leave the packages at a remote boating dock. They paid him cash each day when handing over the packages and promised to keep the money coming as long as the packages were delivered successfully.

I had to intercept this kid one day on his route and inform him he was delivering drugs and weapons for the mob. He was lucky. They didn't even know his real name or where he lived, and he never returned to the pub.

Theo was in the same position as the kid but wasn't as lucky.

"I can't offer you money, Theo," I said. "But I can offer you a life where you don't have to constantly look over your shoulder and bow down to the cartel. I'm sure you heard about those dead bodies at the morgue last week. Do you really want to end up like the guy with his ball sack ripped off?"

A sick realization spread across Theo's face. He knew damn well what I was talking about and was likely envisioning his own privates getting separated from his body.

He cried more but didn't make a sound. Just mute streams of liquid trailing down his face. "They want me to kill the boy."

"Dominic?"

Theo nodded. "I've been going to that hospital every day, hoping to get just twenty seconds alone in the room with him. But there's always someone there."

"You were going to kill him when he was in the coma? What the hell is wrong with these guys?"

"They saw the boy as a threat if he ever woke up. His story has become too high profile. I've kept the reporting to a minimum, but I can't control the TV stations and social media. All the fucking hashtags. Pray for Dom. Wake up, Dom. It's become a national issue. His fucking face is all over every news channel in America. The cartel saw this as a threat. It's only a matter of time before he's getting interviewed by Oprah or some bullshit. If he remembers *everything* that happened, their operation here is done."

"Theo, can't you see?" I said, forcing encouragement into my voice. "This is your way out. Let Dominic live and tell his story. Then the authorities will take care of the cartel."

Theo shook his head deliberately. "They said if I don't kill him before he leaves the hospital, it's my own funeral. I'm tied to his life, Mendez. I don't have a choice."

"We all have choices," I said. "Life is nothing but a series of choices. Each one takes you down a different path. I can't guarantee to keep you safe from these goons, but I can give you a chance. And that might be the best you can get. Those parents aren't leaving Dominic's side. And I won't let you kill the boy."

Theo laughed. "Oh yeah? What are you going to do about it? I'm the one with the gun."

This was it. Theo wasn't budging. No more negotiating. He wasn't dropping that gun unless forced to.

With a sudden flash, I threw out my hand like a whip, the tips of my middle and ring fingers connected with the Ruger's muzzle. The gun fired, sending a bullet whizzing past my head.

Theo's eyes widened as he realized he was fucked. He swung the gun back around, but I was already lunging toward him. I kept low, tackling him around the hips and driving my shoulder into his pudgy gut. The gun fired again, I'm guessing somewhere into the ceiling or walls.

I drove Theo through the open doorway and rammed him into the hallway wall. This collision caused him to drop the gun, but he moved more quickly than I thought he was capable, flailing for his Ruger and getting it back in his grip within a second.

I had stumbled back a couple of steps, my head having bonked into the wall during my tackle. I spun back into the office and snatched my Glock off the desk, immediately holding it in position, ready to fire.

"It's over, Theo," I said, not having a clear view of him through the doorway. He was just to the left, and now we played the waiting game. He was probably still sitting there, gun cocked and aimed at the open doorway, just waiting for me to step into his view.

I considered crouching low. He'd likely be aiming high, and I trusted he couldn't re-adjust his shot too swiftly. But I also didn't know if he had remained on the floor or stood up. The last thing I wanted was to aim low and deal with trying to shoot his legs. Much more difficult than landing a slug in his thick torso.

But Theo decided for me, barreling through the doorway with manic determination in his eyes. He growled like a rabid pitbull, teeth drawn like a lunatic. He actually glided through the air with both hands on the gun. Did he think he was in some action movie? These types of shots never worked in real life.

We both pulled our triggers, the guns exploding in sync and causing a reverberation probably heard all the way down the block. A chunk of drywall erupted from the wall behind me.

Theo landed on the floor, immediately clutching his chest. Blood seeped through his shirt and fingers. I shuffled to him and dropped to a knee, pulling his hands off his chest. My shot landed two inches above his heart, likely severing an artery, certainly puncturing his lung.

"I'm sorry, Theo," I said in a soft tone. "I never wanted to shoot you today, but you left me no choice. You only have about a minute left. Is there anyone else who might publish that fake article about me? I need to know. Blink once for yes, twice for no."

His eyes were already glossy, but there was still a flicker of life in them. He blinked gradually once, then struggled a second time, but the message was received. Blood pooled beneath his body from the exit wound on his back.

A guttural sound came from his throat, accompanied by a trickle of blood. He was trying to talk. I lowered my head toward his mouth.

"Kih...the..." he said.

"Try again," I said.

"Kih...them."

"Kill them?" I asked.

Theo blinked once, opened his eyes, then never blinked or breathed again.

He wanted me to kill them. The cartel. The assholes who had put this somewhat innocent man in this fucked up predicament.

I hadn't given Theo my word, but I was happy to oblige.

Chapter 37

I returned to my hotel shortly after noon. I had waited around Theo's house, unsure what to do. Calling the police would have been the right thing to do, but I didn't trust anyone over there at the moment. Plus, I was fairly certain the cartel had been tailing me for several days now. There was no other explanation for why Theo saw me as a threat. Once I entered his home he had every intent—at least in his mind—of killing me.

If I called the police right now, that would tip off the cartel to Theo being dead. The less they knew, the better. If they knew I called the police, they might double down their reinforcements around the property. They knew I was coming, but did they know when?

Manny knew me. I followed my heart. I'd never leave Lily in their possession, even if it was the easy thing to do.

I brought Theo's laptop and notepad with me. He didn't need them anymore, and I had to make sure there was zero chance of the phony article getting leaked. I ripped out the pages bearing my name from his notepad and flushed them down the toilet.

The laptop was easier. Theo had the article pulled up in a Word document. Written, edited, and ready to publish.

Complete with a candid picture of me sitting in the coffee shop from the other day.

Jesus Christ, these bastards really had been keeping close tabs. They were too many steps ahead of me and probably had eyes on my vehicle parked outside the hotel. I'd no longer be taking that tonight. If I had to slip out the back and walk to the mansion, so be it.

I deleted the document containing the article and searched through Theo's digital fingerprints. Emails, browser history, all the good stuff. I found lots of porn, DoorDash delivery receipts, and a multitude of emails from different residents of Hillcrest. They were all innocent enough. Requests to cover various stories. People wanting to promote their fundraisers and causes. Nothing concrete that tied him to the cartel.

They would never be so reckless as to communicate with one of their patsies via email. They probably gave him a new phone on a private line. Or maybe he had a landline at his house I hadn't noticed.

None of that mattered. Theo was dead and couldn't bring me any closer to the cartel. I wondered if they had backup plans to kill Dominic. If they did, they wouldn't have enough notice to make a move before I arrived at their mansion tonight. For all they knew, Theo was still working on it.

Unless someone had trailed me to his house.

I assumed if anyone learned of Theo's death, I'd get a call from Agent Duncan. Until then, I'd proceed as normal.

Giving up on the laptop, I powered it off and slammed it shut. I'd have to dispose of it, preferably in a dumpster out behind the hotel.

I rinsed off with a quick shower, needing to remove Theo's dried, caked-on blood from my arms. Killing a man was never easy, but I'd learned how to sleep with those demons in my closet.

My phone buzzed on my nightstand only seconds after I had stepped out of the shower and dried off. No way in hell word had already broken about Theo getting killed in his home. If it had, the cartel had leaked the information, and I'm not sure why they would do such a thing.

Sure enough, it was Agent Duncan's phone number. "Hello?" I answered.

"Mendez," Duncan said, sounding as if he was panting. "Where are you?"

"I'm at my hotel. Why, what's going on?"

I jogged over to my window to look out, sensing something boiling over in Hillcrest. All I saw was the usual. The ocean far in the distance. Palm trees swaying from a gentle breeze, although it was a slightly more forceful wind blowing today. The sky remained gray, the clouds pregnant with rain that would continue for the foreseeable future. The raindrops streaked down the window, creating trails that spread in every direction.

"Stay inside and turn on the news," Duncan said.

"Why do we have to play games?" I asked, rushing back to my nightstand to grab the TV remote. "Just tell me what's going on."

I braced for the worst as the TV clicked on. Had they still managed to kill Dominic? Or maybe the man I put in the hospital had died and my face was plastered all over the news as the start of some incorrect manhunt.

My stomach twisted into knots as I flipped through the channels to get to the news, then I felt an immediate sense of relief when I saw the headlines proving I was wrong on both fronts.

The newscaster, Sarah Potter, was back, this time looking like she was on the verge of vomiting. The feed cut away from her in the studio and changed to a bird's-eye view of city hall.

"For those of you just tuning in," Sarah said. "Mayor Tony Reece has been kidnapped. Eyewitnesses saw the mayor walking down Main Street after lunch, when an all-black van with no windows pulled up to the curb. Four masked men jumped out and pulled the mayor into the van, which then sped off. By the time anyone could call the police station, the van was out of sight from those witnesses on Main Street. The police are asking for the public's cooperation during this crisis. If anyone spots a black van with no windows, call 9-1-1 immediately. Do not approach the van, as they believe the men to be armed and dangerous. Do not follow the van."

"What the fuck?" I asked, forgetting Duncan was on the other end of the phone.

"What the fuck is right, Mendez," Duncan said. "We're in deep shit now. The governor has been briefed on the situation. The National Guard will be rolling into town tonight. My hands are tied. The DEA is going to pull me off the case while this matter gets resolved."

"Who the hell are these guys?" I asked. "Kidnapping a DEA agent *and* the mayor? It's ruthless and gutsy. They've got to know the target on their back is growing bigger."

"They're going to make me hand over all the files I have on the case," Duncan said, as if he hadn't heard a word I said. His mind was all over the place. "I won't be able to make any moves without approval from the National Guard. Once they're here, the entire city of Hillcrest becomes their jurisdiction. I'll have to cooperate as much as I can, but their focus is going to be on the mayor, not on Lily."

"Come to my hotel," I said. "Right now."

"What the hell would I do that for?"

"Do you want to save Lily?"

"Of course."

"Then get your ass over here immediately. The Guard isn't here yet, so you may as well go into hiding. You don't need to worry about permission from anyone if they can't get a hold of you. Turn off your phone so no one can track you, then come here and we'll make a plan. We're going into that mansion now. And as long as you don't share any information about the mansion, we'll get to do it undisturbed."

"Mendez, you must out of your goddamned mind!" Duncan cried. "I am a highly respected DEA agent. I can't just go radio silent to hide from the Guard. People will be reaching out to me. And why the hell wouldn't we just want the Guard to raid that mansion for us? They're better equipped than the two of us."

I was making the speaking motion with my free hand, mocking him in private for my satisfaction. These government types were all talk and no action when it came down to the dirty parts of their work. Duncan wanted the soft life of pushing papers at his desk, doing light investigative work to make it look like he was busy. But he didn't have the balls to storm into a house full of the cartel to save his partner. Lily would have done it for him because she was a woman of action.

"If the cartel is willing to go to these extremes, then they're ready for war," I said. "If the DEA shows up at that mansion, it's going to be a shootout until there's one man standing. And we have no way of knowing if that will be a good guy or a bad guy. Do you really want to find out?"

"And your grand idea is for *us* to take on this army ourselves?" Duncan asked. "Are you fucking high?"

"At the moment, no. But when this is all done with, I'm absolutely going to a dispensary."

"God dammit, Mendez, do you really think this is the time for jokes?"

"I'm not joking."

Duncan sighed. "This idea is absurd."

"The situation is absurd. We're just trying to find a way out of it."

"What would you say the odds of us surviving the night are?"

I thought about it. I'd never really put a number on a scenario like this before. "Twenty percent chance of us returning home tonight. Forty if we can free Lily and have her along to help us."

"Our best odds aren't even a coin flip," Duncan said, letting out a nervous laugh. He might have realized his time on this case was over, all his laziness wasted down the drain. Maybe he felt some guilt about Lily being in these criminals' possession—I hoped. Or perhaps he wanted to join me tonight and had never faced such high odds of his own death.

I'd grown numb to the possibility of death. If I had to make similar calculations for my past, I'd say most of my days as an adult left me with a ten percent chance of dying. It was like playing Russian Roulette from the moment I woke up every day. I knew I'd meet my demise eventually, but until then, I'd power through and make the world a better place.

"Alright, Mendez," Duncan said. "I'm trusting you. I'll be there in five minutes."

Agent Duncan ended the call, and a violent crack of lightning shook the world below.

Chapter 38

Agent Duncan knocked on my door exactly seven minutes later. He was dripping wet from the short walk between the parking lot and the hotel lobby.

He wore a long trench coat that had turned dark from the moisture. His graying hair matted against his head. Fear swam behind his brown eyes.

"It's a fucking monsoon out there," he said the moment I opened the door.

"That only works to our advantage," I said. "They might think I'm not coming tonight because of the storm. They're wrong. Even if they think I'm still coming, the rain works to our advantage. It provides background noise and impedes vision. I couldn't have asked for a better forecast. We need to get ready."

I turned around and returned to my bed, where I had my outfit, makeup, and hunting knife splayed out on display.

"You're wearing bright colors," I said when Duncan slipped off his trench coat to reveal a yellow dress shirt.

"I didn't realize there was a particular dress code for tonight."

I chuckled. "Sass? From you?"

Duncan shrugged. "I gotta break the tension."

"We need to be dark. I'll let you borrow a black T-shirt. Try to not get it dirty, okay? And you can use my makeup."

"Sounds like a fun girl's night we have planned," Duncan said, cracking a slight grin.

"Another one? I'm impressed. Maybe you're not the total dud Lily made you out to be."

"A dud?" Duncan asked, raising his brow. "No she didn't! We'll see if I go rescue her now."

I found Duncan's mood swing odd. But everyone reacted to facing death in their own way. Some people shut down; others turned to humor. I was stationed with a guy in the SEALs who always wrote a letter to his wife before we set out. Just in case. For me, I preferred to focus on killing the bad guys. It always brought me peace.

I went to my closet and grabbed the black T-shirt for Duncan. When I tossed it to him, he held it up in amazement at how large it was. If it wasn't raining so heavily, he could have probably used the shirt to go parachuting off the hotel roof.

I stripped down in front of him, and he turned away in a hurry, gazing out the same window I was just looking out minutes ago when he called.

"What's the matter?" I asked. "Never been in a boy's locker room?"

Duncan turned back around, holding eye contact so he didn't have to look down. "Well, yes, I just wasn't sure how much you were planning to take off."

"Chill, man, my boxers are still on," I said. "Your underwear doesn't have to be camo unless you're covering your whole body in the makeup. At that point, you might as well lose the drawers and paint over everything."

"What on God's green earth are you talking about?" Duncan asked, letting out a nervous laugh.

"Don't worry about it," I said. "Just change your shirt and we'll put this makeup on."

I fished my iPod out of my backpack, plugged it into the TV, and went to my 2Pac folder. "2 of Amerikaz Most Wanted" played first, and if that wasn't a song to put you in the mood to go out and kill a motherfucker, I'm not sure what was.

"Is this your hype song?" Duncan asked, and I noticed his head bobbing to the beat. It always made me laugh when the authorities danced or hummed along to songs that were entirely anti-authority.

"I don't need to be hyped," I said. "Just more of a mental state, I guess."

I dressed in my camouflage outfit and shuffled to the mirror above my dresser, ripping open the package of makeup.

It had been years since I had to go full out like this. The last time I wore camo makeup was in Iran to hunt down a group of terrorists hiding out in the forest along the northern border.

I covered my face in black and dark green, using my fingertip to get the job done. After five minutes, I was completely covered and could blend into the night as effortlessly as a bat. Speaking of, I never understood why Batman left the bottom half of his face exposed. Seemed like a disservice to himself.

Duncan changed his shirt and joined me at the mirror. I passed over the makeup. "Do it just like me."

He studied my face, then looked at the makeup, unsure. "You really are treating this like a war."

"They have guns. We have guns. They have a hostage, and we're going to free that hostage. That's essentially war."

Duncan considered this, nodded, then applied the makeup.

The iPod changed to "Me Against the World" and now we were really cooking. While Duncan finished with the makeup, I double checked my backpack. The Beretta was in there and would remain as a last resort. I pulled out the Glock, confirmed it was loaded, and placed it back inside. My new knife went into my front pocket for easy access.

"What kind of gun do you have?" I asked Duncan.

"Glock 17," he said.

"Beautiful," I replied. His was semi-automatic, so we could really make it rain bullets once we got into that house.

"Okay, I'm ready," Duncan said, turning around.

His face was completely dark. If Duncan was a comedian, he'd have all the social justice warriors' panties in a wad for an impeccable blackface. Fortunately for them, we were doing this to save a life.

Lightning burst angrily outside, causing the lights in the hotel to flicker. It wasn't even nighttime yet, but the clouds were growing darker by the minute. The sun wasn't coming back out today, leaving us the opportunity to start our raid early.

"You ready?" I asked.

We stared at each other, neither of our faces recognizable to the other.

"I am," Duncan said.

"I'm proud of us," I said. "We didn't start off on the right foot but look at us now. Fighting side-by-side to save a friend in need."

"I don't need a pep talk, Mendez. Let's do this already."

"My man. Okay. You'll need to drive. These assholes have been following me, and they probably have eyes on my car right now. I'd advise you to drive around to the back of the building and wait for ten minutes to make sure no one follows you back there. If the coast is clear, send me a text message to let me know and I'll meet you out back. If someone *does* follow you, drive to Hamburger Stand and call me from the parking lot."

Duncan nodded. "Got it."

He patted his Glock in the holster on his waist before slipping his trench coat back on. He had thrown it on my bed, and it left a wet outline on my comforter. Bastard.

"Alright, Mendez," Duncan said. "I'm putting my full trust in you. My life. I will do exactly as you say. Can you handle that?"

I smiled. "If you don't need a pep talk, what makes you think I do? I'll see you in ten minutes."

Duncan bit his bottom lip and turned to leave the room. Once the door closed behind him, I pulled out my cellphone to set a ten-minute timer. I was nervous, sure, but all I had to do was think of Lily and know that this would all be worth it.

Chapter 39

Coast is clear.

When I received the text message from Duncan, I turned off all the lights in my hotel room. I unplugged the iPod and allowed the hammering raindrops to be the only sound. Every few minutes, a flash of lightning lit up the world that had otherwise remained dark. If I had seen clouds like this in the Midwest, I'd be taking cover from a tornado. But out here along the beach, there was no such worry. Flooding was more of a threat, but Hillcrest seemed to have a reliable drainage system.

The makeup on my lips left a bitter taste in my mouth, but that was the least of my worries. I slung my backpack over my shoulder and shuffled to the door, looking back at the space that had been my home for the past couple of weeks. I wasn't one to get sentimental, but before heading out on what many would consider a suicide mission, I couldn't help but reflect.

Was this the last time I'd see the inside of this hotel room? If it was, then this would be the last place I lived during my tumultuous journey on this planet. And if it wasn't, what would my return look like? Duncan, Lily and I strolling in late, giggling and drunk after celebrating our survival? Or would Duncan and I return without Lily, trying to understand where it all went wrong? The most sickening prospect was me returning alone. That was always a possibility, and one I had grown used to.

When my Tia Rosa was on her deathbed, I was a troubled teenager struggling to find my footing in life. I asked her why everyone in my life left me.

"Jonny, you sweet, sweet boy," she had said, brushing a frail hand along my cheek. "God only makes the strongest people go through life alone. We're the only ones who can handle it. I went through my life alone, and now I die alone. We all die alone. It doesn't matter who's standing at your side when it happens. I'm dying, *mijo*, and you don't get to come with me. I love you."

My Tia Rosa rarely gave sound life advice, but when she did, it was often delivered like an iron fist into the groin of my soul. Her explanation was harsh but honest.

I'd seen it too many times after too many war battles. Men and women removed from existence. Removed from their families. The fallen soldiers died, and the families grieved. That was the way of the world back then, today, and in the future.

I once told a shrink at the CIA that I had no interest in getting married, or even having a life partner. The doctor suggested this was because of my abandonment issues.

No shit.

But today wasn't the day to reflect on my personal matters. I bid my hotel room adieu and started down the long hallway to the back of the building, opting for the emergency staircase to exit and avoid startling any guests hanging out in the lobby downstairs.

I made it to the rear exit without an interruption. Agent

Duncan waited in his black town car just outside the door, the red brake lights contrasting the grayness of the world.

I hurried into the passenger seat and closed the door, hair instantly soaked from the quick five steps I took between the hotel and the car. Fucking monsoon was correct.

Duncan looked straight ahead, the windshield wipers vigorously swiping back and forth. His hands were steady on the wheel, now covered in black gloves.

"We're really doing this," he said, and I thought it was meant for himself. He put the car into gear, and we drove off.

Neither of us spoke during the ride over. The rain sounded more like hail, massive drops exploding across the car. Duncan couldn't drive over twenty miles per hour without the visibility growing impossible. So we took our time.

What should have been a quick eight-minute drive ended up taking twice as long. He pulled over and parked in front of the dirt road that led up to the driveway.

"You can't park here!" I cried. "Are you crazy?"

"Don't you think we should block off their only exit?" Duncan asked.

"No one in there is trying to leave," I said, jerking my head side to side. "All you're going to do is piss off someone if they're trying to get *in* and can't. Park down the road about fifty feet, and kill the lights."

Duncan nodded and turned the car around, doing exactly as instructed. He really was serious about listening to my every order.

He parked up the road and turned off the engine. I wasn't too worried about being spotted, thanks to rain making visibility nearly impossible.

"Okay," I said. "The most important thing is not to rush

any decision. It's about one hundred and fifty yards from the bottom of the hill to the house. We're not going up the driveway—that's too obvious, and they'll probably be waiting. Have you ever gone hiking?"

"No."

"Good. It's a stupid activity, but one we need to do right now. This area is heavily populated with trees. They probably chose this space because of that. Complete seclusion from the rest of the world. It's going to feel more like eight hundred yards because it's all uphill, and we need to tread carefully. Watch where you're stepping. Every. Single. Step. I'm not expecting any kind of booby traps out here, but you never know. If something looks out of place, avoid it. Are we clear on this?"

"Yes, sir," Duncan said.

"Good. This entire sequence is about taking it one phase at a time. Don't think about the big picture of rescuing Lily. Our first task is to simply get within view of the mansion. Once we have eyes on it, I'll assess our next steps, and go from there. If your life becomes in danger, just shoot. No hesitations. Lily is the only life worth saving in that house. No exceptions."

Part of me wanted to add my nephew to that list, but I couldn't. I'd avoid shooting the kid as best I could, but his life ultimately depended on his decisions in the coming minutes.

"Alright," I said. "Let's roll."

I didn't wait for Duncan to agree to anything and opened my door, stepping out into the rain that had downgraded from a monsoon to a steady pour.

Duncan stepped out and followed me across the street. I jogged down the shoulder of the road, stepping in muddy puddles, and passed the driveway, taking an immediate right into the stand of trees.

Agent Duncan chased after me, panting for breath, and I had to remind myself he wasn't in as good shape as I was. He'd need to figure that out on his own because I wasn't slowing down for him.

When he joined my side, I took twenty steps into the woods, the rainfall lightening up thanks to the canopy the treetops provided. We looked up the hill, seeing nothing but hundreds of majestic redwood trees practically growing on top of each other.

The towering trunks made me feel like a mere ant crawling down the sidewalk, oblivious to how massive the world truly was.

We continued forward. The ground was spongy, and we had to step through a wide variety of shrubbery, weeds, and native plants now drenched with rainwater. My clothes were completely soaked through, like I had jumped into a swimming pool fully dressed.

I looked back at Duncan and saw the makeup on his face was only smeared a bit, but fully intact. They hadn't lied when they called it water-resistant.

I supposed on a day full of sunshine, the cartel might have planted some guards to wander through the woods, but the downpour had surely reduced the radius of the area they wanted to cover. There wasn't a soul in sight. Even if they had a sniper hiding some distance away, they'd never land a successful shot in these conditions.

We needed to take down as many men outside of the mansion as possible. And in silence.

Duncan had no interest in leading the way after my mention of booby traps, but after the first forty yards, we ran into no issues. We kept on, while I looked high and low.

I didn't think they would have gone through the trouble to lay out traps. They'd have only done that if they assumed they would one day have unexpected visitors. And they had life made in Hillcrest. Control over the police department, the main reporter, and a comfy meeting spot at the local diner before I turned it into a crime scene.

And when the DEA arrived in town, they simply kidnapped one of their agents without a second thought. Why not throw in the mayor if you felt invincible?

I refused to let Duncan know that we might have been in over our heads. Any cartel acting this cocky only did so if they had the resources to back it up. But I had no reason to scare the guy off. I'd been in plenty of similar scenarios in the past and loved to overcome the odds.

Thunder boomed from high above, the lightning faint thanks to the trees. I knew you were supposed to avoid standing near trees during a thunderstorm, but did that still apply if there were hundreds of them? Mother Nature couldn't strike them all, right?

We passed the halfway point of our journey up this God forsaken hill, and I saw the top of the mansion's roof.

"We're close!" I called back to Duncan, who was only about ten paces behind me. I figured I would have lost him by now, but he was holding his own.

I waited for him to catch up to me and laughed when I heard his heavy panting for breath.

"This is nuts," he said, planting his hands on his knees as he crouched forward.

"Part of the job," I said. "I take it you don't get into a lot of foot chases in the DEA?"

"Not in years," Duncan replied with a weak chuckle.

"I wish we could spend more time here reminiscing about the past," I said, "but we have shit to do. Let's go."

I started again, my legs moving faster now that the mansion was in view. Every couple of steps brought more of the dwelling into sight. The last time I was here was at night, and I couldn't see shit.

This house had a dark green exterior that helped it blend into the surrounding woods. That was no accident. A portico held up by towering brown columns stretched to the roof, and on both sides were some of the largest windows I'd ever seen. The mansion stood two levels tall, and these windows stretched across both.

We were only fifty yards out now, and I saw chandeliers hanging from the ceiling through both windows. The lights were on, and silhouettes of people walked around inside.

I broke into a jog, and once I reached the area I calculated as forty yards out, the hill turned into flat ground. The entire mansion was within view, granted through the maze of tree trunks. Duncan was still straggling along, so I looked right and saw several cars parked in the same area as the other night. I couldn't see them all, but they appeared tightly packed leading up to the house in sloppy single file. The driveway was too narrow for any other arrangement, and they needed to leave a clear path for other vehicles to pull up closer to the house.

Duncan was closing in, so I started walking. No more jogging. We were within range of being seen. All they needed was a pair of binoculars to spot us. My senses heightened as I readied for anything. A man charging out from behind a tree. A gun firing in the distance.

We were thirty yards out when I stopped again. Duncan ran up behind me, breathing even heavier.

"Oh, good," he said between breaths. "You *do* have a stop button." He placed his hands behind his head and drew in as much air as his lungs would allow.

"Far from stopping, amigo," I said, studying the mansion. Two guards patrolled outside the front door, pacing back and forth with what looked like AR-15s cradled in their arms. They were the first line of defense and probably the weakest. The more skilled guards would be inside, ready to protect my brother.

I wondered if he ever got my message. I'd find out soon enough.

To our right, I examined the vehicles, and saw the black van with no windows. Mayor Reece was here, likely tied up next to Lily.

"What do you think?" Duncan asked, having finally caught his breath.

"Two options," I said. "We can spread out and approach from the sides of the house and each attack a guard. But I'm not sold on that yet. Option two, I'd rather create a diversion that draws them away from the house and out here into the woods. We'll have much better odds and can keep hidden after killing them. Either way, I still want to get a little closer. Our camo is working wonders right now. It looks like the trees end about fifty feet away from the front door. If we can get up to that point, we'll have a better look at what's going on inside."

"How many people do you think are here?" Duncan asked. "There are so many cars."

"It's not as bad as I thought. I'd guess about fifteen

cars, so probably twenty to twenty-five people inside that mansion. They'll all have guns, but that doesn't mean they're all competent at using them."

"Do you think they have cameras?" Duncan asked.

"It does. I'm not sure how else they saw me the other night. Hell, my brother snuck up *behind* me, so we really need to stay alert. Look in all directions. Let's go."

I continued, keeping my eyes glued to the two guards. They kept pacing, passing each other every so often and never stopping to have a word with each other. That told me they were focused. They knew I was coming.

Each step we took was deliberate and calculated. We probably looked like we were tiptoeing through a minefield, and it didn't feel too different in all honesty.

The guards occasionally peered down the driveway, but never glanced in our direction in the woods. We started moving laterally from trunk to trunk, using the redwoods for cover. The rain continued steadily and provided a visual barrier between us and the guards. Just enough to assist us on our trek toward the mansion.

We bounced from tree to tree like kids playing hide-and-seek, until we were just twenty yards away from the front doors.

I could now see the guards clearly. They were dressed in identical all-black tactical gear. Their weapons were indeed AR-15s, meaning they didn't even need to be good shots and could fire a barrage of bullets in our general direction.

Several people were inside the mansion. A group sat on the right-hand side, filling two couches and watching a gigantic TV hanging on the wall. It looked like a spring training baseball game between the Dodgers and Angels. The TV was so big that even from this distance, I felt like I was sitting in the outfield grass at Camelback Ranch.

On the left-hand side, more men huddled around a kitchen table. Most had their backs to the window, and the few I could see were unrecognizable. No sign of my brother.

As I watched, one of those men turned around and strolled right up to the window, gazing out at the woods as he pulled a cell phone out of his pocket.

"Mayor Reece," I said. "Why is the mayor relaxing with these guys that kidnapped him?"

I turned to Agent Duncan, who looked pale with worry. He only shrugged in response.

I looked back at the mayor, who appeared to be dialing his phone before placing it against his ear.

"He's calling someone," I said.

Five seconds later, my blood chilled when the cell phone in Duncan's pocket started ringing.

I turned around to see Duncan aiming his Glock at my face.

Chapter 40

"Get on your knees," Duncan said through gritted teeth. "Or I'll blast your fucking head off."

"You're making a mistake, Duncan," I said, slowly raising my hands above my head.

His phone kept ringing, so he reached into his pocket with his free hand and pulled it out to decline the call.

Big fucking mistake.

"I don't make mistakes," Duncan said. "If I did, you wouldn't be standing here with this gun pointed at your face."

"Let me get this straight," I said. "This whole scheme was put together so you could deliver me to my brother?"

Duncan laughed. "You're full of yourself, Mendez. None of this was about you. All we wanted was a peaceful town to operate in. Then you arrived and fucked it all up. By a stroke of luck, you happen to be Manny's brother, so he saw this as an opportunity to recruit you to the family business."

"Oh, I'm not joining your little gang."

He laughed again, sounding on the verge of a mental breakdown. "Wrong again. You can either join us or die. There are no other options."

"Then you might as well pull the trigger now," I said. "I'd rather be dead than work with you thugs. I can't believe you played all of us. Even Lily. How long have you been working for these guys and betraying your country?"

"Betraying my country?" Duncan asked, letting his jaw hang open. How I wanted to jam a fist through that fucking mouth. "Mendez, the United States isn't a country, it's a business. We're all just here to make money. No other place in the world can give you as much money as America. It's a fucking ATM once you learn how to play the game."

"Wow, I'll make sure my representatives fight to add that to the Constitution."

"Get on your fucking knees," he demanded again.

Duncan was keeping his voice low, like he didn't want the guards to see or hear us. He refused to answer that call from Mayor Reece. This told me he was defying someone or some order. If Manny wanted me to join the family business, then he intended to speak with me. I couldn't know for sure if he gave his goons strict instructions not to kill me, but I got the sense that was the case, and Duncan was prepared to go rogue.

Knowing this, I dropped to one knee.

"Both knees," Duncan said calmly.

"Fuck you, man," I said. "My knees are sore after that hike. I'm surprised you're so chipper considering you looked on the verge of death after walking a whole twenty feet."

"Enough of the remarks," he said, and he seemed to give up on obliging me to get on both knees.

"So how does this play out, Agent Duncan?" I asked. "You're going to shoot me here in the woods and go into that mansion to count all your money? You know all that money isn't going to save your marriage, right? Maybe she doesn't love you anymore because you've become too greedy. Fell out of love with her and in love with the almighty dollar."

"You don't know shit," he said, and reared back his Glock to whip me across the face. I absorbed the blow, but was already making moves in my mind while it played out. After he whipped me, I had a split second where his arm was extended across his body, the Glock pointing nowhere near me. I lunged from my one-legged kneel and tackled him.

He gasped as my shoulder drilled into his groin, and we tumbled to the wet ground.

"Motherfucker!" he shouted, trying to bring the Glock back around, but I punched the gun out of his hand, sending it into the mess of green shrubbery gracing the forest floor.

Even though Duncan wasn't in good shape, he was still big. Not as big as me, but enough to put up a fight.

We wrestled. Duncan tried wrapping his legs around mine, succeeding twice, but I broke free. He hugged my body and tried rolling me over to pin me down. His strength caught me off guard, but after seeing how he performed during the brief hike up this hill, I knew I only needed to outlast him. He'd tire out well before me.

We were both keeping quiet, only grunting and muttering under our breath. He called me a bitch, bastard, and mother-fucker as he struggled to move my body. My mother would have put soap in his mouth for such language.

I slipped my left arm free from his embrace and quickly delivered a blow with my elbow square across Duncan's jaw. A tooth flew out from his lips, along with a stream of blood.

Now, he didn't hold back his wailing, so I clapped a hand over his bloody mouth. "Shut the fuck up!"

I felt his lips part, then he tried to bite my hand. I balled my hand into a fist and jammed it harder into his open mouth. A second tooth popped free, and Duncan shrieked in pain, the sounds trapped in his throat.

I was completely saddled over Duncan's torso, and he rammed his knee into my back. It jutted me forward a couple of inches, which actually made my fist drive even deeper into his mouth. I pinned down his arms with my knees, pulled my fist out of his face, and drew my gun, positioning it on his temple.

"Make a sound and I pull the trigger," I said. Duncan lay on his back and had to keep blinking the raindrops out of his eyes.

He said nothing, licking around his gums to feel the missing teeth with his tongue. "You piece of shit!" he whispered.

"How long have you been working for the cartel?" I asked, my patience depleting. I glanced up to check the guards, and they continued to pace. We were low enough on the ground to remain just out of sight. The rain washed out any of the sounds we had just made, but I knew they wouldn't drown out a gunshot. I pressed my Glock harder into his temple. "Tell me, asshole."

"They found me at the diner after one week in town," he said. "They already knew who I was, and offered me two hundred and fifty thousand dollars to cooperate with them, plus a paid position on their staff. All they asked of me was to keep the DEA off their trail."

"So you let Lily go out and do all the work, just for nothing to happen?" I pressed the gun harder, and Duncan winced.

He nodded, and I couldn't tell if it was rain or tears welling in his eyes. Probably both. "I needed the money. I'm getting divorced and it's going to wipe me out. All this money was off the books, too. My wife would never know about it."

"You're fucking scum," I said.

"This is all your fault," Duncan said, forcing a terrifying smile with his bloody mouth and missing teeth. "If you just minded your fucking business, we wouldn't be in this situation. I could have kept things under control with Lily. She'd still be working the case, and we'd both leave town in a few months. You and Manny. He demanded we bring you here alive. We should have just killed you from the start. *You* complicated all of this."

"Oh, fuck off. I'm not going to apologize for doing the right thing. Maybe you can think about that while you spend the rest of your life in prison."

"Oh, I'll be thinking alright. How I should have shot you in the back the first time we met. I only had them pull Lily off the case hoping you'd leave town, but that clearly backfired."

Duncan's legs flailed around behind me. He kept trying to land a blow, and his knees occasionally brushed against my back. They were growing stronger with each passing minute.

"And you know what?" Duncan said, his grin widening. "You're not even half the man your brother is. He changes people's lives. Puts food on their tables. Helps get kids through college. He's out here making a real difference. Not like you, just some drifting homeless bum."

I chuckled. "Yes, my brother is a real saint, I'm sure. Forget all the people he killed, right? Or worse, the people he corrupted. He relies on weak people like you. What wouldn't you do for a dollar? All this proves is that your soul is for sale to the highest bidder. You're a joke. Just like him."

Duncan laughed. "They're going to kill you. You know that, right? You may have won this battle against me, but all those men inside are waiting for you to show up."

Duncan spit in my face, a clump of bloody mucus landing

on my cheek and dripping down my face.

"I was going to let you walk free," I said. "But you've proven that you'll never change."

"Get off your high horse, Mendez," Duncan said, cackling with delight. "You pretend you're better than us, but you've probably killed more people than anyone inside that house."

"That might be true, but I've never killed someone who didn't deserve it."

Duncan's chest rose and fell with each heavy breath he drew in. His arms tensed beneath my knees, and his damn legs continued to kick at me.

"We could have been in that mansion right now, saving Lily," I said. "But you refused to stray from your crooked ways. The world won't miss you."

His eyes widened while I spoke, then I pulled the trigger.

Chapter 41

The gunshot echoed around the woods, and I had seconds to make my next move.

I jumped up and ran behind the nearest tree, going away from the mansion. The two guards dashed from their posts at the front of the house and charged into the woods. They shouted at each other, but I couldn't make out their words.

They stood with their backs pressed against each other. Because of their tactical gear, I had no clear shot. These bastards were even wearing helmets.

I waited for them to approach Duncan's dead body, and it took them just a few seconds to reach that area. They stopped, one guard lowering his weapon to crouch and examine the body.

"Did he shoot himself?" he asked his colleague.

"Who is it?"

"The fed. Manny's not gonna like this."

"We can't just leave the body out here."

"Wait for Manny to decide. Let's keep searching the area."

I leaned against the tree, listening for their footsteps crunching through the dirt and plants.

"Split up," one said, and the footsteps broke into two distinct directions, one set going away from me, toward the dirt road.

The other, however, was too close, so I circled around the tree, hugging it and craning my neck for a view of where this gunman was.

He stopped directly next to the tree I was hiding behind, opposite my position. I held my breath and stayed frozen like a statue. He was probably listening for anything that would give away my position.

After ten seconds—and it felt more like five minutes—the guard continued forward, down the hill. These split-second decisions were the difference between life and death on the battlefield. And here in the drenched woods of Hillcrest was no different.

I pulled my knife from my pocket, opened the blade, and dashed out from behind the tree toward the unknowing man. The protective vest he wore ended at his waist, so I jammed the knife in the fleshy area between that and his hip bone.

The man howled as my blade sunk into his kidney, immediately dropping his AR-15 to flail around for his wounded back. He couldn't reach and was already tumbling off balance. He spun around like a dazed ballerina before collapsing onto a tree to support his body weight.

I scooped up the AR from the ground and was delighted to find it had a 100-round drum magazine attached. If I couldn't get Lily out with this weapon, maybe it was time for me to hang up my boots once and for all.

Shouting came from across the woods, followed by the rapid fire of the other guard's assault rifle. I hurried behind another tree and waited.

The man kept firing. Bark exploded from the surrounding trees, sending splinters into the gray skies. He screamed,

"*¡Diego! ¿Donde estas?*"

I pulled out my Glock and fired a shot in the air. If I could get this other guy closer, I had a plan.

I listened to the hurried steps now running through the woods, growing closer, and finally coming to a sliding halt when he saw Diego lying at the base of the tree he had fallen into.

"Shit!" he cried. "Which way did he go?"

I dropped to a knee and waited. Both men were panting for breath. One because he had just sprinted across the woods. The other because he was slowly dying.

"Diego!" the man shrieked. "Who was it? Where did he go?"

Diego forced his next words out through drastic heaves for breath. "It's...him...Jonny."

"Manny's brother?" the panicked guard asked, and I heard the concern in his voice elevate to another level. Like he just realized he was alone in the woods with a murderous Sasquatch. Which, I suppose, he was.

"Fuck that guy!" the guard shouted. "Don't die on me!"

I heard his gun clatter to the ground, so I peeked around the tree and saw him taking off his helmet, tossing it aside, and then fumbling to get out of the jacket wrapped around his vest. I knew these two frontline guards were going to be the easiest to get past, but I wasn't expecting them to hand over their lives on a silver platter.

I lowered the AR-15 quietly to the ground and pulled out my Glock, taking one full step out from behind the tree. The second guard was too concerned with trying to stop Diego's bleeding to notice me. Diego's head hung to the side, his eyes glossy and staring directly at me. Blood streamed from the corner of his mouth. I knew he saw me, but his body was already too far gone for him to alert his friend.

He didn't even flinch when I lined up a shot, aimed for his partner's head, and pulled the trigger. The slug caught him square above the ear, and he instantly dropped to the ground, jacket still clutched in one hand, the other falling lazily from Diego's chest and twisting awkwardly as he lay dead on the ground.

Lightning flashed in the sky, yet no thunder followed. The rain softened, but continued, the icy drops hitting my skin like little bug bites.

In front of me was a unique opportunity. I glanced back at the mansion and saw no stirring from within. Those assholes really didn't give a shit for their two guards standing watch. Not so much as checking in on them while they patrolled outside during the worst thunderstorm I'd seen since arriving in Hillcrest.

I strolled over to the two dead men lying next to each other. Neither was too big. Diego was the taller of the two, so I bent over him to remove his helmet, then rolled him over to make removing his jacket and vest easier. Blood streamed from where I had stabbed him in his back, running down his leg like a dark river.

I slipped into the vest, adjusted its straps to fit my wider torso, and squeezed my arms into his jacket. It was a snug fit, but I only needed to wear it for the next few minutes if everything went according to plan. Fortunately, my pants were also black, so I wouldn't need to squeeze into little Diego's blood-stained pair. The helmet fit snugly over my melon head, but it worked and concealed my face.

I patted around the jacket to check for anything, hoping one of these guys had a radio. They didn't.

I grabbed Diego's half-naked body from under his arms and dragged him away to the nearest bush, where I hid his body out of sight. I left the second man where he lay and looked to where Duncan's body remained across the woods. It gave me another idea.

I picked up the second guard's AR-15 he had so carelessly tossed aside moments ago, pulled off the drum magazine, and stuffed it into the front of my waistband for now. The whole thing was about the size of two of my fists, so it wasn't the most comfortable as I headed back toward the mansion, but it would have to do.

I kept calm, my breathing under control. I had no idea if my plan would work and was relying on the knee-jerk reactions of those inside the house. Did they have procedures in place for certain scenarios? If I could just get as many of them outside of the house as possible, that would make the rest of my mission here run seamlessly. Someone would have to stay back inside. It was just a matter of how many people. And who.

I'd even considered entering the mansion and starting to fire away. They'd never see it coming, but I didn't know the layout of the house and anyone smart enough would have the upper hand. The woods I had already become fairly familiar with. The hike up the hill wasn't just to stay covered from wandering eyes. It was to understand the pathways to and from the mansion, the terrain, the layout of the property surrounding this obnoxious house.

When I reached the flat landing atop the hill, I drew in a deep breath and charged directly for the front door, slouching my shoulders and bending my knees to get closer to Diego's height.

I could see through both gigantic windows on either side of the mansion. The men to the right were indeed watching a Dodgers spring training game. And the men on the left had sat down around the table where they were standing earlier. Some drank coffee, others beer.

I ran to the front door, adrenaline creeping into my veins. My heart felt like it was about to leap out of my mouth as I reached out for the handle and pulled open the screen door.

The main door had been left open this entire time, so I took one step inside, looked left, then right. No one noticed me. I counted eighteen men within my immediate field of vision. That was too many perfect shots for me to land in rapid succession. All it took was one of these men to realize what was going on and line up a shot at my head.

With the various conversations taking place, I heard a mixture of English and Spanish. All I could do was trust everyone was bilingual, so I'd go with English. I cleared my throat and shouted, "Man down! Diego's been shot in the woods by the fed! I need help right now!"

The baseball watching men jumped to their feet, startled at first, then focused on the task at hand. Six of them pulled pistols out of holsters from their hips. Two others started for the door empty-handed.

The other side of the mansion was right behind them, guns clacking as they cocked them during their march out the door.

The mayor raced to the back of the mansion, not stopping to look back.

I turned and dashed outside, counting the men as they ran into the woods.

Twelve in total had fled from the mansion, all but two with

a gun visible in hand. They shouted across the woods at each other, and it only took twenty seconds for someone to spot the dead guard.

"Over here!" someone shouted. I walked carefully behind the rows of running men. They all flocked toward the dead body, two men on their knees to examine their fallen colleague. Others looked at the helmet he had tossed aside, while another man picked up the AR-15 now missing the drum magazine rubbing against my crotch.

All twelve men stood in a circle, and this was exactly the moment I was hoping for. I needed to act fast before any of them looked over and saw Duncan's sorry ass lying forty feet away.

I rushed up behind the huddle of thugs, whipped up the AR-15, and started squeezing the trigger. I had one hundred rounds at my disposal before needing to reload, but still was careful to line up the shots as quickly as I could. The gun was a semiautomatic, so would blast as rapidly as I could move my finger.

I had gone through extensive training on the shooting range during my SEALs days. Even though we were issued fully automatic weapons where you only had to hold the trigger down and let the gun do all the work, we also trained on semi-automatics to work finger strength and reflex time. I could usually get out four shots per second, sometimes five or six. With the colder weather, joints moved slower, so I was counting on the four.

Indeed, four men dropped dead within that first second. Followed by another four after the second. Eight for eight in two seconds, and only four remained. I had focused first on those with guns, and as I moved my AR over to start on the next group of men, one of them had already lined up a shot and pulled the trigger.

The bullet whizzed by and scraped my shoulder. Another inch lower and I'd have no use of my right arm. I shot this man square in the chest and moved on to the next three. One had his gun out already, so I fired at him, missed, readjusted, and shot again. That one landed, and so did he.

The two men who didn't bring their guns to this party—stupid asses—sprinted away down the hill.

A gunshot rang out from behind me. I spun around to see another nameless thug I didn't recognize. He fumbled his pistol, and I could actually take my time to blow his head clear off his neck. It was like watching one of those clay plates explode in the sky on the shooting ranges. Poor guy.

Eleven men killed in a matter of fifteen seconds. Two on the run.

I dashed into the woods after them.

An object came whizzing through the air, hitting the ground ten feet in front of me before slowing to roll within inches. It was a grenade. Wasn't expecting that today.

I jumped to my left and tumbled like a ball behind the nearest tree. The grenade burst, sending shrapnel in every direction. A couple of pieces caught my boot, which was still sticking out from the tree, but nothing else hit me.

The gunless men were just sitting on the couch with grenades in their pockets? They really woke up this morning ready for a fight. So did I.

I pulled myself up and poked my head around the tree. Didn't see anyone, and now the rain softened to a gentle sprinkle. I looked up, and the gray clouds filled the sky, although a break in action appeared about twenty minutes away.

When I looked back down, I glimpsed one of the men ducking behind a tree fifty feet down the hill. As much as I wanted to ditch these two clowns and head into the mansion to finish business, I knew better.

If I didn't dispose of these assholes right now, they'd only come back to bite me in the ass later. I refused to make the same mistake twice in my life, so I stepped out and fired a couple of rounds from the AR.

No one moved, so I charged down the hill, weaving through trees and stepping around broad roots protruding from the earth.

I kept my gaze fixed on the tree where I last saw the man cower behind, about twenty feet away. If I could just sneak—

CRACK!

I never saw it coming. From behind the tree nearest me, a branch roughly the size of a hockey stick smacked me across the face. My skin burned with fresh cuts, eyes welling with tears, as I tumbled and tripped over a root. I rolled ten feet down the hill and hurried back to my feet. When I looked up, the second man who I had lost track of tossed aside the branch and sprinted to my right, eyes focused on something on the ground.

Fuck.

My AR.

The Glock in my waistband had almost popped free during my fall, but it remained. I whipped it out at the same time this man dropped into a somersault to pick up the AR and bounced right up to his feet.

This dude wasn't fucking around as he swung the gun in my direction and started pulling the trigger. I fired twice with my

Glock before he dropped, shards of tree bark flying all around me from his errant shots.

I heard the racing footsteps from behind me too late, and soon felt the second man's shoulder ram into my spine. The Glock flew from my hand as we both went down, and within a second of hitting the ground, something thin and sturdy fastened around my neck.

I pushed myself off the ground into a flailing standing position, not gaining steady footing as I scampered around like a drunk stumbling through the house in the middle of the night. Whatever was around my neck tightened to the point I thought my eyeballs were going to pop right out of my skull. I could no longer draw in air and felt around for what was choking me.

A loose vine.

I could feel the blood rushing to my head, my brain and other organs in a unified panic. Heat pricked my face, which was surely as red as the devil's ass by now. I grew lightheaded, strength fleeing my body, but I still had enough left in me.

I couldn't risk swinging a limb behind me and missing, especially since I couldn't feel exactly where this jackass was standing while choking me out. The vine was being pulled downward, indicating this guy was much shorter than me, so I had no choice but to use my sheer size to get out of this pickle.

I fell backward, letting my body turn into deadweight—which wasn't hard to do at the moment. My new friend either had to let go of the vine to stand clear of the falling tree that was my body or go down with me.

He chose the latter, and I felt his bony body crunch beneath my back. His grip on the vine loosened just enough for me to gasp for fresh air, my lungs burning for oxygen. He grunted and pulled tight again, but it was too late.

The air in my body gave me just enough of a boost to roll over and snatch the man's wrists. I pulled his arms in opposite directions, the vine tightening around my neck before it finally snapped in half and was no longer a threat.

The man's brown eyes bulged in an immediate panic. He surely saw his death around the corner, and I was happy to oblige. His feet thrashed freely, but he gained no traction on the muddy ground.

I panted, still recovering from the extended period with no air. He resisted, but I pressed each of his wrists into the ground, my face coming lower toward his like we were about to share a romantic kiss in the woods. Instead, I reared my head back and drilled the top of my skull into his nose.

He screamed as blood spewed in every direction.

By the time I stood up, I couldn't even see his face. Between the mud and blood, he may as well have been wearing the same makeup as me. I had a moment to catch my breath while he rolled back and forth on the ground, clutching his face. Hands on my knees, I watched him squirming, trying to crawl away.

He must have spent all his energy pulling on that vine, because he now moved at the pace of a stoned turtle on vacation. I gave him a twenty-second head start, and he only moved ten feet away from me.

I took three steps toward him, flipped him over on his back, and raised my boot over his face. After the third stomp, he stopped wailing. I stomped twice more, and his body ceased moving. Then four more times because it made me feel better.

If he wasn't dead, he sure as hell wasn't making it back to

the mansion tonight. Good enough.

Thirteen men dead from the initial eighteen I had seen in the house. There would be more, but now the odds had tilted heavily in my favor. I gathered myself, found the AR-15, patted my crotch to make sure the drum mags were still there, and headed up the hill with more scratches on my face than I had woken up with.

Assholes.

I was going to kill everyone left in that fucking mansion.

Chapter 42

I picked up the other dead guard's AR-15 on my way back up the hill and left it outside the front door of the mansion.

The place looked deserted, but I knew it wasn't. I'd just wiped out more than half of these clowns, and the rest were all hiding somewhere inside. No vehicles had left the driveway. The black van reminded me that the mayor was somewhere in the mansion. The coward.

I ripped off the jacket I had borrowed from Diego, my upper body now free to move naturally again. I kept the bulletproof vest on and tightened my grip on the AR-15, finger on the trigger and ready to fire.

I stepped into the house. The table to my left had abandoned beer bottles and coffee mugs. The Dodgers game continued on the TV to my right, so I shuffled over to turn it off. Pure silence filled the mansion now.

I held my breath to listen to my surroundings. Nothing.

They were all hiding.

After taking that blow to the face from the tree branch, my senses were elevated more than usual. I hated getting surprised like that, and I'd be damned if it would happen again today.

This mansion was too big to make a reliable plan. A hallway

broke off from this living room, stretching to the back of the house where an open doorway revealed what looked to be another living room.

I strode to the other side where the men had been drinking at the table. Behind that was a kitchen. A pot of melted cheese sat on the stovetop. I dipped my pinky inside and tasted it. Perfect for nachos, which they were in the middle of preparing. A skillet with pork carnitas was next to the cheese. Ten bags of tortilla chips lined the counter, along with bowls of diced tomatoes, pinto beans, jalapenos, and black olives. I would have much preferred to receive an invitation to this little fiesta instead. All the burners were still on, and I left them that way.

Fuck 'em.

Behind the kitchen was another damned hallway, and no, it didn't connect with the same room at the end. This place was massive. Lily could be anywhere. I wondered if Andres might be hiding somewhere, but he seemed to live at Hamburger Stand. Lucky guy.

The door at the end of the hallway was open and appeared to be a stairwell heading down. I knew basements weren't common in California, which meant they were surely running their illegal operations out of one.

Shit.

These guys could have an arsenal down there for scenarios just like this. No way I could take on a dozen of their men on my own, right?

I heard a clatter from above. Upstairs. I hadn't seen a staircase aside from the one at the end of the hallway and shouldn't have assumed it led *down*.

Starting down the hallway, I raised the AR and swept it from wall to wall, waiting for any sudden movements. My steps were soft and slow, not wanting to give away my position in the mansion. I had my breathing under control as I passed four different doors in the hall. As much as I wanted to open each of them and see what was inside, I couldn't risk exposing my location. I didn't know if the doors might creak and had to play it safe.

I kept my hearing focused behind me as I passed the doors, waiting for the abrupt sound of one opening and some cartel goon jumping out. But that never happened as I neared the end of the hallway.

The door at the end opened to a landing, and from my angle, I could see it split both up and down.

Shit.

The noise had come from above, so I needed to check there first.

Just before I stepped through the open doorway, a man jumped out and shouted, firing a pistol aimed right at my chest. The bullet hit my vest, and I felt the pressure against my sternum. A perfect shot. But he had no reason to think I'd be wearing this. Thanks, Diego.

I pulled my trigger three times and watched three holes appear across the man's chest. He looked down, ran a finger around the rim of one entry wound, then fell to the floor. His pistol clanged against the hardwood. A Desert Eagle. One of my favorites. Bigger than most handguns, so not everyone could handle them. I could. They gave me all the power of a semiautomatic rifle in my fist.

Now everyone in the house knew where I was. No point in wasting time, so I stepped through the doorway and over this dead guy's body and took a right to go up the stairs. I took two steps at a time until reaching the top landing, where another hallway awaited.

This place was a fucking maze.

I no longer gave a shit if the jackasses in this house knew where I was. This hallway also had four doors along the sides, a fifth one closed at the far end.

I opened the first door on my right. I almost shot my reflection in the bathroom mirror but recognized myself in time. Nothing going on in there.

I crossed the hall and opened the door on my left. It was a bedroom with the curtains drawn, and a laptop humming on the nightstand next to the bed. I stepped into the room, first checking behind the doors, under the bed, and inside the closet. The usual places people would hide. No one was in here, so I moved closer to the nightstand, keeping my ears focused on the hallway outside.

Behind the laptop were two baggies of cocaine, but the screen caught my attention. It was a spreadsheet. A contact list of names, phone numbers, and addresses. A who's who of everyone I had encountered during my time in Hillcrest.

Jo's Diner. Mayor Reece. Theo Rambis. Dominic Evans and his family members. There were at least forty names on this list, some highlighted green, others in red. Five police officers were listed, and only Matthews was highlighted in red. The others had no color. Agent Duncan was highlighted green.

I figured they were highlighted based on who was helpful to their cause, and who wasn't. I couldn't help but wonder if Matthews had always been red, or if his color had changed because of recent developments. Duncan was a piece of shit— that much was confirmed.

I heard footsteps pounding up the stairs and promptly ducked down behind the bed.

"Where is he?" a voice whispered when the footsteps reached the top landing.

The bedroom I was in was the only open door. Dammit.

I tightened my finger around the trigger and stood back up. This tiny bed had no chance of hiding me, and I'd have to face these men straight on. But they didn't enter my field of vision, so I scurried across to hide behind the opened door.

I listened and only heard faint whispers coming from the hallway.

Seconds later, a cylindrical object flew into the bedroom, banging against the wall and coming to a rest. At first, I thought it was another grenade and my downfall. But it was only a canister of tear gas. It whizzed smoke, which started filling the room in a hurry. The closet door was behind my back, so I slid it open and slipped inside, closing the door.

The smoke would eventually make its way inside the closet, but this bought me some time. I reached above my head and found a pull string, yanking it down to turn on the light. An array of suits and athletic wear greeted me. I spotted a black hoodie and pulled it off the hanger, wrapping the sleeve around my face to protect my mouth and nose.

I drew in a deep breath to see if any of the tear gas had made its way in. Nothing yet.

A standing fan was tucked into the corner of the closet. The old kind that my mom used to move from room to room during the blistering summers in Texas. It would rotate from side to side while Manny and I tried speaking into the spinning blade to make our voices sound like some sort of futuristic robot. The fan must have been a sign from her in the heavens.

I took in another deep breath and held the air in my lungs, grabbing the fan and sliding the closet door back open. Smoke had filled half the room. I unraveled the power cord and jammed the plug into the outlet under the window overlooking the woods. Quite the view under normal circumstances. I flipped the latches on the window and swung it open, then turned the knob on the fan, moving it to face outward.

It wasn't the most efficient process, but it blew a portion of the smoke out the window. Enough to keep me going. My eyes burned, but I'd be fine as long as I didn't inhale any of this shit.

These pussies in the hallway weren't going to step foot in this room. I had maybe another twenty seconds before my lungs would get pissed off and require fresh air, so I gritted my teeth and darted to the door.

Two men were waiting for me, guns drawn, and immediately started firing. I felt another bullet lodge itself into my vest, then a familiar burning sensation from my leg. One of those caught me in the thigh, but it seemed to have only been a grazing. Hell, I didn't know for sure. Adrenaline was flooding all of my senses.

I fired ten rounds in three seconds, sweeping my AR from side to side until both men were on the floor, splayed out and useless. I stepped over them and immediately recognized them as the two men who fled from the tavern after the shots were fired my first night in Hillcrest. These men were cowards for abandoning their friends who had died that night. I was glad they were no longer part of this world.

I closed the bedroom door, keeping the tear gas trapped in there so it could gradually escape through the open window.

There were now less than a handful of people remaining in this mansion. I was sure of it. If they had more bodies, they would have sent more than two to smoke me out of the bedroom just now.

Resources were running thin for the cartel, and my confidence was rising. I was also growing fond of Diego for letting me use his vest. I'd be a dead man without it.

I checked my leg and saw a chunk of my pant leg missing, a blotch of blood soaking around the tear. It was more than a gentle graze—the bullet had taken a dime-sized amount of flesh. But it wasn't lodged in my leg, had missed arteries and even the muscle. I wasn't a believer in luck, but only needing a couple of stitches after facing all these men with guns was the closest I'd get to calling myself lucky.

I continued back down the hallway, encouraged by the way everything had played out so far. There were two more doors facing each other, and I kicked them both open, no longer giving a shit about playing nice. Fuck their doorframes.

The two rooms were more bedrooms, both of which looked regularly used, judging by the piles of clothes on the floors. I was no longer snooping around. I just wanted to find these crooks and keep dealing them death.

When I reached the door at the end of the hallway, I stopped and reset myself. The adrenaline kept me going, but I had plenty of strength fueled by sheer confidence. Taking on sixteen men on my own amped me up that way.

I reared back and kicked the door open with my wounded leg, just to prove a point. It appeared to be an office.

The floor was covered in a light gray carpet. A wide mahogany desk stood against the back wall and sitting behind it in a swivel chair was Lily. Mayor Reece crouched behind her, holding a pistol against her temple.

Lily's eyes bulged, sweat trickling down her face. A bandanna was tied around her mouth, and she fought to make inaudible noises, jerking side to side in the chair. Ropes tied her arms and torso to the seat, and she could barely move.

The mayor glared at me with a shit-eating grin. "You're finally here."

Chapter 43

"Mayor Reece," I said. "Fancy finding you here."

The gun quivered in his hand. Lily's eyes locked on mine. She was trying to communicate something through vision, but I couldn't exactly give her the focus such a task demanded. I needed to find a way out of this scenario we'd found ourselves in.

My AR was held high, aiming right at the mayor's face. He crouched lower to make my shot impossible, using Lily's head as a shield covering half his face. One eye watched me from behind the blonde strands sticking out messily.

"I could say the same," he said. "Why are you really in Hillcrest? No one's buying this shit that you just wandered into town to spend time at the beach."

I'd had perfect outings at the shooting range several times in my life. Bullseye after bullseye. I once hit forty-nine in a row. Something about the milestone of fifty got into my head, and I missed that last shot by two centimeters.

"Unlike everyone else in this town," I said, "I'm actually telling the truth."

"Bullshit," the mayor said. His calmness surprised me. This wasn't some ordinary mayor. He held the gun with con-fidence, spoke with clarity and purpose. And was obviously a plant from the cartel. "Tell me who sent you, and I'll let your girlfriend live."

"That's where you're wrong, Mr. Mayor. Lily is going to live. Maybe you should quit being a coward and leave her out of this. We can put the guns down and fight this out like men. What do you say?"

His visible eye didn't flinch as he held a burning gaze on me. As did Lily. I hadn't been the center of attention like this in quite some time. Needed to add "All Eyez on Me" to the 2Pac playlist, apparently.

"I say you're both going to die today," he said. "Sounds like a good plan to me. No more DEA. No more Jonny fucking Mendez. And we can all go about our lives as planned."

Mayor Reece was smart—I could give him that much credit. He never kept his head still, bobbing slightly up and down in no particular cadence to prevent me from lining up a reliable shot. He also weaved his head left and right. I didn't know if I wanted to take the gamble. Those two centimeters burned in the back of my mind, and that could certainly make a difference between who lived and died behind the office desk.

"Let me get this straight," I said, taking a step closer.

This movement caused the mayor to pull his gun from Lily's temple and point it at me. "Another fucking step and you're done," he said. Again, so calm. And he kept her as a shield through it all.

"Deal," I said, locking my feet in place. "So you think someone sent me to hunt down this cartel in Hillcrest?"

"We know that's what you're doing," the mayor said. "We just don't know *who*. And we want answers. Was it the Zetas? Sinaloa? Tell me."

"I've been nothing but truthful. This is all a coincidence."

"People like you don't show up at a place by chance," the mayor said. "Not with your skillset. You're a hired hitman. But hunting your own brother—that sounds like something the Sinaloa guys would have you do."

"You clearly have never done your homework on me if you think I'd ever be a part of that nonsense."

"Oh, please. You don't think we have people in the CIA working for us? We have them, the FBI, the DEA. You name it, and we have our bases covered. No one investigates us without us knowing about it. Which is why I know you're working with one of the other cartels. You showed up unannounced. When our guys saw you in the tavern, I didn't believe them. None of us believed them. Your own brother dismissed it, saying it had to have been a lookalike. But then you showed your face all over that camera for us to see, and sure as shit, it's Jonny Mendez live in the flesh. What's the prize for killing your own brother? Fifty mil? Hundred?"

Stay still, motherfucker. But he didn't.

I met Lily's stare. She'd been crying, and it made her blue eyes look extra blue. Absolutely beautiful. If those eyes were the last thing I saw in my life, I'd have no right to complain. The mayor took his gun off me and returned it to Lily's temple.

"I'm impressed," I said. "I show up in town and an entire cartel jumps to all these conclusions and has made up all kinds of stories about me. Makes me feel like a celebrity—and I just left Los Angeles, so believe me, everything you said is a complete lie. I've never met with any cartel. And I thought my brother was in Mexico for the last twenty years."

"Don't play dumb, jackass," the mayor spat. "Manny has been in Mexico. He had to come out here to clean up the mess you've caused."

"I suppose I should ask the questions," I said. "You guys technically started all this."

"What the hell are you talking about?"

"The two guys at the tavern," I said. "If no gun was fired that evening, I would have finished my nachos and margarita, and gone to the beach the next morning. All our lives would be different today if those men were never shot. So, what made them so deserving?"

"Those two were trouble for us," the mayor said. "Slacking in their work. Sloppy in their delivery of drugs. They were always too careless and took pointless chances."

"I see. They were going to risk your operation getting busted, so they had to be eliminated. Makes sense."

"Exactly. Anyone who endangers the greater good will no longer be allowed to breathe. Those are the rules. We run a tight ship."

The mayor was loose. Feeling good about himself and talking. He thought he was in control, but I understood how to flip his confidence to my advantage. His cockiness would keep him talking. These types of criminals took great pride in bragging about how they pulled it all off. That *Aha! Gotcha!* moment that filled their void of satisfaction. Poor Mayor Reece was never told he was enough as a child.

"Okay, so you killed those two men," I said. "But I'm wondering what happened even before that. Did this cartel corrupt you while you were mayor, or were you planted into your position?"

"Winning office in a small town like this is a joke. With the money we have, my name was blasted all over this city. By the time the election came around, most people voted for the only name they recognized. We have politicians in our group, so I had first-class training on how to present myself as a charming public figure."

"So that's the first step," I said. Lily stopped looking at me, her eyes daydreaming. I supposed she was listening to the mayor's words and piecing together how she would use this confession in a future trial. "Win the mayor's office. From there, you choose your police chief. Police chief then directs the force how to deal with particular issues around town. Just like that, you own the local law enforcement."

"They never said you were smart," the mayor said. "Just the muscle doing the dirty work for the brains behind the operation."

"Well, that's just rude," I said. "That's a judgment based on my size. You're right, though, I *do* go out and tear bad guys to pieces. But I also hit the books in my free time. Always curious and learning. It's the only way to live."

"A philosopher, too?" the mayor wondered, cocking the lone eyebrow I could see. "You're nothing at all what I expected."

"Sorry to disappoint," I said, cracking a grin.

Mayor Reece returned a mad smile. In a rapid movement, his hand that had been out of sight whipped out from below and slapped Lily across the face. "This crazy bitch?" the mayor said. Lily's head jerked aside for a quarter of a second and returned to conceal the mayor's face. She squeezed her eyes shut for a moment before looking at me, her gaze full of desperation. "Yeah, this one's been a piece of work. Almost as much as you. We're just happy to see the both of you leaving today."

"Well, that's a tall task," I said. "Seeing as if you pull that trigger, you'll be a dead man. Lily there has more dignity in her pinky than you have in your entire body. She's everything you're not. She's all that's right in this messed-up world."

"No one gives a shit," Mayor Reece said. "Any second now, she'll be nothing but a dead DEA agent, along with her worthless partner."

"That's not nice," I said. "Duncan's job was to bring me to this mansion. And he did that."

"You were coming regardless. All we needed was this blonde bimbo, and we knew you'd come running. That's where Duncan helped us. Intercepting this sweet thing on her way to the airport. That's the problem with you trustworthy people. You never know when you're getting played."

Lily blinked her eyes tightly again, keeping her stare on me. She darted her eyes to the right before returning them to normal.

The move seemed deliberate now, no longer a reaction to getting slapped across the face.

"I'm sorry we're not broken like you," I said. "You've built this world around yourself where you can't trust anyone. As many times as life has burned me, I still trust those who deserve it. Funnily enough, I didn't trust Chief Matthews, and now he's dead. I take it you didn't trust him, either."

Reece laughed. "What a disgrace. Fucking Matthews. We had an agreement, and he turned his back on us. Got soft and caught a conscience. Thought he could toe the line, play the best of both worlds. But we need full commitment. No half-assing."

"Always fully ass something," I said. "I get it."

"Shut the fuck up, Mendez."

Lily did the blinking thing again and moved her eyes to the right. Was she planning to move her head to the right and give me a clear shot? It wasn't entirely obvious, but I thought it was along those lines.

"You're an angry little guy," I said. "Must be from wearing all that makeup. Glad to see you've embraced your feminine side."

"Enough."

"What are you waiting for?" I asked. "You've all made it plenty clear you don't want to kill me. Is Manny wanting to do the deed himself? If you wanted me dead, you'd have shot me by now."

"Enough, dammit!"

"I requested a meeting. Or was it you who called the meeting? Because that morning at the diner when I saw you three clowns, I recall the whole meeting with Manny was your brilliant idea. You tried to orchestrate this meeting, but what was it really going to be? Just another trap where Manny could corner me. Was he going to have you pop out of a closet with a gun? Good little obedient boy."

His lone eye squinted, and I knew I was getting under his skin. The last thing these cocky assholes liked was getting beaten to the punch. *He* wanted to tell me the whole story, not the other way around. What was the fun if I already knew all the answers?

"I'll be honest," I said. "You all had me fooled most of this time. It wasn't until Duncan went along with my idea to join me so easily on this trip. I was expecting a fight, seeing as he hated me. But he agreed immediately. Plus, nothing made sense once I learned Rambis was involved. And if he was sharing a meal with both the mayor and the DEA agent, then you two *had* to be involved, too. Theo didn't exactly have vibes that he could be a double agent. Plus, I know journalists make shit for money, so why wouldn't he take the easy cash to filter what got published?"

"You don't know shit," Reece said, and I heard the vigor slipping out of his voice. So maybe I *did* know shit.

"The only piece I couldn't figure out was you, Mr. Mayor," I continued. "After your tears at the press conference following the chief's death, I took you for an honest man of the people. But you've already admitted you're just a trained monkey. You need to get re-elected, after all, so why not show your vulnerable side? But then you got kidnapped and it all made sense. You used yourself as bait. For me. You knew I already wanted to come free Lily, and couldn't resist the chance to save the mayor, too. As you said, you played me because I'm honest."

"The road to hell is built on the backs of good people," Reece said, seeming to regain some of his confidence. "Bad people can't manipulate other bad people, only the good ones."

Lily did the blink and stare routine again. Without saying a word, she was willing me to trust her plan. I locked eyes with her and gave the slightest nod to show I was following. She responded by blinking three times in steady succession. Like she was counting.

On the count of three.

"It's too bad," I said. "Most bad people I've met are incredibly smart and could do some big things in life if they applied their talents to doing good."

Lily did the three blinks again, and I nodded, lining up my shot on the left half of Reece's forehead. She raised and lowered her eyebrows, which I took as her nodding to me. We were on the same page.

She blinked once.

"Fuck doing good," Reece said. "Good people only make it so far in life. They don't know how to take what's theirs."

Lily blinked a second time.

"There's more to life than money and power," I said, not even listening to my words. All my focus zeroed on Reece's head. Adrenaline pulsed in my fingertips, the trigger beneath my index finger smooth and cool, awaiting my direction.

"Agree to—" Reece began, but Lily blinked the third time and jerked her head to her right, giving me a split second of a fully exposed mayor.

I didn't hesitate and pulled the trigger.

Chapter 44

The top half of the mayor's head burst into a mess of blood and brains. A decent amount landed on Lily, but she didn't seem to care. She'd just been spared.

Lily actually fell over, taking the chair down with her.

I rushed across the office, going left around the desk to avoid the mess of Mayor Reece splayed out on the other side. I whipped out my knife, cut the ropes tied around Lily's limbs, then pulled the bandanna out of her mouth.

She jumped to her feet, gasping for air, and threw her arms around me. "Thank you, Jonny," she whispered in my ear, planting a quick kiss on my lips. She tasted salty from all the sweat that had pooled around her mouth and soaked into the bandanna, but I didn't care. Besides, my waterlogged clothes were already drenching her. She wasn't bothered, either.

"The house is mostly empty," I said. "I've lost track of how many of these thugs I've killed, but there can't be many left. I suspect my brother is waiting for me in the basement. Do you know the layout of the mansion?"

Lily shook her head, wiping sweat from her brow. "No. They've kept me in this room this whole time."

"Okay," I said, reaching into the front of my pants. Lily watched me with plenty of confusion but didn't ask questions as I yanked the drum magazine out and felt like a new man again. "Take this. I left an AR-15 right outside the front door. When you go down the stairs, the first landing is the main level. You'll pass through the kitchen to get to the front. Get the gun and run. You'll see the driveway full of cars. Run all the way down it and don't stop. The AR is just in case anyone is waiting out there."

"I'm not leaving you, Jonny," Lily said. "No way in hell. Especially after you just rescued me."

"They were never going to kill you," I said, not believing my own lie. I thought Reece was absolutely going to kill her but was just biding time to figure how he could do that and stay alive himself. Poor schmuck. "You were bait to get me into this house. This is between me and my brother. No need for you to stay involved. You'll only be putting yourself in harm's way."

Tears rolled down Lily's face. "I can't leave you, Jonny. Please let me help."

I put my AR down on the blood-splattered desk and grabbed Lily by each arm. "This is personal. A family matter. I'm all they want. If you want to help, get as far away from here as possible and call someone. But not your boss, because I'm honestly not sure who to trust right now. Maybe Homeland Security. The National Guard is supposedly on the way, but I'm not sure if that's even true. There's been a lot going on while you've been cooped up in here."

"Dammit, Jonny," Lily said. "Fine."

She grabbed the drum mag out of my hand, gave me one more hug, and started for the door. Stopping and turning around, she said, "This isn't over between us."

She vanished through the doorway. My heart skipped a

beat. Lily was truly one of a kind. I'd never met a woman who would just barge through a cartel-owned mansion with no fear. She completely trusted me when I told her the house was safe, even though I had no way of knowing who might lurk downstairs.

I chased after her, since she wasn't armed yet, and caught up with her by the landing on the main level.

She stopped in the kitchen, examining everything that had been abruptly abandoned.

"Don't cut through the woods," I said. "Lots of bodies. Just stay on the driveway. It will turn into a dirt road and take you to the bottom of the hill."

Lily looked over her shoulder at me and nodded. "Good luck, Jonny."

She ran out the front door, grabbed the AR, and inserted the drum magazine. Seconds later, she disappeared down the driveway and out of sight.

The gentle pattering of soft raindrops falling on the roof echoed throughout the house. I passed through the kitchen and crossed over to the living room, heading down the other hallway. I entered what I had originally thought was a second living room, but found it was actually a game room. A billiards table stood center, and along the outer walls was a fully stocked bar, air hockey, foosball, and a ping-pong table. I would've never guessed one of the cartel's priorities was entertainment, but if you were trapped in a house with almost two dozen other men, some steam needed to be released.

The game room was abandoned. Even the TV hanging on the wall remained off. They wanted to lure me into the basement. I smelled the trap. There was only one way down there, and they could easily have four men lined up with their guns pointing at the door waiting for me to arrive.

At some point, Manny's patience would wear thin, and he'd lose his desire to keep me alive. I'd already cost him plenty by killing a majority of his workforce in Hillcrest. When was I no longer worth the hassle? I had to assume that time had come.

I returned down the long hallway and was greeted by a goon with two pistols who stepped out from around the kitchen. He fired twice, and I shot once. One shot whizzed by my head and planted in the hallway drywall behind me. The other was nowhere close. Mine landed square in the man's right shoulder. He dropped both guns to clasp his left hand over the wound.

"Where's Manny?" I demanded.

"Fuck you!" the man shrieked back through clenched teeth.

I lowered the AR and shot him in the thigh. He dropped to the ground, writhing around in pain, unsure which gunshot wound to grab.

"The next one will be in your head if you don't tell me," I said. "Is Manny in the basement?"

The man nodded, hugging his knee into his body, blood oozing from the shot in his thigh.

"How many people are down there?"

He shook his head. I flipped my AR around and smacked him across the face with the stock.

"I'm not telling you shit," the man said, wiping blood away from his lips.

I put my AR on the floor and hoisted the man up from his armpits, pinning him against the wall that connected the living room to the kitchen.

His feet kicked but had no strength.

"Tell me how many men are downstairs!" I shouted in his

face.

"Put my man down," a calm voice said from my left.

I whipped my head around to see my brother with a cigarette pinched between his lips.

"Manny," I said. "It's about time."

I pulled away from the wall and threw this worthless sack of shit across the living room. He hit the sofa with a grunt, flipping it completely over as he crashed to the floor. His guns still lay there, but Manny didn't so much as look at them, despite only having a cigarette.

"Baby brother," Manny said, flashing a grin. "We have so much to catch up on. Why don't you come join me?"

Manny started back through the kitchen. The stove burners were still on, so I studied them closer. Gas burners.

"You wouldn't happen to have a spare cigarette for me?" I asked. "It's been quite the day."

Manny was on his way to the staircase but stopped and turned around to face me. "Put the gun down, and I'll give you whatever you want."

I hadn't even realized I picked the AR back up after I tossed that little man aside. My brain and body were apparently running on instincts. And my instincts told me to avoid the basement at all costs.

I placed the AR on the dining room table between the scattering of coffee mugs and beer bottles.

"Good," Manny said. This was the best look at him I'd had since we were kids. I remembered my brother as rugged when we were younger. Through high school, he always worked manual labor jobs. Landscaping, working on farms, construction jobs. His hands were calloused, face weathered and worn out by the sun. He claimed to work to help provide for me and my aunt—which he did—but he had secretly kept another stash of money as part of his plan to flee and return to Mexico.

The man in front of me right now resembled nothing of the teenage version of my memories. He had always been darker skinned than me, and that held true. But all the ruggedness had dissipated. Manny looked like he hadn't worked outdoors or with his hands in at least a decade. His face was too pretty. With all his fortune, he paid for a nose job, and some shitty Botox work that looked like invisible hands were pulling his cheeks back. He had a perfectly groomed beard that glimmered under the lighting with each subtle movement.

But his eyes remained the same. Dark brown and full of curiosity. But also scarred. I wondered how many people those eyes had watched die. Probably as many as mine.

Manny wore a gray suit, and I tensed when he reached for the inside pocket of his jacket. All he pulled out, however, was a pack of cigarettes. He fished out a smoke for me and handed it over.

"A peace offering, baby bro," he said.

He always called me that. As long as I could remember. Unless I pissed him off. Then I got my full "Jonathan Christian Mendez!" yelled at me like he was an enraged parent. Which he was, in a sense.

Manny understood he was the only man I had in my life for guidance, and he shouldered that responsibility with pride. In the months before he left, he seemed to teach me new things every day. Looking back, I thought he was trying to clean his conscience before leaving his kid brother behind. He taught me how to change a tire on Tia Rosa's battered Honda Civic.

How to defend myself by both physical and mental means. He even had a sex talk with me and sneaked one of Tia Rosa's bras away to show me how to unsnap it.

I wondered if he ever thought back to those times as often as I did. Back when life was simple, even after losing our mother.

The cigarette trembled so slightly in his grip. I whipped my hand out to snatch it from his fingers and plucked the butt between my lips. Manny reached back into his pocket and brought out a lighter.

I leaned in toward him, jutting out my face so he could light the cigarette, which he did in a swift motion. Two dish rags hung from the oven's handle behind me, so I grabbed one and patted off the sweat from my forehead.

"So," Manny said. "It's come to this."

I shrugged and took a long drag from the cigarette. These cancer sticks were fucking gross, but sometimes you had to put aside your tastes for the greater good, like scarfing down a disgusting dish when visiting a relative you hadn't seen in years. We visited my Tio Antonio every two years in Florida—he came to Texas in the alternating years—and he always prepared a seafood dish. The kind where the fish still had its eyes staring at you while you ate its body.

That shit freaked me out as a kid and still does. I don't eat seafood to this day. But my mom would always pinch my leg underneath the table as I stared at the fish, horror-struck.

And now the cigarette in my mouth was no different from my mom's fingers pinching the flabby part of my thigh. I had to get through this.

"I don't know what you're talking about," I said. "This has all been a giant misunderstanding. I never intended to find you and bring down your operation."

Manny laughed. "Oh, please. That may be true, but if you found out this was my cartel from day one, would you have just left town and let me be?"

"Of course not," I said. "You're killing innocent people in this town, and I was never going to stand by and watch it happen."

"Killing people?" Manny asked, raising an eyebrow. "You make it sound like I'm holding down people and forcing pills down their throats. We've never sold a single drug to anyone who didn't ask for it."

I chuckled. "Get real, Manny. You have no right to act innocent. You know damn well what those drugs do to people. Just give them a sample, and they'll be back for more. They're addictive, and you can only prey on the weak to become your repeat customers. Is this really the life you planned for when you left me behind? Selling drugs to high school kids and addicts? What are you getting out of this? Mom would be so appalled by what you've become."

These last words appeared to have struck a chord, but Manny brushed them away just as easily. "Jonny the Golden Boy. You could never do no wrong. If you got in a fight at school, somehow Mom still questioned me about why I wasn't there to protect you. You hit that baseball through Mr. Martinez's window, and I got blamed for making the pitch too easy to hit. You might not remember these things, because you were younger and reaping the benefits. But I do. And I never held it against you because it wasn't your fault. It wasn't anyone's fault. Mom always saw too much of Dad in me and resented me for it. Don't you think I wanted to be as close to Mom as you were? She was all I had."

Manny's voice wavered. He'd always been a closed book,

and I knew he'd never spoken these words to anyone else.

"I can't speak to that," I said. "You're right, but that doesn't excuse you for becoming a criminal."

"Mom pushed me away. I could only take the favoritism toward you for so long. It wore me down. My mind was made to go to Mexico many years before I actually did. I was gonna go sooner, but Mom's death delayed those plans. I couldn't leave you after all that—I needed to know you were going to be okay."

"You say things like this, and it reminds me there is a good person swimming around in there."

"I am a good person," Manny replied, his voice lowering to just above a whisper. "I care about people. Go to church every Sunday. Even donate money to important causes."

"But your money is earned in the slimiest of ways. You can do all the penance you want, but that doesn't change the fact that you make others' lives worse for the sake of making yours better. It's selfish. Despicable."

"And I'm aware of this. But I don't see any of it. All I see are stacks of cash dropped on my desk once a week. The money is clean and legit by the time it reaches me. I own twelve properties around the world. Over forty cars. One private jet. You may not agree with it, but my lifestyle is the dream. I can do whatever I want whenever I want. I've provided a life for my son that you and I could have only dreamed about as kids."

"Your son," I said, shaking my head. "That's probably the most fucked up part of all this. You bring him in to work for you. Get his hands dirty nice and young. You may have created this glamorous image of yourself in your head, but you're nothing but a joke."

Manny pursed his lips, and he stopped taking puffs. He pointed his cigarette at me. "This is a family business. And there will always be a seat at the table for you. Dad wants you. He had his eyes on us from the day he left. Always looking out. Waiting for the day he could invite us to join him. He is the king of Eldorado. No one is respected and feared as much as him. Royalty. You're a prince and don't even know it yet."

I could feel the disdain coming from my brother's tone and knew I had to make a move soon. I took a step to my left to open a clear view toward the stove on my right. The nacho cheese was bubbling in the pot, hot and ready to make a stomach's dreams come true.

"I'm never joining you or Dad," I said.

I plucked the cigarette out of my mouth and tossed it toward the stove. It landed next to the burner and rolled closer toward it, a cloud of fire erupting in an instant. Then I threw the dishrag I'd been holding on top of it, and watched it transform into a ball of flames.

"*Idiota!*" Manny shouted, and he pivoted away, sprinting out the back of the kitchen and down the stairs.

The stove and kitchen counter were covered in flames. The cheese was burning, a true crime. Fire danced around, touching the bottom edge of the cabinets above the counter. In ten minutes, this entire kitchen would be up in a blaze.

I grabbed the AR-15 from the table and noticed the man I had thrown was no longer in the living room. Through the window, I spotted a figure sprinting down the driveway. He wasn't coming back, and I hoped he wouldn't cross paths with Lily. For his own sake.

I dashed toward the rear doorway, ready to barge down the stairs, but stopped when a gun fired, the wall to my left exploding into fragments.

I looked down the stairs and saw one of my brother's crew holding a TEC-9 with an extended magazine. He jumped back through the doorway at the bottom of the stairs once I swung my AR around and fired four rounds. They all landed in the wall behind where the man had been standing.

I had two choices. Further risk my life by running down these stairs to eliminate whoever remained. Or join Lily, who had probably reached the main road by now, and let this mansion burn to the ground.

I tiptoed down the first step, heart thundering in my chest, the fire cackling in the kitchen to serve as a ticking time bomb. If I didn't kill my brother today, he'd only keep hunting me. I knew too much and had refused to join his team. No cartel in the world would be fine with me walking away from this situation. Throw in my background with the SEALs and CIA, and it was in their best interest to remove me from the equation.

"This ends tonight," I said under my breath, and ran down the rest of the stairs.

Chapter 45

I reached the bottom landing, only two feet between me and the open doorway into whatever this basement was.

My entire body was numb with adrenaline. The AR felt like an extension of my arms as I cradled it, finger on the trigger. I tasted death in the air but wasn't sure who it belonged to. Falling to my brother and father's cartel wasn't exactly a romantic ending to my life. Some might call it ironic. I wasn't sure what to think of the possibility. Bullshit?

If the good truly died young, then my number would be called soon. Funnily enough, I never could picture myself as elderly. I could close my eyes and try to imagine what I'd look like as an eighty-year-old man, but nothing ever appeared in my thoughts. Just blankness. Was that some premonition that I'd never live to be that old? I assumed so.

Heat radiated from the top of the stairwell, and I had no way of seeing how much the fire had spread. Maybe the roof would collapse and kill us all in the basement. Better to go out as a group than on your own.

I stuck the barrel of the AR-15 into the doorway and was promptly greeted by an array of bullets flying into the wall to my right. It could have been one automatic gun, or several. I looked over and counted nine holes in the wall.

These guys had already made a mistake by retreating into the basement. Their position gave me the advantage in the stairwell. I could sit on the bottom step and wait for them to come to me. Only two people could fit through the doorway, so they would have to bottleneck into a line even if there were fifty of them in there. It was the same strategy King Leonidas used for his heavily outnumbered army. And it worked...until it didn't.

But I liked my odds against whoever remained in the basement. They weren't going to charge through the doorway. I couldn't wait them out, either, especially with the kitchen on fire several feet above my head.

I had no choice but to play angles. They wanted me—and probably expected me—to just burst through the doorway where they could open fire and send two dozen rounds into my body. Did they really think I was that stupid?

I lowered the AR to my side and pressed against the wall, inching my face toward the doorway. All I needed was an idea of the layout in the basement to make some sort of plan.

Rows of tables lined the room from front to back. If I didn't know any better, I'd have thought it was a business conference room. But instead of laptops and notepads, these tables had mountains of pills, powders, and cash. I also spotted bags full of marijuana and cocaine. The Eldorado cartel had been selling more than the originally suspected opioids plaguing the community. They were a fully functioning one-stop shop for all drugs.

I counted ten tables in this room, split into two rows of five. Flipped on their sides, the front tables served as shields, and I noticed the top of someone's head propping up from behind the one on the right. The AR-15 rounds wouldn't have any trouble breaking through the table.

At the back of the room was a dark brown door contrasting with the white walls. The entire room was closed off. It was their lab where they conducted their dirty business, and they'd never risk allowing wandering pairs of eyes to see their criminal activity.

The man behind the table on the right stood up and fired three shots through the doorway. I retreated behind the safety of the wall and spit out the dusty aftermath the bullet holes left in the drywall.

"Let's fucking go!" the man shouted, his accent leaning heavily south of the border.

If Manny had an army to defend him, they wouldn't be hiding behind tipped-over tables. They'd have no reason to hide, which meant they were now playing defense. I took one step back from the wall, enough to have an angle of the table's edge, and shot three rounds.

The table splintered around the edges, where I landed three perfect shots on the upper corner. The man fired six more rounds back, and I heard a magazine being smacked into a gun as he reloaded.

I peeked back around the doorframe and saw a second man behind the table on the left. Both wore all-black attire and bulletproof vests. Neither had a helmet, however, so I'd have to go for kill shots to the dome.

I still had around ninety rounds to take out these two guys, plus whatever Manny was hiding out with in that back room where I presumed he had cowered to.

An explosion came from the kitchen. It could have been anything, but I figured the only thing that could combust was the gas-powered stove.

"Shit!" one of the men cried out, so I stepped more into the doorway and started blasting at the two front tables. Within six seconds, twenty rounds made a nearly perfect line of holes across the two tables.

The man behind the left one lay on the ground, clutching his arm and rolling around with clenched teeth. The one on the right had abandoned his post and flipped over a table two rows from the back.

The writhing man grunted as he reached across his body to pick up the TEC-9 he had dropped. He inserted a new magazine in slow motion, groaning through each step of the process.

The man in the back stood up and shot more rounds, a couple of bullets flying past my head. I felt the air move right next to my ear. Two more inches over and I'd no longer have a right eyeball.

I fired back in his direction, forcing him to duck behind the table and giving me the chance to slide in front of the table of the man currently down. I wasn't sure if this man had seen me because of his angle lying on his back, but he shot three more rounds anyway.

They were errant, two of which went through the ceiling.

I kicked the table so it slid toward him, prompting him to shoot again, this time the bullets flying toward the wall to my left. He had no aim, and from the way he was clutching his arm, I had to have landed a shot somewhere in his biceps.

I knelt down and looked over the top of the table. Sure enough, blood oozed from the man's right arm, which held the TEC-9 with every ounce of remaining strength he could muster. But it wasn't enough. He could barely pull the trigger, let alone point the weapon in a particular direction.

"Sorry, amigo," I said. "You picked the wrong crowd to roll with."

I lined up a clean shot to his head and squeezed the trigger. No more arm pain for the poor bastard.

"Is that all you got?!" the last remaining thug shouted from the back of the room. "You'll never bring down the Eldorados! If you kill us all, you'll have to answer to your father. He'll pull your balls out from your throat and hang you from a phone pole."

"As relaxing as that sounds, I think I'll pass," I shouted back. "But thank you!"

Something heavy banged upstairs, like a piano had dropped from the sky. It was entirely possible the kitchen ceiling had collapsed and whatever furniture was above had fallen through.

The man in the back stood up, now with a TEC-9 in each hand, and fired away with little care for lining up a clean shot. I dove back behind the table and watched at least fifteen rounds land all around the room. When I stuck my head over the table's edge, I saw cash and clouds of cocaine powder falling gracefully to the floor.

I stood up and ran toward the back, AR aiming directly at the man's table as I waited for him to stand up again. Even if he stuck just his hand out with the TEC-9, I'd blast that shit to the moon.

I usually trusted my gut when deciding to sneak up on someone. It was more of a decision made on the spot. I'm not sure what compelled me to take the gamble at this exact moment, but I was glad I did.

I reached his table in four seconds and caught him struggling to load a new magazine into his TEC-9. He looked up at me, eyes bulging, as I jumped and soared through the air, leg stiff as I planted my right foot square across his face.

The kick sounded like someone slapping a punching bag.

"Fuck!" he screamed, dropping everything and throwing both hands across his face. Blood spewed out from his nose, and I didn't give him another second. I climbed back to my feet and reared back a fist, imagining I could send whatever remained of his nose to the back of his skull.

He fell silent the second I struck him, arms and legs contorted as he splayed out like a double-jointed freak.

I picked up both his guns and hurled them clear across the room. He wasn't even breathing anymore, so I wasn't worried. Getting my heart rate back under control, I scanned the room. Unless he had more goons hiding behind the door, Manny only had those two men left to protect him, and they were no longer part of the equation.

The fire was raging above, no longer a steady crackling, but a blood-chilling roar. The temperature was rising, and I was incredibly grateful to be standing where I was. Another explosion sounded, and debris collapsed into the stairwell, blocking the path back up the stairs. For now, it also prevented the fire from reaching us in the basement, but that wouldn't last forever. I needed to find a way out but had other pressing matters to tend to.

I strolled up to the door I was certain my brother hid behind and knocked.

"It's just you and me, Manny."

Chapter 46

I tried the doorknob.

Locked.

"C'mon, Manny!" I shouted, balling a fist and banging on the door. "I can just shoot my way through."

"Just go," Manny replied, his voice not as distorted as I expected through the door. "It's over. If you've reached this door, then everyone is dead. The house is on fire. Just let me burn to death in here."

My heart thumped against my ribs. If there was one thing I knew about my brother, he was no quitter. I didn't buy it for a second that he would roll over and let his life end, literally, in flames.

"All that money spent on these men who couldn't protect you, so you're just going to wave the white flag locked in a closet?" I spoke calmly and stepped aside from the door. "Is this like your private bunker? Keep all your money safe and sound in there?"

"I'd rather die in a fire than get killed by my own brother," Manny said. "I should have just brought you to Mexico me with me all those years ago, then we'd never be in this situation. We'd both be living the high life right now. Probably eating caviar on our private jet, taking our families all around the world."

Asshole forgot I didn't eat seafood.

"That was never going to happen," I said. "You can't assume I would've just pissed away my morals because you took me to Mexico."

"Everything would be different, baby bro," Manny shouted, his elevated tone catching me off guard. Desperation dripped from his words. My older brother saw his life approaching its end and hearing that fear in his voice caused me to hesitate. I'd been mentally preparing for this moment once I learned Manny was the leader behind this cartel. I'd killed lots of men in my life, but never a relative. Never the only man I had in my life. "If you met Dad, you'd know that. He loves you. He regrets not bringing all of us with him when he went to Mexico."

"Regret doesn't mean a damn thing."

"Dad had the vision Mom refused to see. He saw the opportunity and worked his way up to where he is. Mom should be alive. All she had to do was agree to join Dad. But she couldn't see past the bullshit society tries to make us believe."

"Mom was an honest person," I shouted back. I hated when Manny brought up our mother. He didn't even cry at her funeral. He had no right to even *think* her name.

"Two peas in a pod!" Manny said, letting out a nervous laugh. "Funny how our family split the way it did. Don't you ever wonder how things could have turned out differently?"

"Like if I was the one hiding in a bunker while my house was on fire?" I replied. "No, I don't dwell on that kind of possibility. You know Hitler died hiding in a bunker, right? Looks like you're no different from the most despicable scum the world has ever seen. You and Dad are the two who deserve each other. Where is he, by the way? Too chickenshit to show his face around here? I'm sure you've told him I'm here."

The door swung open, and I readied my AR.

Manny walked out with his hands raised above his head, a fresh cigarette pinched between his lips, cocaine residue powdered around his nose like a shitty makeup job.

"Really, Manny?" I said. "You face death and only want to get high? How many pills did you take?"

"Enough to not feel the pain."

I kept my AR-15 fixed on my brother, a skeleton of the man I once admired. Gone was the boy who I played baseball with during the long summer days. Skipping rocks across the Rio Grande, wondering what life was like on the other side of the border. Manny was the first person to meet me at the hospital after our mother was killed. He held me, and I cried into his chest for over an hour. He gave me all the time I needed, and when that initial shock had passed, assured me everything was going to be fine. That's just what people said in those scenarios, but those words coming from my older brother gave me hope. My mom's death didn't have to mean the end of my life.

When I wallowed around in depression for two months following the funeral, it was Manny who took me out for a long drive and set up a picnic for us at a park where Mom used to take us when we were little. A park with a pond and a long, wooden bridge you could stand on and throw bread to the ducks.

"You have to keep living, Jonny," he had told me. "Mom is gone, but she wouldn't want you living like this. You haven't showered in two weeks. You eat cereal for all three meals. It's going to be hard, but you need to live. For Mom. You are now her legacy, and you need to make her proud."

I hadn't reflected on these words until now and just realized Manny had always seen me as the extension of our mother. It wasn't *us* who were our mother's legacy. It was *me.*

This memory echoed through my mind as I stared down the barrel of the AR aimed at my brother.

"What happened to you, Manny?" I asked. The basement was growing hotter, the fire fighting its way down the stairs. "You were always so independent and strong-headed. I'll never believe that you sold out for money and a life of crime."

Sweat was already streaking down Manny's face in shiny rows, but I noticed a line of tears intersecting with the moisture.

"Cartels are portrayed unfairly," Manny said. "It's one of the first things you learn once you're in. Yes, there is violence and illegal activity. But behind all of that, it's just a business. Dad is a brilliant businessman. But he's also a monster. The only difference between a cartel, and say, a big corporation, is that the cartels handle their threats directly. We're all just trying to get by and make a living. If you fuck with a cartel, you're fucking with a family. And there is no forgiveness."

Manny's arms trembled as he finally lowered them to his sides. Darkness swept across his eyes, as some level of focus seemed to have filled his body. I tightened my grip on the trigger, heart pounding away as my mind tore itself into two. You can think something all you want, but when it comes time to follow through, that little voice in the back of your head, the one that makes you human, will always push back.

The basement felt like a furnace. It had to be at least ninety degrees where we stood, the temperature climbing by the minute. This also factored into my decision. There was a chance both of us were going to die. So why leave this world with an unclean conscience? Maybe Manny and I could hold on to each other as the universe engulfed our polarizing lives into flames.

Even in the end, with everything on the line, I tried to find the humanity in my older brother.

Then his eyes blazed with rage, and he charged at me, growling like a pissed-off rottweiler. Despite the heat, my blood froze. My finger felt stiff, an impossible task to simply bend the joint in my index finger on the trigger.

Manny was only a couple inches shorter than me, but he'd lost his bulk from his teenage years. We were both running on pure adrenaline.

His shoulder planted into my gut, and we tumbled back. The AR flew out of my hand and clattered to the floor three feet away. Manny didn't even look at it, content to rear back his fists and start swinging.

My compassion got the best of me, and I absorbed six blows from my brother's thundering fists before realizing what had just happened. I had a strong jaw, as they said in the boxing world, and I took the punches with little reaction.

I reached up and snatched Manny's wrist as he swung it toward my face. The force between my hand and his arm was electric, like the final lightsaber duel between Luke Skywalker and Darth Vader. No one gave an inch, and we looked like two men having an awkward arm-wrestling match in the middle of a burning house.

Thick cords bulged out of Manny's neck as his face turned red. He'd gain an inch before I took two back. We went at this for a few seconds before he spit in my face. It landed in my eye, stinging and making me lose ground.

I hadn't even realized our other hands were clenched on each other's shoulders. His thumb was pressing beneath my collar bone like he was trying to snap it in half. He had me pinned down, but Manny didn't really have an advantage. If we were reversed, I'd have been finding ways to choke him. Press my forearm into his throat until he surrendered.

And that's why the cartel and all their guns were bad for fighting. Manny had size and strength, but no plan. I dug deep into my mental well, gathering any traces of energy that hadn't been expelled yet.

With his arm in my grip, I pulled it hard across my body, causing Manny to lose his balance and tumble face-first into my chest. He let go of my shoulder, and I swung my other hand around to punch him in the back of the head.

His head jerked to the side, but he punched back, connecting with my left cheek. I felt blood running down my face, pooling in my goatee.

The blow had pulled us apart, and we both clambered to our feet. Blood covered our faces, but Manny stared at me with a manic smile.

"Not as good as you thought, are you, SEAL boy?" he said, cackling.

We circled each other like two cage fighters waiting to pounce.

"We've always been following you," Manny continued. "From the day you joined the Navy, we've had informants keeping tabs on you. Dad always wanted to extend a hand for you to join us in Mexico. He knew better than to get involved with an active SEAL. Then it was even worse when you joined the CIA. Many of his inner circle urged him to forget about you. To move on. Even I told him it wasn't worth it at that point. But he insisted."

"Well, isn't he just the sweetest man," I said, and we kept circling. With the temperature climbing, the knife in my pocket burned against my leg. Sweat seemed to run down every inch of my body. My clothes stuck to my skin, hands slick. "If you think I'll change my mind because of these bullshit stories, you're wrong. I judge men by their character, not their words."

Manny laughed, his teeth covered with the crimson of his blood. "You better hope you die tonight, baby bro. Because if you don't, Dad will be coming after you. It won't be right away—he's a planner. But once he realizes you wiped this entire team out, he's no longer going to give a shit who you are. He'll find you in the night and make you wish it was you next to that car that blew up instead of Mom."

My body made itself hotter thanks to the rage that had now boiled over. My teeth grinded against each other as I clenched my jaw. Manny's words were the only reminder I needed. He was no longer my brother. That chapter was closed, the book burned and forgotten.

I reached into my pocket at the same time Manny charged at me again. His eyes were focused on mine, and I'm not sure he realized where my hand had gone. Or maybe he didn't care. Manny never shied away from taking a chance.

We were only ten feet apart. Two or three steps. My fingers grasped the knife, hot to the touch, and flung open the blade. After two steps, Manny jumped, arms splayed out to tackle me from my shoulders.

I swung the knife upward as he landed on me, and we both fell down. He landed on top of me again, but this time, he wasn't swinging fists or making any attempt to keep me down.

Warmth spread down my hand clutching the knife. It had sunk directly into my brother's stomach. His body grew heavy as it trembled all around. More blood seeped out of his mouth while his lips wavered. Manny held his head up above my chest, the only thing he could do.

A flood of tears ran down his face.

More banging sounds came from upstairs, and I thought I heard a distant wail of sirens. The first clouds of smoke trickled into the basement, but not enough to panic. Yet.

Manny struggled to lick the blood from his lips. I rolled him over to lie on his back and knelt beside his head, his eyes peering at the ceiling.

I lowered my face to his, hand still on the knife.

The banging from above continued, growing louder. Voices shouted over the crackling of monstrous flames. It was all background commotion. I heard what sounded like the return of a heavy rainfall. But it was too steady.

The fire department had arrived.

"I'm sorry it had to end like this, big bro," I said. Manny kept parting his lips but couldn't get any words out. "I'll never forget you."

I planted a kiss on my brother's forehead, then pulled out the knife from his gut.

Chapter 47

The beauty of being in such a small town was how quickly the emergency responders could arrive at a destination.

Of course, I had Lily to thank for calling the fire department as soon as she saw smoke from the bottom of the hill.

The fireman who was first to clear the debris blocking the stairs told me another ten minutes and I'd have been dead.

"You must have a guardian angel looking out for you," he said, clapping me on the back as the paramedics checked me out in the driveway outside the mansion.

Most of the house was still standing, albeit black and charred. The area above the kitchen had indeed collapsed, and it was a bed and nightstand that had fallen into the kitchen, setting off a ripple effect that led to the stove exploding.

The explosion caused the most damage, taking out the entire kitchen and its surrounding area, which crumpled into a heap on the stairwell. A sheet of drywall landed perfectly to seal off the doorway into the basement and kept the smoke out. If that hadn't happened, both my brother and I would have suffocated to death well before he even burst out of the closet.

I knew who my guardian angel was. This wasn't the first time she had saved me, and hopefully, not the last.

Lily ran up the driveway a moment after the paramedics cleared me. Aside from bruises and cuts, I had no serious damage. Even the bullet that skimmed my leg wouldn't require any stitches and would heal itself in a few days.

When Lily spotted me, she threw her arms around my shoulders and let out all the tears. "I didn't think you were coming out of there. I knew you were in the basement. Then the fire..."

I squeezed her, and despite the several dozen emergency responders now flooding the property, it felt like we were the only two people in the world.

I noticed five police officers on the scene, but the only one I recognized was Officer Billingsley. He strolled over to us, a bashful expression as he kicked the rocks on the ground.

"You okay, Mendez?" he asked.

I pulled away from Lily, but she remained at my side, running her fingers up and down my arm.

"I'm good," I said.

"Rumor has it that you took on this entire cartel by yourself. Is that true?"

"I suppose it is. I was just trying to free Lily. She saved me, though, by making sure the fire department got here."

"Quite the noble work by both of you," Billingsley said, forcing an awkward grin. "You leaving Hillcrest now?" he asked, sounding genuinely curious.

I nodded. "Too much bad blood here. I try to stay off the grid. By now I'm sure everyone in Hillcrest knows me. Can't have that."

Billingsley nodded in return and stuck out his hand to shake. "Well, I'm glad you were here."

We chatted more about the events that had just unfolded

as part of the statements he needed to collect for this matter. I gave him the number to my burner phone if he thought of more questions. When we finished, I shook his hand, and he returned to his colleagues circled around a patrol car.

"What do we do now?" I asked Lily.

She rested her head on my arm. "I have a pile of work to do, but I'll deal with that when I get back to D.C. Are you hungry?"

"Starving," I said, unsure of the last time I ate.

"Let's go."

Lily had driven to the top of the driveway. Thank God I didn't have to walk back down that hill. We got in and she drove us away. I watched the woods out of my window, officers and medics navigating the trees and the dead bodies peppered around the property.

"Can we just grab dinner and take it home?" I asked. "Your place or mine is fine. I just don't want to be out in public right now."

"Of course," Lily said. "I know just the spot."

She sounded chipper.

It was only seven o'clock when we reached the main road, and the clouds had finally given way to the evening sun.

My head spun as it tried to process everything that had happened today. I still couldn't believe I killed my brother and wished there had been another way out of it. Lily must have sensed my deep thinking because she kept silent while we drove back into town.

When she pulled into the Hamburger Stand parking lot, I whipped my head around to her.

"What are we doing here?" I asked.

Lily grabbed my hand and smiled. "Go see your nephew. He's not a threat."

I blinked rapidly, not wrapping my head around this. But I trusted Lily. She knew a lot more about these cartel members than me.

"Are you sure?"

She nodded. "Just bring me a burger, okay?"

I stepped out of the car and stared at the entrance to Hamburger Stand. The place was empty. With all the commotion happening around Hillcrest today, I doubted anyone wanted to go out in public.

I saw Andres through the front windows, wiping down tables with a rag.

He looked up and saw me, then looked around in a panic. I raised my hands and strolled toward the door.

When I stepped in, mariachi music was blasting from the kitchen. Andres remained next to the table and watched me with nervous eyes, like he was expecting me to strangle him.

I kept my hands elevated and said, "Can we talk?"

He looked me up and down. The blood all over my body and clothes couldn't have been a promising sign, but he agreed and sat down at the table he had just cleaned.

I sat down across from him and saw so much of my brother in his face. He was a more handsome version of the boy I had grown up with. No wonder I had thought I knew him from somewhere.

"Have you known who I was this whole time?" I asked.

Andres looked down at his fingers drumming on the table.

"Don't be nervous," I said.

Andres looked up, his eyes heavy, and nodded.

"Are you aware what happened to your dad today?"

He nodded again.

"He's dead," Andres replied in a stiff tone.

"He is," I said. "And I have to come clean, Andres. I killed him. I didn't want to, but it happened. We were fighting in the basement, and things escalated. Only one of us was getting out of there alive."

Andres nodded silently to himself, not surprised by this news. "He told me about you all the time. Tio Jonny, the war hero. The undercover CIA agent. People are afraid of you in Mexico. That's the real reason they never wanted you to join Abuelo's business."

Even though it was obvious, I had never mentally made the connection that my long-lost dad was Andres's grandfather. I struggled to picture my father in that light. "What else did he say?"

"He told me that if anything ever happened to him, that I should look for you. He said if he wasn't around, there wasn't anyone else in the world he would trust with his only son. Not even Abuelo."

The back of my eyeballs burned with tears as I fought them back. No matter how far my brother had strayed off course in life, he still held me in high regard. "Well, Andres, I'm afraid you can't live with me. I don't live anywhere. Just travel from city to city. And that's no life for a young boy. How old are you, anyway?"

"Nineteen," Andres replied. "And that's okay, Tio. I've never wanted to follow in my dad's footsteps. I saw the people he spent time with. The things he's done. I want to go to college, and this is probably my best chance now."

"College?" I leaned back in my seat, eyebrows arched high. "That's an impressive decision. What do you want to study?"

Andres shrugged. "Haven't thought about it. I'm pretty good at accounting. I run all the books for this place and did some for my dad."

I grinned. "Well, good for you. And take your time. There are so many things you can study. Consider all the ones that interest you before committing to anything. You can even try out different things your first two years before declaring a specific major."

"I've thought about joining the military," Andres said, keeping a flat expression.

I wondered if his life growing up in the cartel had scarred him from showing any emotion. He was surrounded by not just luxury and the high life, but also death and threats.

"The military, huh?" I asked. "Do you have citizenship here in the U.S.?"

"I do."

I nodded. "Well, that I can speak from experience. The military is a great way to see the world and learn about yourself as a man. You'll gain lifelong friends and skills. Plus, they'll even pay for your schooling if you still want to go to college."

"Thank you, Tio. That's good advice."

We sat in silence, and Andres looked out the window toward the mansion. "My dad called me," he said. "When he was hiding in the closet. Told me he was probably going to die. He said I shouldn't blame you. That you were only doing the right thing like you always have."

That tingle returned to my eyes. Why couldn't my brother have spoken like this to my face? He was too caught up in the cartel's world to stray from it. I suppose either route he took would have ended in death. And once he realized that, he took the time to clear my name with our only surviving family member.

"You have a good head on your shoulders," I said. "Just like your grandmother."

Andres's eyes widened at the mention of my mother. I had no idea how much he knew about her, and didn't want to get into all that now. We could sit here in the Hamburger Stand for three days telling stories, but we both had places to go. New roads to travel.

"I'll tell you about her another time, okay?" I said. "You've gone through a lot today. Do you have somewhere safe to stay?"

"Yes. My dad always made arrangements for me, in case… " he trailed off and bit his bottom lip. This was the most emotion I'd get from him tonight.

I stood up and clapped him on the back. "Write down your phone number for me. I don't own a cell phone, but I'll get in touch when I can. I look forward to hearing all about your adventures in college. And don't stress too much about which classes to take, or even which school to attend. As your grandmother always told us, 'Trust your gut.' Do that, and you'll be just fine."

Andres stood up and hugged me. I wrapped my arms around his bony frame. He could definitely use some military in his life.

"Oh, by the way, I'm gonna need a couple of burgers to go."

We both burst into laughter.

Chapter 48

We arrived at Lily's house eight minutes after Andres handed me a bag full of burgers and fries, along with two vanilla milkshakes. The full works.

I wished my nephew the best and promised to reach out the next time I had access to a phone. He flashed me a rare smile, and I once again saw that younger version of my brother in his face.

We set up in Lily's living room. She pulled the coffee table in close to the couch, scattered napkins around, and laid out the food. Once we settled in, she turned on the TV hanging on the opposite wall and put on the local news.

Sarah Potter was back in action, a somber expression as she explained the story of what happened at the mansion hidden in the woods. Between that and Jo's, many citizens of Hillcrest believed their small beachside paradise was under some sort of terrorist attack. But Officer Billingsley clarified everything regarding the cartel.

From how long they'd been operating in Hillcrest. To the rise in drug overdoses plaguing the community. And even pinned the blame for Chief Matthews's death on them.

Nothing was mentioned of Theo Rambis. Yet. And there was plenty of outrage over the mayor's involvement with the cartel. Officer Billingsley, who was suddenly the longest tenured police officer in Hillcrest, and the unofficial interim chief, promised a thorough investigation alongside the DEA to uncover all the details of the illegal crimes committed throughout the city.

"That won't be me," Lily said. "I'm still supposed to fly back to D.C. I have a lot to explain to the people above me."

"You're not in trouble, are you?" I asked, chowing down the double burger with a handful of fries.

"Not anymore. With everything out in the open about Hunter and his involvement, I'm looking pretty good. This was quite the elaborate scheme, and he somehow kept me entirely out of it. I'm sure it was more out of fear than respect, because he knew I'd never put up with that shit."

I laughed. "Well, it's good either way. Did you ever have any suspicions about him?"

Lily shook her head. "Nothing like this. We worked together for three years, and I never once questioned his integrity. Even here in Hillcrest, I just thought he was distracted by life and not wrapped up in a criminal enterprise. He played his cards close to his chest, apparently. More power to him, I guess."

"Are you going to call his wife?"

"No. Normally, yes, but their home back in Maryland is going to be raided. Anna—that's his wife—is going to be questioned for any potential involvement. I'm sure she'll be cleared. If he kept it all a secret from me, I'm sure it was a secret from her. We spent more time together than they did. That's just the nature of this job."

The news had gone to a brief commercial break and returned with cameras set outside of the Hillcrest hospital.

Lily grabbed the remote and turned up the volume. A man and woman were walking through the hospital doors, pushing a younger boy in a wheelchair. The boy waved and smiled.

"In positive news," Sarah said, "Dominic Evans has been discharged from the hospital this evening in what has been a wild day of emotions for Hillcrest."

"Oh, thank God!" Lily cried, placing her hand to her chest. "He's going home!"

The feed cut to an earlier recorded segment of Dominic's mother, Michelle, answering questions from inside the hospital.

"We're all going home tonight," she said, a wide smile plastered across her face. "Dominic is well and expected to make a full recovery. It will take time, but we thank the Hillcrest community for their support through these dark days when we didn't know if our son was going to wake up." Tears rolled down her face, and she wiped them away. "We've been following the developing stories on the news and pray that everyone is okay. May God bless those who will continue to investigate these horrific crimes that have haunted our fine city. We ask for our family's privacy in the coming days as we adjust to this new normal. Our first goal is to help Dominic gain the strength back in his legs so he can walk again. Once we're at that point, you'll definitely see the Evans family around town."

Sarah wrapped up the story, and finally gave way to the weather. Lily turned off the TV, most of the food on the coffee table gone like we were rats scavenging a dumpster.

"I still can't believe everything that's happened," I said, leaning back on the sofa.

Lily pulled her legs up on the couch and lay her head against my shoulder. Even though she had been to hell and back, I could still smell a faint trace of that lavender scent wafting from her hair.

"It was chaos from the moment you arrived," Lily said. "Not that you were the cause, but everything really went to hell after that night at the tavern."

"That's for sure," I said, running my fingers through Lily's hair. At this moment, she felt like home. Just us on the couch, no other worries in the world. I imagined a life where this was our routine. But I knew better. Neither of us was cut out for that.

Lily rose from the couch and planted a kiss on my lips. She tasted like the vanilla shake she had just finished. "I need the restroom. Be right back."

She disappeared through the doorway to our left. The side of the house I hadn't explored the last time I was here. She had mentioned two bedrooms while showing me around.

I glanced around the now quiet living room. Not much had been packed up. But Lily had suggested the DEA rented out houses like this one, fully furnished and move-in ready.

I stood up, needing a stretch, and walked over to the kitchen. The counter was cleared off compared to my prior visit. No charcuterie boards. No boxes with chopped off hands in them.

The backyard patio waited behind the kitchen, and I looked out as the sun set, wishing I had known who to trust that night of the barbecue. Chief Matthews had been trustworthy all along. Agent Duncan was nothing but the devil hiding behind a mask.

It almost made me feel sick—or perhaps that was the combination of all the fast food—but I had to remind myself that events played out a certain way for a reason. If I had ever believed Agent Duncan was involved with the cartel, that would have changed everything, including mine and Lily's relationship. I doubt she would have believed me without concrete proof, which had been impossible to come by on this case.

Or if I had trusted Chief Matthews, how might have things played out differently? Would he still be alive? Maybe if he had trusted *me*, we could ask the same question.

All I could ever do was work with the information and resources in front of me. Lily gave me a gun and a car. I took it from there. The cartel was now eliminated from Hillcrest.

My name was never mentioned in the news, and I was grateful for that. I didn't need people flagging me down to give their thanks. That wasn't why I did it. I left the world a better place than it was when I had woken up this morning. And I'd continue doing that as long as my mind and body allowed.

My brother was right, though. The Eldorado cartel would come after me. It didn't matter if their leader was my father. No cartel in the world would just roll over and accept the losses I caused. I killed all of them. Including my father's favorite son. The one who followed him and wanted to work in the family business.

And I knew no matter how much I stayed off the grid, the cartel could always find me. I had many long nights ahead, sleeping with one eye open, pistol under my pillow. But I'd done that before. It didn't bother me.

When they found me, I'd be ready.

For now, I had a full belly, a warm house to spend the evening in, and a beautiful woman to share it with.

Lily's bedroom door creaked open, startling me out of my

daydream. She stood in her doorway completely naked, a wide grin as my eyes couldn't help but admire every curve of her stunning body.

My throat tensed shut. I was speechless.

But she was not. "Care to join me in the shower?"

Chapter 49

Rays of sunshine clawed through the half-drawn shades in Lily's bedroom. I didn't think I'd have the energy for three rounds of lovemaking last night, but that's exactly what happened.

Then I slept like a fucking rock.

Waking up, I was pretty sure I hadn't moved a single inch since dozing off with Lily's head on my chest and arm splayed across my shoulder.

But now, she wasn't in bed, her side of the sheets done neatly.

I saw a piece of paper on the nightstand and knew she was gone.

It didn't bother me. We had known we weren't going to fall in love and have some gushy happy ending. That's not how our lives functioned.

I sat up and reached over for the paper, allowing my eyes a moment to adjust before reading:

Jonny,

I had to fly out this morning. For real this time. Last night was perfect, so I didn't want to ruin it with a sappy goodbye. I'll never forget it. Or you.

By the time you read this, I'll be halfway back to D.C. to wrap up this case...at least my portion of it. I owe you. If you never rolled into Hillcrest, this case would still be stalled and I'd probably be flying back for a reprimand right now. From the bottom of my heart, thank you for all your help. Maybe you'll consider giving up your life as a nomad and join the DEA. We could really use someone with your talent.

I can see you shaking your head already. Silly idea!

You're a good man, Jonny. Your mother is surely smiling down on you for everything you've accomplished not just in Hillcrest, but in life.

I'm glad our paths crossed. We're perfect for each other. We had a real connection and mutual understanding. Sometimes you just need a person to share a moment with. A phase in life. Not everything has to be as drastic as spending an entire life together. We were exactly what each other needed in Hillcrest, and I can easily say these past two weeks were the happiest of my life when I spent time with you...except for that part when I was kidnapped in a cartel mansion.

But you followed your heart and saved me. I wish I could say I owe you, but I know we'll never see each other again. And that's okay. Sometimes perfection needs to be left how it was.

I left you a parting gift on the kitchen counter. A little something to remember me by. I technically have the house for two more days, so you can stay that much longer if you'd like.

I wish you nothing but the best for the remainder of your days. If our paths ever cross again, then maybe the universe is trying to tell us something. Until then, I'll always think of you.

Much love,

Lily

I folded up the paper and held it firm in my grip. The pillows and sheets still smelled like Lily, and I took one last whiff before getting out of bed.

She had taken the time to wash my clothes at some point in the early morning and left them folded on top of the dresser. I smiled as I got dressed, playing through the events of last night.

She had put my backpack at the foot of the dresser, and left the Glock she had originally lent me.

I went into her bathroom, finding it cleared out of every-thing except for a roll of toilet paper and the hotel-sized bottles of shampoo she had left in the shower. I fished my toothbrush out of my backpack, splashed some water on my face, and ventured into the living room a couple minutes later.

The house was exactly how it looked when we arrived home last night. The traces of our dinner on the coffee table were gone, so I shuffled into the kitchen. Sitting on the countertop was a lone peppermint candy.

I grabbed it and stuffed it into my pocket. Lily was more sentimental than I had originally given her credit for. I could have been too, if given the chance. But she'd never mentioned having to fly out before I'd wake. That explained why she was making love like she was running out of time.

I slipped the note she had written into my backpack, did one final look around the house, and decided I had no interest in staying here for another two days. Without Lily, I'd just sit on the couch and watch TV.

I could do that from anywhere in the world.

Besides, my time in Hillcrest had run its course. The

thought of returning to the beach put a sour taste in my mouth. There were other beach towns without the baggage I now carried in Hillcrest. Places where no one knew me.

I'd forever remember Hillcrest as the city that both reunited me with my brother, then took him away from me. While I could always reflect on the success I had in removing an entire cartel from operation, it would forever remain a missed opportunity.

Manny and I should have been going out to dinner, catching up on where life had taken us. Even with all the evil he had done, if he could have shown me any sort of remorse, I would have moved past his criminal history.

I didn't realize how badly I thirsted for family until we crossed paths that night in the mansion's driveway. I had Andres now. But he was off to start life on his own, also probably never wanting to return to Hillcrest.

Too much death and pain were left behind here. If I found myself hitchhiking up the coast again, I'd make sure the driver knew to blow right past the exit for Hillcrest.

I grabbed my backpack and slung it over my shoulder as I pulled open Lily's front door. A beautiful spring morning greeted me upon stepping outside. Birds sang from high in the trees, wind chimes added to the orchestra, and that hint of salt in the air from the ocean filled my nostrils.

It was almost overwhelming. Like the world was tempting me to stay, even for another hour. I wanted a paradise, and had it for an entire twenty minutes until the guns started blasting at the tavern.

That seemed to be the norm no matter where I went. Would I ever get to experience true peace?

I started down the walkway. Lily had taken the car. I

expected as much. A couple of Lily's neighbors were in their front yards, watering their lawns. They smiled and nodded at me as I strolled down the sidewalk, leaving the neighborhood behind.

My journey ahead was full of unknowns. Weren't they always? When I reached Main Street, I saw Jo's Diner three blocks down. Going in there would be a shitshow. Emotions. Questions about Lily. Praise from Jo, who knew what I had done to keep Hillcrest safe.

No. I couldn't show my face anywhere in this town. It was time to go.

I waited at the bus stop across the street from Hamburger Stand. When it arrived, I climbed on, getting all the stares from the passengers as I moved my gigantic body down the aisle and took a seat toward the back. Some things never changed. I'd take the bus as far as it would go, walk until I passed the city limits, and never look back at Hillcrest again.

I Hear You

If you enjoyed meeting Jonny Mendez in *Never Look Back*, don't miss his next thrilling adventure in *I Hear You*.

Join Jonny as he tracks down the truth behind a suicide epidemic plaguing a small Oregon town.

Who do you call when no one can be trusted?

Jonny Mendez finds peace in central Oregon. Until a suicide rocks the local community..

The town is desperate for answers. Then news breaks of a second suicide.

The trend continues, and Jonny can no longer stand by. What is causing this once quiet town to become ravaged with death?

As Jonny digs into the matter, he finds the reality is much more disturbing than anyone could have imagined. It doesn't help the locals keep whispering his name.

As the body count climbs, Jonny must confront a horrifying truth.

Before it's too late...

Order I HEAR YOU today at mybook.to/IHearYou

GET EXCLUSIVE BONUS STORIES!

Connecting with readers is the best part of this job. Releasing a book into the world is a truly frightening moment every time it happens! Hearing your feedback, whether good or bad, goes a long way in shaping future projects and helping me grow as a writer. I also like to take readers behind the scenes on occasion and share what is happening in my wild world of writing. If you're interested, please consider joining my mailing list. If you do, I'll send you a free time travel thriller as a thank you!

You can get your content **for free,** by signing up at bookhip.com/KAWWBK

Author's Note

After twenty-plus books, I wanted to make a slight shift in my writing. Before *Never Look Back* I had never written in the first person. Nor had I written a straight thriller. While some of my prior books lean thriller, they were more of a toe in the water. With Jonny Mendez, I wanted to jump all the way into the pool, and I'm glad I did.

Starting this series rejuvenated me as a writer, not that I was necessarily in a rut. But with everything new to me, it felt like a fresh challenge. Stepping out of your comfort zone always comes with a mixture of fear and excitement. Will I fail, or will I fly?

As I write this, the verdict is still out regarding this novel. But to me, I flew!

I love meeting a new challenge, and Jonny pushed me to write like I've never written. I've also been a pantser my entire career (that's someone who doesn't plot their books before writing—yes, madness!), but I wanted to try plotting, thoroughly, this story. Knowing what twists I wanted ahead of time instead of figuring them out along the way made for a stronger story. I could plant the seeds earlier since I knew what was coming. I'm afraid I'm a plotter now. Or at the least, a recovering pantser.

If you've seen the Disney movie *Soul*, you'll recall the main character experiencing moments when he was in the "zone."

Complete focus, just him and the piano while the rest of the world took a back seat. I experienced this lots of times during the writing of *Never Look Back.* It felt like I unlocked a new skillset in my writing, and truly elevated my craft to the next level. For any artist out there, you'll know that hunger to constantly improve. And like anything, it takes great studying, practice, and repetition.

Perhaps this was all the culmination of the last twenty books I'd written, but I'm just happy to have reached this new level, and I hope I'm not the only one feeling this way. If I'm wrong, tell me, and I'll happily assess where I may have gone wrong in my pursuit of crafting a mainstream thriller. If you agree, tell me that, too. Because if so, I want to keep my foot on the pedal and see how many situations we can put Jonny through.

It certainly feels like I've reached a new chapter in my journey in this wild career, and I couldn't have done it without a strong support system.

Like any book, it takes a team to bring the finished product to you. Thank you to the designers at 100Covers for another beautiful cover. And to my editor, Melissa Prideaux, who always knows the right adjustments needed to make the story pop. Without your touch, this book would only be mediocre at best.

To Arielle, Felix, and Selena, for unknowingly keeping me motivated through it all. You might look back one day and wonder why I was always buried in my laptop during practices, but please know it was all to chase after a better life for all of us. Running a business has no days off!

And lastly, to my wife, Natasha. The heartbeat and backbone of our publishing house (and my final editor). Thank you for all you do, both for the family and the business. I can't begin to imagine what a mess we would all be without you.

Andre Gonzalez
   July 10, 2024

Enjoy this book?

You can make a difference!

Reviews are the most helpful tools in getting new readers for any books. I don't have the financial backing of a New York publishing house and can't afford to blast my book on billboards or bus stops.

(Not yet!)

That said, your honest review can go a long way in helping me reach new readers. If you've enjoyed this book, I'd be forever grateful if you could spend a couple minutes leaving it a review (it can be as short as you like) on the Amazon page below:

https://mybook.to/NeverLookBackJM1

Thank you so much!

Also by Andre Gonzalez

Jonny Mendez Series:
Never Look Back (#1)
I Hear You (#2)

Arielle Lucila Series:
Time Roller (#4)
Dirty Money (#3)
Secrets in the Vault (#2)
Angel Assassin (#1)

Wealth of Time Series:
Time of Fate (#6)
Zero Hour (#5)
Keeper of Time (#4)
Bad Faith (#3)
Warm Souls (#2)
Wealth of Time (#1)
Road Runners (Short Story)
Revolution (Short Story)

Amelia Doss Series:
Salvation (#3)
Nightfall (#2)
Resurrection (#1)

Insanity Series:
The Insanity Series (Books 1-3)
Replicate (#3)
The Burden (#2)
Insanity (#1)
Erased (Prequel Short Story)

The Exalls Attacks:
Followed Away (#3)
Followed East (#2)
Followed Home (#1)
A Poisoned Mind (Short Story)

Standalone books:
Snowball: A Christmas Horror Story

About the Author

Andre Gonzalez is the international bestselling author of the Wealth of Time Series, and co-owner of M4L Publishing.

After surviving the Aurora Theater Shooting in 2012, Andre was inspired to chase his lifelong dream of pursuing a career as an author. This tragedy gave him a new appreciation for life along with a drive to make the world a better place by publishing books readers all around the world can enjoy.

He has written over twenty time-travel, thriller, and horror books after spending many years reading and studying the works of Stephen King and Dean Koontz. Keeping readers up late and their hearts pumping faster than normal is his ultimate goal. Andre was the recipient of the Rocky Mountain Fiction Writers 2021 Independent Writer of the Year award.

When he's not writing, you can find Andre buried underneath a long to-do list or chasing around his three hyper children. He and his wife are raising their family in their hometown of Denver, CO.